For Lee, eternally and infernally.

Madness Heart Press
2006 Idlewilde Run Dr.
Austin, Texas 78744

This is a work of fiction. Names, characters, places, and incidents either are the product of the author's imagination or are used fictitiously. Any resemblance to actual persons, living or dead, events, or locales is entirely coincidental.

Copyright © 2026 Christine Morgan
Cover by Luke Spooner

All rights reserved. No part of this book may be reproduced or used in any manner without written permission of the copyright owner except for the use of quotations in a book review. For more information, address: john@madnessheart.press

First Edition
ISBN: 978-1-967517-20-6
www.madnessheart.press

INFERNAL QUEEN

Christine Morgan

A Madness Heart Press Publication

FOREWORD

Well, here we are again, and who would've thought? I know I sure didn't, years ago, when I humbly reached out to Edward Lee begging permission to publish a little Mephistopolis-noir detective story about a wisecracking gumshoe from the 1930s now plying his trade in Hell. That was Matt Brimstone, P.I., who's since gone on to appear in a mini-book of his own, Damned Lazy, tracking a case into one of the lesser-regarded neighborhoods of that teeming infernal city.

Even being allowed to do those alone would have been honor enough. To also be allowed to spin up my own strange sequel to Lee's series, following up on what happened around a certain Florida lake in the wake of a certain Spatial Merge, was beyond my wildest dreams. Thus, Lakehouse Infernal came to be, which went a step yet further beyond wildest-dreams territory by winning the Splatterpunk Award for Best Novel.

But it still didn't stop there ... once the ball was rolling, he was all in favor of me doing a second, which of course I was only too delighted to do, returning to that messed-up little corner of reality to continue the adventures of characters I'd grown to love, in all their twisted glory. Hence, Warlock Infernal.

A year or so ago, from when I type this, I decided to press

my luck (y'know, like the game show, though just watching it gives me an anxiety tummy ache; I'd never be able to actually be on it). After all, since Lee's original Infernal books were a trilogy, hey, why not do the same? So, I asked. And, again, with a couple stipulations, he agreed.

The biggest of those stipulations was that I not involve the actual Mephistopolis, since he had stuff in the works and didn't want us to get in each other's way. Rather than posing a problem for my planning, it pushed me in a different direction, giving me the chance to explore some hitherto largely uncharted territory ... the flip side of the afterlife, the shall-we-say Upstairs. It, like everything else about these projects, proved to be tremendous fun, and I hope readers will see it the same way.

Meanwhile, of course, I still had some matters to attend to in the vicinity of Lake Misquamicus, the infamous HellZone now under new management. Really bitter, angry, vengeful new management, in the form the titular Infernal Queen. I was also able to pursue a few other unresolved storylines. I like to think I got them mostly wrapped up, with a sense of at least closure if not necessarily satisfaction (because, hey, not every character can have a happy ending, no matter how much I may like them).

Through all this, I was further privileged to become not just a devoted fangirl of Edward Lee, but a friend. He entrusted me with proofreading and editing manuscripts for him, dubbing me his "favorite fuck-up fixer-upper."

He was overjoyed to encourage and give feedback on my collaboration with Susan Snyder, the totally filthy-bonkers Nympho Shark Fuck Frenzy. And, as the ultimate rosette of icing on the cake, he invited me to collaborate with him on a wicked-fun project we ended up calling Cunt-Kick the Witch-Bitch (he really really really wanted to use the c-word in the title, and who am I to refuse him anything?).

If unsuspecting Past Me, getting City Infernal as one of the Leisure Horror Book Club monthly selections back when I barely knew "extreme horror" was even a thing, and then being utterly blown away by it, had any idea of what the future would hold, poor Past Me never would have believed it. Shit, to this day, Present Me sometimes still thinks it's all been an extremely vivid dream from which I'll wake up any minute. Which, if it is, I definitely do not want to; that would suck.

At any rate, here we are again, for a third foray. Thank you for joining me; see you on the flip side!

Heaven Can't Wait

Never in his life would Gregory Nachtwald have expected to find himself kicking open the Pearly Gates with a wounded angel in his arms.

Okay, maybe it wasn't *the* Pearly Gates, the main entrance, the towering edifice of pristine white clouds and columns of pure golden radiance and shafts of divine Light beaming down to the tune of heavenly choirs.

Not *the* Pearly Gates, where Saint Peter manned the grand podium, lording it over milling throngs of hopefuls, like patrons vying to get into the most exclusive upscale club. Saint Peter, with his venerable beard, shining halo, and kind-but-stern eyes, poring over the measureless Book of deeds and misdeeds, chronicles of countless souls in all their sin and splendor.

Not *the* Pearly Gates, where pairs of immense and terrifyingly beautiful seraphim played bouncer, ready to give the bum's rush to anyone who didn't make the cut ... to shunt the unworthy off to Limbo, or Purgatory ... or, in some cases, the express elevator all the way down to the fiery pits of eternal suffering and damnation.

Not *the* Pearly Gates, where various emissary deities waited around, bearing dazzling placards—Ōmeyōcān, Elysium, Valhalla, Aaru, the Happy Hunting Ground, Nirvana, and so on—the way tour guides collected their excursion groups disembarking a bus or cruise ship. Or where a very few served in a manner more akin to chauffeurs at the airport, there to pick up particular special clients.

Not *the* Pearly Gates of a thousand cartoons and comics and jokes, where cats had been granted nine lives because when they were in, they wanted out and when they were out, they wanted in, or where dogs asked if they had been the goodest, or there were stairways to Heaven but highways to Hell in anticipation of traffic density.

Not *those* Pearly Gates, no.

But, gates, yes. Pearly, yes. Just, smaller. The clouds less brilliantly white and pristine, the golden columns less towering, the divine Light and heavenly choirs muted and perfunctory. With no milling throngs, no bouncer seraphim, no grand podium or Saint Peter. A side entrance, as it were, which may as well have had EMPLOYEES ONLY stenciled across it. Maybe even with a sheltered nook off to the side where staff could step away for a smoke break, if such things were permitted here.

Greg didn't know, didn't care. What mattered was they *were* Pearly Gates, and he *did* kick them open, augmenting the physical force with a potent booster of warlockian energy. The septagonal eldritch sigil emblazoned upon his brow—identical to that engraved upon one side of the medallion he wore around his neck—flared bright silver. A backrush of magic caused the hem of his long coat to sweep dramatically, further tousling his hair.

Way to make an entrance, he heard in his memory.

And it might've been, had there been anyone around to see him. Yet, as he kicked open the gates and strode on through, battered and tattered and bloodied and bruised from battle, steely-eyed with resolute determination, a wounded angel cradled in his arms, ready to throw down against whoever or whatever might try to stand in his way, he was met with only a clean, serene, empty space.

It reminded him of a museum atrium, all cool marble and vaulted ceilings, with a library hush and steady, ambient illumination from no readily discernible source. Compared to the elaborate, baroque, or even gaudy adornments of fancy cathedrals, it seemed almost plain, almost spartan, and somehow that much the more breathtaking for it.

Empty, though. Unfurnished. Not so much as a bored security cherub perched on a stool, an information kiosk, even a helpful YOU ARE HERE map.

Maybe he didn't rate a whole welcoming committee, but a warlock busting his way into Heaven itself, let alone with a wounded angel in his arms, should have counted for *something*.

"Hey!" he called, raising his Voice so it rang and reverberated in the chamber's strange acoustics. "Anyone home?"

Way to make an entrance.

Blaze had said it. The crazy fireworks kid, ready and raring to go up against diabolical legions armed with a pyrotechnic arsenal of bottle rockets and cherry bombs.

At the time, Greg and Ethriel had just translocated into a secret tunnel, a liminal space connecting the normally saner outside world to the encapsulated mini-pocket of Hell-on-Earth occupying the environs of what had once been a modest Florida lake.

All of which was its own long and fairly complicated story, involving a Spatial Merge meant to swap out the freshwater contents of said lake with the far-from-fresh, definitely *not*-water, contents of an infernal reservoir. It had succeeded, triggering religious hysteria, rapid government response, and the walling-off of the entire region in the aims of containing and quarantining the corruption, complete with military checkpoints and armed guards.

Inside the perimeter, madness and mayhem held sway, the locals and trapped tourists tortured, slaughtered, hideously mutated, acquiring or being twisted by dark magic. Same for the local flora and fauna; those who already thought Florida a nightmare of snakes, 'gators, skeeters, sinkholes, quicksand, and swamp rats were in for one fuck of a rude awakening as the changes set in.

During those first days, hosts of monsters and demons emerged from the six billion gallons of blood, shit, piss, bile, and pus lapping at the shores of the former Lake Misquamicus. Chief among them, it turned out, was a being known as Favius, who'd started off as a soldier way back in the Roman Empire, been damned for his numerous atrocities, and then worked his way up the ladder in the service of Hell's armies.

He was a specimen indeed, this Favius. Loyal to a fault, nearly every inch of his skin grafted with the still-living faces he'd personally peeled from his victims, a muscle-bound centurion from the crest of his helm to the soles of his sandals, he'd ended up crossing over in the Merge through a series of incidents and accidents more fully described elsewhere.

Once incarnate upon what he called God's green earth, Favius was taken into military custody. After holding and interrogating him for several years, the powers-that-be decided to strike a bargain with him, the better to make America great again and gain the upper hand over all enemies both foreign and domestic.

Or something like that. It didn't work as planned.

Well, it didn't work as planned for the Americans. It worked out fine and dandy for Favius, and for those to whom his allegiance was truly bound.

One thing led to another. Mistakes were made. Ultimately, Favius betrayed his captors—very much to their shock and surprise; go figure—and seized control. The area around Lake Misquamicus underwent yet more drastic adjustments. Lots and lots of people died in some pretty fucking gruesome horrible ways.

Into all of which had blundered one Gregory Nachtwald, who'd then had no idea of his ancestral warlock heritage. No, he'd just been flying along in his Cessna, veered into the quarantine zone, and crash-landed smack in the middle of the whole mess.

Way to make an entrance then too, maybe. Not the most heroic or impressive entrance, reducing his plane to crumpled and smoking wreckage, scattering his cargo, and getting smacked in the forehead by his own lucky medallion so it seared its eldritch sigil into his skin.

Still, it was an entrance.

And an introduction; that selfsame lucky medallion, a gift from his grandmother, proved to be a token allowing his guardian angel, his *literal guardian angel*, to manifest in person.

Ethriel-then bore little resemblance to Ethriel-now. Ethriel-then had been a two-foot-tall sylph, sexless as a fairy from Disney's *Fantasia*, with shimmering dragonfly wings.

The Ethriel he now held in his arms was his own size, lush-bodied and curvaceous and absolutely gorgeous ... with a deep puncture wound in her side and her formerly glorious wings of radiant golden light sheared off into ragged ichor-seeping stumps.

He held her cradled to his chest.

Ethriel, naked and shaking, swathed in an absurdly large

beach towel. A Margaritaville knock-off beach towel, as it happened; the kind of thing vacationers might buy from a roadside stand for cheaper than the actually licensed and better-quality souvenir goods.

Greg could have conjured something more suitable, but he knew he'd need every ounce of power he could dredge up to bring them here, let alone deal with whatever came next.

To think, just a week or so ago, he'd been an average guy, if still something of an outlaw. Running drugs across borders technically fell into the outlaw category, even if the drugs in question weren't heroin and fentanyl but insulin, cancer meds, and other such vital life-saving substances. Big Pharma and the insurance companies really resented would-be Robin Hoods messing with their profit margins; their retribution could make the cartels and kingpins seem reasonable.

There he'd been, flying along. There he'd been, instruments gone wonky, plane out of control. There he'd been, the blameless blue sky swapping places with the crimson grossness of the lake, spiraling, plunging, the sheer stench alone almost strong enough to kill, desperately fighting to at least bring the Cessna down on something approximating dry land.

Then, as he'd hung suspended by his harness upside-down in the wreckage, as he'd worked his way free, wondering what in the world had happened and what he was going to do, there she'd been.

Ethriel. Tiny. Cute. Naked. Sassy. His guardian angel, of the *Custos Viatorum*, in the service of Saint Christopher ... or Saint Menas, depending. Who had, way back, been his grandmother's guardian angel as well, and who ordinarily shouldn't have manifested corporeally. But, as she'd told him, at Lake Misquamicus, the rulebook kind of went out the window; there were no case precedents, and all they could do was play it by ear.

Regardless, her mission and purpose remained the same: guard him along his journey, protect him in his travels. With her main goal being to get him out of there, get him to safety, before something worse happened.

It'd been Ethriel who pointed out his arcane abilities— *Yer a warlock, Greg'ry,* she'd said in a bad Hagrid impression. Ethriel, who helped him navigate his way through the deadly-dangerous and seriously fucked-up terrain. Ethriel, with her affectionate, effervescent champagne cotton candy smooches. Who'd been beside him as he fought the satyr-demon Zilch, and whom he'd already thought he lost ... not just once but twice before.

The way she had faltered when momentous events unfurled and diabolical forces surged ... the way she had faded as if being erased from existence, even as Greg wept and pleaded with her to stay ... at the very end, he'd released her from her duties, giving her the medallion ... and then she'd been gone, gone, leaving him in misery.

Dispirited, caring less for his own fate than for not wanting to let her down, wanting to honor her last wish and get out of there alive, he'd trudged on.

And he'd been within shouting distance of escape when Favius seized power, necessitating a last-minute all-out dash.

A dash for the wall which was becoming a Wall as lines of scarlet fire seared the sky to form an impenetrable Dome of rippling bloodlight, the *Aurora Diabolicus*.

Running faster than he'd ever run before, knowing it wasn't enough, knowing he'd be too slow, too late; he'd fail. He'd fail and be trapped and caught, and—

Then, there she'd been again.

Ethriel. But not sylphlike little Ethriel as he'd known her; a his-sized Ethriel, arrayed in golden armor, with wings of light. A true, full-fledged angel of unearthly beauty.

Ethriel, who'd caught his hands, lifted him airborne, and carried him through the narrowing gap a heartbeat before the *Aurora Diabolicus* closed, sealing everything and everyone within ...

Only to, having saved him, be torn from him again, leaving him all the more desolate and alone.

His recollections of the hours immediately following Ethriel's second disappearance were, he had to admit, somewhat muddled.

Wandering through backwoods Florida nowhere, with little idea of where he was and less of where he was going. Only that it was away from the wall—the Wall, now, with its Mordor-esque parapets and demon-infested pinnacles. Away from the unholy, pulsating bubble of the Dome and the horrors it contained. Away from what was sure to be an inrush of media and military and response teams and an outrush of panicked civilians. Knowing he had to keep moving and could not afford to be caught up in any investigation.

Especially not since he'd become a murderer as well as a drug-runner. Dispatching Zilch hadn't weighed on his conscience much, but the enslaved vineyard thralls he'd also cut down with his newfound magic had been, once, just regular people, undeserving of their fate.

If he'd known then what even worse murder was to be done by his hands …

Blissfully unaware of that much, at least, he'd stumbled on, eventually finding refuge in some old car. There, his memory really betrayed or played tricks on him … he could have *sworn* it was an El Camino, but he'd curled up in the back seat, and he was fairly sure El Caminos didn't *have* a back seat … some cosmic blooper there, someone's fuckup that had somehow slipped past a reality check.

Anyway, it'd been refuge, a place to snag a couple hours sleep, every part of him—body, mind, and soul—a mass of knotted aches and pains. He'd wept for his lost angel, for the people he'd killed, and for his own uncertain future. How could anybody return to a normal life after what he'd seen and done and been through? After discovering what he *was*?

And yet, at the same time, there'd been a strange relief in it. As if a shell or facade had crumbled away, allowing the long-buried truth to emerge. Things would never be the same, *he* would never be the same, but maybe it would somehow still be all right. Maybe there'd even, he'd thought, turn out to be some reason or purpose to it all.

From the derelict car, he'd made his way to a nearly-as-derelict motel, all but forgotten and well off the beaten track. Not entirely abandoned, a neon VACANCY sign had sputtered pink into the darkness, and the front office had been occupied by a man and a dog, both sound asleep in front of a television shopping channel. But it obviously hadn't seen guests for a very long time.

So, refuge, part two. His wallet lost at the crash scene, no ID and just a handful of change to his name, he'd resorted again to the warlocky stuff, raiding a vending machine for stale snacks and breaking into a musty but not too terrible room.

Which was where, much to his surprise—indeed, much to his bare-naked toweling-off *shock*—Ethriel returned to him.

His recollections of what had *then* transpired were crystal clear and to be cherished to the end of his days, thank you very much. Even with the cringing anticipation of being smote by a thunderbolt or turned to a pillar of salt at any second.

Ethriel, there with him, also naked, warm and glorious, the radiance of her wings playing over their entwined bodies …

Worth risking any number of divine thunderbolts. Worth facing a tribunal of judgmental archangels or the very wrath of God.

Worth being tsked and tutted at by his scandalized grandparents? Okay, that part had been fairly mortifying. Still, in the greater scheme of things—his grandparents both being long dead, for instance, their meetings taking place in no earthly realm—he supposed he'd get over it.

After all, there'd been rather more important and urgent matters to deal with. Such as learning to master his powers.

Oh, yeah … and saving the world.

Hell, as he'd been led to understand it, was a city. A vast, sprawling, corrupt, polluted, teeming city of the demonic and the Damned. The Mephistopolis, which had grown apace with the modern world. Made up of its own various districts and principalities, subdivisions by sin, it ran on sorcery and suffering.

Not, in other words, any sort of place Greg was keen to visit. His preview, in the form of Lake Misquamicus, made sure of that.

Purgatory, a corner of which he *had* visited, was disturbing enough. Purgatory, the time-loop of the afterlife, the same span of events over and over, unchanging and unchangeable, and the more aware of it one was, the worse the eternal repetition of torment. It was, he thought, weirdly like having the chorus of "Every Breath You Take" on endless perpetual repeat in your head, forever.

Limbo didn't sound all that great either. The waiting room of the afterlife, the crowded DMV office where the "Now Serving" numbers ticked over at a pace to make glacial seem speedy, being on hold with occasional "your call is important to us" messages until your ear and butt and whole body went numb. Or the aircraft held on the tarmac, passengers strapped in but departure delayed, please remain seated—*South Park* may have been a bit off about Heaven and Hell, but they'd nailed Limbo with that episode.

There were other layers, other places, plenty of them. Myriads and multitudes, from astral planes to humble hauntings to full-scale sanity-shattering cosmic dimensions. Anything and everything. Even, he supposed, nothing ... not a blank or an absence or a vacuum or an emptiness ... a null so null it nullified even itself.

And, of course, there was Heaven. So often imagined, so often depicted. Heaven, its pure panorama of clouds and harps, peace and love, light and joy, reward and reunion. Where no one could be unhappy or in pain. Where all would be washed clean, made blameless, forgiven.

Given what Ethriel had told him, the cynical side of Greg couldn't help but suspect there was more to it than that. Maybe not the cold, aloof, fussy-bureaucracy corporate structure of, say, *Good Omens* (though she'd also said *Good Omens* had gotten a lot right) but more like ... well ... a theme park. Presenting the idyllic ideal for the paying customers. No troubles, problems, dissent, struggle, or unpleasantness. All smooth, effortless, serene perfection.

While under the surface and behind the scenes, the *real* work went on, the grunt work and dirty work and nitty-gritty, the colossal amounts of labor, organization, and minutiae required to keep something of such scale running. To make it *look* smooth and effortless, so as not to spoil the perception, the illusion, the immersion.

He'd long heard of the labyrinthine complex of tunnels and secret chambers below the Disney parks—the urban legend of whether or not they actually had Walt's cryogenically-preserved corpse stashed down there notwithstanding. They were said to be veritable hidden worlds, where the staff could go back and forth, carrying out the necessary daily business of supply restocking, trash removal, cleanup, and such, without being seen. As well as getting into or out of or changing costume and character; couldn't have the kiddies crying if they caught Mickey with his head off having a smoke, or Ariel and Cinderella yelling at each other.

Where, it was also said, anyone stricken by emergency illness or injury could be quickly and discreetly whisked away, rather than disrupt vacationers' fun with grim sights like ambulances, bodies, or blood. Where any altercations, threats, or crimes could be discreetly dealt with, out of sight and out of mind; nobody at the Magic Kingdom needed the buzzkill of police cars or SWAT teams.

If Hell was a city, why not Heaven as a theme park? Maybe minus the rides and gift shops—or, hey, maybe they had those too.

One thing for sure, he was about to find out.

Ethriel, wrapped in the beach towel, shivered against him. She raised her head from his shoulder, her gossamer hair having lost much of its luster, her celestial eyes shadowed.

"You … did it," she whispered.

"Warlock, remember?" He tried to keep it upbeat and confident, however wrenched by dread and worry he might be.

And heartsick; he'd rather have been struck down himself, discorporated or utterly obliterated, than for her to have suffered even the slightest harm.

Not to mention guilt-ridden; she'd been hurt defending *him*. While it was her literal *job* as his guardian angel, it didn't stop him from blaming himself. If he'd been stronger, better trained … if he hadn't gone to pieces over the little boy—

Fuuuuuck.

What a way to think of it, "gone to pieces." Because "gone to pieces" was precisely what had happened to the little boy, the junior warlock, the one who'd caught Greg off-guard with a burst of raw magic, making him reflexively lash out in retaliatory defense. His spell, like a net of diamond-edged wires, had reduced the boy to a pile of red chunks in the blink of an eye.

His horror over what he'd done nearly ended the whole fight then and there, but Ethriel had rallied him, convinced him to finish what they'd started. Which they had, dispatching the Hell-Centurion warlord Favius in a cinematic epic battle, and that should have ended it.

Only, it hadn't. Only, they'd reckoned without Favius's woman. Or consort. Or queen. Who, to say the least, was *extremely* pissed at them for depriving her of her demonic lover and possessed no small amount of dark power herself.

Greg now, in addition to the sigil seared into his forehead, bore a scar across his chin, a scar he doubted would ever heal or fade. A scar left by the point of Favius's gladius, snatched up by the woman, who might've chopped his head off if Ethriel hadn't yanked him back.

What had happened next would live rent-free in the forefront of Greg's mind for the rest of eternity. The woman stabbing Ethriel in the side and then, as Ethriel doubled over in agony, cleaving the radiant wings from her shoulder blades with a single vicious slice.

Somehow, he'd reached her, his wounded angel. Somehow, with the help of a ghost truck and a spectral energy boost from a dead man, he was able to translocate the surviving members of their rag-tag resistance to safety.

This, of course, being mere minutes before the rest of the day's events unfolded. Save the world? Ha, yeah, no, not quite. Fell far short, as a matter of fact.

They'd gotten rid of Favius, yes, and taken out a good-sized chunk of his legions into the bargain. A costly blow, a real setback, but …

But then there'd been the business with the nuke. Intended, no doubt, to eradicate the Dome and the Wall and everything within, as well as possibly half of Florida, its energy had instead been diabolically absorbed, converted, and rebounded in a globe-sweeping wave of absolute ultimate *PAIN*, affecting nearly every human soul in its encompassing path.

The results must have been catastrophic, apocalyptic. If not quite extinction-level, certainly devastating, causing massive loss of life both in the immediacy and the aftermath. Critically disrupting society, shattering civilization.

Those surviving members of their rag-tag resistance had been spared, as were others in similar liminal spaces. Passed over, as it were. Those sheltered by the *Aurora Diabolicus*, presumably likewise. For everyone else? Six seconds of sheer, incomprehensible, unbearable *PAIN*. To be followed by death, destruction, chaos, and collapse.

Way to make an entrance? Okay, couldn't deny, he had a knack for that.

Way to save the world? Yeah, not so much.

Unable to do anything or help anyone else, once ensuring the others were more or less all right, he'd focused solely on what mattered most.

"I'm going to fix this," he'd told Ethriel. "Somehow. Whatever it takes."

And now, here they were.

Perimeter Check

The Painwave, rolling relentless over everything outside the Dome, had indeed been a doozy.

Millions dead within the first few minutes, millions more in the subsequent hours. No natural disaster since the comet that wiped out the dinosaurs even came close, though this was far from a "natural" disaster by any reckoning. Manmade disasters like Chernobyl and Hiroshima, pandemics, climate change, and genocide? Small beans by comparison.

As far as supernatural disasters went, never mind Sodom and Gomorrah, or the plagues of Egypt; this ranked right up there with the Deluge. You know, the Flood, forty days and forty nights of planet-drowning rain, Noah's Ark, and all that.

Now, arguably, the Flood could be considered worse because it basically eradicated all nonaquatic life except for the two-by-two specimens gathered onto the Ark, plus Noah and fam. When really, the animals hadn't done a damn thing to deserve it; the Big G had been pissed off at *people*, and all the other species were just innocent bystanders.

In that regard, the Painwave was, if not *kinder*, at least more *fair*. Yes, many animals also were and would be indirectly affected, but the majority went more or less unscathed. Which was a better deal than they got during the Flood, and a better deal than eventual Armageddon would have in store for them. What's outlined in Revelation essentially fucks everything up for everybody, from mankind to microbes.

Because the Big G, for all He's supposedly so loving and benevolent, could be one petulant mean-ass prick when He got His robes in a twist. The undisputed master of table-flipping, screw-*you*-guys, take-My-ball-and-go-home hissy fits, some might say.

None of which is meant to justify the Painwave in any way, of course. It was vicious, brutal, over-the-top, excessive, and insane. Sheer, undiluted, capital-E Evil. Intended solely to hurt and punish and show humanity, in the stirring words of Favius's final oration, *the folly of **fucking with Hell!***

Mission accomplished.

After the Painwave, no one, not even the craziest gung-ho fanatic, was about to make a single move against Lake Misquamicus. Partly because, well, they were far too disorganized and busy dealing with other stuff, but mostly due to fear.

Okay, abject terror; call a spade a spade. But those still able to rationalize and justify made it seem more like sensible caution … itself often a rarity in such cases.

If a single nuke had done *that* much damage, they reasoned, what would a full-scale assault do? Who wanted to risk it when the entire global situation was more precarious than a bull on a tightrope?

Especially when that single nuke hadn't so much as scratched the Dome. Instead of the anticipated blooming mushroom cloud and total annihilation, instead of Marvin the Martian's yearned-for "Earth-shattering KABOOM," leaving a charred ashscape crater strewn with bits of demons, it'd done fuckall … except backlash the Painwave, and the last thing anybody wanted was an encore.

Shame, really, because—little did they know—a second attack right on the heels of the first *could* have done the trick.

Without Star Wormwood and the Ameri-Golem to facilitate the absorption and conversion, with Favius obliterated and hosts of demonic underlings discorporated in a messy whirlwind of spectral energies and untethered souls, with the diabolical anchor-points shaken and the defenses in disarray, with the balance of power teetering, the HellZone had never been more vulnerable.

Another nuke just then, even a small one, and, *hey presto alakazam*, problem solved!

But they *didn't* know, didn't even suspect. And, after fucking around and finding out once, were in no hurry to try again. Not when they had a complete shitshow of a mess on their hands already.

So, to overload metaphors, the critical window closed. The golden opportunity slipped through their fingers. They dropped the ball, missed the boat. The ship sailed. They were fuck out of luck.

The moment, basically, was lost.

The *Aurora Diabolicus* remained intact, the Wall and its multiple checkpoints still held fast and strong.

Sort of.

A few of the checkpoints hadn't been, strategically speaking, such of a much to begin with, even before Favius's ascension. They'd been there for years, and the more remote ones had gotten kinda … casual, if not lax, over time.

By the time the government had decided to reveal the modern marvel of their patriotic super-soldier Ameri-Golem prototype to a shock-and-awed world, only two of the checkpoints had still been operating as proper military bases at full capacity. The others routinely staffed anywhere from two to ten or so, sleeping in shifts like forest rangers.

Then, well … *ECCE, NOVUM PRINCEPS DE INFERNO, NOVUS REX TERRAE!* Favius had returned to Lake Misquamicus, seized power, and reshaped the perimeter and checkpoints to suit his purposes, rendering them no longer under the auspices and control of the United States military.

The wall itself, now the Wall, responding to a new master, rose and grew in a colossal surge, somehow volcanic and earthquake-ish and calving-glacier-in-reverse all at once. Forget prison movies and war movies; it reared up in the kind of looming, violent, domineering edifice only seen in epic fantasy trilogies, bristling with towers and parapets and pinnacles, topped in razor-sharp spears of obsidian instead of weak-ass barbed wire, pocked with arrow-slits and murder-holes and ramparts from which could be dumped cauldrons of boiling oil, molten iron, corrosive acid, toxic demon-puke, or gallons of festering bloody shit.

Instead of a few gun turrets, war machines bulked ominous and huge along its length. Catapults, trebuchets, ballistae, and other fiendish devices dreamed up by the most insane minds in Hell stood positioned to rain down punishment on anything within range.

Nazareth and Bethlehem, the two biggies, underwent the most impressive and effective transformations, becoming fortified strongholds with full dungeons and armories.

At Nazareth, the Gargoyles—dense and heavy, ogre-like, no longer remotely human, their bodies were solid stone overlaid with iron plating and spikes. When they moved, it was with a rough and grating menace, perpetually shedding grit the color and consistency of coarse-ground ore. Set deep beneath overhanging ridges were eyes like orbs of polished jasper, swirled and banded. They spoke in growling, guttural earthquake rumbles.

Though they needed no other weaponry than their brutish fists, that didn't stop them from gearing up in full equipping montage. Nazareth's arsenal of high-grade military hardware had also been given sinister Hell-style upgrades, supplemented with swords, maces, mauls, spears, axes, and other medieval and horrific implements of death.

Being bulletproof and almost invulnerable, they didn't technically need any additional armor either ... but, again, that wasn't going to stop them from buckling on whatever suited their fancy. At the very least, it only made them look more badass.

In the fuming bloodlight of the Aurora's baleful glow, they lined the battlements above Nazareth's main gate, which was now made of interlocked razor-edged iron blades, and waited with unbridled eagerness for any foolish mortals to attack.

At Bethlehem were the Blackwings, the airborne jack-boot lock-step flying squadrons initially under the command of double-headed Nazi-eagle bitch-harpy Captain Veronica Adler.

They had, however, sustained heavy losses in the battle at Bighead Rock, including the very untimely and ignominious rendering of Captain Adler herself into bloody, smoking, burnt-feather confetti. A substantial number of her troops had fallen to the combined efforts of magic, divinity, pyrotechnics, and hillbilly ingenuity.

Following such a defeat, the remaining Blackwings at Bethlehem had only strengthened in their disciplined fascist resolve. Anything—be it stealth bomber, spy-drone, stray kite, bird, or bumblebee—invading their airspace would be swiftly, decisively, and *thoroughly* brought down.

Their smug, lofty superiority and sneering disregard of the non-winged made them less than popular among the lake's other denizens, not that they cared. They swore unwavering fidelity to the dominion—if, interestingly, no particular personal oaths to Favius's successor.

So yes, Nazareth and Bethlehem may have held fast and

strong, but what about the other four?

Such as, oh, say, Checkpoint Moses, for example …

Due to a series of unfortunate—or, fortunate, depending on perspective—events, there'd only been a single guard on duty at Checkpoint Moses when Favius had claimed his dominion.

Normally, their complement numbered six, but one had been on personal leave (death in the family), and four more figured it'd be fine if they skipped out to find some Spring Break action over toward the coast. As long as someone covered for them, shouldn't be a problem, right?

Which, normally, it wouldn't have been. Moses, located in a particularly boggy and swampy region of Lake Misquamicus, rarely saw any official traffic. The closest they had to a road was a long-defunct hiking trail, reclaimed by nature after too many also-defunct hikers had bad run-ins with local wildlife.

Punts and inflatable rafts were their primary means of travel. Their supplies came in quarterly by airboat. Their main job was to patrol potential weak spots, where the government quarantine wall had been built across sluggish waterways coursing toward the lake. Each such spot included corrugated culverts reinforced with grates and mesh, in theory to keep anything nasty from swimming upstream and escaping the 'Zone. Snakes, 'gators, mosquitoes, leeches, and other such natural hazards were nothing to be sneezed at, but the unnatural ones spewed from and spawned by six billion gallons of shit, blood, bile, and piss—football-sized Copro-Leeches, vampiric imps with needle-nose proboscises, carnivorous lily pads, lamprey-snakes thin as wires and eager to slither into any orifice, salamanders that exhaled actual liquid-fire napalm, semi-sentient blobs of corrosive slime, cyclopean giant frogs, and so on—were the real concerns.

Oh, and there was also that fucking creepy awful tree-thing, with its fucking awful squelching pulsations and spongy throbbing heartbeat. That fucking creepy awful tree-thing, which had once snatched a guard clean out of a punt with a veiny, viny tentacle of a branch, wrung him like a wet rag, and then fucking *ate* him as his screaming partner rattled off an entire magazine into its tumorous, boled, and knotted trunk. Dark sap oozing like black blood from the wounds in its fetid bark, more branches writhed and roots humped up from the murky not-water, so he'd chucked his weapon overboard and poled that punt like a motherfucker.

Later that night, back at Checkpoint Moses, after having related the details to the others, he went and blew his brains out in the storage shed …

Yeah. Patrols after that? Those regular patrols of the waterways and weak spots? Went from regular to occasional to sporadic to hardly ever. Oh, they filled and filed the required reports, just as they filled and filed the duty log, but it wasn't as if anybody came to check. Surprise inspections were not really a thing.

As for the sole guard left on duty that fateful day? Shit, he'd been just as glad to be on his own for a while. It wasn't easy, stuck in close quarters with a bunch of other guys, most of whom were noisy assholes prone to stupid jokes, video games, and pranks.

So, sure, it'd have meant trouble if they got caught, but in the meantime, he could get some damn *sleep*. Had turned off the radio and communications too.

Not like any important announcements were going to be made. Not like anything was going to happen. Same shit, different day.

Certainly not like there'd be a whole broadcast of sacrifice and consummation followed by dominion-shaking transformations and a new regime.

Sleep. Blissful, quiet, uninterrupted *sleep*. Several hours of it. Deep sleep. Sound sleep. Dreamless, if he were lucky.

He'd been sleeping so deeply and soundly, in fact, that when he became aware of the rumbling vibration of the Wall reforming and the Dome descending, his first muddled thought was that he'd wakened himself snoring, with no idea he snored so loud!

It was also his last human thought.

His next thoughts only involved swimming, stalking, prey, defending his territory, and ravenous *hunger*.

In the days since, he'd rapidly acclimated to his new purpose … which wasn't so different from his old purpose: patrol and protect.

And *feed*.

The urge to feed may have been strongest, but it tied in nicely with the other two.

He barely cared that Checkpoint Moses had changed from a cluster of basic utilitarian prefab buildings perched on the shores of or on stilts above the brackish, swampy bayou to a half-submerged labyrinth of flooded, dripping catacombs. He paid little attention to the collapsed and broken archways, tilted columns, and monstrous graven images of leering, toothy, aquatic and semi-aquatic beasts or entities.

And he certainly didn't bother with any of the supplies and equipment still stored in its dank, sunken chambers. What did he care about weapons and ammo when he had jaws powerful enough to wrench a grown man's leg off at the hip? What need had he of body armor, Kevlar vests, or helmets when his own thickly scaled hide was tough enough to stop bullets? What use were punts and poles when sweeps of his muscular tail propelled his tripled mass with far more speed and ease?

He cruised silently, nostrils poking above the surface to guide him through the damp, tepid darkness by scent. Any fish-things, frog-things, or turtle-things he encountered, he snapped up and gulped down ... but their flesh was pale and unsatisfying, their blood tepid and thin. He craved *red* meat, craved *warm* blood!

Eventually, he made his way out of the catacombs, becoming aware for the first time of the baleful Dome pulsing above and the newly-arisen Wall. It had been rusty metal— poles, chain link, barbed wire, occasional sheets of humidity-warped steel—ten or twelve feet high at the most. It was now rearing slabs of moist, ancient-looking limestone, ruins slick with slimy fungus.

A deep, dim, buried part of his mind thought, *Mayan, Babylonian.*

A deeper, dimmer part thought, *Atlantean, Lemurian.*

A part so deep and so dim, so primal and primordial as to seem to come from somewhere else entirely thought, *R'lyehan, Dagonian.*

The merest suggestion, the faintest whisper-brush, of these concepts in his altered consciousness sent a chill through him, ectothermic or not.

Along the cracks and crevices of the limestone slabs, boneless creatures oozed and slithered. These, he did not snap at, but kept clear of, despite their smaller size and unprotected, gelatinous substance.

The "weak spots," where the old wall had crossed the meandering waterways flowing to the lake, were no longer marked by simple corrugated culverts blocked with grates and mesh.

He possessed enough sentience to wish they had been left unchanged, "weak spots" or not. Some sights, even for the HellZone, were just *too* disgusting.

Such as, say, the rear end of a huge, bloated Vore-Vole.

Now, a Vore-Vole was by no means a pretty picture from any angle, but especially not from behind.

Nor had any of them simply gotten stuck in the culverts, trying to squeeze their immense flabby mass through. They had been placed there, wedged there, held by slick, semi-organic-looking chains fused into the slick limestone.

Each was covered with wrinkled, finely-hairy skin like that of a naked mole rat, sickly-colored and bumpy. Stubby, nearly useless nubs of legs ended in splayed squishy-toed paws. Short, wormy, rudimentary tails sprouted above …

… above noisome, noxious, flexing, puckered sphincters a good yard in diameter. Flatulent burbles and dribbling seepage issued from them at irregular intervals, trickling into the stagnant bayou.

Their head-ends, he knew, would be blind-eyed, flap-eared, and consist primarily of yawing mouths ringed with wavering, questing, anemone-like pallid growths. Anything even remotely edible that came within range would be seized, tucked into a cavernous maw gurgling with digestive fluids, dissolved, and eventually shit-squittered out.

Honestly, ravenously hungry as he was in his new form, it put even him off his lunch.

But nothing would be entering or exiting the HellZone via any "weak spots" at Checkpoint Moses now, that was for sure.

At Checkpoint Gabriel, like at Moses, there had also been only one guard present when the bloodlight of the *Aurora Diabolicus* filled the sky.

Not, btw, because of anybody being on leave or sneaking off in hopes of scoring a little Spring Break action, expecting someone else to pick up the slack and cover for their AWOL asses. No. In their case, it was less a matter of abandoning post than of doing the right thing.

Or, trying to, anyway, for as well as it worked out.

Gabriel rarely had more than two on shift at any given time, being the smallest of the checkpoints and considered of the least importance by higher command. If they didn't get much in the way of external communication and support, well, that was fine by them; they were content to have the brass stay off their backs.

This was particularly true of Ryder, who wore a tie-dye t-shirt with his camo fatigues, sported a long grey ponytail, had a peace sign dangling from the same chain as his dog tags, and hardly seemed the type to be manning a military checkpoint, let alone holding down the fort on his own.

If not as out-of-the-way and hard to get to as Moses, Gabriel was a long-ass difficult drive from just about anywhere. Even back in the days before AllHell, when Lake Misquamicus had been a passable tourist destination, the scenery and amenities in the vicinity also left much to be desired.

About the only site worth mentioning was a campground once known as Bible Creek, which clearly had been established with more of the roughing-it kind of camping in mind. The terrain was rocky and rugged, scarce on nice flat, even motorhome parking, water and power hookups, or flush potties. A few run-down docks and piers jutting from the lakeshore did not a fancy marina make, the nearest place to rent a jet ski or speedboat was miles off, and the fishing wasn't great.

And since AllHell ...

Well, suffice to say, Bible Creek went downhill fast. A clan of inbred red-eyed mutant freaks worshiping the giant ram-horned skull of a deposed demon lord tends to do that. There goes the neighborhood, there go the property values.

None of which stopped the occasional attempted foray from the outside. Plenty of people, for plenty of reasons — thrill-seekers, do-gooders, journalists, etc. — wanted to get into the HellZone, and some of them figured a remote checkpoint like Gabriel would give them the best chance of finagling their way through.

Earlier, Ryder and his partner, Garcia, had gone ahead and let a church bus full of Holy Rollers pass their gate.

The ultra-religious types were always the hardest to dissuade; God had sent them, God would protect them. They were on a *Blues Brothers* style mission from God. Just couldn't talk sense to those people. Sometimes, it was easier to let them have a peek. Most, upon seeing what they were really up against, wasted no time turning tail and hauling ass back for the safety of the real world.

This particular group had other plans in mind, judging by the ensuing fusillade of gunfire and grenade blasts shortly thereafter. Seems they hadn't, as Ryder had put it, come to "pray the Sa' away" after all, but meant to wage actual war against Lucifer's minions.

So Garcia took the ATV and went to "investigate the disturbance" … and the next time Ryder saw her was on TV, getting her guts stomped out by a hulking clay behemoth.

Up until then, watching the Special News Report Live Broadcast, he'd been kicked back, drinking a Doctor Offbrand and thinking how glad he was the important hotshot military convoy had crossed at Nazareth. Too much pomp and circumstance and pressure for him; all that saluting and "ten-*hut!*" and "sir-yes-sir" left a worse taste in his mouth than the cheap cherry cola.

He'd sat up fast, though, when the scene on the screen went from freaky to FUBAR.

Not cool, man. Not cool at all.

He wasn't old enough to have been a *real* hippie. His parents had been, though. Ryder's earliest memories included caftans, beaded door-curtains, and Red Zinger tea. He'd been raised on a steady diet of Flower Power, Make Love Not War, and Give Peace a Chance.

How he'd ended up in the military remained a mystery even to him. "Seemed like a good idea at the time" was the best he could do. If he pressed himself, maybe—*maybe*—there'd been some lofty notion of changing the system from within.

But for every famous photo of a flower child poking daisies down gun barrels, a thousand others got rifle stocks to the face. The top brass weren't interested in peace and love. Peace and love didn't bring in the big bucks. The war machine made a fuckload more money than the Age of Aquarius ever would.

He'd signed on for sentry duty at Checkpoint Gabriel because it had sounded low-stress and because shooting demons seemed preferable to shooting fellow human beings.

Not that he'd had to do much of that either; on the occasions something monstrous ventured too far from the lake, Garcia was always glad for target practice.

Now, though, the situation had undergone a drastic what-the-fuck. *He* was something monstrous, warped by demonic energy into a hellish camo/tie-dye hybrid of machine gun and man, fused with his M4 so that he couldn't put it down if he tried. The entire checkpoint had become a bastardized Vietnam POW jungle camp that hurt Ryder's brain just to look at.

It hurt his brain more when, an unknown amount of time later, several figures in ghillie suits had come creeping from the cover of the Florida scrub-woods, attempting some sort of covert-op sneak attack.

Weren't they all on the same side?

Wait, what side was he *on*?

Did he *have* a side?

He didn't want to open up on them if they were just regulars like himself, serving their country, doing their job.

But he couldn't let them broach the gate, the Wall, threaten the glorious infernal realm! While they would likely have had no moral qualms about scragging *his* lanky ass on sight.

Before he could decide what to do, a sniper shot him in the chest. He'd pitched backward, his tie-dye re-tie-dyed with oily blood.

The only reason it hadn't finished him off was too cliche to be believed: the sniper's bullet had struck the amalgamated cluster of peace sign and dog-tags he wore around his neck.

Still, not cool, man. Not cool at all.

As he'd fallen, thinking how much this whole thing was one major bummer of a bad scene, the surrounding vegetation reared up. Inhumanoid plantforms moved in on the attackers. Ryder was again weirdly reminded of the photos of protesters sticking daisy stems down rifle barrels.

Only, instead of daisy stems, they were long spiky-blossomed spears, and they went a lot further than down rifle barrels. They went into throats, into bellies.

Thorn-studded vines whipped around ankles or necks, hauling thrashing, bleeding, screaming bodies into the tree canopy. Sharp shafts of bone-colored bamboo, slicked vile green with vegetative toxins, sprang up in impaling punji-stick booby-traps.

The soldiers had tried to fight back, tried to retreat, for

all the good it did them. The ghillie suits, despite being made of artificial stuff, adapted and merged, sprouting new profusions of growth. Their wearers found themselves literally rooted to the ground, immobilized and taken over, forcibly converted to a different cause.

These new recruits may have been unable to move very far or fast but were quite able to lash out against the as-yet-unconverted with tough ropy tendrils, barrages of barbed cactus-like needles, clouds of choking spores, gouts of acidic sap, and nasty little sticker-burrs.

Gunfire-shredded leaves and fronds mended, flourishing on a nutrient-rich diet of blood. Mangled corpses, falling to the overgrown earth, rotted to mulchy fertilizer fast as a time-lapse video.

Flower Power, motherfuckers!

The hermit, Solomon Shoop-Shoop the Most Fervent and Penitential, had a sad.

He sat atop his mountain at Checkpoint Uriel—he had not come to the mountain, the mountain had come to *him*, in a dramatic upsurging fashion, lifting him so fast he shrieked and pissed himself—at its lonely apex, in front of his humble cave.

It was perfect. Ideal. Exactly as he'd envisioned and always wanted.

His bed was a board studded with nails. His bathroom, a dark crack at the back of the cave. He had no blanket, no fire or candles against the night. His only source of water was a rank-smelling trickle from a cleft in the rock, of which he had to drink by catching it in his scabbed hands; he had neither cup nor bowl. His only food was in the form of pallid, yellowish wormy extrusions that squeezed up like thick pus from the dry, dusty sandstone. Manna from Heaven, it certainly wasn't. It tasted of ammonia and rancid cheese curds.

His garment was a literal hair shirt, coarse and itchy, greasy, speckled with dandruff, crawling with lice. His feet were bare. His own hair whipped about his head in dirty, matted dreadlocks like macrame snakes. His beard straggled to his knobby knees.

A hank of rope girded his scrawny waist, a knotted scourge hanging from it for whenever he felt the need to flagellate himself. As the latticework of old scars, half-healed welts, and freshly raw and oozing open wounds crisscrossing his back attested, this need struck him with considerable frequency.

Perfect. The whole scene. Perfect in its penitence.

Yet, he had a sad.

Here he was, at his most fervent and everything, waiting to dispense his wisdom to those worthy pilgrims who made the ascent, passing the tests and surviving the obstacles ... but no one had come.

He'd set it all up like those devil-dungeon games he used to play—his father had always told him those games, along with comic books and rock-and-roll music, would end him up in Hell; the old man had been right about that much at least!— and those Indiana Jones movies, especially the one with the Holy Grail.

Though, thinking on it now, he might've gotten a little mixed up with that other Holy Grail movie, such as at the bridge where his minion was supposed to ask pilgrims their favorite color ... either way, though, he'd put in a lot of work, and it was disappointing to have it go unappreciated.

Once, early on, a vehicle *had* approached, but it was just that no-account troublemaker Heck Bodean. Heck could have been, Solomon knew, a real first-rate sinner if he'd put his mind to it instead of chump-change dicking around with alcohol, gambling, and pornography. He had the potential, lacked the conviction. There he'd been, seeking not wisdom but escape! Wanted them to let him and his harlot-Jezebel kinswoman—the harlot-Jezebel kinswoman Heck hadn't even *fucked*; honestly, did someone have to draw him a map?—through the gate, forsaking this, their glorious new kingdom of Hell!

Well, the mistake had been Heck's. The original gate had ceased to exist, replaced by the mountain with its narrow path, up one side and down the other, loaded with pitfalls and puzzles. No one was getting through without earning it!

Except, then, Heck just turned and walked away, the lazy cheater! So Solomon's semi-mummified minion Curtis had to shoot him, and then the harlot-Jezebel beat the stuffing out of Curtis, hefted Heck back into the truck, and drove off!

Long story short, here he was on top of his mountain, minus one minion—sort of; Curtis had been subcarnated into a desiccating sand sponge, capable of sucking the moisture from a man-sized target in a matter of seconds—peering vainly in all directions from his high, lonely vantage point.

Yea verily, Solomon Shoop-Shoop the Most Fervent and Penitential sat, unappreciated and disappointed, having a sad.

Not all of his sad, though, was because nobody had yet come to test themselves against the challenges of his mountain, which he'd worked so hard on and was so proud of.

Part of what really got his goat was how, here he'd been, all this time, embracing the new cause. He wasn't some Johnny-Come-Lately who'd only hopped the bandwagon after Favius rose to power.

Years, he'd done the hermit thing! *Years!* Years of deprivation and penitence! Flogging himself raw (in the knotted-scourge sense, not the fun way, tyvm). Living on locusts and nettles! Finding locusts wasn't easy either; sometimes, he'd had to settle for crickets, cicadas, and beetles … but in his heart and mind, they'd been locusts, and it was the thought that counted.

What had he gotten for his pains? His literal, very *very* literal, pains? His suffering and servitude?

Scorn and mockery, that's what he'd gotten. Being laughed at. Made fun of. Called fucking "Shoopie." Having his own men roll their eyes and twirl their fingers behind his back.

Then, boom, a whole revamped dominion of unholy transformations, the new Wall, the Dome, the Checkpoints and their personnel, and they're strutting around as if it's the latest craze … when he'd been here, fervent and faithful, all along! Didn't he deserve at least a little recognition?

True, he'd gotten his mountain, the hermity mountain of his deepest desires. And he hadn't been turned into a gargoyle, pyroclast, harpy, or other monstrosity like everyone else, but was allowed to retain his wretched human form, the better to continue his penance and misery.

Still, something more would've been nice. Pilgrims would've been nice. Followers. Awestruck humble admirers. He'd just had a few underlings, who'd been desiccated and beef-jerky mummified into mindless—again, literal; their heads were as hollow as Halloween jack-o-lanterns— obedient thralls.

Maybe a sacrificial lamb or two; was that so much to ask? His son showing up, them doing a take on the Abraham and Isaac thing? If he'd had a son ... but he *had*, in his previous life, hadn't he? Yes, yes he had. A lazy, whiny, sullen brat who'd probably grown into a lazy, whiny, sullen youth by now.

Do the boy good to be pinned to a sandstone slab of an altar by his own father, the jagged edge of a bone-handled knife held to his throat. Teach him some fucking manners and respect, knock some sense and humility into his entitled ass!

What a reunion that'd be! Downright prodigal!

Probably too much to hope for, but could a man not dream?

In the meantime, he took a slight measure of consolation in the knowledge of what his son must've experienced during the Painwave. Consolation, if mixed with covetous envy. What exquisite, excruciating agony it must have been! Sheer, pure, undiluted *PAIN*, of a sort to make beds of nails and flaying the skin from one's back seem like a mother's kisses.

He had, from his mountaintop, witnessed a portion of its effects. Among his meager possessions was a pair of military-issue high-tech binocs with the lenses replaced by cyclops corneas; these cynoculars had near-telescopic range and a zoom feature to put the fanciest cameras to shame. With them, he'd tracked the course of the nuclear missile, its arcing contrail etching the sky, its lethal glint as it bulls-eyed in on the Dome.

And he'd seen, sweeping around his full field of vision, plenty of people as the resulting backlash washed over them.

Fleeing evacuees, clogging the highways and byways with traffic jams of epic proportions. Families unable or unwilling to leave, huddled in their homes or community shelters. Members of the media, sharing the universal delusion their press credentials made them untouchable. Eager lookie-loos, top brass, and government officials, who thought they were at minimum safe distance.

He'd seen, all right. He'd witnessed, praise Satan!

But he himself had missed out. Missed out on the ultimate torment.

Lucky fuckers. No wonder he had a sad.

Last but not least, Checkpoint Jericho … events at which may have been described in more detail elsewhere, as bonus material in a limited edition, or something. The particulars, therefore, need not be gone into, but a summary may be in order.

In terms of the four classical elements, if Nazareth represented Earth, Bethlehem Air, and Moses Water, Jericho got Fire. Leaving Gabriel with plants and Uriel with … with whatever the fuck Shoopie was up to; they can't all make sense.

Anyway, Jericho. Fire. A roiling wall of **FIRE**, not just fire or even *fire* but **FIRE**. Smoking fissures spitting cyclonic whirls of sparks and embers. Sudden jets of incandescent flame. Choking ash and soot. Expanses of red- and white-hot coals, the air above them distorted with heat-ripples.

Flash-furnace. Crematorium. Incinerator. Furious, fuming, searing, scorching.

FIRE.

Of them all, really, the one the most like Hell was, to the common person's understanding, *supposed* to look. Needing only the stereotypical little capering red devils with pitchforks to complete the picture.

Jericho had previously been among the better-known checkpoints, being located not far past a nameless wide-spot-in-the-road townlet. This townlet, following AllHell, enjoyed a brief touristy-trap revival after rebranding itself as Area 666, offering souvenirs, sightseeing, local produce, and minor magics.

It was also home to, fittingly, Peterson Pyrotechnics, a generational family-run outfit claiming to produce "Florida's Finest Fireworks" … many of which were at least semi-legal. Though plenty of Area 666's businesses had since closed down, the Petersons were still going strong. At the time of recent critical events, most of them had been hunkered down in the company's warehouse, a low-slung, heavily reinforced bunker of cinderblock, steel, and concrete made to withstand explosions, preparing to "ride out" the threatened nuclear missile strike. Whether they could have survived it or not was rendered moot; what mattered was, while they did get hit with the Painwave, they came through undamaged, able to quickly bounce back from and walk off the effects.

Checkpoint Jericho *also* happened to be where an SUV of college students, on their way to celebrate Spring Break at the fancy lakehouse belonging to the parents of the spoiled-rich-kid Carmichael twins had—courtesy of cash bribes from Trevor and a tit-flash from Chelsea—entered the HellZone just before Favius rose to power. They'd thought the demonic stuff an exaggerated hoax and weren't about to let it ruin their fun.

Their entrance had further been facilitated by the fact Trevor Carmichael knew one of Jericho's gate-guards from when they'd gone to school together. Knew and, seeing him again now with his trim, fit, buff-and-toned military physique, was plenty eager to refresh their acquaintance, Trevor being the sort who appreciated a fine form regardless of minor details such as gender.

In other words, Trev thought Jason was hot as fuck.

Perhaps, as it turned out, a poor choice of words.

When Jason—in hopes of getting another look at Chelsea's tits, if not more—decided to pay a visit to the lakehouse after his shift was done, he'd borrowed/rented a sweet-ass Trek Procaliber mountain bike from a fellow soldier and set out on a harrowing cross-country ride. As a result, he'd been a good ways away when Jericho's section of the Wall erupted into roaring, seething *FIRE*.

To say he'd been stunned would be to put it mildly. He'd stood there, astride the bike, gaping at the conflagration, trying to tell himself it had been a terrible but ordinary disaster. Terrorist attack, tanker-truck crash, the fireworks factory blown up. Trying to tell himself but not buying it. Not with Star Wormwood flaring overhead and the bloodlight of the *Aurora Diabolicus* flooding the sky.

Stunned and undecided.

Go back? And do what? If he could even get within a quarter-mile without being barbecued alive? When his fellow soldiers must have been fucking *carbonized*?

Or go on? Find Trev and Chelsea and their friends, get drunk, get wasted, get laid while he still had the chance?

He had still been standing there, astride the bike, stunned and undecided, when the ground began to smolder at his feet.

To smolder, then to fracture and split with fuming cracks,

then to bulge as a lumpy mass pushed its way up.

It was human-like in shape, pumice-grey in color, pumice-rough in texture, with an ashen coating flaking away to reveal the sullen pyroclastic glow of banked coals. As it forced itself higher, freeing head and shoulders, arms and torso, something about it seemed horribly familiar.

Dropping the bike, he stumbled backward.

It raised molten lava eyes to him. "You're AWOL, soldier," it said in a crackling, smoky voice.

A searing hand shot out and seized his ankle.

"We have strict penalties for desertion," it told him, and dragged him, screaming, into the smoking earth.

So, yeah, Trevor thought Jason was pretty hot?

Well, he sure was now, all right!

Much hotter than before. Too hot. Far, far too hot. Hot as in "suspended in a cage over a bubbling caldera of magma in a fiery cave" hot.

The cage's bars glowed an incandescent yellow. Whenever any part of his body made contact, his skin instantly sizzled, blistered, crisped, and peeled off in charred curls ... but never to the point of destroying the nerve endings and stopping the pain. He healed almost as fast as the damage was done, trapping him in a vicious cycle of agonizing punishment.

His clothes and body hair had burned away, leaving him more naked than he'd ever been. Even his pubes were gone, having ignited in a brief but brisk inferno, damn near frying his dick off. It hung like a blackened bratwurst against his scrote and baked-potato balls.

If he stood on the cage floor, the tender bare soles of his feet cooked like steaks on a grill. If he hung from the bars above him to give his feet a brief reprieve, his hands took the branding-iron brunt of it until his upper body could no longer bear the strain of supporting his entire weight. Then he'd have to lower his feet again, the tender new skin fresh meat for the cooking, leaving scraps of burnt tissue from his palms and fingers.

Rising superheated fumes singed his nasal passages, scorched his lungs. Sweat evaporated with a teakettle hiss from his pores. The water from his protesting eyes did the same, and how the eyeballs themselves didn't just burst or boil away, Jason wouldn't have known, even if he'd been able to think about it.

When he *could* think, of anything beyond how goddamn

much it hurt, it was along the lines of how this, at least, was what Hell was *supposed* to be like. This was the scalding cavern, the Lake of Fire, the sputtering torches and fumarole gas-jets, the cackling crackling flame-gremlins cavorting on sulfurous outcrops. This was the Hell a childhood of Sunday school and Saturday morning cartoons had led him to expect.

Instead of pitchfork-wielding devils, though, he had Nora, Russ, and Shae. Or rather, the creatures that used to be Nora, Russ, and Shae. He could still recognize each of them, tell them apart despite the similarities in their new inhuman humanoid pumice-and-lava appearances.

Russ was still a slobby bastard, for one thing, his fat-rolls coursing in lava-orange ripples, a perpetually slow-erupting volcano flow oozing down his body to somehow absorb again and recycle itself.

"Mmm-mmm-mmm, smells like barbecue in here!" he'd chortle. "Making me hungry!"

"You deserted your post, soldier," Nora continually reminded Jason. "You deserted your post, and traitors must *burn!*"

At this, the flame-gremlins would spring down, screeching, monkeylike, swarming his cage and pelting him with gooey wads of igneous shit that struck, adhered, and clung like hot tar.

As for Shae …

"You lost my bike, you asshole."

Jason always tried to choke out explanations, apologies, and pleas, but the best he could do was a series of hoarse, ashen croaks, and the burning agony went on and on.

Juno Regina

Never in her life would June Goldsmith have expected to find herself ruling over a demented, disgusting, depraved pocket kingdom of actual Hell-on-Earth.

Of course, never in her life would she have expected a lot of what had happened to her in the past couple of weeks.

Such as jabbing a long-handled campfire marshmallow-toasting fork up her aged mother's aged hoo-hah and yanking out, in a messy gynecological evisceration, the entire reproductive works responsible for June's own existence. Forget Freudian castration fantasies and Oedipus/Electra complexes; there was fucked-up and then there was *fucked-up*.

Even now, as she reclined on her throne, the sun-bleached skeleton of Margaret Goldsmith still hung by the wrist bones from the gantry where the deed had been done. It'd become, in a weird way, a shrine of sorts. Denizens of the realm had taken to lighting candles and leaving little offerings. Matricidal martyrdom, relics of an anti-saint … June didn't care to know or ask. Let them do as they would.

The old bitch was dead and gone, which was what mattered. Dead and gone by her only daughter's hand. The marshmallow fork had finished the job by piercing its tines up through the underside of Margaret's wattled chin, stapling her relentless critical tongue to the roof of her mouth and skewering her judgy contemptuous eyeballs.

It had been the most satisfying moment June had ever known.

Until a few minutes later, when she'd finally been relieved of her burdensome virginity, there on a dais in front of a wild crowd, on a televised broadcast for all the world to see. She had been stripped naked, splayed out, and *fucked*. Fucked harder, faster, better, and more thoroughly than she'd even imagined possible. The very first thrust brought on a shattering climax, and she'd come so many more times she'd lost count … before losing consciousness.

Fucked by a demonic brute of a man, a musclebound centurion no longer in the legions of Imperial Rome but of Hell, oath-sworn to Lucifer, nearly every inch of his skin patchworked with the horrifically living faces of victims he'd personally peeled from their red and screaming skulls.

Never in her life would she have expected that either, but she had loved every single grunting, sweaty, flesh-slapping, cock-throbbing, cunt-clasping, fluid-gushing second.

And the encores? The many, many torrid lascivious encores over the following days? Having him finger her, feast upon her with his thick and broad delving tongue? Fellating him, discovering both her innate knack for the act and her hunger for it? Being wanted, desired, lusted after? Being fondled and filled and sated?

Oh, she'd loved all that too.

She'd also loved—which she *certainly* hadn't expected—*him*. Favius. Her lord, her king, her master, her husband, her soulmate, her lover … no single word could encompass what he was to her or what she was to him. They had somehow found, in each other, destiny and completion. Happiness.

Then that asshole warlock and his whore-slut angel just had to barge in and ruin everything.

One more on the list of things she never in her life would have expected, though in a way, she supposed she should have. Why *wouldn't* the universe, or fate, or God, finally give her what she'd craved and wanted and needed for so long, only to then tear it away from her? A big cosmic gotcha, the mean joke to transcend all mean jokes. Another pointing, jeering HA-HA in a long line of pointing, jeering HA-HAs.

Well, she'd scored some revenge points, at least, by drawing warlock blood and angelic ichor. Another for the "never would have expected" column, the way she'd taken up Favius's gladius and hacked that divine whore-slut's wings right from her back.

Some revenge points, yes. Some, but by no means enough. After what they had taken from her? After what they had done? Oh, she owed them plenty more. But they'd gotten away, they'd escaped her furious wrath, and she would not let it stand.

Among the many other things she never would have expected was to be literally backstabbed.

By the girl who was *supposed* to be her dutiful handmaid.

Okay, June maybe *had* been having a bit too much fun rubbing her nose in it … Chelsea, young and sexy, rich, privileged, with her perfect tits and better-than-you attitude … it'd stuck in her craw bigtime to be relegated to handmaid status, let alone handmaid to a flat-chested homely spinster twice her age. Having to wait on and be ordered around and treated as "the help" … oh, the way it made Chelsea's teeth grind, even as she'd tried to put on a subservient smile!

So, yeah, really, June probably shouldn't have been all *that* surprised by the betrayal. Someone used to being the star of the show finding herself a bit player while the most unlikely candidate took center stage? Doing demeaning work, getting no attention instead of having admirers salivating all over her? Of *course* she'd instantly hated June. Of course she'd wanted her ousted, cast down, even dead.

To personally pick up the self-same marshmallow fork which had been remade into a symbolic scepter/weapon of power and run June through? From behind, no less; the cowardly literal backstab? That, one would think, Chelsea'd lack the nerve to do. Or be too afraid of the repercussions.

Well, water under the bridge; she'd done it. All the worse for her, she hadn't done a good enough job. Although the impalement had *hurt* like ice-lightning, although it'd been seriously unsettling for June to look down and see the bleeding tines protruding from her chest, and although she'd been in such a weakened and vulnerable state after smiting the angel the blow that took her down, it hadn't been fatal. Had, somehow, managed to miss puncturing the heart or nicking the aorta, or so she was told later by the medics and healers who'd tended to her.

Still … traitorous little bitch!

The events leading up to her injury, that momentous day atop Bighead Rock, remained clear in her mind. How quickly the tide of battle had turned, their glorious triumph gone so suddenly sideways,

Not that she cared about most of it. The Wyrds, the pukey boy-warlock and his mother, the Blackwings, the Senators; for none of them did June give a shit.

But what had happened to Favius ... *her* Favius ... seeing him torn apart, seeing him fall, seeing him obliterated and annihilated ... much too clear, every detail vivid and sharp-focus.

She wondered, sometimes, late at night, if she'd have been better off *had* the traitorous little bitch killed her. So she didn't have to remember and relive.

Her rage, the seething redblack cloud of her vengeful rage, argued otherwise. Only when the asshole warlock and his whore-slut angel, and anyone who'd allied with or aided them, was dealt with—harshly, permanently dealt with—could she seek the comfort of her own oblivion.

Until then?

Until then, it looked like she'd have to be the goddamn infernal ruler of this goddamn infernal region.

There'd been no coronation, no official transfer of title or power, no ceremony, no ritual. Nor any other claims, any rivals seeking to usurp or take over—might've been a different story had that Nazi cunt Adler survived. Just an overall, unspoken, unanimous consensus from the masses. *The king is dead, long live the queen, ipso-facto cock-a-doodle-doo.*

Fine. Queen. Queen without a king, without a crown.

Queen of what?

Queen of six billion gallons of demon-infested blood, bile, piss, and shit. Surrounded by acres and acres of demon-infested swampland, scrubland, and backwoods, full of demon-infested flora and fauna. With a demon-infested population of retirees, vacationers, hillbillies, soldiers, and witches.

And, let it not be forgotten, the entire United States government and every other nation and living soul outside the Wall and the Dome wanting—perhaps not unreasonably, given the circumstances—them all wiped from the face of the Earth.

If the events leading up to the backstabbing remained crystal-clear in June's memory, the events immediately following it, she'd missed and had to be told of later.

She remembered Juggernaut, her Golem bodyguard, stomping toward the warlock. What had her order been? "Bring me his *heart!*" in the best fairy-tale wicked queen tradition.

She remembered that ridiculous Ameri-Golem in its star-spangled loincloth, poised below Star Wormwood waiting for the incoming missile. She remembered the other two Golems, Thing kiln-baked by a fireball and Hulk an inert lump without its empowering LIFE glyph-stone.

She remembered the chaos and destruction all around her, burnt and bleeding and broken bodies everywhere, the half-finished senatorial rotunda taken out by a flying junkyard-reject, the chariot-slaves rebelling, the angel wounded and crippled, the warlock desperate and drained.

Then she'd fallen, and aside from a brief semiconscious resurfacing, the next thing she knew, she was once again reviving in the master bedroom of the supersize luxury RV serving as the royal residence.

Favius's toady-in-chief, the skeev-o local known as Spot, had filled her in on the rest of it. Some of which hadn't made a whole lot of sense at the time—ghost truck? seriously? He told her how the warlock and angel had escaped, how Juggernaut wrenched the traitorous bitch handmaid's arms from their sockets, how it went with the nuke, and the hectic aftermath.

It seemed, however, the traitorous bitch handmaid had survived the garishly violent de-limbing.

"I'se may've overstepped, Yer Highness," Spot had said, groveling for all he was worth, "but I'se figgured, see, y'might as be wantin' her alive, y'know, t' settle her hash personal-like. So's I called off that there Golem an' had 'em patch her up enuff's t' keep her alive."

It also seemed the traitorous bitch handmaid's pretty-boy brother, Favius's first appointed Senator, had made it through the day's events mostly unharmed. He'd wasted no time pleading to June on Chelsea's behalf ... though not exactly in the spirit of family loyalty and filial affection. Trevor Carmichael, already notorious around the lake as an orgiastic sadistic hedonist, was said to have a real, uh, *interest* in amputations, and, well ...

Tempting as it would have been to "settle her hash personal-like," June found the prospect of turning Chelsea over to her brother's "care" far more vindictively satisfying. Incestuous nonconsensual mutilation and stump-fucking was probably worse than anything she could have devised anyway. Let the pretty-boy have his playtoy. Served the little bitch right.

Besides, if she was to make a go of running this crazy shitshow, she'd need an administration, and he was the only Senator currently left standing. One, Favius had dispatched himself; the others had still been in the rotunda when it simultaneously collapsed and exploded. So, keeping Trevor content and on her side, a person of authority to the masses, was in the best interests of herself and the realm, until such time as she decided what the fuck she was going to *do*.

All of which was a lot to think about, a daunting and overwhelming list. Delegate, take charge, make decisions, lead. From large-scale stuff such as maintaining the Wall and commanding the troops, to a billion bits of bullshit bureaucratic and diplomatic minutiae.

She'd have to deal with whatever was going on in the wider world beyond the Dome—the initial reports after the Painwave provided some relief; it'd be a good while before anybody got their shit together enough to try anything else. She'd have to deal with internal matters as well, picking up the pieces, seeing to the well-being of her subjects, and whatever fucked-up sense of community helped them more-or-less function.

Not to mention the asshole warlock, his whore-slut angel, their idiot allies, and any other possible would-be dissenters, rebels, or troublemakers.

When, really, she just wanted to curl up and cry. Cry for her lost love, her Favius and his magnificent cock, and all the glorious fucking she'd never be able to enjoy again.

Oh, she *could* have gotten sex, plenty of it, and readily enough; she'd not missed the lustful way gazes followed her now. She would've had no shortage of volunteers, could have commanded anyone within the realm to her bedchamber and had them comply.

Which was also something she never in her life would have expected; she'd always been, since childhood, drab and unattractive.

A plain-Jane, as her mother put it.

Often.

Almost every single fucking *day*.

Usually with a tone of there-there condescension.

"Oh, Juney-June, some girls just aren't cut out for being pretty or popular."

Puberty hadn't brought her much in the way of curves, leaving her narrow-hipped and small-breasted.

"Fancy clothes and makeup would just make it seem like you were trying too hard."

A lifelong litany of it. *Don't draw attention, don't highlight your flaws, spare yourself the heartache, boys aren't going to be interested in you anyway, you weren't meant to be special but that's fine, nothing wrong with it, nothing wrong with being a plain-Jane* ... on and on until she could scream.

Decades of failing to get laid. Couldn't even give it away to some drunken trucker. Having men look right past or through her as if she were invisible was bad enough; having them elbow each other and snicker and make remarks was worse.

Then, joining the church group for their trip to Lake Misquamicus. Knowing their plan was reckless and dangerous if not downright stupid. Knowing there were demons and monsters and inhuman brutes in the HellZone, eager to ravage and ravish anybody, even a plain-Jane spinster virgin like her ... and how pathetic was *that*? Reasoning it might be her last and only shot?

Pretty goddamn pathetic.

Pretty goddamn pathetic to be bound naked and spreadeagle to an altar beneath the giant ram-horned skull of an Archduke of Hell, whose spirit had possessed the body of one of her fellow crusaders in order to defile her, hot and wet and ready and waiting, only to be inspected and met with the comment, *"ENH, IT'LL DO."*

And even then, even *then*, having a couple of other crusaders bust in at the last minute to "save" her from violation?

At the time, it'd been just about the ultimate salt in the wound, insult to injury, slap in the face. At the time, she'd yet to meet Favius, yet to find her true destiny.

Once she had, once he'd claimed her and fucked her and made her his queen, she could look back and be grateful for the previous rejections and intercessions. Better to be the willing virgin, offering herself freely and eagerly after proving her dedication by an act of vicious matricidal sacrifice.

No regrets, as the pithy saying went. No regrets.

People had looked at her differently after that. Men *and* women. With admiration, desire, jealousy, respect. No more the awkward and self-conscious plain-Jane, she'd felt wanton and wild and confident and free. *Favius* craved and enjoyed her body, *Favius* couldn't keep his hands off her or his cock out of her; what possible more ego-boost could she need?

Now, Favius was gone, and while, yes, she *could* have taken other lovers, there didn't seem to be much point. How could anyone else even *hope* to compare? How could she ever be satisfied by some lesser being?

Besides, then she'd have to kill them.

A promise was a promise.

Thus she'd sworn to Favius, his only condition to their … arrangement.

Kill them after or have them killed. Casual. Meaningless. Disposable fuckmeat. Throwaways.

So long as no other, he'd said, fingers buried deep within her slick heat, pressing at her G-spot, thumb persuasively massaging her clit, *man, demon, or beast, be allowed to go on living a single day more with the flesh-memory of this hot, hungry cunt.*

Those had been his terms, to which June—nearing orgasmic overload—had readily agreed.

And would have had no compunctions adhering to, but it still just wouldn't be the same.

The first few days following the battle, she'd stayed confined to the RV, recuperating and trying to come to terms with incalculable grief, fury, and loss.

Spot, with his customary sleazy deference, handled most matters, or at least put them off until she was in a better state of mind. Various grievances, such as those involving relatives of the recently discorporated or deceased, could wait. So could the appointment of replacement Senators. New construction projects were back-burnered in favor of cleanup and repairs.

In the lakeshore war camp, now called Camp Favius—not by any vote or decree; it just organically and naturally *was*—the abattoirs, smokehouses, and mess tents bustled, processing resources before they could go to waste. Salvaged and scavenged items were inventoried by the quartermasters. The medics' tents saw to the wounded; the detention facilities saw to the prisoners of war.

The soldiers had adjusted their chains of command

without fanfare, the competent stepping up or being promoted as needed, the weak links disciplined with extreme sanction. Couriers—Blackwings, mostly—took messages back and forth, brought in reports from the Checkpoints, and performed security sweeps on the lookout for deserters and dissidents. Though some of the reports from the Checkpoints were … odd, to say the least …

Matters at the RV itself were going smoothly; Ma and Pa Riggers—the animate heads of an apple-cheeked matron and jovial muttonchopped man, grafted into the sides of their portly, club-footed son—were longtime caretakers to many properties in the vicinity, including the Carmichael house, and had arranged for adequate domestic staff.

As a further bonus, the top brass's former Michelin-star chef and his team had been located, hidden in one of the convoy's refrigerated supply trucks. Once thawed, they'd returned to active duty, under only modest threat.

The civilians, for the most part, carried on as they had since AllHell, with Crawdaddy's roadhouse still being the primary node of information, trade, and communication. If the famed Hock Parties were on hold for the time being, if a lot of people preferred to stay home and lay low and see which way the wind was blowing, that was considered fair enough.

"It's them Bodeans you'se gonna wanna keep an eye on," Spot told June. "First Zeke, then Maybelle, then fuckin' Heck an' Lorlinda up an' siding with the opper-sition? Clarabeth, 'leastways, knew what side the bread was buttered on, but she's deader'n shit, an' no tellin' what the rest of 'em might be thinkin'."

Her sole Senator was in full accord. "I only met a couple of them, and then just the once, but … yeah … totally rubbed me the wrong way."

For whatever that was worth, coming from someone whose idea of being rubbed the *right* way involved nice, fresh, juicy, fleshy stump-jobs. Still, to each their own.

Nor did it help that, since his very obvious death atop Bighead Rock, it sounded like Heck Bodean was already well on his way to becoming a rustic urban legend. Cruising the backroads in his ghost truck with a load of 'shine, his brother's severed head riding shotgun.

"An' Lorlinda?" Spot went on. "Got away, din't she? Poof in a silver flash, her an' the warlock an' the angel, an' that fireworks fucknut—must'a been a Peterson, him; they's all crazy as possums on meth."

There was also, June knew, the naggy loose end of a possible tunnel, a secret way in and out without crossing any of the Checkpoints. The boy-warlock and the Wyrds had been able to glean that much from their divinations, suggesting it was where the warlock and angel, and their allies, had launched their attack from.

Spot, however, claimed to have heard of no such thing, though admitted it wouldn't surprise him. "If'n there is," he allowed, "fer-fuckin'-*sure* it's gots t' do with the Bodeans ... ol' Jeb had his fingers in a lotta pies, an' no tellin' whatall he might'a passed on t' his kin."

Clearly, Spot had a real bug up his butt about those Bodean people. The only Bodean June had personally met was the butch blacksmith woman who'd presented Favius with a severed head in a lettuce keeper. She'd been a character, all right, and it was a shame she'd met a messy end; of all the Senators, she was the one June had gotten along with best. Rather have still had her around than the pretty-boy, but, oh well.

The hillbilly sexpot tramp who'd escaped with the warlock and angel would have to be caught and face an especially nasty fate as a message to anyone else tempted to switch sides. June, having heard more than she cared to about "Hock Parties" and their "cham-peen," was already thinking that might be the way to go ... drown the tart in demonic redneck spit and snot. Like a stoning from the old days, but far grosser.

As for the rest of the clan, however much of a grudge Spot had against them, June was content to wait and see. If they toed the line, good for them. If not, they'd get what they deserved.

"I guess, if'n that's what Yer Highness wants," Spot said.

Downcast and disgruntled, it was plain he'd have just as soon seen every Bodean dragged from their shanty-shacks and shitty trailers, flayed alive, rolled in sulfur-salt, then staked out screaming with buckets of devil-ants dumped over them.

If it came to that, June supposed there'd be no harm done in letting him have his way. Despite his skeeviness, he *had* served Favius with unswerving loyalty. Knowing nearly everyone, and nearly everything that went on around the lake, he was a great asset and a useful advisor.

He'd also retrieved some key items from atop Bighead Rock, including Favius's gladius, her own marshmallow fork, and the defunct glyph-stones unearthed from the rubble of Thing's hard-baked, broken body. And he'd seen to it that Hulk's inert clay mass got moved to a secure location in the war camp; it was theoretically possible for the Golem to be reactivated, but most of those with the appropriate knowledge were no longer with them.

The closest they had to experts were the Meltzers, an elderly couple who'd parlayed their hobby of making dolls for their grandkids into a prosperous side-hustle selling to tourists. Then, after AllHell, they'd moved on to crafting homunculi, simulacra, and manikins for various magical purposes. Including, as she was led to understand it, the ones a certain local horror writer used in his homebrew torture-porn snuff movies for extra-realistic special effects.

That guy, June hadn't met and wasn't at all sure about, no matter how much Favius had admired his work or how Senator Trevor raved about him. She'd seen some of his books in the RV and picked one up once, out of idle curiosity, only to fling it aside in a hell of a hurry. How fucked-up did a person have to be to imagine, let alone *write*, such sick, sick shit?

She was just as glad, really, he had no political aspirations, no interest in joining the Senate or being involved in community affairs. If he wanted to keep to his lakeside cottage, with his ... bosom-buddy, or whatever that boob-creature was ... fine by her.

Eventually, though, yes, she would need more Senators. The retired veterinarian, who'd been the closest Lake Misquamicus had to a doctor before the military medics showed up, and the florid mogul who'd run the region's largest boat-rental place (also jet skis, inflatables, pop-up cabanas, and more!) were both dead, flattened under the ruins of the rotunda. Their families had accepted June's condolences and showed no signs of holding it against her.

Nor, to her knowledge, did anyone else seem to be nursing bitter resentment or discontent. Aside from Spot's Bodean butt-bug, which he would just have to suck up.

In the meantime, she still harbored a particular grudge of

her own. One even now nearing, so to speak, *fruition.*

Accompanied by Juggernaut, she went over to the pavilion near the central square of the war camp.

There, two of her former companions, fellow passengers on the Holy Roller, lolled in wooden troughs, attended by medics and under armed guard around the clock. IV tubes, feeding tubes, breathing tubes, catheter tubes, and other tubes fed into or out of various orifices. Their out-of-shape sixty-something nakedness and distended gravid bellies were on display for all the world to see.

And a sight, indeed, it was; their abdominal skin had stretched so tight it seemed about to split, while restless movements within caused hideous bulgings and undulations. Every now and then, the internal press of what might have been a hand, or a foot, or a root, or a hoof, or a malformed and lumpy freakish head could be seen.

"My, my," June said. "So active, aren't they? So ready to be born!"

She beamed at Mr. and Mrs. Shinn, a smile of benign malignance, poisonously sweet and deliciously smug.

The effect was rather lost on Mr. Shinn, who lay catatonic and drooling. He'd given up and checked out shortly after the removal of his testicles—double orchidectomy, such a lovely phrase! Though the retired veterinarian protested, having never done such a procedure on a human before, he'd made a fine, deft, professional job of it. June thrilled to recall how the loose nodules had slid around, wobbly and pathetic, in a surgical pan, and how they'd felt in her hand as she'd crushed them to squeeze out their fluids. Like juicing underripe lemons.

Mrs. Shinn, thanks to a virulent melon allergy, was puffy and swollen, covered head to foot with bright-red, oozing hives. She was all but unrecognizable, as if someone with mumps had been stung thousands of times by bees. But her eyes—reduced to squinting slits though they were— remained hateful and aware. If she could have shot daggers, or laser beams, from them, June might've been in danger. As it was, only impotent, furious tears trickled from their corners.

Paralyzing the vocal cords, which had initially been Trevor's idea to keep Chelsea from yelling at him, proved to work just as well on Mrs. Shinn. Shut her up, the cantankerous hag; June had heard more than enough from her long before any of this.

More than enough from both of them. Hypocritical, sanctimonious crap. Right-to-life this and abortion-is-murder that, pregnancy was God's will and even rape-babies were God's silver lining, so on and so forth.

Shoe was on the other foot now, though, wasn't it?

Thank you, Lucifer and all the powers of Hell, for utero-gourds! For their seeds, which could be "spunked-up" with any sort of sperm and rapidly grow to full-term hybrid monstrosities!

The sperm in this case, of course, June had personally hand-squeezed from Mr. Shinn's sorry excuses for balls. The seeds had then been forced into the mouths and down the throats of both Shinns, very much against their will, with no respect for their personal choices or bodily autonomy. Thus turning them into vessels, into incubators, for the unwelcome and extremely unwanted bundles of joy currently squirming and kicking inside them.

The guards and medics on duty were primarily female; for some reason, amusingly, even with everything else they dealt with around here on a daily basis, the miracle of impending motherhood tended to squick the guys right the fuck out. They couldn't handle it, begging for *any* other assignment no matter how low or debasing. Many of them had been present for Mr. Shinn's initial un-balling, and the savagely gleeful reactions of the women in attendance had only made it all the more traumatic. His "pregnancy" and the prospect of birth had them eager to be as far away as possible.

"You will be able to bring him around when the time comes," June said, not as a question.

The lead medic saluted smartly. "Ma'am, yes, ma'am. Be a real shame to have him miss all the fun."

Mrs. Shinn glared even harder, impotent tears streaming rather than trickling. Her restraints—as much to keep her from scratching the agonizingly itchy hives as from trying to escape—creaked as she struggled.

"Tsk, Mrs. Shinn," June tutted. "It'll be over soon. And

think of it this way ... you've only had to endure it for, what, a couple of weeks? It isn't as if you've had to do the whole nine months, now, is it?"

She administered a condescending pat to Mrs. Shinn's belly, where something rolled as if in response. Mrs. Shinn shuddered.

"I mean, really, compared to what you protesters made other women go through?" June went on. "Teenagers? Little girls with bad daddies? Never mind if they had medical conditions putting their lives at risk, never mind if they had other children they already couldn't afford."

Angry, vindictive mutters arose from more than a few of those gathered around the pavilion.

"How many of them did die, I wonder? From complications, or botched back-alley procedures, or suicide? How many of them would you and your kind have had executed, given the death penalty, even for an accidental miscarriage?"

"Docs too," a medic said. "Threatening the docs, bombing clinics, for doing their damn jobs."

"Because, *God*," June declared, lifting her palms skyward. "That's what you told yourselves. That's what you told the rest of us. So, Mrs. Shinn"—she patted the baby-bump again, for all it was more boulder than bump, and not exactly a baby—"is this His will? If not, well, where *is* He?"

At that very instant, as if by divine providence or diabolical mockery, what could only have been a contraction hit, making Mrs. Shinn lurch, belly rigid as stone, body wracked with pain.

"Goodness me, that was a *big* one!" June said with a note of saccharine congratulations. "Won't be much longer now, will it?"

She stepped back to let the medics do their thing, checking for cervical dilation and fetal positioning and such. Which wouldn't matter for Mr. Shinn; as interesting as it'd be to see how the utero-gourdling might make its own way out—gut-burster a la the *Alien* movies held the lead, with ass-baby a close second, and passing it through his sorry old dick like a nine-pound kidney stone in third—any of those would likely be almost instantly fatal, and June wanted to make sure Mr. Shinn had plenty of opportunity to behold God's silver lining in all its squalling glory. So, C-section it'd be ... once they'd roused him so he could fully experience the experience.

"Serves them right," said Duval, a sergeant who stood high in June's personal regard. Aside from the devil-horns curving up through her severe military haircut, she still looked human, tough as nails and take-no-shit. "Should do the same to every one of those ignorant fucktards. Let them see how *they* like it!"

June glanced at her, sidelong, speculative but not prying.

Duval caught the glance, grinned wryly, spat, and cleared her throat. "Not me, no. Had a sister, though. Eight years older. Sweetest, most loving, most caring goddamn person in the universe. I fuckin' idolized her. She and her boyfriend were still in high school when, well, y'know. They were going to go to college together, get married, had it all planned out. They did want kids, yeah, just, not right then."

"Ah," June said.

"So, they made the hard decision. Both families backing them on it, respecting their choice. Then, they're on their way to the appointment, and what should happen?"

The devil-horns weren't the only transformation after all; June could have sworn a hellfire-red glow briefly lit Duval's eyes.

"People like *them*," she sneered. "Beat her boyfriend with their 'Choose LIFE' signs as he was trying to protect her. Beat him so bad he was left paralyzed and brain-damaged, a damn vegetable. My sis lost the baby anyway and died six months later. Overdose; maybe accidental, maybe not."

A combination of alchemy and electroshock snapped Mr. Shinn to alertness in plenty of time to witness his wife silently bellowing in the throes of labor, thrashing and straining as she was instructed to *breathe*, to *push*.

Some fathers, even not in sitcoms, fainted in the delivery room. Mr. Shinn was not allowed the luxury. He was forced—as in, his head turned and pinned in place, his eyelids held open—to watch the entire grueling, squelchy process. Whatever his feelings for Mrs. Shinn's genitalia might have been, back in the early days when she was more tight and youthful, could hardly compare to what he must've felt watching her droopy, hairy meat-curtains splay apart, viscous semi-amniotic/semi-slurry mucoid gushes lubricating the emergence of a slick, lumpy, misshapen head.

Then a slick, lumpy, misshapen body, about as humanoid

as a mandrake root, trailing stringy slime-tendrils reminiscent of pumpkin guts. It was so orange and squashy and puling and bleating, it might've—

No. No. June was *not* going there.

"Eew," someone said.

"Eew, fuckin'-A," Duval agreed.

The medic, making a face akin to someone handling rotted roadkill, held the newborn up for Mrs. Shinn's inspection—or, rather, for Mrs. Shinn to take one look and start bucking so crazily, fueled by a surge of super-adrenaline, that she tipped her wooden trough over sideways. Tubes ripped loose, flying about all wiggle-worm, spattering assorted liquids. Equipment got knocked every which-way.

And somehow, it broke the vocal-cord paralysis spell; Mrs. Shinn's shrieks and bellows rang from one end of the war camp to the other, probably echoing so people on the far side of the lake would think someone was chainsaw-slaughtering howler monkeys.

It took six soldiers to right the trough, two other medics to grapple Mrs. Shinn enough for a third to inject her with a horse-sized hypodermic, and way too long for it to kick in ... but finally, the struggling and screaming stopped. Mrs. Shinn went limp, though still conscious. The grotesque gourdspawn was placed upon her chest, where it snuffled about until it located the side-saddle sag of a breast and latched on greedily.

"Birth, such a beautiful thing," another soldier said, then bent double and barfed profusely on her own boots.

Tempting though it was to do likewise, June kept it together, gulping down a throatful of sour bile. She fixed her benign, malign smile on her lips again and spoke saccharine to Mrs. Shinn.

"Look who's a mommy now," she crooned. "What a wondrous blessing. You never did tell me if you'd decided on a name."

"Don—" someone began, then went "oof!" as if given a firm elbow-dig to the ribs.

"Shut your mouth, soldier," Duval said.

June looked to the medic. "Is it a ... boy, or a girl, or ...?"

"Fuck if I know."

She returned her attention to Mrs. Shinn. "Well, we can worry about that later. Whatever else, you have a strong, healthy baby. God's silver lining."

Mr. Shinn appeared to be on the verge of checking out again, so with a nod, June indicated the medics give him another jolt. He blubbered, snot-bubbles repeatedly forming and popping at both nostrils, breath hitching in wet, choking sobs.

"And here's the proud papa," she said, moving to him, giving him the whole beaming benefit. "I don't really see much of a resemblance, but it's too soon to tell. They all look funny when they're just born."

"Please, Junie ..." he managed. "Please don't. Haven't you done enough?"

"Haven't I done enough?" she echoed, tapping a thoughtful finger against her chin. "Haven't I? Hmm. Honestly, I don't quite think I have. Not yet."

"Just ... just kill us. Kill me, before ... before ..." His gaze, more pitiful than anything in those guilt-trip ads about abused and neglected animals, flicked briefly in the direction of his middle, then flicked away.

"Oh, Mr. Shinn," she said. "Oh, poor, poor, dear Mr. Shinn. We both know that's not going to happen."

"So, uh, Your Highness—" Sgt. Duval began as they moved back to give the medics space to prep Mr. Shinn for surgery.

"June."

"Ma'am?"

"And not ma'am. I get enough of that already. Call me June."

Duval paused, working it over, as if unclear about such a casual breach of protocol.

"I insist," June said to make it easier on her.

"Okay, so, uh, June ... about all this ... about her in particular ..." She made a vague gesture in the direction of Mrs. Shinn, the nursing gourdspawn now appearing to not just be suckling but gnawing.

"What about it?"

"How it ... look, these seeds, they swallowed them, yeah? So how come his is in his stomach, but hers came out ... down there?"

Spot could have explained it better, if in his crass vernacular. But Spot had spun some feeble excuses and made himself scarce, along with most of the male-types.

What had he told her before, when she'd asked a similar question? Something to do with the seedlings seeking out the best place to get nutrients, able to permeate the barrier membranes protecting different organs, forming their own "placenters," as he put it. A womb, of course, was best suited, but other organs served in a pinch.

"Magic," she said with a shrug. "Hell-powers. Who even understands how *any* of this works?"

Duval strayed a hand to her devil-horns. They were the classic Halloween-costume model, but no headband held them in place. Curved upright crescents, four inches from base to tip, dark red with blackish striations. "Yeah, true," she said. "I sure didn't have these before. Then, crackle, there they were."

"Did it hurt?"

"Thought for a second my fuckin' skull was gonna shatter, but other than that, nope." She grinned. "And, gotta admit, they look pretty badass."

"That they do."

"Sure could've been worse. You've seen Pork Chop?"

"The soldier with the, ah ..."

"Pig face? Yup, him. Was his nickname before, since he used to be a hog farmer and butcher. Had the temper of a wild boar when he was riled up. Now, he's got the tusks, snout, and bristles to go with it."

"Does he ... mind?" It hadn't really occurred to her to wonder; so many people undergoing so many drastic transformations. Most, as far as she could tell, simply took it in stride, as Duval did.

"Loves it." She snickered. "Just don't ask if he has a curly little tail or corkscrew dick."

"I will keep that in mind, thank you," June said.

"Ma'am?" interrupted a medic. "We're ready."

"Excellent!" She clapped, and went over to Mr. Shinn, who was still weeping and incoherently babbling a mixture of pleas and prayers.

At her order, they'd slathered his midsection with a numbing salve, the alchemical equivalent of a local anesthetic. Not enough to fully dull the pain, because she wanted him to feel what was happening, but just to take the edge off so he wouldn't be too distracted by it to miss the rest of the proceedings.

Such as having to watch them slice a long incision, blood

welling in a crimson line, skin and flesh and fatty tissue parting. At which point, he left off his babble plea-praying and commenced screaming even louder and shriller than his wife had.

"Man up, pussyboy," Duval said scornfully. "Didn't you embarrass yourself enough when they cut out your nuts?"

"I like you, Sergeant Duval," June said. "Would you consider being my military advisor?"

"Excuse me? I … I'm no officer. There's lieutenants and captains—"

"I like *you*," June repeated.

"Well, uh, you're the one in charge, you're the queen; if that's what you want … sure?"

"Good. Consider it done."

The scalpels worked their way deeper, the incision gaping wider, exposing the glistening pinkish sac of the stomach itself. It looked like an overfilled, churning water balloon as the creature inside strained toward freedom.

"Stand back," warned the medic through a clear plastic visor. "This might—"

Whatever the medic said next was lost, because at the first touch of razor-sharp surgical steel, Mr. Shinn's stomach really did pop like an overfilled water balloon.

Only, it wasn't water. It was a bomb-blast geyser of acidic digestive fluids, whatever they'd most recently pumped down his feeding tube, and amniotic slurry similar to that which had gushed from Mrs. Shinn's abused birth canal.

Boooosh! patter-patter-splort-patter.

Accompanied by shouts of disgust, rapid backing up from the splash zone, and a spate of revolted swiping and shaking off.

Nobody said "eew" this time; "eew" fell far short. And it *stank*, even by the standards around Lake Misquamicus. It stank like spoiled eggplant puree and vinegar and ammonia.

As they all reeled, gagged, or swore, a small pudgy fist punched defiantly into the air. It was yellowish-white and yellowish-orange and orangish-white, with a slightly nubbly texture, and reminded June of nothing so much as those weird squash sold as harvest decorations.

A second fist followed. Both fists unclenched into itty fingers, gripped the sides of the incision, and levered into view the upper portion of a …

… of a surprisingly cute, big-eyed, chubby-cheeked baby.

A yellowish-white and yellowish-orange and orangish-white baby, with a nubbled texture to its skin and a wet tuft of fibrous, cornsilky stuff atop its head.

It clambered halfway out of Mr. Shinn's belly, blinking those big round innocent eyes. His screams had choked off; he stared at it in utter incomprehension and disbelief.

So, for a moment, did everybody else.

The *cuteness*, June thought, was what really threw them all off-kilter.

And then the way it peered at Mr. Shinn, cocked its head, and gurgled, as if to say, "Hi, Dada!"

"Aww," someone said, instead of "eew."

The squash-baby wobbled precariously as it tried to further extricate itself. It was going to fall, going to tumble head-first to the hard ground, and smush into pulp—

A nurse, perhaps on pure reflex, darted forward and caught it a split-second before disaster. It gurgled again, chortled, and snuggled against the crook of her neck and shoulder. Now fully freed from its father's guts, they could all see its plump little legs and its adorable rounded baby-bottom.

"It's a girl!" the nurse said.

There were a few cheers, and then a flurry of activity as the medics belatedly realized they should probably do something about the blown-out wreckage of Mr. Shinn's guts. It was a puddled hollow of noxious liquefied stew in there, Lake Misquamicus in miniature, and the monitors tracking his vital signs were making the kind of beepy noises that always indicated bad news on the tense prime-time medical shows.

"Okay, I've seen some weird shit since I've been here," Sgt. Duval said, "but, for real, what the hell?"

Mrs. Shinn, doped though she was, had been with it enough to observe the entire process. June couldn't be sure, due to the swollen mask of puffy hives, but caught a fleeting glint of what looked like bitter jealousy … there she was, having birthed the fugly mandrake-root creature toothlessly gnawing at her sagging breasts, while her *husband* went and produced a downright adorable—if not quite human—baby girl?

*Going to be **some** fucked-up family dynamics there.*

Until then, she hadn't put much thought toward what to do with the Shinns when all was said and done; subjecting them to a heaping helping of humiliation, objectification, trauma, and poetic justice had been the main goal. Forcing upon them what they, and their kind, had been forcing upon girls and women for centuries. Taking away their choice, their control, their bodily autonomy. Really ramming the point home. Beyond that ...

"What happens to them now?" asked Duval, as if reading June's mind.

"Good question. I wasn't even sure they'd survive. But I'd kind of like to see how it plays out."

"My guess?" Duval looked back and forth between the new parents and their offspring. "Not well. Not very fuckin' well at all."

Later, after giving orders to have arrangements made for relocation of the Shinns to more suitable housing—with round-the-clock supervision—and meeting with Duval's CO to take care of whatever red tape needed be taken care of to facilitate the sergeant's promotion and transfer, June returned to the RV, Juggernaut plodding in her wake.

The sentries snapped to attention and saluted, opening the doors for her. The household staff bustled dutifully. All was spic-and-span, even the bathroom the boy-warlock's puking shitfest had damn near rendered uninhabitable.

But, no handmaid to fill the tub for her, alack and alas, oh woe, oh no. What *was* a queen to do?

Do it herself, that's what a queen was to do. Though Spot said he and Ma Riggers were putting together a list of possible candidates for a replacement, June was in no real hurry. She'd seen too many of those elaborate period-piece courtly dramas where the ruling elite didn't even wipe their own butts, and where royal women stood like department store mannequins while servants took care of putting on everything from undergarments to jewelry.

Ugh. Screw that. It *had* been fun, yes, ordering Chelsea around, giving her menial duties, but only because it was Chelsea. Treating some lowborn local the same didn't sit right.

Immersed to the chin in steaming lavender-scented water, the jets busily thrumming the stiffness from her neck and shoulders, June tipped her head back and sighed. For a few hours, she'd had distractions to take her mind off of other matters, but her grief, loss, anger—and rampant horniness— quickly returned.

Had Favius been there ...

But Favius wasn't. Wouldn't. Never again.

Her own fingers, slicked with bath-oils, and a bit of contortion to bring judicious application of the tub's jets to the proper angles relieved some of the physical aspects of her need.

It was only the old, normal kind of orgasm, though, the kind she'd been so accustomed to self-inducing during her lonely spinster existence. The feel of his cock, the girth and throbbing of it, the pressing fullness and thrilling sensation of each thrust ... slow and languid, almost lazy ... or vigorous battering ram pounding relentlessly into her ... the sheer weight and presence and muscle mass of him ... the anguished flexion of the faces stitched into his skin ... the rough huskiness of his hot breath, his impassioned words ...

She brought herself off twice more with those memories in mind and still was left wanting.

Rinsed, dried, powdered, groomed, and adorned in a fresh robe—regal purple trimmed in gold, silken and flowing—she rang for her dinner and went to the room she'd designated as her private workspace.

It was cozy, originally intended as a den or home office (motorhome office?), with a couple of plush comfy chairs, a grand desk capable of withstanding some fairly ambitious and acrobatic sex acts, a minibar, and the usual accoutrements. Most of the books, she'd had cleared out, the built-in shelves holding instead a collection of gifts, mementos, relics, and trinkets. From its window, if she so desired, she could take in a view of the lakeshore, with the matricidal shrine where her mother's bones hung, the dragon-topped monument pillar marking the place where Favius had first emerged to set foot upon God's green earth, and, of course, the dais where he had so utterly fucked her brains out and changed everything forever.

The desktop, once put to such better use, was now strewn with lists, notes, messages, reports, and paperwork.

Regarding it, June couldn't help wishing the "secretary" the political bigwigs purportedly brought along hadn't gone missing during the turbulent events, or had been found afterward, like the kitchen crew. However much of a "secretary" she had actually been—dubious, given some of the outfits left in one of the RV's guest rooms—it would've been better than nothing. At least to help organize; not as if goddamn shorthand was required.

"*Juuuune* Goldsmith, *this* is your *life!*"

Her exhalation landed in the overlap of a Venn diagram of "laugh," "sigh," and "sob."

Yeah, this was her life. Eating alone in her office because, unless some meeting or other occasion was going on, she couldn't bear having servants standing around watching her, ready to leap in and refill a glass or retrieve a dropped napkin. Much too *Downton Abbey.*

Food was good, though. Much better with Chef Emilio and his team back on the job, even if he did constantly bemoan the dearth of choice ingredients. How a diva of his caliber was supposed to function without ready access to fresh mussels flown in directly from a particular cove, or artisanal cheese dry-aged by monks, or whatever the fuck else he went on about … doing the best he could under such restrictive circumstances … on and on.

She'd probably get sick of it and have him executed eventually, but for now, it was more amusing than annoying.

As she ate, she sifted through messages and memos, trying to prioritize what had to be handled promptly and what could be put off. Some of the renegade chariot-slave POWs had been recaptured and should probably be made a gory public spectacle of … Favius had intended to build a coliseum for just such entertainments, but the plans—along with those for the palace, temple, and Roman-style bathhouse—were on hold. The parking lot at Crawdy's hardly seemed fitting for gladiator duels … maybe march them in chains to the top of Bighead Rock, site of their betrayal, have them hamstrung, blinded with hot pokers, and then hurled into the lake?

Not that she was any too keen to go back there herself, but she knew it was expected of her. To make an appearance. To honor Favius and those who'd fallen in battle, to reassure the people, to quell further rebellion.

To make a fucking *speech!*

The very idea gave her heartburn and anxiety-jitters.

A surprise natural at fellatio, she might have been, but

other sorts of oration? Addressing the masses? Speaking in front of a crowd? The #1 phobia of the majority of the population, surpassing even death and spiders?

Had to be done, though. Had to be done.

And, longshot, but maybe the dark muses who'd inspired Favius with stirring rhetoric might favor her as well. He'd told her how he, just a common soldier, had not previously been so gifted. Then the words had come to him, flowed through him.

Oh, and she'd loved it, hearing him, his Voice, its power and potency spurring her to spontaneous knee-buckling climaxes without a single touch.

He would have wanted her to carry on, she felt sure. To not let what he'd begun go unfinished, the glory of his triumphs fade and falter.

For him. For Favius.

And, okay, for the might and majesty of Hell … but mostly, for Favius.

In Lucifer's name, so be it.

Even if it meant making a fucking *speech*.

Resolved, she moved on to the next memo, and grimaced.

The little girl, the boy-warlock's sister, daughter of the decapitated snake-lady Senator; something still had to be done about the little girl. She couldn't just be left on her own indefinitely, with only her agonicitized, insane father.

A father who, as it happened, was not unfamiliar to June. Brother William had been a passenger aboard the Holy Roller, one of the last survivors alongside herself and the Shinns. Not an unhandsome man, with a kind of "careworn George Clooney" thing going on, she wouldn't have kicked him out of her sleeping bag, given the opportunity.

When he'd disappeared, the rest of them wrote it off as bad luck; the creeker-freaks or some other hazard must've gotten to him. That he'd been conning them all along and ducked out on their mission to go look for his estranged family? Who could have guessed?

You'd've been better off with the creeker-freaks, "Brother" William, she thought.

At a discreet tap on the office door, she looked up. "Yes?"

"My queen?" It opened, and instead of a servant there to collect her dishes, a young soldier peeked in.

A disturbingly young soldier, the kind you'd see in old war movies, when fourteen-year-olds would lie about their age to get shot at and mustard-gassed in dismal muddy trenches. How the hell he'd been allowed to accompany the military convoy to a place like this …

"Private Hurst," she said. "Is there news?"

He'd been, she was told, a military messenger before, a runner, small and fast and agile, able to weave through a combat zone to deliver orders without getting hurt. Since the Blackwings did most of that via airmail now, his current assignment was to the RV household guard, as a sort of all-purpose page and errand-boy.

"Sergeant—I mean, Major—Duval to see you, ma'am."

"Ah! Please show her in."

He did so, stepping aside to let Duval pass, saluting.

"At ease, Meep," Duval said, giving him a slanted grin. "It's just me."

He grinned back, then darted a glance at June and clearly remembered it wasn't *just* Duval; he was still in the presence of the *queen*. He snapped to, squaring his shoulders so precisely a builder's level wouldn't have found them off by a millimeter.

June chuckled a little and shook her head. "Thank you, Private. Dismissed."

Hurst was gone in a blink, the door closed.

"That kid." Duval chuckled as well, then put on a serious expression. Aside from shiny new insignia, her uniform hadn't changed. "I was told to report to you before going to my new quarters."

"New quarters?"

"They moved me to the camper van Captain Adler had been using; hope that's all right."

"Certainly all right by me, if it's all right by you."

She scratched at the base of a horn. "A little weird, but I'll get used to it. I mean, major? That's a jump."

"I have every confidence in you," June said. "Feel free to hand-pick your own staff of assistants."

"Will do."

"As my military advisor, I'll basically want you to, well, advise me on military matters. Or, anything else, really. I'm new to all this." She met Duval's gaze frankly. "And fully expecting to put my foot in it. If you can help me not make a *total* ass of myself, I'll appreciate it."

"Don't think you've got a lot to worry about in that department," Duval said. "As far as the troops go, at least; can't speak so much for the civvies."

"Really?"

"Shit, yeah. The way you manifested and went after that angel? Talk about badass!"

"Huh. Well." Not sure how to react, she noticed her half-finished plate and changed the subject. "Have you eaten? I can ring for—"

"Grabbed a bite at the mess on my way over, thanks. But if you've got any beer around here, or something stronger, I wouldn't say no."

"By all means." June waved to the mini-bar.

Duval poured herself a hefty knock of bourbon over a whiskey stone and raised the glass. "Highness."

"June."

"June. Right." She settled into one of the comfy chairs. "Nice digs."

"Major Duval, may I ask you a personal question?"

"My kill-count? I'd have to think—"

"No, no. I'd like us to be on first-name terms, since we'll be working so closely together."

"Oh. Oh, sure. Okay. I usually go by Xanne."

"Zan?"

"X-a-n-n-e," she spelled out.

"Short for … Alexandra?"

She sipped and savored. "Roxanne. But, once people start calling you Roxy, it's only a matter of time until some smartass starts in with 'Foxy Roxy,' and then you gotta break a few bones."

June opened her mouth, wasn't sure what to say, and closed it again.

"Bad enough when it's high school," Xanne went on, "but then, ROTC and boot camp? Need to nip that shit in the bud early on, or those swinging dicks will *not* let it go."

June decided a drink of her own wouldn't be out of order. As she mixed a gin and tonic, she asked, "Have you had to break very many bones over it?"

"Not a lot. They get the message pretty quick." She leaned back with a nostalgic look. "Especially after my high school PE teacher. Typical type, right? Failed ex-jock taking it out on teenagers. Called me 'Foxy Roxy' in front of the whole class, so I cleaned his clock right there on the basketball court."

"Good for you," June said. "Family?"

"Told you about my sis. Mom and Dad kinda lost it after that, drifted apart. My brother fell in with a bad crowd, and me? Guess I was always kind of a hellraiser, but I managed to stay out of prison. Took me a while to get my head on straight. You?"

"You know about *my* mother. Some far-flung other relations, but, otherwise, no."

Xanne raised her glass again. "Who needs the aggro anyway, right?"

"Right. I take it you're not married?"

"*Haaard* pass. Same for having kiddos. I tell ya, when everyone else was going ga-ga over that baby-thing earlier … eyugh. Yeah, it was cute, but, nope, not my jam. I have got, like, zero maternal instincts."

June raised her glass in turn. "Hear, hear. We were stuck with that warlock brat for, what, a week? I barely had anything to do with him, and I still wanted to feed him to the dino-turtles." She scowled and flicked at a sheaf of paper. "Now there's the sister, as if it's *my* responsibility to ensure she's taken care of."

"What, so you're not gonna adopt her and make her a princess?" Xanne snort-laughed sardonically. "Pork Chop and I went over to the house to give her the news about her mom and bro, and that right there is one *severely* screwed-up little girl. You should've seen the dad!"

"I read your report."

"And *they* did it to him, his own kids. Welcome home, Pops, let's just jab these fishhooks into your dickhead and wire you up to play video games!"

"Arguably, he is still her father, and he *is* still there—"

"Not for fuckin' long, he won't be. Guy made leprosy look like a case of the shingles. He'll be rotted to sludge in no time."

"Be that as it may, I'm *not* adopting her," June declared. "This war camp is no place for children."

"This HellZone's no place for children."

"Also true. But I'm sure someone around here will be able to take her in. I'll ask the Riggerses for suggestions. They seem in the know and handle caretaking and housekeeping for plenty of the locals."

"Good call."

"They're also looking into finding me a new handmaid," June said. "Since it didn't go so well with the last one."

"No shit. I heard you turned her over to her brother, Senator Stump-Humper."

"He did ask so nicely."

"He's a piece too. Did you know he's been making inquiries to the top brass about someone stationed out at Checkpoint Jericho?"

"I did not. What for? What kind of inquiries?"

"Claims the dude is a friend, wants to pull strings about having him reassigned to his security team."

"Hmm."

"Anyway." Xanne drained the last of her bourbon and stood. "I should probably get unpacked, and let you get back to your dinner and queenly shit. Send Meep—uh, Hurst—if you need me?"

"I meant to ask … Meep?"

"Like the Roadrunner, from the cartoons? Y'know, 'meep-meep' and *zoom*!"

"Oh, of course. With the coyote."

"All the more since we came here. He'll be outrunning bullets, just you wait!"

June got up to walk her to the door. "Thank you, Xanne," she said with genuine sincerity. "It's nice to have someone to talk to. The others all seem either … ingratiating or intimidated."

"Hey, I'm plenty intimidated," Xanne replied. "Badass Queen Juno the Vengeful, Patron Anti-Saint of Matricides, Smiter of Angels? You're fuckin' terrifying!"

Never in her life would she have expected to find herself having such a reputation, but …

Well, she could hardly complain.

After Xanne left, June finished her meal, rang for dessert—*crème brûlée* with grilled peach slices, *spécialité de la maison* (chef's kiss, "muah!")—and ventured into the RV's spacious main chamber, which was a combination of living room, lounge, conference room, and throne room.

Because, while she may not have had a coronation or a crown, she did have a throne. Or, at least, a big grandiose chair, which a local craftsman had made from blood-bleached driftwood and blackened mosa-gator bone. It had a flared back, imposing armrests carved in the likeness from that famous screaming painting, and suede cushions stuffed with what she'd been told was emu-raptor down, sourced from a ranch near the outskirts of the lake.

Juggernaut, as was customary when not accompanying her someplace, loomed bulkily beside the chair, clay features impassive as ever, eye slits at a steady banked-coal glow. Two sentries flanked the exterior doorway, with two others outside. The heads of Mr. and Mrs. Riggers, grafted onto their son Ronny, were huddled at a side-table with Spot, poring over what must've been handmaid applications. They rose as she came in. A few members of the household staff, seeing to their various tasks, paused and did the subservient dip-bob-bow she wished they really wouldn't do.

She indulged them all with a nod and a wave. Then, eschewing the throne for the time being, approached the side-table.

"Any luck?" she asked, keeping her tone light.

"Ain't *too* bad, I reckon," Spot said. "We gots half a dozen or so we figgur y' might wanna inner-view, see if'n any of 'em strikes yer fancy."

"We thought we'd keep it a more narrow field at first," Mrs. Riggers simpered. "Decent, humble, hard-working girls who'll …" She trailed off.

"Who'll know their place and mind their manners," her husband took over. "Not, Highness, to say anything bad about the Carmichaels; Satan, no! Been looking after them a long time, we have, and they always been fine, fine people."

"The finest!" Mrs. Riggers jumped back in. "Just, well, Miss Chelsea, Lilith love her, might not have had the right … temperament for such a position, if'n you takes my meaning."

"I do indeed." Which had been the fun part, but she'd had her fun and could now move on.

"Now, these here gals …" Spot fanned out the pages like playing cards. "All's come from respek-ter-bal backgrounds, long-time lakefolk stock, goin' way back."

"No Bodeans?" she said, just to see what he'd do.

He looked fit to spit. "Re*spek*-ter-bal, I done tol' ya, Miz Yer Highness. Girls what ain't got crim'nal records an' trampy-ass cum-dumpster reppertayshuns."

June bit back a smirk.

"'Sides," added Mr. Riggers, "Senator Carmichael, young

master Trevor, he already hired on most of those."

The smirk almost escaped, especially when Mrs. Rigger rolled her eyes. "I did try an' warn him, so help me Lucifer. Nothin' but trouble from such sorts. But him bein' so ... appreciative of certain characteristics, shall we say ..."

"He couln't see past their titties," Spot said. "Or mebbe was their arms an' legs he was more lookin' at."

"Harumph," went Mr. Rigger. "At any rate, the ... the predilections of the Senator aside ..."

"Yes, of course." June skimmed the applications, some of which had photos attached.

Not studio-quality glamour shots, for sure, but not mugshots either. Polaroids, and candids, and bathroom selfies. One was even a cap-and-gown graduation portrait, showing a rather drab young woman looking dead into the camera as if staring down a firing squad. She had lank, limp, dishwater hair in an unflattering cut. A prominent nose, narrow lips, and weak chin.

And her eyes held a flatness that catapulted June straight back to her own senior year.

Smile, now ... come on, just a little smile ... your parents will want a nice picture to put on the mantel, and it'll be in the yearbook for all your friends to see ...

"Her," she said. "This one. This one right here. Her."

Never in her life, either, would June have expected to find herself back at the hidden clearing in the hills above Bible Creek, gazing down from on high at the altar where she'd once been bound.

The view was fragmented, fractured, split with jagged distortions, as if seen through a broken kaleidoscope, but she recognized the place well enough. Remembered it well enough, the stone slab beneath her all wet and tacky with Mrs. Gabelman's blood, the possessed Brother Lucas looming over her.

Someone else was bound there now, someone June didn't recognize but deduced, from the tatters of his expensive suit, was a politician from the original government convoy that had escorted Favius to Lake Misquamicus.

His little Florida vacation had, clearly, not gone well. He was filthy, haggard, unshaven, covered with scrapes and bruises and cuts. His shoes were missing, his socks in rags, his feet bloodied. His tie, probably Hermes or Ralph Lauren, was clumsily wrapped and knotted around one upper arm, as if in a makeshift attempt at a bandage or tourniquet. On the wrist of the other arm, glint-hints of gold suggested a Rolex caked in layers of muck.

How he had made it all the way over there, alone and on foot, had to be some kind of testament to his fortitude and luck. Both of which must have finally run out, because the creeker-freaks had him now.

Some of *them*, June *did* recognize, and none too fondly. Many had died during David and Ramon's valiant rescue attempt—she'd killed plenty herself—but the rest of the clan still seemed to be going strong.

They gathered around the altar-stone, deformed pallid mutants with albino-like red eyes and straggly black hair, swaying in herky-jerky unison as they chanted. The chant, even garbled, was also familiar, skin-crawlingly so.

Az-bun-ael, Az-bun-ael.

Beside the captive politician, on a crude stepladder, stood a dwarfish, twisted figure with squat bow-legs, elongated arms, and an undersized head set at a perpetually neck-crooked angle. Scraps of a silver-mylar camping blanket—remnants of the previous shaman's ceremonial garment—partially covered what appeared to be an ill-developed, hermaphroditic nudity, the vestigial breasts and multipurpose genitalia not anything June wanted a closer look at. And was just as glad, really, for the fragmented distortions preventing her from seeing too clearly.

It occurred to her, in a flash of unease, that the perspective from which she was observing the scene would have aligned with the huge post upon which the ram-horned demonic skull of the Arch-Duke had been mounted. As if she now had that very same ringside seat.

Impossible, since Ramon had blown the skull to bits with a grenade. A Major Relic, destroyed. Azbunael's hold on this place, broken, his power dispersed. Game over, cocksucker. Back to Hell with you and good goddamn riddance.

Only here they still were, the creeker-freaks, worshiping and preparing to make sacrifice to their idol.

She tried to turn, to pan the camera as it were, and was surprised when it worked. Briefly, only for an instant, but an instant long enough to show her another fragmented, fractured image—a cracked and charred jigsaw of bone, cobbled together, held by sticky-sap glue and coarse twine. Like a shattered china plate someone had tried to repair, despite its missing pieces.

The skull, the ram-horned demon's skull, smoky redblack energy seething in hollow sockets.

Az-bun-ael.

Except ... except the chant was different.

Az-JUNE-ael.

Startled, she lost her grasp, lost sight of the skull. Her vision panned automatically around to the altar again as the creeker-freaks contorted more violently, working themselves into a frenzy. Waving hands with too many fingers, or fused flipper-fingers, or no fingers at all ... bodies writhing and bending and twisting in ways no human spines were meant to move ...

The chanting reached a fevered pitch as the dwarfish shaman seized a fistful of hair, wrenched the politician's head backwards, and ripped a serrated blade across his throat.

June bolted upright, gasping.

Tried to tell herself it had just been a bad dream.

Didn't buy it for a second.

If she needed more proof, she got it when she switched on the bedside lamp and saw smoky, redblack tendrils curling and dissipating around her like a fading aura. By the time she reached the full-length mirror, only wisps remained, vanishing before her eyes.

"Ohh fuck," she exhaled shakily.

Physically, she was otherwise unchanged; aside from her newfound confident posture and carriage, she was the same ol' plain-Jane Junie-June she'd always been. No horns, no tail, no fangs or wings or cloven hooves.

But there was no denying the truth. Favius had even anticipated it, explaining to her how, when Ramon had destroyed the Relic in God's name, Azbunael's lingering essence had been siphoned into him, there imprisoned like the spoils of war to the Opposition. Then, when June killed Ramon, that essence had been reclaimed, with her as its vessel. Not possessed, no; not as a puppet. More as a legacy. The power was hers.

Which, she couldn't deny, she'd already tapped into more than once, whether on purpose or by sheer instinct. The way she'd called upon it in the fight versus the warlock and angel, for instance. And, quite possibly, the way she'd survived Chelsea's backstabbing.

She just ... wasn't too sure how she felt about those depraved inbred creeker-freaks sacrificing people to her. Seemed a bit much.

"Az-june-ael?" she muttered, testing it out. "Yeah no, I don't think so."

If for no other reason than it acknowledged that dickhead Arch-Duke, Mr. ***"ENH, IT'LL DO."*** He could fuck off and be forgotten, as far as she cared. If his power was to be hers, it'd be *hers*, and she'd use it her own way.

She returned to bed, to the rumpled king-sized bed far too big for her alone, not nearly as rumpled as it had been and hardly for the same reason. They'd put it through its paces, that bed. The RV too; for all it was sturdily built, its shock absorbers had been given some workouts.

The rest of her sleep, as far as she could tell, was uninterrupted, and a red-tinged daylight, filtered through the *Aurora Diabolicus*, crept around the edges of the curtains by the time she awoke. She breakfasted—Emilio was also a master of Eggs Benedict; how could he whip up such a creamy, tangy Hollandaise under these conditions?—and attended to routine morning matters, then beckoned to Juggernaut and went over to see how the Shinn family was doing in their new abode.

An unscrupulous real estate agent might have listed it as a "tiny house," taking advantage of the craze and charging an exorbitant amount. As far as June was concerned, a rose by any other name may smell as sweet, and a shed from Home Depot was a shed from Home Depot.

And this was a shed from Home Depot, which was still nicer than the Shinns probably deserved. Certainly nicer than some of the shanty-shacks and beat-to-shit trailers many locals lived in. A hell of a step up from being strapped into wooden troughs in an open-air pavilion, the way they had been.

They, though, seemed rather less than appreciative, and not at all thrilled by her visit. Mrs. Shinn's melon-allergy hives had diminished since the birthing, looking much less inflamed and itchy, but she didn't act very grateful for that either.

"They won't have anything to do with the babies," the on-duty guard told June. "That, or they try to kill them."

Mr. Shinn flinched. Mrs. Shinn glared.

In the cribs—repurposed supply crates—the little gourdspawns wailed, the needy and demanding nature of their cries the sort that drove right into your ears.

"Kill their own *babies*?" June asked, overloud, in aghast exaggeration, privately thinking she'd want to strangle the noisy little shits too. "But that would make them baby-killers, which they were always so *against*!"

It further amused her to learn that, with the Shinns continuing to refuse choosing names for their bundles of joy, the nurses had taken to referring to them as Manny (short for Mandrake) and Melony (not Melanie, but Melon-with-added-Y).

And the Shinns fucking hated it. Particularly the mock birth-certificates one of the medics had drawn up, complete with ink-stamp footprints. Or, in Manny's case, rootprints.

"Are you really going to leave them with these people?" a nurse asked.

"They are their parents," June replied.

"Unfit, terrible parents." The nurse picked up Melony, doing that soothy-bounce thing. "There, there, sweet girl. It's all right."

Melony hiccupped and burbled and made cute noises, and June could not get out of there fast enough.

"Keep me updated," she said, beating a hasty path for the door.

Accompanied by Juggernaut, she made the rounds of the war camp. Favius had impressed upon her the importance of maintaining connections and contact, of not being aloof and haughty. It was all fine and well to talk about country and duty and causes and grand ideals, he'd said, but when push came down to shove, soldiers fought and died for each other and for leaders they could respect. Who earned and deserved their deathless loyalty.

Whether that was her or not … whether she could inspire anyone to do anything, let alone fight and die … Major Duval, and others, might hold such opinions now, but what would happen if and when push *did* come down to shove?

Spot caught up with her at the mosaic, an ongoing labor of craftsmanship being painstakingly assembled from vertebrae, teeth, knucklebones, lakeshore pebbles, bullets and spent casings, and other beachcomber battlefield souvenirs. Depicting key scenes from the past fortnight or so, it made her think of that famous French tapestry, except far more graphic. And, of course, William the Conqueror hadn't celebrated his victory with a wild public fuck.

Had to admit, though, it was a work of art. Some license and liberties taken, maybe; the images of her were rather more flattering than reality warranted. Almost made her look pretty good. They'd really captured, too, the vindication of the marshmallow-forking.

"Miz Yer Highness," Spot said, "that girl as what you wanted to see, the handmaid cand'date? She's on her way. Lester Riggers done went t' fetch her. Tol' him, I did, t' keep his manners an' his pants on, an' his pecker t' hisself. Not so's I 'spect it t' be a problem, since't ..."

He shut up abruptly, the curdled-milk shade of his skin beneath his rash of freckles going even more curdled. His lumpy Adam's apple bobbed in his scrawny throat. One hand twitched as if he desperately wanted to clap it over his mouth.

"Since't?" June prompted mildly after an awkward pause.

He gulped. "Nuthin' ... since't nuthin' ..."

"No, do go on."

"I jist ... I jist ... beggin' yer pardon, Miz Yer Highness, I din't mean nuthin' by it, jist, my tongue runned away with me; my granny allus said it flapped like a sheet on th' warsh-line in a windstorm."

June only kept looking at him, eyebrows arched expectantly.

Spot's whole face twisted as if he'd bitten into a rancid lemon. She noted his knees were pressed together, whether because he suddenly had to pee or because he was vividly recalling Mr. Shinn's double-orchidectomy. While she'd seen him grovel and—not literally, thankfully—kiss Favius's ass often enough, this was the first time he'd seemed on the verge of trepidatious panic.

"Since't?" she repeated, not letting him off the hook.

He crumpled into abject hangdog misery. "I'se only sayin', if'n ya do sign her on, ya prolly won't's have t' worry much 'bout ... 'bout the likes o' Lester or anyone ... messin' with her ... or, y'know, her foolin' aroun' with them soldier-boys an' neglectin' her 'sponserbilities."

"Ah," June said with a sage nod. "Because she … how would you put it, Spot? Because she *ain't purdy*?"

Which, of course, she wasn't. It was with the air of one who knew it all too well that the girl was shown into the largely-vacant throne room sometime later.

Her outfit might've been a hand-me-down from the Dust Bowl era, the kind of thing an extra would wear in a community theater production of *The Grapes of Wrath*. Drab, simple dress, ill-fitting and shapeless. Apron over it, some dingy shade of once-white. A matching bonnet—a for-fuck's-sake *bonnet!*—and scuffed lace-up ankle-boots, probably with wads of old newspaper stuffed into the toes.

She held herself like someone from the Dust Bowl as well, head slightly downcast, hands gripping a patched purse in front of her waist. Weathered hands, more accustomed to menial tasks than to manicures, the nails bitten short.

"Iris Tate," June said.

"Yes'm. Thank you for seeing me."

She had a low, unassuming voice, with only the barest trace of an accent.

"Please, have a seat."

After a glance at Juggernaut's bulk, placid and passive in the corner, Iris did, with the mannerisms of a church-mouse not wanting to draw any attention as she slipped into a pew. She set her purse on her lap and folded her hands atop it. She had yet to lift her head, let alone meet June's eyes. Everything about her posture suggested she was only waiting to be dismissed.

"Tell me about yourself, Iris Tate."

"Not s'much to tell, really. I'm twenny-three, or thereabouts; it's been hard to keep track after AllHell. Finished high school, did all right. My family's from over by what folks call the Shallows, near what's now Checkpoint Moses. My momma passed when I was young. My daddy, he was a county clerk, a notary and such, did licenses and legal documentation. He also passed, a while back. I have an aunt and uncle still out that way, on my daddy's side, who helped raise me up. Some cousins. A couple relations on my momma's side, gettin' on in years. That's … well, that's it, I reckon."

Recited as if by rote, without emotion; just the facts,

ma'am.

"Iris, look at me," June said.

The girl did, not skittishly but not boldly.

"What kind of job experience do you have?"

She drew a breath and dropped her gaze again. "Well, I took care of the house and such for my daddy. Cooking and cleaning and laundry and all, and when he started gettin' sickly there toward the end, I took care of him too. I did chores over to my aunt and uncle's place, especially come canning time. Took in some seamstressin'. Would go sit with and read to a blind neighbor-lady, fix her tea, write letters for her. That kind of thing."

Although she hardly needed to ask, June did anyway. "Boyfriend?"

Iris dug her short-bitten nails into the seam of a patch on her purse and shook her head, brusque and quick. "No'm. I ... never been popular that way. My cousins, now, there's another story, but I ... no'm. Not me."

"Not at all?"

She raised her head again, and this time did meet June's eyes. "If you mean, am I a virgin? No'm. There was a time or two, which I'm not proud of but did happen. More a ... a joke, to the fellers. Like a dare, or someone lost a bet, or they were having a dog show kind of party. Where they'd laugh about it later."

June brought a hand to her own cheek, which had flushed hot. She almost didn't trust herself to speak, finally saying, "I see. Yes, I ... think I understand."

"Hope I'm not out of line," Iris said, "but I had the feelin' you might. That's why I put in the application. I was there that day, on the lakeshore. I saw you. What you did. Heard what you said, whatall you said. And from that very moment, maybe it's presumptuous and all, but I just *knew*."

"Just *knew*," June echoed, thinking of how she'd felt as soon as she saw the girl's unsmiling graduation photo. How she'd just *known*.

"All my life," Iris went on, "growin' up, seeing people in the movies and on the teevee and in the magazines ... the way they, 'specially the women, were always so pretty and perfect and happy ... and if there was one who wasn't so much, well, they'd be the friend at best, or the comic relief."

June smiled bitterly. "Or it'd turn out she was done up to look plain so she'd be only a makeover away from suddenly being gorgeous and getting the man of her dreams."

Iris nodded. "My whole life, I seen that. Everywhere. All the time. They never got to be ... *somebody* ... confident and powerful and strong, not givin' a hoot what the rest of the world thought, not ashamed, not hidin'. Then ..." She tipped her head toward the window. "Out there, that day, I saw *you*."

"I think you're giving me too much credit—"

"No'm. You stood tall, and defied that bullshit—pardon m' language—and you *won*. Now, look at you. Forget bein' a pretty princess; you're a goddamn *queen*."

The girl really *was* giving her too much credit, but the tremulous admiration in her voice and the unshed tears brimming in her eyes made June reluctant to disagree.

"So I knew, from right then on, I wanted to be near you. To be part of what you were doing, what you were making happen. To help, if I could, even if in the smallest way."

And here was something *else* June never would have expected. It left her speechless, nearly unable to wrap her mind around the concept. Having someone look up to her, idolize her, see her as a ... a fucking *role model*? That, she was flat-out *not* prepared for.

"And maybe," Iris continued, ducking her head again shyly, "to learn from you. Learn to accept m'self, 'stead of always being down on m'self so bad. To be proud of who I am, and—"

June held up a palm. "Iris, enough, please. Or your queen is going to cry."

"M'sorry—"

"No, no, nothing to be sorry for. I just ... no one's ever ... Iris, listen to me, I *do* understand. Everything you described about growing up, being bombarded by movie stars and supermodels and beautiful people, being made to feel not up to standards, not good enough. Oh, believe me, I *totally* understand! I spent a lot of years angry about it too. Shit, I'm *still* angry about it!"

She found herself on her feet without intending to get up, pacing with tight, aggressive strides. Iris watched her as if awestruck.

"Having them dismiss you, pity you, mock you!" June clenched her fists. "Telling you no one will ever want you, love you! Even those who should care and be kind, your own family, your own *mother*, saying it's *fine* to be plain and ordinary while treating you like garbage!"

"I … I didn't mean to upset …"

"You didn't. *They*—" She waved wildly, as if encompassing the entire universe. "*They* did. Men! Other women! The media! Cosmetic companies! Building on our insecurities from the time we're old enough to walk. Tearing us down, making us feel bad, making us hate ourselves. Wrinkles, oh no! Grey hair! Varicose veins! Crooked teeth! Cellulite! Arm flab! Imperfect tits! Even creating *new* insecurities out of nowhere—special creams for unsightly fucking *elbow* calluses because, Lucifer Almighty, you can't go outdoors with *those* showing; get back in your bell tower, Quasimodo!"

Iris slid from her chair and landed on her knees, her previously unshed tears streaming, reaching up as if in supplication.

June stopped short, panting. She'd heard the phrase "seeing red" before, but never quite like this; the smoky redblack aura surrounded her again, wreathing her limbs and obscuring her vision.

And it was *glorious*!

The RV and its environs had fallen library-quiet. Much of the war camp too, for a considerable radius. Everyone within earshot or magically sensitive had frozen stock-still in whatever they were doing, hushed and apprehensive. As if nobody dared move, speak, or so much as blink.

Closing her eyes and catching her breath, June stayed as she was until her thundering heart slowed to a more reasonable pace. The adrenaline surge ebbed in increments, taking the rage and tension with it.

She inhaled deeply, smoothed her hair, straightened her robe, and opened her eyes again.

The redblack was gone.

Iris Tate lay prone at her feet. At first, June thought she'd killed her, but the girl was exalted, silently weeping.

After a perfunctory tap at the door, Major Duval poked her head in, wary, as if ready for anything and bracing for a real horror show. The sight of an unbothered Juggernaut took her off high alert, and her tone was casual as she addressed June. "Not to intrude, but, everything okay in here?"

"Yes, thank you, Xanne," June said. "Our, um, discourse got a bit spirited for a minute there, that's all."

"Roger." Xanne sketched a brief salute, ducked out, and shut the door again.

"Iris?"

"Yes'm?"

"I, uh, apologize if I scared you—"

"No'm, no, not hardly!" As if anticipating a rebuke but determined nonetheless, Iris clutched the hem of June's robe, kissed it, pressed it to her forehead, and kissed it again.

"Oh, hey!" June said. "What's that for?"

"It's my honor t' be here, and my honor t' serve, if you'll have me."

"Would you get off the floor, please?"

Iris did so, adjusting her apron and bonnet.

"The job's yours if you want it," June told her.

"Yes'm, I do, more than anything!"

"With a few stipulations. For starters, let's not have all this … robe-kissing stuff. I'm not some bishop or pope."

Iris smiled faintly and bobbed her head. "Yes'm."

"Good. As for pay, I … actually have no idea how that works around here, but it comes with room and board, at least, and whatever else you need, within reason; just ask one of the household staff or quartermasters. Speaking *of* room, there's one down the hall where my previous handmaid stayed. I don't know what she might have left in there, but feel free to go through it, keep what you like, ditch what you don't."

Her face had lit up, and while it still didn't do much for her looks, June supposed it was the happiest Iris'd ever been. "And my duties?" she asked.

"Just help me out where I need help," June said. "Clothes, looking after my personal effects, that sort of thing. Though, you mentioned your father was a clerk?"

"Yes'm, for the county. He'd hoped to be a lawyer or judge someday but never had the money."

"Did you, by any chance, assist him?"

"Sometimes, sure. Like, with filing and correspondence and appointments and such."

"Thank Satan," June muttered, thinking of her desk with its stacks of paperwork. "Then I should have plenty to keep you busy."

"I won't let you down," Iris said. "I appreciate this so

much, more'n I can possibly say."

"One more thing, though?"

"Yes'm?"

"When it's not an occasion or something, or when it's just the two of us, I'd prefer it if you called me June."

At that, Iris looked somewhat more dubious, but agreed. They even shook on it, which had the girl dazzled again, as if she'd just shaken hands with an A-list celebrity.

Handmaid acquired. One more check-mark on the to-do list, so far so good. June turned her over to the head housekeeper so she could get settled.

However, it seemed she now needed to have a little chat with one Ritchie "Spot" Wilkins. To set him straight on the way things were going to be done around here, informing him in no uncertain terms what would and wouldn't be tolerated.

At marshmallow fork's point if necessary.

She could have had him taken to the main stockade, or stuck in a pillory in one of the main pavilions, but thought it might be better if they handled this more privately. Without an audience. Without making a big deal of what his precise offense had been, which could come off as overly sensitive, maybe even be taken as a sign of weakness.

All that said, he was in for it, and he knew it too. He sat on a fallen log in a clearing behind the RV, where she'd told him to go wait, like a guilty schoolboy on a bench outside the principal's office. Shoulders slumped, lower lip pooched out, sulkily kicking at dirt clods.

As she and Juggernaut approached, Spot immediately fell to groveling his ass off, whining it'd only been talk, he hadn't meant no offense, plenny folks said worse all'a time, why'd ever'one gotta take it all personal—

"Hold him upside-down by the ankles," June ordered.

Juggernaut obeyed.

Spot's freckled face went maroon as the blood rushed to it. His gingerish hair hung in greasy clumps. His dangling arms pawed for purchase.

"I am well aware," she began, sitting on the log herself to better bring them near eye level, "of how dedicated and invaluable your service has been. Favius spoke well of you, the way you swore yourself to him, the way you handled things in his absence and made ready for his return."

"Tha'ss right!" he said. "Tha'ss right, weren't no one 'round this whole lake more—"

She gestured, and Juggernaut bounced his head on the ground. He squawked, then got the hint and shut his yap.

"You've been of great assistance to me as well," she went on. "Without your knowledge, familiarity, and connections, none of this would be running as smoothly as it is. I would hate to lose such a vital resource."

His eyes bugged.

And bugged more when she idly drew the marshmallow fork from the loop on her belt-cord.

"I would hate," she said, calm as if discussing the weather, "to have Juggernaut snap you like a wishbone."

The Golem shifted its grip, tugging Spot's legs apart just enough to suggest how effortless it'd be to split him from crotch to sternum. Spot cringed, the message clearly not lost on him.

"Actually, no," June said, after a pensive pause. "I wouldn't *hate* it. I might *regret* it later, and it might cause more problems than it solved, but I don't think I'd *hate* it. It's entirely possible I'd enjoy it. You know how that is, don't you, Spot? I'm told you have quite a fondness for seeing people suffer. I'm told you really get a kick out of it."

He tried to nod, a challenge when hung upside-down.

"Which is why I *did* find it odd when you skipped out on the Shinns giving birth," she remarked. "Considering the utero-gourd seeds were, in fact, *your* suggestion in the first place. And a wonderful suggestion, at that; couldn't have asked for anything more fitting."

She doodled idly in the dirt with the fork's bronzed tines, then looked at him again.

"But it's a guy thing, isn't it?" she asked. "Being squeamish about all that girly stuff. Periods, pregnancy, birth. Funny how, as much as so many of you claim to just looove you some lady bits, they're only for sticking your dicks into. As soon as their actual, oh, purpose and function is involved, you can't cope."

Spot wheezed. The effects of his inverted position on his circulatory system and lungs were taking their toll. He'd pass out sooner or later, probably sooner.

"It's also funny—and, by 'funny,' I don't mean 'funny;' I mean stupid and obnoxious—how many of you judge women solely by their looks, when, frankly, you may not be anything to write home about yourselves. Yet there you still go, entitled, like the universe *owes* you hot babes, and shitting all over anyone who doesn't fit."

Spot's eyes rolled woozily in his lolling head, so June had Juggernaut turn him right-side-up again. The Golem's thick clay hand held him by nape and shirt collar, scruffed like a kitten, and gave him a jostle to encourage circulation along.

"And maybe," June allowed, "it isn't altogether your fault. You men, I mean. You've been as saturated with it as we have, just in different ways. All those movies where the nerd-dork-loser gets the girl, sitcoms with slobbo husbands who have sexy wives. Maybe you get hit with other kinds of pressure … how much money you make, if you have a nice car. But you know what?"

A side-to-side wobble could have indicated a no, or it could have indicated he was still about to pass out or puke; June didn't care.

"Even then," she said, rising from the log to look him square on, "even then, you find ways to make it the woman's fault. We're always the bitches, aren't we? Oh, she won't go out with anyone less than six feet tall? Shallow bitch! She only wants a guy with a job, who doesn't live in his parents' goddamn basement? Gold-digging bitch!"

She paused and took a deep breath, feeling the smoky redblack wanting to seethe over her again. Her grip had gone white-knuckled on the marshmallow fork. So easy, it'd be, to stab the tines into his groin, skewer his nutsack, and *twist!*

Spot must've seen it in her face, because he shivered and sniveled, and a wet patch darkened the front of his trousers.

"But worst of all, worst of all, is the ugly bitches, the fat or skinny or old bitches, who have the nerve, the fucking *nerve*, to *exist*. Exist while not being hot babes, not up to your standards!"

Smoky redblack wreathed her arm, gloved her hand, swirled and danced along the length of the marshmallow fork. She leveled it at him, not at his groin but a half-inch from the end of his nose so he had to go cross-eyed to keep it in view.

The temptation, oh, the temptation was terrible and delicious. So seductive. His terror, intoxicating.

She lowered the marshmallow fork and relaxed her grip, letting the smoky redblack dissipate into wafts and wisps.

"I suggest," she said, "in the future, you choose your words more carefully. And, perhaps, examine your attitudes."

He bobbled a weak nod, still quaking.

"Well, Mr. Wilkins? Anything to say?"

"'m ... 'm sorry," he mewled.

"Sorry?"

"Won't do it again, won't hear nothin' of the sort outta my mouth, I swears t' Satan, an' an'body else go spoutin' off such bullshit, I'se'll makes it my bizniss t' put a stop t' it right quick!"

At her curt nod, Juggernaut let go. Spot dropped six inches, his feet hit the ground, his legs buckled, and he landed in an ungainly, groaning heap.

"See that you do," she said. "I hope we need never repeat this discussion."

Not waiting for a reply, she turned and swept out of there as grandly as she could muster, sliding the marshmallow fork back into its loop. Juggernaut followed, and though the Golem's features were impassive as ever, she liked to think there was a quiet, satisfied approval.

Judging by some of the looks she got as she returned to the RV, her desire to handle the matter more privately and without an audience may not have been altogether successful. It could, quite possibly, backfire on her and bite her in the ass if Spot's shame fermented into resentment ... but somehow, she didn't think it would.

If it did?

Well, there was always the wishbone option. Or the marshmallow fork.

Once alone in the master suite, she went again to the mirror and regarded her reflection. As before, she appeared physically unchanged, no ram's horns or cloven hooves, no spectral aura or demonic skull superimposed over her image.

But she could feel it. Oh, yes. She could feel it.

And it really did feel pretty goddamn glorious.

Almost Paradise

So, this was Heaven.

The backstage, behind-the-scenes, working machinery part of it, anyway. The part the paying customers didn't see. Mustn't ruin the experience with mundane, gritty reality.

Well, not that it *was* mundane, gritty, or reality. It was very much *not* that. Even apparently empty, without so much as a stray cherub in sight, the undeniable fact of the matter remained: it was Heaven.

Greg chose a hallway at random, Ethriel cradled to his chest, a Margaritaville beach towel burrito. Her head lay against his shoulder, her eyes closed, her breath shallow.

"They all at fucking *lunch* or something?" he grumbled to himself, then flinched.

Swearing in Heaven, probably not cool. Minor league, for sure, especially stacked up against the other sins and transgressions on his roster, but no sense pushing his luck. Ethriel may have surprised him by using such language upon their first acquaintance, but as she'd told him, at Lake Misquamicus, the regular rulebook had been thrown out the window. Such might not be the case here. Here, the rulebook could very well be in strict play. If so, he was violating it more than enough already.

For all it seemed empty, as he progressed through a windowless maze of unmarked intersections and chambers with purposes he couldn't begin to identify—in one, suspended in mid-air, hung a giant faceted globe, a disdyakis triacontahedron, revolving on multiple axes and beaming intermittent golden rays from its 120 triangular sides—he felt more and more a sense of presence and activity. And a great deal of it.

He thought again of vast networks of hidden service

tunnels, hospital basements, the below-decks of luxury megaships. Engine rooms and boiler rooms, laundries, pantries, archives, vaults. Harp storage. Janitorial closets full of halo polish and cloud cleaner.

Then he turned a corner and almost collided with a mass of wings and eyes and rings of fire. He yelped, jumped back, stumbled, and landed flat on his ass with Ethriel in his lap.

Way to make an entrance ...

The mass of wings, eyes, and rings of fire, fully a yard in diameter and awash in coruscating radiance, wafting with scents of sandalwood and myrrh, zigged straight up so fast its uppermost cluster of wings hit the ceiling, and emitted the kind of shrill sound a cartoon housewife might make when seeing a mouse.

Greg gaped at it. At the angel, at the biblically accurate angel, divine and unearthly and otherworldly and all but beyond human comprehension.

Its myriad cerulean eyes all fixed on him. At the warlock, in his rumpled trench coat, eldritch sigil branded upon his brow, scruffy and battle-scarred.

"Hi," Greg said.

Myriad eyes blinked in erratic succession, myriad wings fluttered, myriad rings of fire flickered. More sounds issued from it; these, unlike the startled shriek of a moment ago, were composed of a thrumming buzz overlaid with a series of harmonious notes.

"Sorry, I ... I don't ..." he tried, but words failed him. After all he'd seen and done and learned these past weeks, he'd figured he was ready for just about anything.

Guess not.

The angel scrutinized him again, buzz-thrummed as if in consideration, and, although it had no discernible mouth, spake unto him.

"By the Seven Trumpets!" it said in a prim, fussy voice, like Roddy McDowell at his prissiest. "*You* shouldn't be here!"

Greg managed a weak grin. "Yeah, story of my life lately. Still, it is what it is, and, uh, here I am."

"A *mortal*! A *warlock*, no less! *Here*! Well, I never!"

"I know, I know, but it was an emergency." He nodded toward Ethriel. "She's hurt. She needs help. Please."

The myriad eyes shifted to her. Following another spate of erratic blinks, some of them widened in shock, while others narrowed in suspicious accusation.

"That's one of *ours*!" it exclaimed, Roddy McDowell at his most highly-affronted. "Recently promoted from the *Custos Viatorum*, unless I miss my guess. What in the Unutterable is she doing with *you*?"

Some awkward, careful explanation later, the angel—Icaiah—finally got its wings and rings in gear, and the next thing Greg knew, the hallway was swarming with low-tier ishim and rasul. A cherub or two flitted in, then a seraph.

If he'd tried to make sense of it all, he would've gone insane, his mind blown like a dandelion puff. The various divine beings defied description, and only thanks to his grandfather's tutelage could he even roughly categorize them. They buffeted him aside in a brisk whirlwind, making him think of first responders who had neither the time nor the patience for bystanders.

Ethriel was whisked off to the celestial equivalent of the ER. The seraph, taking the form of a humanoid figure of pure white flame, barred Greg from following, needing no words to do so. A single stern extended flame-limb, pointing, like the Ghost Of Christmas Yet To Come directing Scrooge to his own tombstone, got the message across.

He went, without protest, to the designated area. It was not a waiting room per se but a kind of spacious alcove, with cloudy walls and crystalline skylights admitting soft, clear rays.

Icaiah accompanied him, though in precisely what capacity, Greg wasn't sure. Guard? Escort? Babysitter? He got the strong impression Icaiah wasn't very sure either. Luck of the draw; you found him, you get to keep tabs on him.

"This truly is most irregular," Icaiah remarked.

"Tell me about it."

"Tell you about it? What could *I* possibly tell *you* about it?"

"Figure of speech, sorry." He poked at a fluffy cloudbank vaguely shaped like a sofa and, when the poke elicited no hostile reaction, went ahead and sat down. He slumped, exhausted, burying his face in his hands.

"Guardian angels incorporating on Earth," Icaiah tutted. "Warlocks. Fornication."

Greg winced. Here it came, the lecture, the thunderbolt, the pillar of salt ...

But Icaiah just kept tutting. "Liminal spaces. Greater Relics. The whole messy, nasty business with the lake; what a headache all *that* was to begin with, and *now*? What with these latest developments? Millions dead, worldwide chaos, and crises of faith. I daresay, it's got everyone in an absolute kerfuffle."

"What, um, if you don't mind my asking, actually happened? We kind of missed it. Those liminal spaces and so on. I knew there'd been talk of a nuclear missile, and I felt *something* go by, but ..."

"The Painwave, they're calling it. At least with the Deluge, we had advance warning, could be adequately prepared. This little monkey wrench caught us blindside, and do you have any idea how difficult it is to catch *us* blindside?"

"Yeah, I bet," Greg said, hazarding a peek at the angel's myriad eyes. Which, while still cerulean, were now also indignant.

"Made us look a load of incompetent blunderers." Icaiah huffed. "Which must be why *you* were able to simply waltz in here uncontested. Had our hands full, didn't we? The sheer amount of *prayers* coming in, the rush of unprocessed souls at the *Gates* ... it's been triple-duty and extra assignments ever since! We'll be centuries sorting out the backlog. *Centuries!*"

"Then I show up?"

"Then you show up, as if we didn't have enough to do. I'm sure you didn't *know*, didn't *mean* to add to the workload, but we can't very well just have *you* traipsing around. A mortal warlock? A *Nachtwald*, no less? Why, it's a public relations nightmare waiting to happen!"

"I really don't want to cause any trouble," Greg said. "I'm only here for Ethriel. It's my fault she got hurt. She was defending me. I owe her so much ... I ... love her so much ... I had to do something."

"Hmph, *love* indeed."

First, his dead grandparents, and now this? True, this was one angel, not a complete tribunal such as Ethriel had had to answer to, but still ...

"Yeah, *love*." He lifted his chin defiantly. "If that's a sin, fine; strike me down."

"Oh, very dramatic," Icaiah said, managing a passable sarcastic little slow-clap despite not having actual hands. "Not, I'm afraid, my department."

"Whose department is it?" Greg asked.

"Never you mind. You'll find out, I'm sure, when the time comes."

"Great, thanks." He slumped back on the couch-cloud, gazing ceilingward at the crystalline skylights. "So what happens now?"

"I'm not altogether certain. This is a most irregular situation."

Despite the anxiety knotting his guts and the tension tightening his nerve-strings to the breaking point, he tried to relax. Tried to let some of the stress and insanity of the past couple weeks melt away.

No doing.

It was all right there with him, vivid as ever. The plane crash, the lake, Zilch, Ethriel, the Wall, his grandparents, the tunnel, the truck, Heck and Lorlinda, the screeching Nazi death-flock, Blaze, the junior warlock, the Golems, Favius. And the woman, that terrible, vengeful woman … Hell hath no fury etc. … he'd rather go up against an entire legion than have to face *her* again.

The worst of it was, now he'd had a chance to think about what she'd said, he could—kind of, almost—relate. Whatever she and Favius had had going on, he believed her. She'd been happy for the first time in her life, and then they'd come along and fucked it all up. She didn't care about the big picture diabolical plan and the greater scheme of things; they'd robbed her of the man she loved. It was *personal*.

In fact, strike the "kind of, almost" … he could absolutely relate. Given the choice between saving Ethriel and saving the world, it'd be a no-brainer.

Selfish? Short-sighted?

Well, so what? He was, still and all when you got right down to it, only human.

A trill of harp strings and a thrill of tingling divine energy brought him upright and aware again. Another presence, a Presence, had entered the alcove, and if his eyes told him he was seeing an ordinary guy in a white coat with a stethoscope slung around his neck, his warlock-senses told him otherwise.

So did the way Icaiah dipped as if in respectful deference,

then drifted back as if to give them some space.

Greg got up. Any self-consciousness about his disheveled appearance, or the transgression of him even being here, got swept aside by a far more overriding concern.

"How is she?" he asked without preamble or polite introduction. "Is she going to be all right?"

"It is soon yet to tell. The injuries, they are severe." The "doctor" consulted a golden clipboard. "Indications are that which inflicted them had been imbued with considerable unholy energies. Of Viscount, or perhaps Arch-Duke, levels. What was the weapon?"

"A sword. Favius's sword; he'd dropped it. Roman-style. A gladius."

"And the wielder?"

"A woman. His queen, I guess. Mortal, as far as I could tell, but there was something about her ..." He described the impressions he'd gotten, the smoky redblack energy, the suggestion of a demonic skull.

The "doctor" made notes with a crystal pen. "Azbunael."

Icaiah twitched but kept quiet.

"An Arch-Duke," the "doctor" went on. "Overthrown and deposed but by no means destroyed. We'd suspected some Relic of his made its way across. If this woman you mention has acquired even a fraction of his power, it bodes very ill indeed."

"But what about Ethriel?" Greg persisted. "Can you help her? Can you heal her? If there's anything I can do, *anything*, my life, my soul—"

The "doctor" rapped him smartly on the forehead with the crystalline pen, dead-center of the sigil. A silvery burst rang through Greg's head like a chime.

"Do not insult us with bargains and deals. I assure you, the raphim shall do all possible. It has been long since one of our own confronted the Adversary's forces so directly, let alone been wounded. Her valor, service, and devotion will not go unacknowledged. Nor shall yours, Gregory Nachtwald. Despite the ... circumstances."

As the "doctor" left, clipboard tucked crisply beneath an arm, Greg sank back onto the cloud-couch rubbing his brow.

"Who *was* that guy?" he mumbled.

He'd meant it more rhetorical, and talking to himself, but

Icaiah answered anyway, with prim, lofty haughtiness.

"For your information, that *'guy'* happens to be the Archangel Raphael, the Healer."

Greg practically choked. "*The* Raphael?"

"None other, so I'd suggest you mind your manners."

He didn't have anything clever to say to that, so he just sat there. It gradually occurred to him how much better he felt, physically, anyway. He regarded his hands, which had been badly abraded scraping against the rough promontory edges of Bighead Rock, several nails ragged or torn off entirely, and found them still dirtied and bloodied but otherwise unhurt. He was no longer bruised, achy, and banged up from the battle. As if simply being near the archangel had eased him of his pains.

Even the gash on his chin had, if not fully healed, at least gone from an ugly, throbbing, crusted sore to a pinkish, tender scar.

Icaiah hovered on the far side of the alcove, keeping a dozen or so eyes on him while refraining from further commentary. Which was fine by Greg; he may have had plenty of questions, but this was hardly the time. Whatever Icaiah's role here was, however accidental, it wasn't to play Virgil to his Dante and give him the guided tour.

Now and then, other angels—ranging in shape from twinkling spheres to plump dove-winged naked babies to a four-faced figure with the body of a sumo-wrestler (the faces, as best Greg could make out, were of a man, an ox, an eagle, and a lion, but he didn't dare look too closely)—came in, and they'd converse with Icaiah in their buzz-thrumming language. Nobody bothered to translate. Some ventured over to inspect him, twinkling spheres flitting around like hummingbirds, and a powder-scented cherub right out of a Renaissance painting poking chubby fingers at his face, but most regarded him from a distance, wary and unreadable.

Finally, what he presumed was one of the raphim appeared, this one in the form of a stout matronly woman in pale-blue scrubs and a surgical mask. She shooed away a couple of cherubs who'd been whispering and smirking at Greg, then approached him herself.

"Mr. Nachtwald? I am Blianthis." She removed her mask, revealing a gentle, kind smile. "I've been sent to update you on Ethriel's condition."

He got up again, somehow more apprehensive than ever.

"Is she ...?"

"I won't sugarcoat it; she was very seriously injured. Nearly discorporated, and in a way which wouldn't have sent her back here."

"You mean, obliterated?" he said, thinking of Favius.

"Or worse."

"Worse?"

"Sent somewhere else." Blianthis made a slight downward gesture.

A cold hollow opened inside him in the vicinity of his heart, giving the blood in his veins the temperature and texture sensation of a convenience store slushie.

"Oh ..."

"Had the blade pierced her side an inch or two deeper, we wouldn't be having this conversation. We've been able to cleanse the wound of corruption, but she'll be facing a long and difficult recovery."

He pounced on this merest hint of hope with desperate eagerness. "But she *will* recover? She'll survive?"

"She will."

Relief nearly collapsed him on the spot. Saying "thank God" or something similar seemed inappropriate, a given, because, well, *obviously*, thank God, and he couldn't think of anything else to say, so he exhaled a shaky, tearful laugh-sob.

"However ..."

Annnd snap, dread had him in its clutches again.

"However ...?" He swallowed thickly. "Her ... her wings?"

"Her wings. The only way they could be restored is beyond our means. If she goes on as she is, she'll have to do so as she is, unable to fly, greatly diminished in her capabilities. After consulting with our team, we've concluded the kindest option may be a complete discorporation and renewal."

"What ... what does that entail, exactly?" he asked.

As if he didn't know; when he'd been about ten years old and the family dog got hit by a car, the vet had sounded pretty much the same way. Yes, Baxter *could* live, but with such a diminished quality of life and in constant reminder of what had been lost ...

"It would entail," said Blianthis, "returning her to the most basic elements of her divine essence and giving her the opportunity to begin her existence anew. A blank slate, if you will."

"Starting over from scratch?"

"Yes."

"As she was before?"

"A different being. A different form."

"But she'd still be Ethriel?"

"Not Ethriel as you know her. Not Ethriel as she knows you. A blank slate, as I said. Without knowledge or memory of—"

"No!" Greg flung up his arms. "No, not that, there's got to be a way, there's got to be another way! Shit-shit-shit-*shit*, I *hate* it when they do that, save someone's *life* at the expense of their *self*, who they'd become and what made them who they are, who they're proud of being; I was so pissed, I almost quit watching *Doctor Who* after Donna! Stephen King pulls that crap all the *time*, rob them of what's important, wipe away their memories after they've been through so much—"

He broke off, realizing what he'd done, realizing he was shouting, awash with arcane energy, eldritch sigil ablaze.

Icaiah had retreated as far as the confines of the room would allow, Blianthis had drawn back with a shocked— almost frightened—expression, and a modest host of other angels popped in out of nowhere. Among them was the white-fire seraph who'd directed him with the silent, stern pointing gesture, and the four-faced sumo-wrestler.

And Raphael himself, the archangel having abandoned his white coat and stethoscope for more traditional biblical robes and majestic swanlike wings.

"I *told* you he'd be nothing but trouble," Icaiah said smugly. "A warlock, in Heaven? Why, the impertinence! Ought to fling him straight back to Earth this very instant."

The white-fire seraph made a move as if to do just that. The four-faced sumo-wrestler cracked beefy knuckles.

"Enough."

The single word from Raphael quelled them all, including—and especially—Greg. His arms dropped to his sides, his arcane energy fizzled out, and he hung his head.

"I'm sorry," he said, sounding as broken as he felt. "I know it doesn't mean anything, I know it's not enough, but I shouldn't have shouted, I shouldn't have done that, I'm sorry."

"Her fate is not your decision to make," Raphael told him.

He nodded without looking up. "I understand. If you're going to throw me out, go ahead, do it. Just, please, let me see her first. Let me say goodbye."

"The cheek! I hardly see why we should—"

"Hush, Icaiah," said Raphael. "Be off about your business."

"You're dismissing me? *Me*?"

"I'm excusing you. And the rest of you as well. It isn't as if there aren't plenty of matters demanding your attention."

They dispersed, leaving Greg alone in the alcove with the archangel and the raphim—Blianthis still in matronly human guise, down to the sensible white-soled nurse's shoes.

"Your passion is admirable," Raphael went on, not without sympathy. "As is your dedication. This, I promise you, on my Oath, no drastic measures will be taken until you've had the chance to see and speak with Ethriel."

"Thank you," he whispered, unable to raise his gaze higher than their feet.

"Once she is in a fit state to do so, you will be sent for. Until then, you are, within reason and so long as there are no further disturbances, free to move about these halls as you will. We ask only that you refrain from passing through any of the Golden Doors. A living mortal could prove quite … upsetting … to those with whose eternal happiness we are entrusted."

He also never in his life would have expected to find himself in a dive bar in Heaven, two stools down from someone he was pretty sure was either Clint Eastwood or the Angel of Death.

Since Eastwood, far as he knew, hadn't yet passed on, ninety-something and tough as nails …

Had the look, though. Leathery and weathered, his entire face a narrow gunslinger's squint.

No jeans, boots, cowboy hat, or duster, however. No voluminous hooded black cape either.

He wore a basic grey sport coat, anonymous and average, the kind that'd blend right in and fade into the background almost anywhere. Ordinary wristwatch, nothing fancy. His only notable accessory was a ring on his left forefinger, brushed titanium inset with a band of glossy black stone—onyx was Greg's guess.

To the casual observer, aside from the striking Eastwood

resemblance, he could have passed for just another commuter on the subway or city street.

To the not-so-casual observer—to a warlock, for instance—it was another story. The dense, dark, turbulent aura hanging compactly about him was a giveaway. If he didn't radiate Presence as openly as Raphael, it was because he chose to play it close to the vest.

A shot glass and a bottle rested on the bartop before him, and he had the fill-it, toss-it-back, refill-it down to a precise routine. The liquid was indigo whorled with diamond flecks and shining streaks, as if distilled from entire galaxies and the vastness of space itself.

In his memory, Greg heard Ethriel: … *think Azrael's not still fucked-up over the firstborn of Egypt? Shit, if angels could be alcoholics …*

"Listen, kid," the grey-sport-coated figure said without so much as turning his head in Greg's direction—and damned if he didn't *sound* like Eastwood too, that raspy, grizzled gunslinger drawl. "If you've got some score to settle or are looking to make a name for yourself, save it. I'm not in the mood."

"No, sir. Sorry. Didn't mean to offend."

He grunted noncommittally and threw back another shot. Refilled. The bottle seemed unemptying.

Greg forced his attention to focus on his own drink. Walking into any sort of bar, let alone a dive bar, and asking for water might have been a good way to get ridiculed—if not as much as asking for a glass of milk—but he had no idea how well his mortal body would handle whatever they used for booze up here. A single accidental mouthful of Zilch's demonic black-grape wine had left him reeling, and he'd seen the effect a gulp of lake-brewed hellshine had on Blaze; the spirits served in this place could only be *more* potent.

So, water it was.

The bartender—a nephilim, unless he missed his guess; nearly nine feet tall and oddly Sasquatch-esque, covered with silky pale-blond fur—had set before him a flat alabaster ring with a hole in the center, and balanced in the hole, a perfect bubble-globe with archaic Aramaic lettering. It read, as best he could decipher from his grandfather's crash-course lessons, "Eden Springs." Into this bubble, a slim reed that might have been plucked from the shores of the Nile where Moses was found among the bulrushes could be inserted and used as a straw.

Not that using a straw seemed much manly-mannier than asking for milk, but he wasn't sure how else to drink it without popping the bubble and spilling it all over himself. Which would also not make the most favorable impression.

So, water it was and straw it was ... and the first sip proved above and beyond any water he'd ever experienced. No alpine stream or glacial pool could have been purer, cooler, more refreshing.

He wanted to guzzle the whole thing; he wanted to nurse it slowly and savor every drop.

"Go ahead, kid, drink up," not-Clint-Eastwood said, pushing some celestial currency across the bar. "On me. Haphthiah, keep them coming."

Prior to finding himself in what may have been Heaven's only dive bar, he'd wandered the network of halls and chambers, trying to stay out of the way and not intrude or interrupt.

He had a visitor's pass in the form of a scroll-shaped ribbon pinned to the lapel of his coat, and a pager-like device in his pocket. The pager-like device, he suspected, also functioned as a tracker, the equivalent of an ankle monitor, to make sure he kept his word and didn't go snooping anywhere he wasn't supposed to.

Through any of the Golden Doors, for instance. Which were almost as impressive as the Pearly Gates, done in designs of filigree so delicate and beautiful as to make a Tolkien elf weep. Tempting as they were, however, Greg steered well clear.

And it wasn't as if he lacked for amazing sights and vistas to behold, once he'd reached the bustling and populated areas where the real work was done. His earlier ponderings about theme parks and luxury resorts hadn't been so far off the mark after all. The infrastructure, organization, and labor required to keep Heaven running smoothly was monumental. Boggling.

From a gallery overlooking an immense space that appeared part call center, part medieval monastery scribe hall, and part mail-sorting room, he'd watched prayers coming in, being processed, and routed to the proper channels. Gratitude prayers, bedtime prayers, pleading and beseeching prayers, even angry and demanding prayers.

It was hectic, nonstop, rasul rushing back and forth like newsboys, ishim operators bent over clusters of spheres resembling those static-electricity balls, a dump truck-sized wheelie bin labeled General Delivery, missives stamped for same-day priority to one saint or another, items flagged as potentially hazardous and turned over to a team of elohim for inspection.

He wondered if they had phone-trees, recordings, and hold music. *Your prayer is very important to us, please stay on the line and a cherub will be with you shortly. We are currently experiencing unusually high prayer volumes; to leave a message, light a candle at the beep. For inquiries about reincarnation, press 7. If you know the extension number of your theology of choice, enter it at any time.* And so on.

Even with his visitor's pass, he got plenty of startled double-takes and suspicious looks. He didn't blame them; it was hard not doing some double-takes of his own. Right when he figured he was getting used to the divine array of diversity, along would come a new form or configuration.

In another section, he found what appeared to be a security control room crammed with an infinity of rippling quicksilver screens, through which could be seen an infinity of camera-angle views from every part of Heaven proper, where the worthy souls enjoyed their eternal salvation in an infinity of ways. Multiple angels of myriad-upon-myriad more eyes than Icaiah floated there, each watching a million screens at once, missing nothing.

Warlock who'd seen some shit or not, it was enough to give him a headache, and damn near an existential crisis. He'd decided that finding someplace quiet, where he could try and get his head back together, was more important than any further sight-seeing.

With that in mind, he'd detoured away from the main thoroughfares, onto more subdued side-passages. Then he'd spotted a pair of ishim exiting a doorway, and everything about them—despite the fact one was a six-winged torso-face and the other a humanoid owl—told him they were regular blue-collar joes who'd stopped off for a drink or two after their shift.

The doorway through which they'd exited supported this notion, with a circular stained glass window above it depicting a trio of chalice-type cups pouring into each other, and small posted placards advertising various brands of wine, ambrosia, whiskey, and cider.

So he'd ventured down a short flight of steps, into a dimly-lit space, where rows of bottles glinted dully from shelves and the scent of sandalwood incense hung smokily in the air.

Haphthiah brought Greg another sphere-bubble of Eden Springs, took the celestial currency to the till, and would have made change but was waved off.

"Keep it," said not-Clint-Eastwood.

The bartender nodded, then—in the time-honored tradition—retreated to the other end of the bar and commenced wiping pint glasses with a scrap of cloth.

"Thanks." Greg lifted the sphere to his benefactor.

Those narrow, slitted gunslinger eyes flicked briefly toward him. "Look like you could use something stronger, kid."

He laughed uneasily. "I probably could, but I doubt it'd be a good idea."

"Yeah." Down went another slug of liquid galaxy, and chug-a-glug went the refill. "It rarely is."

There weren't many other patrons at the moment, and not much room for them anyway. A few booths along the walls, a couple tables with chairs, the barstools, and that was about it. The dim lighting had no discernible source, lending the place the feel of an overcast autumn day, as opposed to the perpetual sunny springtime-summer ambiance Greg had noticed elsewhere. Music, also with no discernible source, played low and soft from somewhere—not harps and choirs, not Gregorian chants, but ... unless his ears were deceiving him ... classic rock?

In the middle of the room was a billiard table, its racked-and-ready balls not done in numbered solids and stripes but as planets and moons, including a white-frosted blue-green Earth and a Jupiter with its great red spot. For this solar system in miniature, the cue ball was a glowing golden Sun, and he really didn't want to think about the cosmological or astronomical implications, so he didn't.

Off to one side, a hall led to what, in a normal bar, probably would have been the bathrooms; whether they had bathrooms here or not, he couldn't say. All he knew was he hadn't needed to "go" since he arrived, and those functions seemed inappropriate for Heaven anyway.

Off to the other side was a nook with a couple of—strange but true—pinball machines, a coin-operated incense dispenser, and a dartboard with a cartoon caricature of a devil pinned to it.

Mustering his nerve, he swiveled on his stool. "I don't mean to be nosy, but … are you who I think you are?"

Down went another shot. "Who do you think I am?"

"Either Clint Eastwood or the Angel of Death." The words just slipped right out of him, and he winced, bracing himself.

"Clint Eastwood or the Angel of Death." In a musing echo, followed by a half-amused snort. "You flatter me, kid. I've sure never won an Academy Award."

"So … you *are* …?"

"Azrael, yeah. Head honcho of the memitim, Destroyer-in-Chief, and His holy hitman." He nudged the bottle aside and signaled the bartender. "Break out the Spirytus Sancti, Haph; *I* could use something stronger. And spare me the sermon. We both know I'm not going to get blotto, no matter how hard I try."

"If I'm bothering you—"

"Nah, kid. I don't often have the chance to actually talk with a mortal. Might as well make the most of it. And a celebrity, at that."

"Celebrity? Hey, whoa, wait a minute—"

Azrael snorted again. "Blessed warlock, demon-slayer, foiler of diabolical plans, chosen consort of an angel? If that's not celebrity …" He glanced at Haphthiah, who held a stoppered and wax-sealed jug old enough to have been on the Ark. "Am I right?"

The bartender nodded and threw Greg a commiserating smile.

"You're famous, Nachtwald," Azrael went on. "Nothing like this has happened around here in ages. And with no chariot of fire or Hand of God either. Just up and did it on your own."

"Only for Ethriel. I had to do something. I couldn't lose her again."

"Be as it may, you did it." The wax seal broken, the stopper unstoppered, he filled his glass to the brim with a viscous, oily syrup like Everclear on steroids. "Ah, there's the stuff."

"All that, though," Greg said, morosely swirling his half-finished second sphere of Eden Springs, "and I'm going to lose her anyway, aren't I? They want to discorporate and renew her. Erase who she *is*, make her start over. With no memories ... no *Ethriel*."

"For some of us, might not be so bad. Plenty I wish *I* could forget. But I see your point, kid, and I agree. It sucks."

"Whether or not I deserve to lose her, or she deserves to lose me, she doesn't deserve to lose herself. They tell me it's not my decision to make, okay, but whose decision is it? Hers? Will they *ask* her, or will they just ...?"

"Easy, kid. Your forehead's starting to light up."

"I love her. There's got to be another way."

"And if there was?"

"I'd do it. Whatever it takes."

"There *are* ways. None of them a walk in the Garden, granted, but there are ways."

"I don't care what it costs, how dangerous it is. Anything for her."

"Careful. Proclamations like that have a way of biting you in the ass. What if it was a life for a life? Not yours, no; someone else's, someone innocent. What if it was a thousand lives for a life? What if it was every mortal life on Earth?"

"Uh ..."

"See? Already had a taste of it too, haven't you? The boy. Billy. His name was Billy. Sure, he was an enemy. Sure, it was self-defense. You're still going to carry him on your conscience the rest of your days."

"I ..."

"Haph, give me the clicker."

The bartender, wordless as ever, slid over what looked like a gilded remote control. Azrael aimed it at a crystal globe suspended in an upper corner, where a regular bar might've had a television tuned to a sporting event. The globe shimmered alight and began scrolling through images of children of every nationality and race. Newborns. Toddlers. Laughing. Crying. Chasing butterflies. Playing. Hugging their mommies.

Greg buried his face in his hands. "Stop, okay? Don't. Please. I get it."

"Do you?"

"Yes! Damn it, I *get* it!"

"Not trying to be cruel to you. Voice of experience, here."

"I understand."

"Good. So you have to watch what you say, what pledges or promises you make. Don't forget Whom you're dealing with."

Haphthiah shifted uncomfortably.

Azrael's thin lips gave a wry twist. "Oh, smooth your fur; I'm not criticizing Anybody. Just stating some home truths."

"What *can* I do, then?" Greg asked. "You said there were ways. What ways?"

"First off, you wanted to know whose decision it was if not yours." He was at least four shots into the Spirytus Sancti, the fumes of which alone made Greg woozy, but didn't seem to have so much as a mild buzz on. "It's complicated. Normally, the heads of her order would have the final say, but, she's no longer under the auspices of the *Custos Viatorum*, strictly speaking. At the moment, she's about the closest to a 'free agent' as the hierarchy recognizes."

"You mean it's her decision?"

"Subject to a consensus from the higher-ups, but yes. Which, in my opinion, is as it should be for all of—"

Haphthiah stirred again, making a rumbly little throat-clearing noise which could only be interpreted as a warning.

"Fine, fine, fine," Azrael relented. "If she chooses renewal, no one's going to deny her and force her into a continued existence in her diminished capacity. No one, Nachtwald. Not even you."

"I ... I wouldn't." It hurt to say, felt as if his inner foundations were crumbling to dust. "If it's what she wants ..."

"Now, if she does choose to go on, it gets trickier, because those higher-ups will have several factors to evaluate, assess, and consider."

Greg bit his tongue and willed his sigil not to flare. If she was still *useful*, in other words. What kind of duties she'd be fit for, a crippled angel who couldn't fly.

"I take it," he said stiffly, "the ADA and United Nations Convention rulings don't apply up here."

Azrael shrugged. "Lo, the lame shall walk and the blind shall see, all infirmities and afflictions swept away, and so on."

"That's bullshit."

Haphthiah directed the warning look and rumble his way, but Greg didn't care.

"What is this, *The LEGO Movie*?" he went on. "Everything is awesome? Everyone is perfect?"

"Kid, I don't make the rules."

"Well, it's still bullshit!"

"Hey, I'm not arguing. You ask the hard questions, you have to be ready for the hard answers. Hear me out, though. This has been an unusual set of circumstances. We've never dealt with anything quite like it before, and it's got wings in a tizzy clear to the top. You and your girl, now, you're the talk of the town. What you did down there? Especially this ..."

He pressed the clicker again, and Greg died a million internal deaths as the scene in the globe rippled, reforming. It was going to be, he just knew it, he just goddamn *knew* it, the motel room. Him and Ethriel, naked on the bed, her kneeling astride him and lowering herself onto—

It wasn't the motel room.

It was Bighead Rock. And it was him and Ethriel, but it was him and Ethriel crouched on the precipice, hands clasped, Favius towering over them. A mountainous, giant-sized Favius, all muscle and Hell-forged armor, the agonized faces grafted into his skin silently shrieking their anguish.

"Go get him, tiger," that Ethriel told that Greg after infusing him with divine energy to augment his own powers.

He watched himself rise to the confrontation, from this perspective not able to perceive the pattern and flow of magic, including the interlaced spellcraft around Favius, but remembering it and knowing it was there.

He watched himself, with brilliant silver-gold scissor-blades of light, snip through the arcane webwork, cutting the stitches holding those suffering faces in place. Cutting them loose, to tear themselves from Favius's skin, a host of disembodied screaming rage whirling and wheeling to swarm over their tormentor.

They tore him to fucking *shreds*.

Until there was nothing left but a heap of empty, steaming armor. Even the dark demonic essence of him was gone, having been dragged along with the liberated through a gateway Ethriel had opened.

"You, uh, you all saw that, huh?" Greg couldn't help cringing a bit, the way he always did when he saw himself on video or heard himself in a recording.

"Not just us," Azrael said.

"You mean …"

"Oh, yeah, down there too. Upset a lot of apple carts. But, here, look …" Another click changed the scene to a hall of shining splendor, where formless souls spun and wheeled in a dance of jubilation.

"Is that … them?"

"Still to be judged and processed, of course, and some will probably do stints in Limbo or Purgatory, but even the worst should be granted a fair degree of clemency, on the grounds they'd already endured so much. Think of it as time served. Many would have otherwise been totally lost to us forever. Now, they can be saved. Thanks to you two."

"Wow …" It seemed weak, but he didn't know what else to say.

"So, you see, kid, you've got a certain amount of clout on your side right now. You're popular. You've got fans. Up here, anyway; down there, I guarantee you're top of a *lot* of shit lists."

"Okay …" Not something he particularly wanted to dwell on, the prospect of the actual Devil knowing his name, or being on Hell's Ten Most Wanted. "But what does it mean for Ethriel? If they … if they do want to write her off as a … detriment, or liability?"

"Be bad optics, I'd say. You do this great thing, and here's your 'reward'? Not a good look. There'd be protests and complaints. Can't have that, not here in Heaven, the biggest happily-ever-after of all."

Maybe, he thought as he left the bar, he just should have gone ahead and tried something stronger after all. It wouldn't have taken much to get him blasted out of his skull; even a single drop of watered-down ambrosia would have done the trick.

But he hadn't, and it was just as well because the pager-thing the raphim had given him went off almost as soon as he turned the next corner.

Four stirring notes—*AHH-le-lu-jah*—accompanied by pulses of soft white light from his pocket.

"Seriously?" he asked no one. "*That's* the ringtone?"

Someone answered anyway, someone sounding totally

prim and fussy and Roddy McDowell. "Do you have a better suggestion?"

He jumped, whirled, and there was Icaiah, wings ruffled in annoyance.

"*Sexual Healing*, perhaps?" Icaiah continued.

"Funny," Greg said. "They sent *you*?"

"I hardly volunteered. 'Plenty of matters demanding your attention,' they tell me, but then as soon as the time comes to fetch *your* wayward backside, they pull me from those matters without so much as a by-your-leave." Myriad cerulean eyes took in their surroundings. "Of course, you just *would* find your way *here*, wouldn't you?"

You're popular, Azrael had told him. *You've got fans.*

Yeah, well, the sentiment clearly wasn't unanimous.

He pushed that aside. "How's Ethriel? Can I see her?"

"Well, that is why they sent me, isn't it? Take hold of my ring."

"… excuse me?"

"My *ring*, mortal. Unless you'd rather walk."

"Uh …" He looked at the revolving fiery rings within rings. "Which one?"

"Does it matter?"

"Hey, I didn't want to just grab something I shouldn't."

"Certainly didn't stop you from grabbing something you shouldn't before."

"Can we just get on with it, please?"

"Then take hold of my ring," Icaiah repeated, enunciating each word with crisp precision.

Steeling himself, he extended a hand and folded his fingers around the first ring he touched. It did not feel like fire, or metal, or fiber, or plastic, or flesh; it did not feel like anything he'd ever felt in his life. It vibrated in his grasp, and the vibration went all through him, blurring his vision, buzzing his hearing, and sending galvanic pins and needles along every nerve.

"You may let go now," said Icaiah, barely audible over the tinnitus buzz. "*If* you don't mind."

He did so, still tingling, and blinked a few times, and saw he was once again in the alcove with the crystalline skylights and cloud-couch. Blianthis, in her pale-blue scrubs and sensible white-soled shoes, offered him another of her kind, gentle smiles.

"Mr. Nachtwald," she said. "Thank you for being so

prompt."

"Thank *him* for being so prompt?" Icaiah blustered. "*I'm* the one who—"

"Yes, yes, thank you as well, Icaiah." Blianthis took the pager-device, and it stopped flashing. "You may go."

"Just like that? Dismissed? Again?"

She raised an eyebrow. The message, even to a being who lacked eyebrows entirely despite having myriad eyes, was clear.

"As if I hadn't anything better to do than hang around this place all day." With a huff, off Icaiah went, passing through the cloudy wall as if it was made of … well, cloud, which it was.

"I don't think he likes me very much," Greg said.

"Nonsense; for Icaiah, that's positively warm and cuddly."

"Really?"

"No, that was a fib." She crossed herself, though not in a way with which he was familiar. "Mea culpa. Now, shall we?"

Trepidation closed his airways, making it a challenge to breathe. "To see her? Ethriel? Is she all right?"

"Come along." She turned, and he followed.

Instead of passing through the cloud-wall as Icaiah had, the clouds parted with a wispy swishing, finer than gossamer, opening onto a cylindrical vastness, extending as far as he could see. Beams of light angled through it in every direction. Golden pathways spiraled its interior, a combination of DNA double-helixes and Moebius strips as designed by M. C. Escher.

"Yeah, no," he said, and passed out.

He revived to a host of angels hovering over him, fascinated and inquisitive, and someone speaking in a scholarly lecture-hall tone.

"—the autonomic nervous system, which continues to carry on with vital functions such as breathing and blood circulation, without conscious control—"

"Gahh!" Greg jerked backward, or would have, except he was already flat on his back on a solid surface.

His sudden movement startled the entire host, causing a flurry of wings as they—successfully, unlike him—*did* jerk backward, allowing him a glimpse of his surroundings.

Which disconcertingly resembled an operating theater, doing little to help his state of mind.

"And here," the scholarly speaker continued, sounding pleased, "we see the dramatic effect the return of the conscious mind has upon the cardiovascular system—"

"What the h-h-h-h ..." He caught himself. "What's going on? What is this? Where am I?"

"Apologies, Mr. Nachtwald," said the scholarly speaker, in form similar to Icaiah but larger, with darker wings and vivid green eyes. "We so rarely have the chance to observe a living mortal being."

Greg sat up, relieved he was able to do so instead of being strapped to an exam table, and even more relieved to find he was still fully clothed. The space around him really did resemble an operating theater, white and pristine, bathed in light.

An operating theater, or an alien abduction scenario ...

"Are ... are these med students?" he asked. "Is this some kind of ... raphim university?"

"The healing arts must be learned and curated," the professorial angel said. "I assure you, no harm was intended."

"We weren't sure what had happened." Blianthis nudged the host aside. "One moment, you were fine, and then next ..."

"Oh, that, yeah." He rubbed his temples, remembering. "I think it just all caught up with me at once."

The professor resumed lecture mode as the students listened attentively, some even taking notes. "An example of what might be called synaptic overload, wherein the human brain, unable to process excessive stimuli as perceived through the limitations of the five inferior senses—"

"Hey, I'm right here," Greg said. "Could we not?" He swung his legs over the side of the table.

"Of course," said Blianthis. "So long as you are feeling well?"

"Fine; just maybe warn a guy next time?"

"Apologies." She helped him down and led him to a doorway, leaving the class engrossed in a lively Q&A session about the "physical peculiarities" and "biological functions" of "the specimen."

"Are we really that weird to you?" he asked as they proceeded through a much less mind-blowingly impossible area than the vast cylindrical chamber with its spiraling golden helix pathways. Still far from normal, by any means, still clouds and pillars of light and unknowable artifacts, but much less mind-blowing.

"Are you not? You are born, you develop and grow, your corporeal form changes of its own accord, you must eat and sleep and eliminate, you can age and sicken and die—"

"Well, yeah, but ..."

"You are so terribly fragile yet so terribly precious. So powerful yet so ignorant. Your earthly lives are so fleeting yet so profound. Is that not, as you say, weird?"

"Maybe I'm only just now starting to understand *how* weird."

She patted his shoulder. "What's the saying you have? Tip of the iceberg? All things considered, you're coping remarkably well. Most mortals would have gone entirely mad by now."

"Let's not rule it out yet."

"Nonetheless." Blianthis paused at another doorway, and her mood turned more somber. "Now, before you see her—"

"She's in here?" He took an eager step.

Her hand on his shoulder squeezed in a firm, implacable grip. "You must know we have done all we can for her. What Raphael and I told you holds true, Gregory. If renewal is decided upon, you *shall* abide by that decision."

He looked down, clenching his fists. "I hear you."

Blianthis released him. "Then you may go in."

Yes, the entire room was a cloud, a dawn-cloud of soft pastels, brushes of palest pink, lavender, gold, and blue against pearlescent white.

Yes, it had a window, overlooking a view normally reserved for immortals, a view no manmade telescope would ever be able to capture.

Yes, the bed was more of a spun-crystal cocoon, like a magical sci-fi cryogenic sleep/stasis tube, bands of light rippling along its exterior, its interior swirling with cool mists, suspended on a glowing haze that waxed and waned in brightness as if to the steady rhythm of an unseen heart.

But none of it was worth a second look just then, because there was Ethriel, as motionless and peaceful as a princess in an enchanted fairy tale.

Her eyes were closed, her face wan. Through the swirling

mists, she appeared naked, arms at her sides, fingers slightly curled.

Greg approached, clutching his medallion so tightly he felt every line of the sigil on one side and every letter of the script on the other. *Never drive faster than your guardian angel can fly …*

"Ethriel," he murmured. "Oh, Ethriel."

Her eyelids fluttered open. Her lips moved. "Hey," she whispered.

"Hey, yourself." He tried a smile, wavery but sincere. "How are you?"

She considered. "I don't hurt," she finally said. "Other than that, no idea."

"Not hurting is good."

"You brought me home."

"I didn't know what else to do."

"How much … trouble … are you in?"

He shook his head. "Don't care. Doesn't matter."

"No … thunderbolts?"

"They can thunderbolt me later."

One slim hand rose through the swirling cool mists. He grasped it, folding it between both of his own.

"You're so warm," she said. "Still alive."

"Still alive. I guess they're not used to that here."

"Not usually, no. Are they treating you all right?"

"It's you we should be concerned about." He brought her hand to his mouth and kissed her knuckles. "Has anyone talked to you yet?"

Shadows filled her eyes. "Raphael was here."

"He told you? The, uh, prognosis?"

"He told me."

"Ethriel, I'm so sorry this—"

"Greg, shh, Greg, don't. We both knew the risks."

"Yeah, but you were defending me—"

"After you saved me. Anyway, we're not keeping score."

"We're not?"

"I'd win anyway."

"You would. All the times you got me out of some jam and I didn't even know it?"

She laughed a little. "So, what've you been up to?"

"Me? Oh, wandering around, not making the most favorable impression, seeing things beyond the scope of human understanding. Had a couple drinks with the Angel of Death. Y'know, stuff like that."

"You went drinking with Azrael?"

"No, hey, no, didn't *go* drinking … I just happened to stop off at a bar, and he just happened to be there, and we got to talking." He paused, then added, "Interesting dude."

"Greg …"

"Besides, I only had water," he said. "Eden Springs. Which, even that, by the way, was amazing."

"Got to talking? You and Azrael? *The* Azrael?"

"None other. Though when I first saw him, I thought he might be Clint Eastwood."

Ethriel laughed a lot more than a little, until she winced and arched her back and went, "Ow, ow, okay, ow."

"Shit, sorry—"

"Just don't make me laugh. And watch the potty-mouth, mister. Remember where we are?"

"Sorry," he said again. "I know. I'm trying."

"He *does* look like Clint Eastwood, though, doesn't he?"

"Sounds like him too."

"Did he ask if you were feeling lucky, punk?"

"Hey, who's not supposed to be making who laugh?"

She cute-crinkled her nose at him. "My turn to say sorry?"

"And, for the record, no, he didn't. Though he did call me 'kid' a lot."

"That's not so bad."

He leaned over and rested his sigil-marked forehead against her wan, smooth one. "Ethriel … all this, what they're saying … I know it's not my decision; it's yours, and *theirs* … but there might be a way."

Toyed With
Chelsea

Never in her life would Chelsea Carmichael have expected to find herself mute, de-limbed, and getting bukkaked as the centerpiece of one of her own twin brother's hedonistic mutilation orgies.

To think, just a couple weeks ago, she'd had it all. Looks, money, clothes, privilege, freedom, great tits ... arms ... a voice ... legs below the knee ...

At least she still had the great tits, even if they were being doused in cum-jets courtesy of the sex-crazed doped-up weirdos prancing around her in a circle-jerk.

She, or what was left of her—*Trevor, you prick, if I ever get my voice back, if I ever get the chance*—lay on a raised dais in the sunken center of a large circular room. Called "the passion pit," it was lined with padded platforms and strewn with cushions, where all manner of activity went on in every possible combination, permutation, and position.

From the passion pit rose terraced tiers, dedicated to other forms of indulgence and excess. There were fountains of booze, lavish buffets, veritable cornucopias of drugs, a mirror-tiled dance floor crammed with more writhing bodies. Music thumped and throbbed. Laser-like beams etched wild patterns of color and light. A disco ball roughly the size of a compact car hung above it all, casting off scintillating glints. Graphic, carnal murals covered the walls and vaulted ceiling.

Her brother had turned out to be a total fucking psycho. She'd always suspected he was a little on the bi-poly-kinky spectrum, but the amputation fetish had been something of a surprise.

The incest aspect, okay, maybe not so much ... though they'd never actually done anything before, the underlying tension had always been there. And why not? She was hot, Trev was hot; he seemed to get a kick out of it when she flashed her tits to gain them access to a club or concert if a cash bribe alone didn't do the trick.

When they'd first arrived at Lake Misquamicus—seemed forever ago now—for some Spring Break hardcore partying, she and their friend Kayla had almost gotten into a drunken slap-fight over which of them was the better at dick-sucking and were on the verge of having Trevor play judge to settle the matter once and for all. It hadn't actually gone that far, but, shit, Chels had been ready to throw down and go down. Never mind it was her brother; it was the principle of the thing!

Then, later, during the whole bonkers demonic scene at the lakeshore, she'd been fully prepared to outright fuck him if it kept her from being claimed by some hillbilly grossness like Lester Riggers. If fate, in the form of Favius, hadn't intervened, she would've ridden Trev's dick like a pogo stick.

Now, bitterly looking back, she wished it *had* happened that way. Or, shit, if Lester had gotten ahold of her; he may have been a filthy, disgusting brute who probably fucked like a selfish jackhammer, but then she might not have ended up being singled out as *handmaiden* to the goddamn *queen*!

Which, tbh, was where it really had all gone to shit. Handmaiden. Her. Chelsea Carmichael. Waiting on, kowtowing to, and kissing the skinny ass of that forty-something titless bitch! Being treated like a servant! Having the smug bitch lord it over her! When, if anyone should have been tapped to be infernal queen …

Not that Chels had been any more eager to fuck Favius than she was Lester Riggers; the Hell-Centurion may have been buff as a gladiator and hung like a beast but was still a ghastly freakshow monster covered with other people's faces; nope city!

Again, though, it was the *principle* of the thing. Being out-sexied by trailer-trash-tramp Lorlinda had been insult enough; being passed over for queen in favor of some flat-chested old maid? Too much to bear.

Leading to resentment, leading to literal backstabbery, leading to having her arms torn off, leading to *this*.

Now, here she was, once again being drenched with

bodily fluids.

As if she hadn't already had to deal with more than her share of them. Being blood-splashed, having to clean up the warlock-brat's piss and shit and puke, being directly puked *on* by the warlock-brat, catching a faceful of ichor and paralytic venom from the warlock-brat's decapitated mother …

At this point, really, all she needed was participation in one of those quaint and lovely rustic "Hock Parties," spit and phlegm to complete the collection!

The splattery seminal barrage continued, raining onto her bare skin warm and wet, only to cool and congeal and become tacky as it dribbled down her ribs and hips to puddle beneath her. It pooled in her belly button and gooped her naval piercing. It pearl-necklaced in the hollow of her throat and along her collar bones. Her tits were more glazed than Krispy Kreme donuts. Her thighs might have been slathered in lotion, and her entire groin area was damn near flooded. She could feel runnels trickling over her labia and did her best to keep the works clenched closed … last thing she needed was for any of it to seep inside. Bad enough she already had it in her eyes, up her nose, and leaking into her mouth. Also in her hair and both ears.

And, of course, liberally coating her stumps.

Her arms had been wrenched off at the shoulders, moments after the literal backstabbery, by one of those damn Golem things. They didn't hurt anymore, but the phantom sensation of feeling like she still had them, could move them, could lift her hands, wiggle her fingers, scratch her nose, or wipe her eyes, was its own kind of crazy hell. She also hated the sight of their absence, avoiding turning her head as much as possible because the stumps were right there in her peripheral vision, kind of pink and soft and spongy.

They had been numb at first, but to her revolted horror, the nerves seemed to be recovering. She didn't want them to. *Knowing* that Trevor was standing next to her, aware of the pressure and motions of his body, hearing his heavy breathing and satisfied groans even if she couldn't see him with her eyes cinched shut, was bad enough. She really didn't want to be able to fully *feel* his hard and eager cock rubbing against the healing flesh. Or to speculate what it'd be like if he got tired of simple stump-humping and decided to have incisions made so he could …

He wouldn't do that, though, really, would he?

Similar to how he didn't actually fuck her or stick it in her mouth. On some messed-up level of his twisted, depraved mind, rubbing against or jacking off onto wasn't the same as genuine penetration. Didn't technically count as all-the-way incest and was therefore somehow okay.

While her arms had been a rough and ragged job, quick and crudely done, the recent removal of her lower legs was handled with nice, neat, deliberate precision. Just above the knees, with tourniquets to minimize blood loss. She'd also been given what passed for a spinal block, some kind of spiny lake crustacean latching onto her lower back. Like acupuncture, they'd told her, though Chelsea seriously doubted acupuncture felt like a thousand drill-bits burrowing into her tailbone. As much as it hurt—with her larynx still paralyzed, she couldn't scream—being temporarily numbed from the waist down spared her having to feel the rest of the procedure.

Feel, no. See, yes. They made her watch, and made her watch Trevor watch, as they cut into her with a weird magical hacksaw-like device, its thin blade a purple-white electric blur. *Zoooop*, there went one leg … and then, *zoooop*, there went the other, and Trev had ejaculated like a geyser.

She did not ask, did not want to know, did not *ever* want to know what they did with the remaining leg-parts afterwards.

The lakehouse, which once belonged to their parents, had never been like this before. Somewhere along the way, after what the locals called AllHell, it had undergone a gradual but strange transformation into something that wasn't really a lakehouse anymore.

Not that they'd initially noticed when they showed up with some friends, a carload of alcoholic beverages, and assorted illicit substances. By the time they reached it, they were just too glad to escape the sights—and smells!— to pay attention. Then, there'd been the giant dino-turtle double-pronging their SUV to scrap metal, and Madison disappearing, and Andy being bitten by a mutant swamp-rat so his leg rotted right off, and Kayla cracking his head open with a fireplace poker, and Chelsea pushing Kayla from the height of Bighead Rock …

What a fucked-up day that had been.

It certainly wasn't how they'd thought their little Spring Break getaway might go, and it had only continued to get weirder and more fucked-up from there.

Especially for Chelsea. Trevor, the sicko prick, had fared much better. He'd befriended the horror writer / snuff-film maker, he'd been made First Senator by the Hell-Centurion Favius, he had the entire Riggers family fawning over him, and the lakehouse—or what had been a lakehouse—accepted him as its rightful lord and master. As a result, it reshaped itself to his wish and whim, in ways their parents would not have recognized ... or, probably, approved.

Since being brought there, Chelsea had tried time and again to exert her own will upon the house, make it obey her too, her being a Carmichael as well, every bit as entitled to it as Trevor was. But the house ignored her efforts, as if as content as her brother to just see her used and abused and made a plaything.

Trev had turned it into a combination party pad and sex-dungeon, staffed with studboys and slutgirls recruited from local denizens and corrupted tourists alike. All of whom were missing at least a toe or finger knuckle as proof of their dedication, many of whom had willingly volunteered other body parts or consented to be publicly mutilated as the highlight of one of Trevor's banquets or orgies. They flaunted their stumps with brazen pride, the way Chelsea had once flaunted her tits.

Her brother, her goddamn sicko prick brother!

It was no rare occasion to find Trevor lolling on a lounge chair like an emperor, being serviced by three or four attendants with raw and bloodied ankles from which their feet had just been chopped, or see him kneeling to receive a handless forearm elbow-deep up the ass, or neck-fucking a beheaded corpse while finger-banging the severed head ... or the other way around.

God, but she hated him. Hated him almost as much as she hated the queen-bitch bitch-queen, who had survived the backstabbery instead of dropping dead. Survived, and taken over! It was also thanks to *her*, the bitch-queen, that Chelsea was now in Trevor's oh-so-brotherly devoted care.

Someday, damn it, someday, she would get back at them. Never mind she had no arms, no legs below the knee, and couldn't talk. Someday, it would be payback time. Maybe see how Trev liked losing his own limbs a bit at a time. Maybe see how he liked losing his *dick*.

As for Her Royal Highness …

Nothing she could think of seemed vicious enough.

The bukkake deluge had finally ended, leaving her soaked and sticky on the dais. Seemed like gallons of it. Abnormal, unnatural, almost cartoonish amounts of cum, like something not just out of bad porn but out of a bad porn parody of bad porn. She was lucky—or maybe unlucky—she hadn't goddamn *drowned*.

The thumping music and sounds of feasting and dancing and wild copulation continued, but for the moment, no one seemed nearby. Chelsea peeled a cum-caked eyelid open to look …

… and regretted it immediately.

"Howdy, Miz Chelsea." Lester Riggers' grimy, unshaven face filled her vision, looming over her with a goatish leer and a malevolent gleam in his silvered eye. "Mr. His-Senatorship says t' getcha all cleaned up nice, an' with ev'rone else bein' busy, I vol'nteered t' lend a help."

Chelsea shuddered and shook her head.

"Aw, now, no need t' thank me," he said. "Least's I could do, given yer fam'ly's allus been so good t' mine."

She shook her head again, frantically, and squirmed her torso as much as possible, but there was nowhere to go. Even if she rolled off the dais, what then? Thump to the floor; not like she could get up and run on the stumps of her half-legs.

"Ho-leee dang, lookit you," Lester went on, sweeping her with his lecherous gaze. "Ain't seen s'much jizzum since't I was twelve years old an' first learnt what t' do when my pecker got stiff. Tellya, I fair t' painted the walls with it, I did. Musta spent most my wakin' hours that entire summer floggin' the hog, an' still woked up t' soggy sheets. Ma got some annoyed, me neglectin' my chores an' such, but Pa? He laughed, an' tol' her how boys would be boys, fact of life an' truth of nature."

While making this nostalgic speech, he'd circled the dais, inspecting her from various angles. She pressed her thighs closed and yearned vainly for arms to cross over her tits.

Was this finally it? Had Trev finally decided to allow their brutish oaf of a handyman to have his way with her?

His huge, grubby, callused hands reached out, and

Chelsea did hurl herself sideways in a desperate roll, dais or no dais, thump to the floor or no thump to the floor.

Off the side she went, a clumsy tumbling fall, but given the amount of semi-congealed fluids she was coated with, and the amount that had also missed the target to saturate the surrounding area, it was more of a squish than a thump.

"Oh, hey now, careful," Lester said. "Cain't have ya hurtin' y'self, can we? Don' want no bruises on them there sweet milk-melons!"

He picked her up, rough palms against the sides of her ribcage, the pads of his thumbs pressing coarse and lewd against underboob. She twisted and writhed.

"Din't I just say careful?" he chided. "Slipperier'n a buttered piglet, y'are. Hate t' drop ya."

Chelsea jerked her upper body forward, thinking to headbutt him or something. It only made her tits jiggle in a way he quite appreciated. He bounced her up and down, wobbled her side to side, and licked his lips. So she spat in his face, but he just laughed.

"Feisty! When here I thought ya done lost yer spirit. Shoulda know'd better. You'se a hellcat through an' through, Miz Chelsea."

Lester slung her onto his shoulder in a fireman's carry. He wore his customary denim biballs with no shirt, his bare and hairy skin loathsome against her. Unwashed, unshaved, he stank of sweat and livestock and cheap liquor. He held her in place by clamping a hand to her ass, fingertips digging uncomfortably into the crack.

In this undignified position, he toted her through the house, which was indeed fairly busy—servants rushing around, Ronny Riggers clomping clubfooted from room to room so his parents' heads could supervise, hectic kitchen activity, deliveries being made. A heightened sense of urgency and importance hung in the air, as if preparations were underway for some even bigger occasion than yet another of Trevor's mutilation orgies.

Of her sadistic, pervert prick of a brother, she saw no sign, but she did hear his voice coming from somewhere upstairs, snippets of a conversation she couldn't quite make out. Something about ... Jason? His buddy Jason, one of the gate-guards who'd let them in. The hot one, not the fat bastard she'd flashed her tits at.

Then, very clearly, the words "good impression" and

"royal visit."

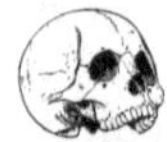

Royal visit?

Royal-fucking-*visit*?

As in, here? As in, *her*? As in, that high-and-mighty bitch-queen queen-bitch? Coming *here*? To this house?

Chelsea strained to hear more, but Lester kept right on going, carrying her out of earshot. He brought her not to a bathroom or even to the hot tub on the deck but onto the back patio.

It, unlike the rest of the house, was largely unchanged. Retractable pergola, slate tiles, the massive BBQ-grill-smoker their father had bought and then rarely used, the firepit. Their mother's choice of indoor/outdoor furniture, the bright tropical patterns of the waterproof cushions rather weathered and faded over the years. Citronella candles and tiki torches to deter Florida buglife ... well, normal Florida buglife from back in those days; what flew and crawled now needed stronger measures. Flamethrowers and holy water, maybe.

At the edge of the patio was a concrete slab where they'd once had an aboveground pool, long since dismantled. At the center of the slab was a rusty metal drain, which was where Lester set Chelsea down. The humid red-tinted sunlight filtering through the Dome was alien and awful; what she would've given right then to see clear blue skies, to be on a warm golden beach with the surf foaming white on the sand, with a complete set of limbs and a host of fratboy admirers.

Instead of ... this, this truncated half-person feebly inchworming in useless futility, with Lester-goddamn-Riggers standing there, grinning, a substantial lumpy bulge tenting the crotch of his biballs.

"Y'know, Miz Chelsea," he said, "there's no reason why we cain't be more friendly-like, you'n'me. I mean, we'se know'd each other how long? An' you ain't 'zactly in such a lofty place anymores, is ya? Sure, the Senator's sister an' all, but that don't count for s'much after what you done. Lucky t' be alive, really."

She rolled over and shot him a glare.

"Just sayin', I c'd make it some easier for ya, if'n you was so inclined. See as you was better treated. Better took care of. Allus did have a fond regard, though weren't hardly my place t' say so. Now as your sitch'ashun's changed, y'might wanna consider takin' more kindly t' a feller."

If he was suggesting …

Her vocal cords may have been paralyzed, but her expression spoke volumes.

Lester heaved a sigh. "So that's how it is, huh? Still thinkin' you'se better'n us reg'lar folks? Lissen here, Miz Chelsea, if'n I spread you open right here'n now an' fucked you inside out, wouln't be no way you'd stop me. Half a mind t' do just that. Y'might even like it after a while, high-steppin' slut as y'are."

Chelsea cringed and recoiled and attempted silent pleading with soulful eyes instead.

"Doubt as I'd get in too much trouble for it neither," he said. "What's the ol' sayin'? Better t' beg fergiveness? Yer brother, he'd unnerstand. Might punish me some, but … Satan's sake, it's pure temptation is what it is. Cain't fault a feller fer that."

Tears welled and spilled, not manufactured crocodile tears but the genuine article. Until this moment, she'd been aware of her total helplessness but not so starkly, *vividly* aware of it. He could do whatever he wanted to her, and she couldn't stop him, couldn't fight him off.

He unhooked the straps of his biballs, and terror burst full tilt into Chelsea's heart as he let them fall around his ankles. He wore nothing beneath but a dense coating of grease and grime and body hair. His cock stuck out, ten or so inches of crooked, scabby meat, its uncut head purplish and crusted. He curled a loose fist around it and gave it a couple preliminary strokes. Droplets oozed from its slit. Lice the size of pill bugs scuttled visibly through a wild tangle of wiry-looking pubes.

Chelsea began crying harder, wracked with sobs as she tried yet again to inchworm away from him. But she could barely move, and there was nowhere to go anyway.

"Still, damn an' bless it all," Lester said, heaving another disconsolate sigh, "now ain't the time; I'se s'posed t' be gettin' you cleaned up. An' Ma, she'll scold my nuts off if'n I don't hop to it."

With that, he stepped closer, aimed his filthy, disgusting cock, and pissed. Pissed in a stinging torrent, hot and dark yellow, using it like a pressure washer to hose the half-dried residue of the bukkake party from her tits.

Chelsea would have screamed but couldn't, and didn't want to open her mouth anyway as the backsplash wetted her face. Then the direct stream moved from her tits up her neck, spraying her chin and lips. She barely got her eyes shut in time. The stink of it filled her nose, ammonia and asparagus and recycled hellshine.

She gagged, and her mouth *did* open, but no piss got in because it would have been going upstream against a flash flood of puke.

"Now, how's'm I s'posed t' clean ya if'n ya just makes more mess?" chortled Lester, continuing the hose-job.

How one man could piss *so* much? He must've been holding it all day, waiting for this moment. It went on and on, sluicing over her, rinsing away as much cum and vomit as possible before the flow finally tapered to a squirt-and-shake.

"There," he said. "Ain't that some better?"

No. No, it wasn't; it was miles from better, light-years from better. His piss was all over her, and it burned. Not in the way scalding water burned but in the way iodine burned. Her tenderest places were already reddening from irritation. Her eyes gushed tears; her nose gushed a mélange of mucus and urine. Despite the outrush of puke, a trickle must've gotten into her mouth anyway; she could *taste* it and would have puked again but had nothing left to throw up.

Lester remained as he was for a moment or two, feasting his lecherous gaze on her while continuing to idly work his cock with his fist.

"Gaw-*damn*, Miz Chelsea, but you surely are the finest piece of ass I ever did see," he remarked. "Y'sure you wouln't like a nice nasty fuckin', right here an' now? Just part them legs, show me that dee-lectable cunt-hole, an' your Lester be more'n glad t' fill it up for ya."

She did her best to curl up and tuck in on herself, and if she could have done the thing those self-devouring snakes did and swallowed herself whole, she would have.

"Aw'right, guess not," Lester said in a mock-sulky disappointment. He unspooled a hose—a regular garden hose this time, the one they'd used to fill the aboveground pool back in the day—and let her have it with a blast of actual water.

It wasn't cold, was merely cool if not tepid, but the shock just about jolted her out of her skin. He kept at it, moving to get her from every angle, using his foot to nudge her over to access those hard-to-reach places, including *there*. He pried her thigh-stumps apart and spent much more time than was strictly necessary giving her groin a thorough rinse despite her struggles.

When he shut off the hose and set it aside, Chelsea lay atop the gurgling drain, soaked and shivering but clean.

Lester hunkered down by her pelvis, silver eye glinting. "Oughta check the nooks an' crannies, see that I done a good job, din't miss anything," he said. He licked his lips again, a long, slow, slobbery pass of his thick wet tongue. "Whatcha say, Miz Chelsea?"

Crying some more, she shook her head again, trying to press what was left of her legs together so tightly they fused into a single limb.

"Y'sure?" he asked. "Might be yer last chance t' have some fun before'n Her Majesty gets here. Who knows what kinda shape y'll be in after that? Way I hears it, yer brother's plannin' t' swap ya out for some soldier-boy."

Andy

Of all the horror subgenres out there, he just *would* have to wind up in the creepy-kid kind. Nor did it help that he himself was currently, basically, a possessed talking doll.

How had it come to this? What was supposed to be a nice relaxing Spring Break road trip with friends, a swanky Florida lakehouse, plenty of beer and booze, plenty of weed, hot tubs, girls in bikinis ...

Okay, so maybe they should have paid more attention to reality and not dismissed the whole transplanted-pocket-of-actual-Hell thing as a giant hoax, but still!

And maybe they should have turned back as soon as they saw for themselves. Andy recalled lobbying for that very option, suggesting they detour over to Orlando instead, hit the theme parks. Getting high as fuck and going on Space Mountain was always a good time.

But Chels and Trev were too stubborn, too determined. It was their parents' lakehouse, their goddamn *property*, and nothing was going to stop them from enjoying what was rightfully *theirs*. Never mind the freaky wrongness, worsening and weirdening the closer they got to the lake. Never mind the lake really did appear to be blood and bile and shit, not a red dye-job publicity stunt as Chelsea had insisted. Never mind the way the plants seemed to be trying to grab at the SUV, or the way the bugs splatting across the windshield were huge and gross and unnatural even by Florida standards.

No, on they'd gone, like every group of idiots in every bad movie, despite warnings and red flags and foreshadowing like whoa. Only when they'd finally reached the Carmichael place and emerged into the face-slapping wallop of abattoir-sewer **stench** were they forced to acknowledge the truth.

If they'd jumped back into the SUV and hauled ass out of there, it might've been a different story. They might all still be alive, and/or in their original bodies.

Instead, after a bunch of crazy fuckery, here he was, stuck in a knock-off Baby Yoda carnival prize ... which was an *improvement* on the magical pod he'd been trapped in before, when his soul had floated up from his mangled corpse—bitten by a swamp-rat with flesh-rotting venom, his "friends" trying to save him by hacking off his leg as it melted down to raw bone, and then his so-called "girlfriend" generously putting him out of his misery by bashing open his skull with a fireplace poker—and gotten caught in the web of a spiderlike demon-thing that wrapped him all up to save for later, when it would drink his essence ...

Crazy fuckery indeed. Too much crazy fuckery to try to explain or understand; you kind of had to be there. Even being there didn't help a whole lot, since Andy *had* been there and still wasn't sure how the hell it'd all happened.

Anyway, there he'd been, conscious but stuck in the demon-spider's pod, his "friends" having no idea and just leaving him, only to be found and rescued by the most beautiful backwoods goddess with lush cleavage, short-shorts, and a honey-twang drawl.

Lorlinda. Lorlinda Bodean, and was he smitten? Oh, forget Kayla—skull-cracking bitch—and every other girl. Lorlinda, who'd called him her "sugarbun" and "sweetie-pie" and promised to look after him, though he could only communicate by pantomime from inside the pod.

Lorlinda and her cousin Heck, in their hodgepodge frankentruck, and yet more crazy fuckery had ensued. Some pretty damn hot and awesome crazy fuckery too, like when Lorlinda pleasured herself with the pod, using it as a sex-toy and giving him the ultimate first-person view …

Then a bunch of other shit happened, Heck got shot, they found the tunnel, one thing led to another, and an old Black lady voodoo-witch was able to transfer his soul from the pod into another vessel. Into this knock-off Baby Yoda carnival prize, the best choice available.

Far from ideal, but at least he could move and talk again.

And do things with Lorlinda. Not everything he wanted, sadly—lacking a dick and all—but the doll's blunt, fingerless arms and somewhat movable mouth sufficed. If he couldn't actually get off, he could get *her* off, which was what mattered.

He would've done anything for her, anything to make her happy, anything to make her feel good, anything to make her smile.

Strange time and place and way to fall in love, but, well, so what?

While it might've been nice to get re-situated into a different vessel more anatomically compatible, he wasn't about to complain.

Then, though, the crazy fuckery got cranked past eleven when the warlock and the angel showed up, and the whole big flying-frankentruck battle happened, with black-winged Nazi bird devils and a wild crash-landing, and somehow in the course of the chaos, he got separated from the others. Torn away from Lorlinda, flung clear, tottering upright and shaken …

Only to run into, of all people, Trevor-fucking-Carmichael, who was somehow in good with the big demon-centurion dude; Andy wasn't sure on the deets and didn't care. All he cared about right then was giving the leg-cutting bastard another well-deserved punch in the nose. Even if it was only with his stubby Baby Yoda doll arm.

Trevor's astonishment in the moment of revelation and recognition had been priceless. More priceless, even, than the satisfying crunch of cartilage and spurt of blood.

Except wouldn't the prick just *have* to go and respond by hurling Andy ass-over-teakettle? A quarterback's Hail Mary that sent him sailing far past the edge of the high rocky promontory and plunging what felt like half a mile straight down into the maroon morass of the lake.

The shit-filled, bilious, monster-infested maroon morass of the lake.

Where, Andy discovered, he couldn't drown because he didn't technically need to breathe. He also discovered the doll's cheap greenish cloth/vinylish "skin" was semi-waterproof enough to keep the spongy foam stuffing from becoming fully saturated—same couldn't be said for its burlap-coarse robe—and buoyant enough to more or less remain afloat.

He *also* discovered that, although he could sort of froggily swim by moving the doll's limbs, active motion tended to draw the attention of various lake denizens, who would investigate anything potentially edible. While he was *not* edible, he got nibbled at, spat out, swallowed, and horked up so often he figured it was best to just stay still and bob along, letting the sluggish currents take him wherever they would.

How long he drifted, he couldn't say. He lost track of day and night and the passage of time. All he could think about was Lorlinda, whether she'd survived, whether she was okay, whether she might be searching for him even now.

Eventually, he washed up into driftwood-choked shallows near the shore, amid half-submerged rocks shaped like skulls and other flotsam and jetsam, and been found.

Not by Lorlinda, his beloved backwoods beauty. No Lorlinda plucking him from the foamy pinkish surf to cuddle him to her bosom, overjoyed to be reunited, never to be parted again.

No, that was when the creepy kid entered the picture.

A little girl, maybe five or six, snub-nosed, freckled, gap-toothed, cute. A mass of curly hair held in half a dozen unkempt corkscrew clumps by 1970s-looking elastic bands with colorful round plastic beads. Wearing a Dora the Explorer t-shirt.

Maybe not so creepy on first sight, as she exclaimed in delight over finding a dolly, a talking dolly, who was going to be her new bestest friend. Hardly Damien or one of those glowy-eyed *Village of the Damned* weirdos, or even the annoying shit from *The Babadook*.

But then she'd lugged him into the house—an older, funkier, more retro-style, less-upscale lakehouse than that belonging to the Carmichaels—chatterboxing all the way, and Andy knew he'd landed in some deep psycho-town trouble.

Even before she proudly took him over to show her new toy to her daddy.

The little girl's name was Sherri—with an i, as she declared—and her daddy was some poor asshole bound upside-down to a big wooden X in the family room.

Bound naked and ball-gagged, covered with oozing sores and gangrenous ulcerations. A leper, a still-living zombie, who might've once born a resemblance to a careworn George Clooney but now made the Crypt Keeper look like the cover of *GQ*.

He was pierced all over with fishhooks, fishhooks attached to wires, wires which plugged into a junior scientist's kit. Way more fishhooks than Andy cared to count were embedded in the guy's dickhead, a crown of steel thorns. More lined his shaft and punctured his scrote. Others went through his fingertips, the skin between his fingers and toes, his nipples, lips, nose, eye brows, and eyelids.

As best Andy could determine from what he'd gleaned of the local state of affairs, the wires were to conduct and convert his pain into energy, which … which was being used to power an old-fashioned cathode ray television and a VCR … currently running a Disney Sing-Along tape he vaguely remembered from his own childhood.

Seriously, what the surreal fuck? Baloo instructing Mowgli on the bare necessities while this guy hung here upside-down with fishhooks in his dick???

Unless he was mistaken, there was also a vintage Atari 2600 hooked up, surrounded by equally vintage game cartridges. *Asteroids*? *Missile Command*? Fucking *Joust*??

"—in the lake, and I know he's kinda oogy and I'm gonna put him in the wash machine, but, Daddy, he can talk!" Sherri shoved Andy at her father's face. "Go on, Mr. Goblin, say hi to Daddy!"

"Hi?" Andy peeped in the doll's robotic voice.

The tortured man's eyes rolled insanely. Spit dribbled around the ball-gag. Glottal, muffled noises issued from his throat.

"Finders keepers, losers weepers, so you're mine-mine-mine!" crowed Sherri, and dance-hopped around, waving Andy triumphantly. "Bratty-brat Billy can't doll-nap you either, because bratty-brat Billy is dead-dead-dead!"

She really had then taken him to the laundry room and dumped him into a washing machine with a scoopful of detergent. He sudsed and churned, once again glad he couldn't drown—or maybe drowning would be a mercy, all considered—and then the spin cycle flattened him against the inner barrel, pressed him there, reminding him of the kind of sketchy carnival rides they'd have on the kind of midways where a cheap knock-off toy like him could be won.

The dryer came next, and it was a bumping, tumbling, disorienting nightmare. If he could have bruised, he would have been purple instead of green, clear to the tips of his pointy Yoda ears. He was almost glad he lacked the capacity to barf. Somehow, none of his stitching split, and he did come out of it actually clean, but it took his head hours to un-discombobulate.

Since then, he'd been in creepy kid psycho-town, as much a prisoner as Sherri's dad. He'd heard all about their family, how Mommy brought them here after she got so mad at Daddy for putting his wiener-neener in the babysitter, how the lake went poopy-bloody and the monsters came, how Mommy hadn't let them grow up but made them stay little kids, how Billy got yellow goat-eyes and warlock powers, how Mommy lost her hair and grew scales and turned into a snake-lady, how Daddy finally showed up so Mommy did the dirty-dirty with him to make new babies and then let them agonicicize him, how Mommy laid a bunch of eggs in the downstairs warm room and the snake-babies hatched and fought each other and escaped, how Billy sneaked out one night because of the big magic and got to stay with the demon-king, how Mommy left for an important meeting, how Mommy and Billy never came back, and, finally, how soldier-people showed up to tell Sherri that Mommy and Billy had died and the queen would have to decide what to do with her.

"The queen should 'dopt me," Sherri had said. "Then I could be a princess! But that's okay if she doesn't. I can take care of myself! I've got Daddy, and now I've got you, and we can have all kinds of fun!"

All kinds of fun. Yeah. Like her other toys.

Being named Andy, of course he'd had to see all the *Toy*

Story movies as a kid and endure his share of ribbing from schoolmates. So naturally, it was that neighbor character, that motherfucker Sid, he'd thought of whenever he saw what had been done to most of Sherri's other dolls and stuffed animals.

At least none of them were animate like him. None could move of their own volition, or talk besides what recorded pull-string dialogue they'd been programmed with. He didn't need Mr. Potato Head or Buzz fucking Lightyear to keep him company.

Though, if any had been able to move, maybe they could have made an escape attempt or something. On his own, he couldn't reach the doorknobs or jimmy open a window screen. Even had he been able to do so, what then? Where would he go? He only had the vaguest notion of where he was—the hippie-house, Trevor and Chelsea called it, visible from the deck of their parents' place ... and their parents' place, he definitely did *not* want to go. Busting Trev's nose may have been satisfying, but he'd had surprise on his side and doubted he'd get another chance. Further revenge wasn't high on his agenda anyway. Far as he was concerned, Trev and Chels could both FOAD.

What he wanted, *all* he wanted, was to find his honey-twang goddess, his Lorlinda. Or, at the worst-case minimum, learn what had become of her. It seemed impossible, though. Assuming she, the angel and the warlock, or any of them had survived, they'd have either gotten the fuck out of Dodge or been captured. He'd been to Zeke Bodean's shitty trailer but couldn't pinpoint it on a map, and had no idea where to find other members of the Bodean clan. The secret tunnel, as far as he understood the local geography, was way the fuck over on the far side of the lake from here.

And really, for all he knew, the others might have gotten away for real, gotten out of the HellZone the same way the warlock and angel had gotten in. Liminal spaces or whatever. They could be anywhere by now.

So, yeah, he knew it was hopeless. He knew clinging onto even the thinnest thread of hope was a sucker's move. Lorlinda was lost to him. If she, by some miracle, was alive, she had to believe he was just as lost to her.

This was his existence now. This was his world. A foot-tall knock-off Baby Yoda doll, hostage to a psychotic kindergartener.

Some Spring Break it had turned out to be, that was for sure.

He was musing on it, sitting in front of the old television and not-too-terribly manipulating the Atari 2600's simple controls—one button, simple joystick, didn't require a whole lot of manual dexterity—when he heard the grumble-rumble of an approaching engine.

Sherri, who'd been in the kitchen, rushed back in with a plate of peanut butter crackers and a cup of something purple. "Someone's coming, Mr. Goblin! Maybe it's the soldier-lady with the cool devil horns. I wish I had cool devil horns! Or maybe it's the queen, and I really will get to be a princess!"

He put down the controller, heaved himself upright, and tottered after her to the front door. *She* could reach the doorknob just fine. Every time she opened it, he considered making a break for it. He knew she'd easily outrun him, but …

The door swung open. Andy shoved Sherri with all his tiny might. As she fell over, yelping in surprise, he took off just as fast as his stubby little Baby Yoda legs would go.

"Help!" he squeaked, waving his fingerless arms. "Hey! Help! Get me out of here! She's nuts! A total psycho! Help!"

"Mr. Gaaaaaaahblin!" Sherri wailed from behind him.

The soldier reacted the way anyone might, seeing a possessed talking doll rushing at them while a creepy kid howled in the background—he raised his assault rifle and opened the fuck up.

It didn't hurt.

That was something, anyway.

Oh, he felt the initial impacts, felt them punching through and shredding. There just wasn't any pain.

All of a sudden, Andy was untethered, observing from a detached distance, as scraps of cloth and wads of stuffing flew in all directions. He saw one green leaf-shaped ear spin away like a playing card and a large dark plastic eyeball bouncing through a shrapnel-spray of walkway gravel.

Holy shit, blown to bits, he thought.

The barrage ceased. For a moment, aside from echoes rolling back and forth across the lake, all was silent. The soldier—not a lady with cool devil horns but a thickset dude with a tusked and bristly boar's head—lowered his gun and peered in disbelief at the strewn tatters of the toy.

Another soldier, also not a lady with cool devil horns but a thin normal-looking guy, had emerged from the jeep parked at the end of the walkway. "Mary's tits, Pork Chop," he said. "The hell was that?"

"I dunno," snuffle-grunt-snorted the one called Pork Chop. "Was coming right at me."

Sherri burst out of the house, teary and red-faced. "You shot Mr. Goblin!"

"Hey, kid—" Pork Chop began, sounding almost contrite.

"Mr. Goblin was my bestest, bestest *friend!*" Dropping to her knees, she gathered some of the larger pieces and hugged them to her chest.

"Aww, man," said the other soldier, approaching. "Look what you did. You made her cry."

"I didn't *know!*"

"What're we gonna tell the queen?"

"It was an accident!" Pork Chop scuffed a foot. Or, rather, scuffed a trotter; he wore no boots, his feet reshaped into porcine cloven hooves.

Am I dead? Andy wondered. *Like, again? Or, for real? Am I a ghost this time or what? I can see and hear and think, but ... I'm not in another pod or anything. How does this stuff even work?*

Releasing her sad armful of doll fragments, Sherri got up. Sniffling, she wiped her nose and wiped her eyes, then turned to the soldiers with her chin and lower lip trembling.

"You killed Mr. Goblin," she said.

"Hey, kid," Pork Chop tried again. "I'm sorry. I didn't—"

"You pigface meaniebutt!" She punched him where she could reach, which was right at junk height.

"Urk!" Pork Chop doubled over.

"I hate you!" Sherri screeched, kicking him in the shins. "I hate you, I hate you, I *hate* you!"

He tried to scramble backward while still bent double, tripped on a length of driftwood, and went down hard. Sherri kept at him, kicking and slapping and hollering.

"Stupid ugly pigface! Someone oughta shoot *you!* Shoot you in the wiener-neener!"

The other soldier grappled her but was so busy trying not to laugh he made a bad job of it and couldn't hold on. Pork Chop curled into a defensive position, covering his head as Sherri went for his fleshy snout. When she hooked her fingers into his nostrils and pulled-twisted, he really did squeal like a piggie. The other soldier utterly lost it then, falling over and literally rolling on the ground, hooting gales of laughter.

Andy, meanwhile, wasn't sure if he should do something … if he *could* do anything … so just kind of kept floating there to watch.

Maybe it was his partner's mirth that pushed Pork Chop over the edge; he went from curled and cowering into lunging upright with a bestial bellow. He seized Sherri, his hands still more like human hands than trotters, and heaved her squirming, struggling little body high overhead as if to do a piledriver.

"Porkie, no!"

The other soldier punctuated his shout with a warning shot.

If it *was* a warning shot; it might have been a near miss. Either way, it passed close enough to singe Pork Chop's bristles and sure got his attention.

He froze, Sherri held high.

"Put the girl down," the thin soldier said. "Nice and easy. Come on, you know our orders."

Snorting a great, steamy gust of breath, Pork Chop lowered Sherri to the ground and released her. The other soldier snagged her by the collar before she could resume her kick-slap attack.

"You too, missy," he said. "No more of that."

"But he killed Mr. Goblin!"

"And he's very, very sorry. It was a mistake. An accident. Okay?"

"No! It's not okay!"

"We're not here to hurt anybody or cause trouble. The queen sent us. You know about the queen, right?"

Sherri nodded but warily. "Do I get to be a princess?"

"Would you like to be?"

"Maybe."

"Well, it's not up to me, but she does want us to bring you to see her. How does that sound? We can take you for a ride in our jeep."

"Is it a real army jeep?"

"It is, and we're real army soldiers."

"*He's* a pigface meaniebutt." She scowled at Pork Chop, who scowled back while massaging his shins.

"Yeah, he is, isn't he? My name's Corporal Lewis, but you can call me Tony."

"Does the queen have a castle?"

"Not yet, though she's got a really nice motorhome."

"Are there ponies?"

"I'm not sure about ponies."

"What about a unicorn pony?"

"Haven't seen any of those."

"For shit's sake, Tone," snorted Pork Chop. "Throw her in the jeep already and let's get a damn move on."

"You shut your meaniebutt pigface mouth!" Sherri told him. "*I'm* gonna be a *princess*! And live in a castle and ride a unicorn pony."

"Yeah, yeah, whatever."

"Don't worry about him," Corporal Lewis said. "Is there anything you'd like to bring along?"

"Mr. Goblin, but *he* shot him."

"Besides that. Clothes, or other toys?"

"I can get my suitcase," she said. "What about Daddy? He's on the X with fishhooks in him so we can use the TV."

Lewis and Pork Chop exchanged a glance. Andy almost could've felt sorry for them. No matter how weird it got around here, just when you thought you'd seen or heard it all, along came a whole new level of WTF.

"We'll send someone back to take care of your daddy," Lewis finally said. "You go pack your suitcase, huh?"

With one more sad look at the ruins of the Baby Yoda doll, Sherri scurried back into the house. The beach-imps and manatee-things who'd ventured close to investigate, evidently sensing the show was over, dispersed. If there had been a snake-baby spying from the tall grass, it, too, had moved on. Only the soldiers, and unseen intangible Andy, remained.

"A princess?" Pork Chop said. "The hell'd that come from?"

"All her, not me," Lewis replied. "I'm just trying to get the goddamn job done. They want the kid. They want the kid in one piece, which she almost wasn't, thanks to you. You nearly fucked the whole works."

"Hey, I didn't mean to scrag the doll-thing. It was—"

"Coming right at you, yeah, I know."

"You would've done the same, some freaky green—"

"Save it." Lewis shook a cigarette from a crumpled pack,

lit it, and took a drag, gazing out over the lake. He loosed a long, philosophical exhale. "SNAFU is as SNAFU does."

The sight made Andy suddenly, keenly aware of how long it'd been since he'd gotten his own kind of smoke on. It couldn't hit him as a physical craving, given his noncorporeal state, but oh, how nice a well-packed bowl or fat spliffy would've been right about now.

Sherri emerged again, wearing a Care Bear backpack and trundling a bright-pink flower-patterned wheelie hardshell suitcase.

"When they sacrifice the little snot," Pork Chop muttered, "I want a front-row seat."

Sacrifice? Andy thought. *Dude, yeah, the kid's creepy total psycho-town, but **sacrificing** her? Might be a bit much ...*

Not that he could do anything about it anyway, even had he been so inclined. Discorporated as he was, he could only watch as Lewis buckled her into the back seat of the jeep, stowed her luggage, and got behind the wheel.

She'd wanted to sit up front, of course, but Pork Chop had balked. Wasn't giving up shotgun no matter how hard she pouted. She didn't pout for long, though; it must've been a while since she went for any sort of car ride, and she goggled around excitedly as they drove off, as if they were going to the park or on a day trip to the zoo.

If he'd had a stomach, the whole scene would have left Andy with a sinking sensation in it. He may not have liked Sherri, may have been creeped the hell out by her, but to be fair, she *had* pulled him from the lake and gotten him cleaned up. And despite the condition of her daddy and her other toys, she hadn't done anything horrible to him. All that had been her brother anyway, or so she'd said.

Jeez, now he felt bad.

Whatever else, creepy psycho-town or not, she was still just a kid. A kid left pretty much on her own in a seriously fucked-up situation. Instead of trying to help her, to actually be the friend she thought he was, he'd had to go and bolt.

Getting himself shot to shit in the process too. Smooth, real smooth. Had he kept his cool, he'd at least still have his doll-body, rather than ... whatever this was.

What *was* this, anyway?

Shouldn't *something* be happening?

When he'd died the first time—what a nutso thing even to think!—his soul had risen from his body the way they said it was supposed to in all the woo-woo religions. But it had been snared, intercepted and stored in the pod before … before *what*?

Moving on, crossing over, *go into the light Carol Ann there's peace and serenity in the liiiiight*, some beckoning welcoming afterlife? He sure hadn't experienced any urge of that sort.

Neither had he sensed any, like, bony chill finger of the Grim Reaper or gaping fiery pit of eternal torment. Or a delivery room, some newborn baby being squeezed into the world, ready to start life all over.

No, for him, the natural process—or, supernatural process—had been disrupted, interrupted. And now that he'd presumably died again, was the glitch still in the Matrix?

Was he a ghost? If so, he seemed to be a pretty crappy, ineffective one, unable to move or act or rattle a chain. Not even haunting a house—which was right *there!*—but haunting what? This stretch of walkway? This patch of yard?

Then he sensed something different. Some very slight, very faint draw … almost magnetic … maybe sub-magnetic … the barest whisper of a pull … although he'd never been one for fishing, he imagined a fish nudging at the bait, not yet taking it but checking it out, the merest tremor on the line … a brush and a bump and a quiver …

It didn't seem either good or bad. Not a call, not a command or order. A suggestion. An indifferent well-there's-this, neutral, neither exciting or intimidating.

A why-not, a can't-hurt, a might-as-well-give-it-a-shot.

So, he did.

Tentatively, with impressions of teeter-totters at their balancing point, the sensation of when the wheels of a plane leave solid ground, the vertigo pause at the top of a waterslide or rollercoaster, the momentary weightlessness when a fast-driving car goes over a bump just right …

Then he was in an amorphous, grey space filled with amorphous, grey shapes waiting in amorphous, grey lines. And he himself was an amorphous, grey shape waiting among them.

Waiting, and waiting.

And waiting.

Lorlinda

"I don't reckon how I'se c'n take much more of this," Lorlinda said.

Oh, and to be sure, she knew it was plumb silly, a grown-ass adult woman her age—however indeterminate that age was, given the way things'd been all funky-like since't AllHell—talkin' out loud to a stuffed toy. One what couldn't even talk back; damn sorry subst'ute as it was for her gone an' lost sugar-pie.

Prolly pathetic, her sittin' here mopin' an' whinin' an' bemoanin' her dang fool head off anyways. But she was *grievin'*, saints bless it; the holy fuck else was she s'posed t' do? She was goddamn *distraught*, an' with plenny good reason! Lost ever'thing, hadn't she? Near ever'thing what mattered.

Some might scold her how she had *not* lost ever'thing; still had her *life*, din't she? Life an' health an' limbs an' all. When there was others couln't say the same. Oughta be grateful!

Oughta, yeah, mebbe ... but *how*? Wasn't nothin' left for her now. Couln't go home; to the entire rest of her famb'ly, she might's well been dead, as dead as Heck was.

Heck, an' Zeke, an' Maybelle. An' even Clarabeth, traitor-ass kin-killin' brown-noser as she turned out t' be. Been a bad run of days there for the Bodean clan, losin' so many.

"It's our mommas I fret 'bout," she told the knock-off Baby Yoder doll what she'd gotten from Brad's stash of assorted bootleg merchandise.

He had tons of it down here, from food an' supplies to souvenir-stuff an' DVD-movies. Picked it up cheap off'n boats an' trucks, sold it for a tidy profit. Between that an' Dan runnin' his veggie stand what peddled peculiar diabolical-mutated produce t' tourists, thrill-seekers, an' fancy chefs, they'd done none too bad, makin' a decent livin' even when not doin' business with Heck. But all them old days was lookin' apt t' be done. No more runnin' hellshine an' other goods through the tunnel. Likely not much cause for tourists or anybody t' be in the market for much after what they was sayin' 'bout the effects of the Painwave.

The missing of which, she knew she also oughta be grateful for. Best as she unnerstood it, when the guv'mint went on and dropped their nuke, it hadn't blown the bejeezers outta Lake Misquamicus with its magic Wall an' Dome but backfired on 'em sommat fierce. All that noo-clear energy converted t' *PAIN*, rollin' cross't the entire planet.

Done a number on the rest of the world, all right. But they, bein' here in the tunnel, in a liminal space as it were, got spared. Passed over. Could also be the presence of the angel at the time had a tetch t' do with it too.

But weren't no angel here now. No warlock neither. They'd lit out not long after, on account of how the angel'd been some sore hurt, an' the warlock went frantic over gettin' her some help. For which Lorlinda surely couln't as begrudge him; a for-real *angel*, beautiful an' holy as anything … she would've done the same, had it been in her power.

So away they'd went, and weren't nothin' else for it but for Lorlinda t' stay put, least's for now. What else could she do? Hardly go home. She din't dare. Be crazy as fuck, a risk not only for her but for ever'one she cared 'bout.

"Think on it, girl," Brad had said. "You was there, right? At the big battle, when they brung down that there Favius. Folks seen'd ya. Includin' folks as likely reckergnized ya."

"Bein' s' well known, Hock Party cham-peen an' all," Dan had added. "Not t' mention bein' there with Heck; shit-fire, ever'one for a hunnerd miles around knew Heck."

"So? What of it?" Lorlinda'd demanded. "Why's that mean as I cain't—"

Before she'd finished askin', the bleak truth sank in. She'd sided 'gainst the rule of Favius, an' though he may've been oh-bliterated, them as followed him still held power.

"Which I guess makes me an outlaw," she told the doll, for all's it was an inert lump, jist cloth an' stuffin' without no Andy-spirit animatin' it an' makin' it walk an' talk an' do sexy-sweet things t' her.

An outlaw, a criminal, an en'my of the state. Whoever was in charge now—that there queen of Favius', it seemed—wouln't have no mercy. It'd be a grisly death sentence at best, more likely after a longtime slow torturin'.

"Not jist for me neither," she said. "They'd go after anyone's I cared 'bout. Shit, they's prolly doin' that already. Punishin' even those what din't have nothin' t' do with it."

She thought of their mommas, hers, an' Heck's an' Zeke's. Of Jammer an' Sadie an' the li'l'uns. Of ol' Pap-Pap an' all the other Bodeans scattered 'round the area. Had they already been 'terrogated? Made t' confess whatever as they knew 'bout her an' Heck's involvement in that momentous showdown 'top Bighead Rock? Had they been made t' suffer solely on account of that blood c'nnection?

It tore at her heart, it did. Their mommas was good an' loving women, innercent! And while innercent weren't a word nobody would use t' describe, say, Jammer, the li'l'uns wouln't know for shit 'bout nothin'! To 'magine them all dragged off t' some dungeon an' put t' the rack or hot pokers or worse, solely for havin' the bad luck t' be related t' her an' Heck, that was a plain terr'ble thing! Bein' put through such agonies? Why, even their own dear mommas'd be cursin' their very names!

The onliest hope as she could cling onto was that them in charge might see there was no point tryin' t' get information as what wasn't known. But even that hope made a mighty fine thread. Like as not, they'd do it anyways, 'cause they could an' 'cause it'd be a firm lesson for anybody else who might be havin' wayward leanin's.

"I cain't even send them a message, let our mommas so much as know I'm alive. Don't dare. Don't know who as t' trust carryin' it. Prolly do more harm than good anyways."

The doll's empty, plastic eyes held absolutely nothin'. No compashun, no symp'thy, nothin'. It din't move its stubby arm t' pat her hand or touch her cheek. It din't tell her, for what-so-ever it was worth, she weren't entirely alone.

"You ain't *Andy!*" With a harsh sob, Lorlinda swatted it away. It fell to the floor, staring blankly at the ceiling. "You ain't, an' you never will be! He's gone too, jist as gone as Heck, dead an' gone! I gots no one!"

She flung herself on the cot and had a full-blown uglycry. Even as she was doin' it, she felt 'shamed, since't she knew it wasn't true. She'd lost Heck an' Andy, but there was still Brad, an' Dan', an' crazy-Blaze the fireworks kid, an' Miz Delilah. An', somewheres, mebbe, Greg an' Ethriel, who still might come back … it weren't impossible.

In the meantime, though, here she was, in this liminal place, unable t' go home, unable t' go anywhere. This cluster-phobic tunnel, which, d'spite it havin' some bigger chambers, was still unnerground an' all closed in. Especially when she hadn't never stayed indoors for days an' days at a time, not even when she'd caught the strep as a girl and weren't s'posed to go outside—easy for the doc to say when's his house had a proper indoor bathroom with flush toilet an' all.

"Why'd'ya have t' go an' 'bandon me like that, y' donkeydicker?"

It was Heck her weepy words were aimed at; Heck, mortal wounded, who'd on-purpose smashed his truck into the cracked columns an' brung'd the whole building down atop hisself.

Heck, who'd then reappeared, ghostly, truck an' all, in the very nick of time. Rammin' that Golem, savin' them, an' then drivin' off, just like a movie hero cowboy ridin' into the sunset.

Once't she'd cried it out—again—Lorlinda made another effort t' pull herself t'gether.

Lordy-Lucifer, but it was a chore, all right. Din't help neither, bein' on her own case for crybabyin'. Sure, plenny people had it plenny worse, but she was the only one feelin' what *she* was feelin'. Whether or not it was small p'taters in the greater scheme of things, what with the whole world an' Hell an' such, this here was her own sorrowin', and she knew she shouln't oughter have the guilts 'bout it.

Nonetheless, she got up, warshed her face, bird-bathed the rest, pulled on a clean sundress from Brad's stores—it had flamingers on it— an' headed out t' the main room t' see what was what.

Which wasn't much. They had no way now of gettin' word from the inside, on account of how it used t' be Heck what brought the local news. The furthest any of them had ventured from the tunnel on that end was when Dan went t' check an' see the camouflage disguise on the openin' still held. True, there weren't but a handful had even know'd 'bout it in the first place, and few as had ever visited, but no point takin' needless chances.

As for that handful, best they could do was hope nobody decided t' blab. Well, that an' have Miz Delilah do some more hoodoo, settin' tripwire hexes so's to give an alert should anyone come snoopin' around.

Miz Delilah had been among those who'd 'vacuated the vicinity before the nuke an' the Painwave, but she'd come back right quick, provin' a sight tougher than most. Certainly tougher than her grandkids had given her credit for, an' more stubborn too.

She was, in fact, sittin' right there when Lorlinda entered what they'd desergnated as the main livin' area of the unnerground complex. It had a kitchenette, a dinin' nook, an' a TV what got cable an' was currently set to the National 'Mergency Network broadcastin' round-the-clock updates.

Rest of the world'd gone tits-up, judgin' by the info scrollin' along the bottom of the screen an' the montage of clips. Death toll continuin' to climb, riots, lootin', r'ligious hysteria, martial law, mass sacrificin', commerce collapse, shortages, economy down the shitter, abs'lute chaos.

T' think, weren't so long ago when the HellZone as had been the crazyplace, which now looked sane an' stable by comparison.

"Come on over here, girl," Miz Delilah said. "Need to see you fed before you fall away to a shadow."

Lorlinda weren't the least bit hungry, but there'd never been no arguin' with Miz D when she was their schoolteacher, and was no arguin' with her now. Petite an' plump, in her caftan an' headscarf, her clunky jewelry an' big earrings, she coulda been anywheres from fifty to ninety and was known as a mojo-woman well before AllHell, when magic got more common here'bouts.

"Where's Brad an' Dan at?" Lorlinda asked as she dutifully took a chair.

"Oh, somewhere up to no good, I'd imagine. Like usual with those two." Miz Delilah bustled over to the kitchenette, where kettles steamed an' pots bubbled an' oven aromas made Lorlinda start t' figure mebbe she was a bit hungry after all.

"I guess I ain't been much help ..."

"Hush on that, now. You've gone through the wringer, child. Seen and done a lot, lost a lot. No one should be faulting you, least of all yourself, if you need to take some time. Especially when there's still a ways to go."

"... there's still what?"

"Later. First, you eat." She bustled back, placing a laden tray on the table in front of Lorlinda. "Hot sassafras, fried catfish, collards, biscuits."

"*Real* catfish? Not—?"

"Not those monstrous worm-faced slimebags you're used to, no. Real Tooawhatcha River catfish."

"I ain't had real catfish in *years*!" She dug in with a sudden surge of gen-u-ine apperite an', in a matter of minutes, had cleared her plate.

Miz Delilah hadn't been kiddin' about seein' her fed; she dished up seconds an' then thirds, which Lorlinda polished off like a starved dog.

At last, when one more bite would've made her pop like a tick, she leaned back, rubbin' her full food-baby belly an' stiflin' a bone-rattlin' burp.

"Prolly a downright sin t' say so, Miz D, but damn-an'-bless if'n those wasn't the best collards I ever did eat, better even than my Aunt Beddie's!"

"Very kind of you."

"An' that *catfish*!" She rolled her eyes. "'Bout fergot how food's s'posed t' taste! Better'n sex by a *mile*!"

"Wellnow, let's not get carried away." Miz Delilah winked. "As I remember it, sex could be mighty fine too."

Lorlinda giggled, which, an hour or two ago, she wouldn't have thought herself capable of. "You'se surely is a one, Miz Delilah."

"As are you, Miss Bodean. Now you're feeling better, though, I do have to tell you some things, which you won't be glad to hear."

The words and tone quickly sobered her. "Is it 'bout my famb'ly? I ... I already been told why I cain't go home, or send 'em any messages, an' how they's in danger anyways ... if'n sommat worse has happened, 'cause of us, 'cause of me an' Heck, I ... I don't know as I could ..."

"I truly do wish I could set your mind at ease in that regard, girl, but afraid I can't. Auguring and far-seeing's not so much in my wheelhouse. It's the spellwork I did for you a while ago."

"The tripwire hexes?"

"No, though I do expect those'll be found out sooner rather than later, and this here sanctuary won't be a secret for long. I'm talking about the soul-transference, the one to move your friend from the Catch's pod into the doll-vessel."

"Andy?" She sat up straight. "My sweetie-pie sugarbun? You c'n sense him? He's all right? I thought sure he was a goner—"

Miz Delilah patted the back of her hand. "I thought so too, because I couldn't sense him, but then I felt the spellwork break. Just a while ago, it was. The doll-vessel's been destroyed, the spell undone. He's moved on now, child, moved on to the Beyond."

"Whatcha mean? He … he made it through the battle an' all? He weren't in the truck with Heck when the buildin' come down an' blowed up?"

"Must not have been. How, and where he was in the meantime, I can't set your mind at ease about those either … but worldly concerns are over for him now."

Lorlinda bowed her head. Poor Andy, an' here she'd promised t' look after him. "D'ya happen t' know which, um, way he got sent?"

"Best as I can tell, he's not suffering. He's at peace, more or less. Apart from that?" She shrugged. "Not for me to say."

Miz Delilah refilled their tea, and they sipped in companionable quiet for a while.

"I miss him," Lorlinda said. "So nice an' polite, differ'nt from most fellas here'bouts. Mebbe I wouln't've thought so if'n we'd met when he was his 'riginal carnation, but, as t'was, he were special t' me."

"The way it is sometimes. We can only hope to make the best of what comes our way."

"Only, I miss Heck too, an' Heck been a jackass peckerhead t' me my whole livelong life. How's that fair?"

"Also the way it is sometimes. Heck, despite his many faults, *was* your kin, your close kin. You grew up together. You had a true bond. And, from what I've heard, maybe at the end there, he wasn't such a jackass peckerhead after all."

"He were brave. He went out one'a the good guys, doin' the right thing. I bet he ain't never 'xpected that." She smiled wanly. "Y'hear how him an' his truck come back ghost on us?"

"I did," Miz Delilah said. "And I daresay we haven't seen the last of Heck Bodean yet."

They passed a span of silence fer Heck's mem'ry, an' then Lorlinda bolstered her nerves to look Miz D in the eye again.

"Said y' had some *things* t' tell me, like, plurl? More'n one?"

"Well, for instance, this tunnel. Might be best for everybody to shut it down a while. Lock it up and leave it be. In case it does get found out."

"Y'mean, goes somewheres else?" She bit her lip. "Me?

Satan's sack, but where? How? I ain't been more'n thirty miles from the lake all my life, an' mosta that was when BoJo used'ta cart us to school in that rattletrap ol' bus!"

"I know, child, but you won't be safe here for long."

Lorlinda indicated the television. "By th' look, ain't *noplace* safe anymores! It's all a shitshow, it is!"

"It is," agreed Miz Delilah somberly. "May get better, may get worse. Told you, I don't go in so much for auguring. Still, I have no doubt, if you get found here, it'll go poorly for you."

"What 'bout Brad an' Dan?"

"They've both got their own places, outside, and I'm sure either of them would be glad to take you in. You'd also be welcome with us; we have a couple spare rooms since Sondra hitched up and Sonya went off to her fancy academy. Or, I daresay you could refuge with the Petersons—"

"After I give their boy such a hit o' 'shine he fuck-near blew hisself t' Mars? They done grounded him a whole week f'r drinkin'!"

"As I understand it," Miz D said, "they would've grounded him six months, but for how he confessed up ... plus the fact he fireballed an entire flock of Nazi bird-demons and helped save the day. A week's barely a slap on the wrist."

"Reckon so," she admitted. "Still ... it don't seem right, somehow, me goin' off safe when others is neck-deep in it with no way out. 'Specially our mommas, mine an' Heck's. I'd feel lower'n a burrowbug's butthole."

Miz Delilah went over to bustle some more at the kitchenette. She shot Lorlinda a kinda crafty glance over a shoulder, an' there was a sly kinda edge t' her tone, put on too innercent, when she asked, "Well, girl, what more options have you got? I suppose you *could* try going home ... it'd be a spot dangerous, yes, but there *are* ways to minimize the risks."

"What ways?" Lorlinda pounced. "Ever'body been tellin' me nope, no chance in Heaven; even if'n I weren't nabbed by soldiers, it'd be a long-ass haul through bad critter country, just beggin' t' be raped, killed, et, or all'n th' 'bove. But if'n there's *ways*, Miz D, I needs t' hear 'em!"

"For starters, you've already got some talismanic items that would help."

"Me? Taliswhatsis? Ain't got mucha nothin', 'xcept what of Heck's pocket-junk he left b'hind, a li'l foldin' knife an' a matchbook. Lost his 'pocalypse bat, I did; got stuck in that big clay-man monster. 'Less'n you mean stuff from Brad's inv'tory, but them cheapo souv'neers—"

"What about angel's hair?"

Lorlinda stopped short, feelin' a hot, tingly blush creep over her skin.

"Don't play coy with me, Miss Bodean. I heard how fascinated you were, and with good reason. An actual angel? Who wouldn't have been?"

"I din't mean nothin' creeper-like," she mumbled, head bowed. "It were jist, her bein' so beautiful an' perfect an' … well, dee-vine … I din't steal it neither! I din't go, like, snippin' a lock when she weren't lookin' or …"

"I'm not accusing you."

"I only c'llected it from a hairbrush what she used. She weren't 'cusstomed, Ethriel, t' bein' corporeal. Curious 'bout, well, mortal things. The human 'xperience. Food an' sleep an' … y'know, fuckin' an' such."

Yes indeedy-do, they'd had them some *innnnterestin'* girl talk, durin' the time it took t' make ready for the 'ttack 'gainst Favius.

"But you *do* have some," Miz D persisted. "You have some angel's hair?"

No point askin' how the ol' hoodoo woman knew. Lorlinda surely hadn't told no one, since't Heck would've ragged her t' the dogs an' back for fangirlin'—oh, but what she'd give t' have him here now doin' so!—an' the rest might've thunk it weird.

She fetched the fanny pack hidden under her cot. It'd also come from Brad's cheapo souv'neer stash, bright sunset colors with FLORDA spelled wrong.

Inside, she had the rest of Heck's pocket-junk, a couple pom'granate bombs Blaze had given her, a few nifty bottle caps, some elongated pressed pennies, a Minnie Mouse head 'tenna topper with red-an'-white polker-dot bow, a tin of gingermints, a pina colada lip balm, an' various other odds an' ends she'd picked up magpie-like here an' there.

Tucked securely at the bottom was a sealed plastic baggie, in which were curled sev'ral long gossamer-silken strands. This baggie, she presented with utmost care t' Miz Delilah, who regarded its contents with a look somewheres 'tween fear an' awe.

"I both wish I'd been here to see for myself," Miz D said, "and am glad I wasn't."

"Won't never forget it so long's I live," Lorlinda said. "Tol' me she had faith in me. Her, a for-real angel, tellin' that t' *me?*"

"Now, here's what you're going to do." Miz D handed the unopened baggie back. "You're going to take those hairs, and some of your own, and you're going to weave them together. The way you girls used to do with embroidery floss, remember?"

"Makin' friendship bracelets! I do 'member that!"

"Yes, usually when you were supposed to be paying attention to your history lessons."

"All them dates an' dead folks; y'gotta admit, it *was* dull as dirt."

"I'm not too old to swat your knuckles, Miss Bodean."

"No, ma'am. Jist sayin'."

"Well, see that you do pay attention to the incantation I'm about to teach you, because you'll want to recite it seven times while you're weaving the bracelet, and you won't want to get it wrong."

"What kind of 'cantation?"

"A protective charm. Should help you pass unnoticed by, or be immune from, any but the most major magics or demonic mischiefs. As long as you watch your step and don't do anything foolish, you should be able to make it home."

"Home? Really?"

"*If* you're careful."

"Oh, Miz D, it'd mean th' world t' me!"

"Then see you weave it strong and sturdy, girl. Snug too; you don't want it loose enough to slip off."

"Yes'm, I sure will."

"While you work on that, I'll find those two troublemakers and see what they can rustle up in terms of transportation. Better if you didn't have to hike it, but the roads present their own challenges."

The thought of goin' back out there, alone, into the Dome's baleful glow, with a price on her ass, weren't 'xactly a comfortable one. But th' prospect of the homeplace, of her momma an' Heck's, of bein' able t' grieve proper with her kin? Far outweighed it, 'specially if she could borrow even a smidge of guardian-angel mojo t' look after her.

When Miz D headed off lookin' for Brad an' Dan, Lorlinda set t' work pluckin' strands of her own hair from her scalp. They looked coarse an' low compared t' Ethriel's, like burlap twine next t' fine angora, but they wove together eas'ly enough nonetheless. She incorporated a kind of seven-sided angular pattern into the weave, which reminded her of the sigil Greg wore on his forehead an' on the medallion 'round his neck.

As she fashioned the narrow, intricate, but surprisingly sturdy bracelet, she recited the 'cantation what Miz D had drummed into her. Despite not havin' much of a grasp of the words or their meanin', she reckernized their inherent power, their rightness, an' made sure not to fuck up the pr'nunciations.

If it truly could help, could see her safely home an' with her famb'ly again, why, wasn't that worth any 'mount of risk?

Royal Matters

Just whose suggestion the tour had been in the first place, June couldn't recall, but her advisors and inner circle agreed it was a good idea. Familiarize herself more with the lay of the land, as it were. Inspect her domain. Acknowledge the loyal troops, thank them for their service, motivate them. See and let herself be seen by her subjects.

The fact many of her subjects had already seen damn near everything there was to see of her, in graphic X-rated detail no less ... that was another matter.

If she was to make a go of this, she had to get out there, do the public appearances, give speeches, and similar queenly shit.

So, okay, fine.

Motorcade, armed guard, full processional. Almost a fucking *parade*, complete with marching band and equestrian unit.

Well, "equestrian" might be pushing the term. It seemed there hadn't been many horses in the Lake Misquamicus area to begin with, and of the few who'd survived since AllHell, most had undergone their own transformations and metamorphoses. Horses with side-tentacles ... horses with gator jaws ... two-headed horses ... ghost-eyed skeleton horses ... bat-winged horses ... a darker-than-dark demonic unicorn.

Others hadn't even started out as horses. From his ranch, a local named Keene had sent as tribute a half-dozen of what might have once been emus. Might have once, but were now ten-foot-tall, patchy-feathered, tailless, long-necked bipedal terrors with high-stepping, raptor-clawed saurian legs and serrated beaks easily capable of shearing through a human femur. Despite their vicious appearance and temperament, they *could* technically be saddled and ridden, and some among the troops were gonzo crazy enough to volunteer. Once they got the hang of it, they were quite a sight, moving in precise formation like a mounted drill team.

"Now all we need are a couple floats, some Shriners in go-karts, and a giant helium Bullwinkle balloon," June remarked, surveying the preparations with a mix of amusement and skepticism.

"Clowns," Major Xanne Duval said, standing at June's right hand. "Don't forget the clowns."

"I draw the line at clowns. Baton twirlers if you must, but I absolutely draw the line at clowns."

"Good," muttered Iris Tate, on June's left. "I hate clowns."

"Then who's gonna throw candy to the kiddies?" Xanne asked.

"Fuck's sake." June pinched the bridge of her nose. "What next, a t-shirt cannon?"

"We could probably rig something up."

"No clowns, no candy for the kiddies, no t-shirt cannons."

"You're the boss." Xanne snickered. "If you do want baton twirlers, though, I'd say put them right after the bearers of the dragon standard—"

June groaned. "Let's not. This is already beyond absurd. I'm supposed to ride around in that ... that ... gaudy-ass popemobile ..."

Xanne's grin widened. "Aw, c'mon. The greasemonkeys in the motor pool are really proud of how it turned out. You gotta admit, it makes an impression."

Which was one way to put it. They'd converted the largest and most luxurious of the armored limos, elevating it on cranked-up lifts and bulky all-terrain tires. Removing the roof, they'd installed a clear bulletproof enclosure, inside of which was mounted a pedestal and thronelike chair. The entire thing was bedecked with bloodflowers, banners, bone garlands, and bunting.

"I'm going to look ridiculous," June said.

"You're gonna look awesome," Xanne said. "Totally badass."

"Regal an' majestic," added Iris.

"Sitting there, doing the stupid little wristy-wave? Smiling like it's the goddamn Tournament of Roses? What next, I have to wear a sash? A rhinestone tiara?"

"Actually ..." Iris shared a glance with Xanne. "We were

thinking … something different."

"Oh, you were, were you?" She narrowed her gaze at the two of them. "And just when were you planning on letting me in on it?"

"Well, today," Xanne said, unperturbed. "We wanted it to be a surprise, but we wouldn't spring it on you last minute."

"Wouldn't never." Iris placed a sincere hand over her heart. "But it's ready now, if'n you want to see."

What had they said? Awesome, badass, regal, majestic? All that and then some.

Beautiful. Wonderful.

Fucking *magnificent*!

For a while, struck speechless, barely able to breathe, June could only look.

Then she touched. Tentatively at first, as if it might not be real, or if it would burn her, blister her fingertips, sear them down to the bone.

It was real. It did not burn, blister, or sear.

"How …?" she finally managed. "How did … where did …?"

"Had it made special," Iris said.

"From *his*," Xanne added. "What was left behind, after … well, after. Thought he'd have wanted it that way."

"Checked first with some pr'gnosticators, though. To make sure. To not transgress or overstep."

"Oh …" June reached out again, tracing the contours of the embossed metal.

The Hell-forged bronze, reshaped, resized into a slender corselet. Separate shoulder pieces and forearm bracers and gauntlets, thigh guards and shin greaves. The Roman-style battle skirt, strips of infernal leather edged by more bronze. The open-faced helm, its crownlike crest inlaid with baleful gems. The footgear, neither boot nor sandal but something between, banded in flexible bronze plating. The jeweled war belt. The cape, a flowing, dusky, dark-crimson sweep with a high, flared collar.

"There's a lightweight kevmesh bodysuit that can go under it too," Xanne said, "if you're really expecting trouble. But it's all padded and lined, so it won't chafe even if you wear it over bare skin."

"And this was his," June marveled. "Favius's armor."

He *would* have wanted it this way, she felt certain. To protect her, keep her safe. No more traitorous backstabs now, thank you very much! But also to let part of him still be with her, in a sense. To be near her. To not be entirely gone. To carry on his memory, his legacy, his purpose.

She turned to Xanne and Iris, both of whom seemed somewhat apprehensive. Worried they *had* overstepped or transgressed, regardless of the prognosticators' reassurances. Afraid they'd upset or offended her.

Too choked up to speak, all she could do was hug them. Which probably startled them as much as it startled June herself; she had never been one prone to impulsive displays of affection.

But then, no one had ever done anything so kind and thoughtful for her before.

She tried the outfit on, only needing a little help to get everything properly buckled into place.

Perfect fit.

Not the least bit uncomfortable. Not heavy, not bulky, not constricting. She could move freely, full range of motion.

And when she looked in the mirror …

"What did I tell you?" said Xanne. "Totally fuckin' badass!"

She'd expected to see something laughable and pathetic, some sorry excuse for an aging wannabe Xena. Instead, she saw a fierce demon-goddess, an avenging warrior-queen, tall and proud, strong, capable.

Totally fuckin' badass indeed!

"I knew it," Iris breathed, teary-eyed. "I just *knew* it."

"Assemble the camp," June told Xanne. "I want to address everyone."

"You got it." She snapped a salute on the way out.

Like Chef Emilio and the missing "secretary," June knew a few cosmetics professionals had been brought along in the initial convoy. The bigshot politicians and news media, expecting plenty of photo ops, screen time, and sound bites, had to look their best on camera, after all. Of course, once the chaos and carnage began, once blood was flowing and heads were flying and faces were getting peeled off, *nobody* had been looking their best. The viewers at home wouldn't have given half a shit at that point how a hairdo was holding up or whether someone's foundation wasn't well blended.

Some of those professionals, however, were still around,

and since neither she nor Iris had a lot of experience when it came to hairstyles and makeup, June dispatched Meep to find someone qualified.

Or, overqualified, as it turned out.

Forty-five minutes and one shamelessly flamboyant stereotype later, as the anticipatory murmur of the crowd outside swelled, June yet again could hardly believe what the mirror showed her.

As much as she hated that damn movie trope where the right makeover was all it took, June had to admit maybe there really might be something to it.

Maybe. With the help of a self-described fairy godfather, in the form of a trim silver-fox Black man named Lyle, who'd worked on several Broadway productions—including *Cabaret, Hedwig and the Angry Inch, Kinky Boots,* and *La Cage au Folles*—as well as *Ru Paul's Drag Race* and *Queer Eye.*

He had, he said, left that lifestyle way behind him ages ago, but some skills, you just never lost.

"Got older, got married, settled down, started a family. Didn't have the energy anymore. Or the legs; sweet Jesus, you should have seen my legs back in the day. Tina Turner legs, *all* the way up. If I'd had any talent as a performer, I might've *been* someone. But, backstage was good enough for me."

He kept up a steady stream of amiable chatter the whole time he was working on her. Though June thought it would make her more tense, it put her oddly at ease.

And when he, with a triumphant flourish, spun her chair so she could see the results, she was damn near stunned.

Wild windblown tresses streaming from under the helm, savage smoky eyeshadow with sharply winged Cleopatra eyeliner, deft strokes of rouge to highlight cheekbones she didn't even know she had, and poison-ripe lipstick …

She still wasn't "pretty" by any sense of the word, but the effect was dramatic, theatrical, and striking.

"Is that me?" she asked, raising her hands to her face but not making contact for fear of smudging it to ruins.

Lyle beamed, camping it up. "As the saying goes, *yaaaass queen.*"

"Isn't it a little … over the top?"

"You're not going on a date. This is a production. This is

showtime. You *own* this, got me?"

"I … I guess …?"

Iris was agog. Xanne, when she popped her head in to announce the camp was assembled as instructed, did a double-take, then whooped, clapped, and whistled.

"Bad-*ass*!" she declared. "You're gonna knock them dead!"

"Unless I get out there and freeze up, make a fool of myself."

"You won't," said Iris. "They'll love it. Sure as sin, they will."

June rose from the chair. The armor moved with her as naturally as if it was part of her own body, not awkward or clumsy at all. She felt the way she had when she'd first held a gun, and the first time she'd taken Favius into her mouth. Innate talent, only waiting to be discovered and utilized.

So far, so good, and if all she had to do was strike a pose, she'd knock it out of the park.

But she'd still have to *talk*, to address everyone, and the prospect made cold, squirmy sensations in her gut, and other places where she more customarily had warm, slippery sensations. Her mouth felt dry; her palms felt clammy. She wasn't sure whether her body wanted to run, faint, puke, or piss. Or all simultaneously.

Favius, she reminded herself. Favius had chosen her, loved her, made her his queen. By all the devils in Hell and angels in Heaven, she was *not* about to let him down.

"Give me a moment," she said to the others.

"You want any sort of fanfare or intro?" Xanne asked.

"No, just … just give me a moment."

They left. She heard the crowd-noise wax and wane as the RV's main doors opened and shut again. Only Juggernaut remained inside, waiting implacably in the front room.

Alone, June gathered her breath and her nerves.

Despite her many years of church-going and external displays of piety and devotion, she'd long since lost her taste for actual prayer. What was the use when there was never any answer and nothing ever changed? When God was absent or indifferent, or simply cruel?

Now, though, it wasn't God she prayed to. Not anymore.

No, now, she closed her eyes and bowed her head, directing her prayers downward. With far more heartfelt sincerity than she'd ever implored higher divine intercession.

Help me do this. Help me get through it. For Favius and all he believed in. Let the dark muses he spoke of send me the words to say, guide me in how to say them. Help me find my Voice, to use in Your Name and Your Cause.

A warm serenity fell over her, filled her, suffused her.

As if being heard, listened to, understood.

Not ignored, or brushed off, or let float away into an eternal void.

With the warmth, however, there came also an awareness, a demand.

Expectation. Obligation. An offering to be made, a price to be paid.

"*Ave Luciferos,*" she finished aloud. "Thy Will be done."

She opened her eyes and smiled at her reflection.

It both pleased and saddened her to think, had Favius been here to see that smile, how he would have reacted.

"You've got this," she told herself. "You can goddamn *do* this."

Then she strode from her bedroom to the main living area of the RV. Juggernaut stirred and obediently fell into pace behind her. The soldiers flanking the front doors from inside snapped to attention and swung them open for her.

Red-tinged sunlight through the *Aurora Diabolicus* bathed her in a patina of blood as she emerged, gladius at one hip, marshmallow fork at the other, cape belling in a humid breeze off the vile churn of the lake. She paused at the top of the steps, head high, chin raised.

Inside, confident self-talk or not, she was scared shitless, having panic flashbacks to school spelling bees and holiday recitals. The entire auditorium looking at her, smirking at her dowdy appearance and Kmart clothes, waiting for her to fuck up and make a fool of herself. Right after, usually, some pretty bitch like Deanna Philbrick—who got boobs in fourth grade!—had performed perfectly. With, of course, dreamboat Carter Bryce and his jockboy friends in the second row, sniggering, horsing around, elbowing each other. And her mother watching from the back of the room, lips pursed in anticipatory disappointment.

No!

She violently flung such memories aside, facing the crowd. A sea of hushed, expectant faces. Most still human, more or less. Some, decidedly not. Military, media, medics, staff, civilians. Chef Emilio and his team. Even the prisoners had been brought out, in chains or under guard. The Shinns were there, broken and miserable, with a nanny pushing a makeshift double-stroller.

Spot, who had shown no signs of resentment from the earlier scolding, only abject and apologetic ass-kissing, gazed up at her with soulful wounded-puppy contrition, clearly so desperate to be back in her good graces he'd do anything, anything at all.

We'll see about that, June thought.

Iris, if none too comfortable even in the second-hand spotlight, bore her own first public appearance as queen's handmaid bravely. She had upgraded her former Dust Bowl attire to the current century, at least; no more bonnet and apron but a simple calf-length skirt, button-down blouse, and slip-on flats. Her dishwater hair was pinned back in a bun.

Lyle—definitely going to have to keep him around!—stood with Xanne and Iris, just about glowing with pride as everyone got their first gander at her new look. Meep, stationed nearby, was jaw-dropped, his mouth hung open far enough to fit a billiard ball. The boar-faced soldier called Pork Chop leaned over to mutter something to the man beside him; June couldn't make it all out but was pretty sure she caught the words "like to snuffle *that* truffle!" followed by a lusty grunt-snort.

The man beside him, with a corporal's stripes, had a little girl boosted up onto his shoulders. The sight of her, excited as a kid on her first trip to the fair, gave June an uneasy twinge.

Oh, well. Omelets and eggs, baby. Omelets and eggs.

Someone from the media division had rigged a quick microphone setup, and cameras began rolling as June approached the podium.

She had no idea if they were broadcasting as well as recording, or where they'd even be broadcasting to, given the dubious state of affairs and whatever was going on outside the Wall, but they were on the job. One crew commanded a drone-operated unit, though the drone had recently been refitted with four sets of buzzing waspish wings, and a weird reptilian eyeball in place of a regular lens.

Every helpful tip she'd ever heard or read about public

speaking had evaporated from her mind. Open with a joke? Imagine her audience naked? Hello, my name is Inigo Montoya?

Favius had preferred the Marc Antony route, all *friends-Romans-countrymen*, but she didn't know if she could carry it off convincingly.

Dearly beloved? My fellow Misquamicans? S'up, peeps? Four score and seven years ago?

All of them, watching her. Waiting. Anticipating.

"Well, here we are," she heard herself say. "Crazy how things turn out, isn't it? I'm sure none of us expected this. I know I sure didn't. Yet here we are. Here we still are, despite everything, against all odds. Here we still are ... and here, so help me, and in Satan's name, we will *stay!*"

People cheered, clapped and cheered, actually *cheered*.

"Despite all that we've lost," she went on, "all that was taken from us, all that we've suffered. They tried, in their righteousness, to destroy us, but they failed."

"The *folly of fucking with Hell!*" several chorused as if on cue.

"The folly of fucking with Hell," June agreed. "I would like to tell you they paid the price, learned their lesson, and will never bother us again ... I would like to tell you we are safe, free from their small-minded hatred and tyranny ... but as much as I would like to tell you, I can't. We do not fully know what happened out there—"

Understatement; they didn't know jack shit about what happened out there.

"—or how long it will take them to recover. Nonetheless, we cannot and must not think it's over. As much as they feared and hated us before, they'll now do so a thousandfold, and blame us as well. Never mind they brought it on themselves, launching a nuclear weapon at us when we had done nothing to warrant such an attack! They wanted to eradicate us from the face of God's green earth, at any cost. Just because it brutally backfired on them doesn't mean they won't try again."

Angry rumblings, fist-shakings, and a scattering of vile expletives greeted this.

"We must remain ready and vigilant," June said. "If we let down our guard, grow complacent, our enemies are sure to turn it against us." She paused, sweeping a gaze over the crowd. "Our enemies ... both foreign *and* domestic. Because, yes, as much as I hate to say it, we'd been, and may still be, harboring traitors in our midst."

The angry rumblings became all the more ominous and deadly.

"Was not I myself struck down from behind in a cowardly backstabbing assassination attempt by my own handmaiden? Were not the forces of the Opposition aided and abetted by renegade members of this very community?"

The dark muses *were* with her. She surrendered herself to their inspiration, letting her Voice and their words pour forth, ringing with power, strident with emotion.

"I myself was not, I admit, a member of this community. I have no longstanding blood ties, no history here, no roots. Like many of you now gathered before me, I came from outside. And under other pretenses, misled, harboring erroneous ideals and beliefs. I came here blind, ignorant, unaware."

The majority, those from the military convoy, nodded fervently. She caught Mrs. Shinn shooting her another patented death-glare.

"Then," June said, "we *beheld*. We beheld Hell's glory in all its might and majesty, embraced it, and accepted it into ourselves."

So she was exaggerating and paraphrasing, so what? Hell's glory or Favius's cock, tomayto/tomahto. Might and majesty either way, which she'd certainly embraced and accepted into herself.

Eagerly. Vigorously. Often.

If still nowhere near enough. She'd been robbed, and she would have personally sacrificed every single soul here on the lakeshore for one more night with him. Forget good and evil and angels and demons, forget any grand purpose or divine rivalry. One more night. One more torrid, pounding, delirious night!

"We were chosen," she went on. "Infernally chosen, diabolically blessed. We had our leader. Our savior, if you will. Our anointed king. *Ecce, novum princeps de inferno, novus rex terrae!*"

"Hail, Favius!" they roared.

"Who was taken from us! Taken before his time, cheating us of our rightful ruler, leaving his plans unfinished and his purpose unfulfilled!" Her Voice faltered, near to breaking. "Taken from us … taken from *me* … his woman, his lover, his … queen."

She let a solemn, somber moment pass, during which she glanced at the gantry bearing her mother's picked-clean skeleton, now a shrine surrounded by many candles and offerings.

"Honors I never expected, scarcely deserved, and never could have dared in a million years to dream," she said. "Just as I certainly never expected, deserved, or dared to dream to be with you here now, as I am. To be called upon to carry on in his stead. I … I was not made for this, trained for it. I confess to you freely, I have felt weak and uncertain and afraid. I have doubted myself, as much if not more than I'm sure you have all doubted me."

As ripples of protest and vehement denial stirred the crowd, June drew her marshmallow fork from its loop on her war belt. Spreading her arms wide, she held the fork in her right hand and braced its tines against her left palm.

"But this do I swear unto you!" she cried, letting her Voice roll forth again in full resonance. She jabbed the tines into her palm, piercing skin and flesh, and held her wounded hand high. "By my own blood, I swear to you … if you grant me this honor, I shall uphold it, I shall serve you and lead you to the best of my abilities, until my dying breath!"

She clenched her fist, maroon rivulets streaming down her forearm, as everyone burst into thunderous approbation.

"*Juno Regina!*" Xanne shouted. "Long live the queen!"

Others took it up, and then they were all chanting it—well, almost all; the Shinns sure as shit didn't join in, though some of the other prisoners had been caught up in the moment.

A seething surge of energy blossomed in the center of June's chest and shot up her raised arm, erupting into a towering smoky redblack supernova with a heart of brilliant, terrible light.

"Then so it is, and so let it be!" she intoned. "In memory of Favius and those who fell in our defense, in the unholy Name of Satan and the forces of Hell, *so let it be!*"

The supernova burst with a thunderclap loud enough to make the Dome itself seem to tremble. When the echoes faded and the aftershocks stilled, she lowered her arm and again regarded the sea of faces turned toward her.

Adoring, admiring, worshipful faces. And more than a

few lustful ones; she suspected she could have had her pick of any or as many ready cocks as she wanted. Even if they knew full well they'd have to die afterward, they'd line up halfway around the lake to volunteer and go out smiling.

"Tomorrow," June said as the hubbub settled, "I undertake a tour of visitation around our realm, carrying this message of strength and solidarity. I trust each of you to continue to do your part. I charge each of you with due diligence, especially against treachery from within. What say you?"

"JUNO REGINA!!! JUNO REGINA!!! Long live the queen!"

At sunset, they gathered again, by June's decree, on the lakeshore by the monument marking the place Favius had first emerged.

Atop that monument, impaled on a spike, the rotting yet still animate head of a former five-star general raged mutely. His face had been peeled off—by Favius himself, no less—and the sinewy striations of muscle beneath were putrid and teeming with maggots. Both eye sockets gaped hollow, their contents long since plucked out. His decaying jawbone worked, the slimy remnants of his tongue writhing like a cluster of worms.

Torches lined the beach, and bonfires blazed, and eldritch lanterns cast eerie glows. The *Aurora Diabolicus* pulsed above, throbbing scarlet and violet, a vast inhuman heart.

"Tonight," June told the assembly, "we honor Favius, without whom none of this would have been possible. We feast for him, drink to him, and remember him."

She lifted a goblet brimming with potent black-grape wine—product, she'd been told, of a now-defunct local vineyard, and did it pack a kick!

"Favius!" she cried.

"Favius!" the crowd responded.

They drank deeply, all as one.

It was all she could do not to break down in anguished sobs, but somehow, she managed. If anyone noticed her struggle, they had the wisdom, or sufficient sense of self-preservation, to keep their mouth shut.

Six stout posts had been erected, piles of driftwood and kindling at their bases. To each post was chained, naked and helpless, a prisoner of war. Some pleaded for mercy. Others were stoic or defiant. It didn't matter either way. As the pyres were lit, as the flames caught, they all burned, shrieking, the same way.

The wild, brutal revelry went on far into the night, another riotous cacophony of fighting and fucking, cannibalism and carnality. More prisoners were sacrificed, tortured and toyed with, or simply slaughtered wholesale. Various types of music competed for decibel dominance. Dancers cavorted in throes of obscene abandon. Sporadic outbursts of spontaneous gunfire rattled the air.

June herself retired early, retreating to the somewhat quieter confines of the palatial RV once the festivities were in full swing. Only Juggernaut accompanied her, the Golem resuming its customary station in the main living area. Iris would have gone along, and without complaint, but June insisted her dutiful handmaid take the rest of the evening off. The next few days of appearances and visits would likely prove exhausting for them all.

Alone in her private quarters, she removed her armor, setting each piece carefully aside. She washed off the makeup and combed her hair and slipped into a comfy robe.

The twin punctures in her palm had already healed. No scars, no bruises, hadn't even hurt. She wiped away the dried blood. Then, gazing at her hand, she concentrated and curled her fingers. A small, smoky, redblack mass formed, flickering with jagged wire-thin bolts of energy, a miniature storm cloud in her grasp. As she spread her fingers, it enlarged, softball-sized, then grapefruit, then bowling ball.

She twisted her wrist this way and that, watching the stormy sphere revolve. As insubstantial as it looked, she had the feeling it would smash right through a brick wall or flatten a tank.

As for what it might do to a living target—a human being, for instance—well, she wasn't quite sure but figured it would be fairly impressive. And probably pretty messy.

What it might do to, say, a certain warlock asshole and/or his whore-slut angel ...

Oh, how she would love to find out!

This was probably the point in the proceedings—or, really, well past the point in the proceedings—when she was supposed to stop and contemplate, in horror, what was happening to her. If she was becoming a monster. If she was corrupted, fully caught in evil's clutches. If there was still time to turn back. Atone, repent, be redeemed, be saved.

"Fuck that," she said. "You can take your damn redemption arc and shove it up your ass."

The next morning found most of the camp hungover and half-dressed, which didn't stop a sadistic bugle-blower from blasting "Reveille" at skull-splitting volume.

Repeatedly.

With great, maniacal glee.

*Doot-**doot**-doodle-oot,   doot-**doot**-doodle-oot,   doot-**doot**-doodle-oot-**DOO-DOO-DOO**,* until a burly ogre of a staff sergeant snatched the brass instrument from him, crumpled it like a frat boy would an empty beer can, and threw it into the lake.

Which, being a violation of military code—interfering with a bugler in the course of his duty—got the staff sergeant written up, though many felt he should have been given a medal instead.

Regardless, however, of headaches and hangovers, a new day was upon them. And a busy day it was to be too.

"You ready for this?" Lyle asked, putting the finishing touches on June's hair and makeup. Smoky and savage, wild, dramatic.

"Ready or not, I don't have much choice." She'd slept better than anticipated, no creeker-freak visions or other bad dreams, though the anxiety of public speaking was beginning to creep in again. What would be the demonic equivalent of butterflies in her stomach? Devil-moths?

It helped a little that Chef Emilio had outdone himself yet again at breakfast—crepes *a la* Bananas Foster, rum-soaked, brown sugar flambeed to caramelized perfection, filled with a decadent blend of pureed banana and thick whipped cream.

"You did awesome yest'day," Iris said.

"Total badass, like I told you," Xanne agreed. "This'll be a breeze. Whistle stop at the roadhouse, quick ceremony on the Rock, then an evening at Senator Stump-Humper's."

"I hears he's goin' all out," said Spot, who had been probationally let off the hook. "Speshul ennertainments an' such."

"Oh joy," June said dryly. She caught Xanne's gaze in the mirror. "Do make sure I keep all my limbs and digits?"

"No worries."

"What 'bout that sister of his?" Iris asked, polishing the crown-crested helm to a brazen shine.

Spot grinned. "Purt-sure she's part of the speshul ennertainments. If'n there's even much left they can cut offa her."

"I guess we'll see." June examined her reflection, amazed once more ... that this fierce, striking figure could be *her*, plain-Jane Junie-June Goldsmith ... "Lyle, I'm hereby appointing you official court cosmetician."

"Majesty." He did an elaborate foppish bow, needing only a velvet cap with feather plume.

The bunting-bedecked popemobile limo, with its contingent of armed guards, waited outside the RV. June, in full Hell-bronze regalia, cape flowing in the sulfurous breeze off the lake, climbed aboard and took her raised seat.

The transparent bulletproof shielding served akin to a greenhouse, making the balmy, humid, Dome-filtered daylight that much sweatier and stickier. Thankfully, someone had had the presence of mind to rig a portable AC, agonicity-powered by way of two generators ... okay, okay, two lobotomized, mindless, pain-wracked torsos stashed behind the driver's compartment. The moderately cooler wafting air provided welcome relief in the otherwise somewhat stifling confines.

Iris rode with her, albeit lower down and nearly out of sight, to tend to whatever needs might need tending to. The rear of the vehicle dipped appreciably as Juggernaut plodded onto a reinforced platform attached to the back bumper. If the Golem's presence, in light of the other precautions, seemed superfluous, well, better safe than sorry!

The limo driver's smart uniform, complete with cap and epaulets, could not hide the fact the driver's skin was a leathery jaundice-yellow, or the way his elongated ears tapered to points, or that his extra-toothy mouth opened on the vertical rather than the horizontal. He wore polarized aviator sunglasses and had the casual, outgoing manner of a Secret Service agent during a bomb threat.

On some level, June still could not quite believe she was doing this. She remembered watching Elizabeth II's Golden Jubilee on television and thinking how pompous and silly it seemed. Now, here *she* was, about to embark on a royal tour of a pocket of Hell ... like to see Anne Hathaway tackle *that* one in a future *Princess Diaries* movie.

They joined the rest of the motorcade, or parade, or processional, or whatever they were calling it, at the edge of the camp. Equestrian and emusaurus units, standard-bearers, marching band, the works.

Minus, of course, clowns, baton twirlers, Shriners in go-karts, floats, Bullwinkle balloons, and t-shirt cannons.

Plus, of course, a fuckton more weaponry, from bayonets and lances to machine guns and heavy artillery.

The pace car, in which Xanne would be taking point, must have once been some Florida retiree's midlife-crisis splurge, a sleek, sporty jet-black convertible, before receiving the HellZone custom treatment. It now resembled a Ferrari as imagined by H.R. Geiger, chitinous and xenomorphesque. Moving not on tires but on multiple omnidirectional mecha-organic-looking treads lubricated by secreted oils, it had neither steering wheel nor driver

Lends new meaning to the word "autonomous," June thought. When the crew from the motor pool had first shown it to her, they'd popped the hood, revealing uncomfortably organ-and brain-shaped engine components suspended in arcane, alchemical fluids. She'd decided then and there she didn't really want to know more.

Xanne gave the order to prepare to roll out. Everyone got into position or snapped to attention. The mounts pranced in place, tossing their heads. Those not actively involved lined both sides of the road to see them off, many still showing the effects of the previous night's debauchery. A squadron of Blackwings in tight formation did a flyover, far lower than the Stealth Bomber or Blue Angels ever did. The marching band struck up a fanfare, then launched into a jaunty number June found weirdly familiar but couldn't immediately identify.

Then it hit her—Queen's "Killer Queen" by way of John Philip Sousa—and she wasn't sure if she should have the band leader executed or exalted.

The crowd, hungover or not, loved it. So, she supposed, she wouldn't execute anybody just yet. It *was* pretty clever, and they sounded great.

They kept it going all the way to the first stop on the itinerary, a place June had heard about often enough but never visited in person: Crawdaddy's Roadhouse, aka

Crawdy's. Even if it was technically now Spot's, Crawdy's it was, Crawdy's it "allus" had been, and Crawdy's it would remain.

Ah, Crawdy's. *The* happenin' joint for local yokels since time immemorial. World-famous—well, lake-famous anyway—for pool tables, cheap beer, bad music, homebrewed 'shine, parking lot fistfights, bathroom blowjobs, and the three-dollar deep-fried crawdad bucket happy hour special.

But most of all, host venue of the celebrated Hock Parties! Where patrons hawked, hocked, snorted, and spat copious quantities of mucus, saliva, "t'baccer chaw, lung butter, snot rockets," and other substances onto the bared breasts or naked bodies of young women. Between buy-in fees, bets, and cash prizes, more money passed through Crawdy's on a Hock Party night than the till might otherwise see in a month.

Spot had described it for her in vivid, sometimes *too* vivid, detail. He'd taken charge of the place after Ol' Man Crawdy's death and maintained it as the social hub and landmark it surely was meant to be. A landmark especially since AllHell and the momentous day when Favius first made himself known to the denizens of the diabolically transformed Lake Misquamicus.

Indeed, even the cause of Ol' Man Crawdy's death was none other than Favius, who'd "popped th' smelly geezer's head right th' fuck off'n his neck stem," as well as staving in the brittle ribcage of a haggard barfly and bending one Zeke Bodean over a pool table to "do him the roughest raw-doggin'-est cornholin' ennybuddy ever seen'd in all their born life."

Having never met Zeke Bodean, unless seeing his severed head in a lettuce-keeper counted, June pictured him as another Lester Riggers type, a hulking redneck hayseed with more teeth than brain cells. She imagined his shocked, indignant bleating as Favius slammed him face-first into the ratty green felt and ruthlessly let him have it.

What a glorious, fucked-up scene it must have been!

The roadhouse hove into view, every bit the rundown and rustic cliche Spot had described and then some. Weedy dirt-and-gravel parking lot littered with broken glass from beer bottles, spent cig butts, and random garbage. Weathered, splintered boards. Corrugated tin sheets. Tattered tarpaper.

Peeling paint. Cracked, grimy windows.

A genuine Grade-A shithole, in other words. The kind of place that, if you saw it in a movie, you knew would be nothing but bad news for any wayward travelers who stopped to ask for directions.

On a normal day, at this hour, Crawdy's would have been at low ebb, not yet open for business, the regulars sleeping it off at home … or in their cars, or on the filthy floor, or in the bushes where they had fallen, depending.

Such was not the case today. The parking lot was packed with junkyard vehicles, everything from pickup trucks to station wagons to a vintage VW van, all heavily "modderfied" with defenses and "critter deterrents." The roadhouse's doors were chocked wide open. A banner hung between the porch supports, HELL SAVE THE QUEEN spray-painted on an old once-white sheet.

A veritable throng of what could only loosely be called "people" awaited. They spanned a spectrum of human, semi-human, human-ish, former human, and downright inhuman. While some of the more recent arrivals had already undergone drastic changes, these were the long-termers, upon whom the infernal environment had had *years* to take effect.

And, whoa nellie, did it show! Pork Chop's new look had nothing on a trio of four-hundred-pound bristly boarmen, whose long and thick twisty corkscrew-dicks jutted erect on prominent display. Xanne's cute little devil-horns could hardly hold up against the array of spiky draconian headgear sprouting from numerous distorted skulls. The limo driver's leathery yellow skin and sideways mouth paled in comparison to a scaled behemoth with gnashing alligators for arms and a ring-toothed lamprey maw taking up most of its chest. There was someone looking for all the world like a shitslug-centaur, human head and arms and torso, but mushy turd from the waist down, leaving a wet brown trail while undulating along. There was a rugose Lovecraftian mass of tentacles and eyestalks. A living visible-woman with jelly-clear flesh and translucent organs and a bony skeleton.

If the members of the military contingent also conducted themselves with rather more stringent discipline and sense of ceremony, such was not the case for the regular folks, the civilians, who whooped and hooted and hollered up a storm as the procession approached. They waved crudely hand-lettered signs, eviscerated themselves to offer up steaming-stinking piles of their own guts, slit each other's throats so carotid arteries spurted like shook champagne, hurled a macabre confetti of dried nipples and foreskins, crowd-surfed bloated corpses, and beachball-batted inflated stomachs with the esophagi and intestines tied off.

Among this crowd, also, were many more senior citizens and kids, many more out-of-shape or disabled bodies, and much more evidence of inbreeding, poverty, and deprivation. Yet, at the same time, an awful lot of the women were, to put it mildly, abundantly stacked, bodaciously bootied, or both.

For fuck's sake. Was it something in the water? When it had been water, anyway? While June saw no one quite so egregious as Jubblies, the ambulatory boob-creature who kept company with that sicko horror writer, she could hardly miss the topless werewolfy Amazon with triple-decker tits, or the sweet young thing in velour short-shorts and a tube top that did not seem up to the challenge.

"I must be out of my mind," June muttered.

She did the little wristy-wavey-wave, and her public went fucking gonzo nuts. They surged toward the popemobile, not an angry mob but a frenzied Beatlemania one.

Their advance line met her guards in a hockey-game clash that rocked the vehicle on its oversized wheels. June held on, ironically glad for the bulletproof shielding. Death by admiration rather than assassination suddenly seemed far more likely; these psychos would adore her to fucking *pieces*!

After a brief but energetic skirmish, a few scuffles, a couple warning shots, one not-a-warning shot, and assorted minor casualties, some semblance of order was restored.

"Everybody chill now?" Xanne inquired through a bullhorn. "Everybody chill, or do we have to carpet-bomb some fuckin' manners into you people?"

It got a laugh rather than offending them, which further helped bring the situation under control.

The popemobile limo had not been overturned, though its shield was no longer clean and pristine but covered in handprints, smooch-marks, tongue-slobber, and other smudges and smears the origins of which June preferred not to dwell upon.

Who was that actress finally getting her award? "You like

me! You really like me!"

Shit, if this was them liking her, June sure hoped she never pissed them off.

Iris stayed hunkered down in the classic duck-and-cover pose but risked a wide-eyed peek around once the tumult subsided. "Son of a bishop," she breathed. "An' I thought *I* was fangirlin' too hard."

"Not nearly," June said. "Unless you're creeping into my room at night to sniff my hair and watch me while I sleep."

"I would never—!"

"I know, only teasing."

"Well, I still would never."

The wounded—mostly bruises from blunt-force trauma—were seen to. The shot civilian insisted, "ain't nothin', jist a skritch," and, when they dug the bullet out, was thrilled to have a souvenir.

At Xanne's okay, with guards at the ready, Juggernaut looming nearby, and the driver going heavy on the dark-glasses Secret Service role, June emerged.

"That was quite a welcome," she said, eliciting another laugh. "I'm glad to see you too."

She delivered a quick speech, a condensed version of the one she'd done the previous night, more tailored to this specific audience. They ate it up, so she followed with a Q&A. Most of the Qs turned out to be not actual Qs but praise and pledges of fealty: *we'se luvs ya, Yer Highness! ... any fucknugget outsiders come at us agin, we'll show 'em what-fer! ... anythin' you need, you say's the word! ... my life for you! ...* and so on.

As she did a quick armed-escort walk-through, they pressed as close as would be allowed, clamoring to give her gifts, shake her hand, touch her cape, get her autograph. A woman thrust a swaddled newborn at her, begging her to "kiss 'r' kill it as y' will, m'lady, in Satan's name heller-loolyuh!" (unsure about either, June settled for sketching an inverted cross on the baby's forehead, which sent the mother into fits of effusive gratitude). A former-fratboy-type asked if she'd sign his dick, and got a gun butt to the teeth from Xanne instead. One of his buddies remarked she would've had to write real small anyway, a bimbo with them adding, "even though her name's only four letters," and the rest of their friends busted up. Some grubby kids presented June with a human heart wrapped in wax paper, explaining, "was our ma's, and we din't even think she had one 'til we follered yer 'xample an' had done with the mean ol' bitch." She thanked them kindly, promising to add it to the matricidal shrine at the lakeshore.

Returning to the limo, she found Spot waiting in the company of the sweet young thing she'd noticed earlier, plus a pair of hulking guys holding a bundle of gunnysack and twine between them—a suspiciously man-sized and man-shaped bundle of gunnysack and twine, moving in fitful struggles and twitches.

"Miz Yer Highness," Spot said, putting on his most servile, formal airs. "Might'n I innerduce Miz Maisy-Sue Kellerman an' her brothers Abel an' Abner? Long-time Crawdy's celebertees, all three. Miz Maisy-Sue's been Hock Party secon-placer some five years runnin', whilst Abel here holds the acc'racy record, an' Abner won a speshul judge's trophy fer the freestyle. They's here t' pay theirs r'spects an' prove their loyl'ty."

"Yes'm, we most surely is!" chirped the girl. "We's done brung'd ya a skunk-fuck traitor Bodean!"

Xanne raised an eyebrow at June as if to ask whether she should intervene or let this latest little stage play of weirdness unfold. June indicated it was okay for now, then turned her attention back to the "celebertees."

Up close, Maisy-Sue's lime-green velour short-shorts proved not only shorter than short but tighter than tight, camel-toe city, and her tube top must've held on by a wing and a prayer. She was maybe five foot two, cute, curvy-verging-on-chunky, with caramel-colored hair tied up in a bandanna, a wide mouth, and myopic brown eyes that probably could've used glasses.

Her brothers each topped six feet, built like tractors and none too bad to look at. Abel had longish blondish hair like straw and a gingery scruff of beard. Abner was darker, with rockabilly sideburns and greased pompadour. They both wore baggy jeans and battered work boots, Abel with a plaid flannel unbuttoned halfway to show a crop of gingery chest hair as well, Abner in a sweat-stained white tee-shirt with a tin of chewing tobacco rolled into one sleeve and a pack of smokes into the other.

"A Bodean, you say?" June glanced at Spot, who was puffed up as proud as if he'd made the capture himself.

"Heared how they was wanted fer questionin'," Abner said. "So, when we caught this here happy asshole peepin' 'round our sister's windah, we figger'd as we'd turn him over t' y'all rather'n string him up by the nuts."

"Though we did work him over some," Abel chimed in. "As a matter of famb'ly honor an' all."

"Of course," June said.

"Some nerve he had, all right," Maisy-Sue asserted. "Like he ain't seen me in the alt'gether plenny times here't this very place an' hocked his share'a loogies on me? He still gots t' try an' get an eyeful while I's takin' a bath? Some nerve indeed!"

"Indeed," June said. "So, who is he?"

Abner held the gunnysack while Abel undid the twine, and together, they dumped a disheveled figure onto the ground. His clothes were filthy. He was missing a shoe. Duct tape wrapped his wrists and ankles, with a strip of the grey adhesive plastered across his face as a gag. He had thinning hair, jug ears, and evidence of the brothers' working him over some was very apparent.

"Well, shit my britches!" Spot exclaimed, rocking back on his heels in delight. "Y'boys must be the early birds; caught you the *worm*!"

"What?" June asked.

"This here's none other'n Wormy Bodean," Spot said. "Real name's … Wayl'n, I think … but ever'one's called him Wormy since't even before AllHell."

Xanne regarded the captive dubiously. "Do we want to know why?"

"Prolly not."

"Oh, go on and tell us," June said.

Spot grinned. "Wellnow, y'know how's there's allus that one kid who'll eat worms? Like, alive an' wrigglin'? Not jist reg'lar earthworms neither but big ol' nightcrawlers? Give him a nickel an' he'd do it in front of the girls, t' make 'em go eew?"

Xanne snorted. "A worm-eater? Is that all?"

"Hell's bells it sure ain't!" Spot seemed insulted. "I weren't done yet. There's allus *that* kid, is what I'm sayin', but Wormy here? He took'd it a ways further!"

"Okay, okay, sorry," Xanne said. "Please go on."

"As I's sayin', when's he's 'bout 'leven or so, ol' Wormy's earnin' him some pocket change c'llectin' worms by the bucket, sellin' 'em as bait for tourists an' fishermen. Only, then, see, one day he gets him a stiffy, th' way boys do, an' takes it inta his head t'—"

"We get the picture," June said, but it was too late.

"—t' stick it in there, like, balls-deep, an' feels them worms all squirmin' all clammy 'gainst his pecker, an' he blows his first real load of dicksnot."

The duct-taped Wormy hunched in shame.

"Changed his whole blammed life! Why, fr'm then on," Spot said, "not even lee-git girl-snatch'd get him hot an' bothered half s' much as a packed-full can o' worms."

"That *is* pretty disgusting," Xanne said. She kicked a dirt clod at Wormy. "You're pretty disgusting. But if it's worms that get you off, what're you doing peeping in people's windows, you perv?"

"Had a jarful with him when we's found him spyin' on Maisy-Sue," Abel said.

"Tell 'em 'bout the gal from Luntville," Abner urged Spot.

"You tell 'em 'bout the gal from Luntville, you'se so revved up!"

Abner shook his head, slicked pompadour gleaming. "Cain't. Makes me near t' puke jist thinkin' it."

"I'se'll tell!" Maisy-Sue shot Wormy a spiteful smirk. "I'se'll tell *alllll* of it!"

Wormy made muffled imploring noises, writhing pitifully on the ground.

"So there's this gal from Luntville—" Spot began, and Maisy-Sue stomped on his toes. "Ow!"

"I said *I*'se'll tell it!"

"Fine, tells it already!"

"Hmf!" She turned to June and Xanne with a poison-sweet smile. "See, m'lady queenship, them Bodeans been trash goin' ages back, an' it got so's decent gals from better famb'lies wouln't as have much t' do with 'em. But then one day, this gal rolls through. This Luntville gal, hitcher-hikin', an' a real lowbrow slut, she was. Do anythin' for some 'shine or some smack or a dollar. Don't ask me how, but she sets her sights on Wormy here as if he's any kinda prize meal ticket. So they hooks up. Only, he's got his … whatchercall it … kink with the worms. C'n barely pop a boner otherwise. Well, he talks her inta lettin' him stuff her babymaker clear t' the brim with 'em!"

Abner had turned a sickly shade, and his gorge hitched, but he managed not to puke.

Maisy-Sue continued her spirited recitation. "*Then* he's good to go a fuckin', an' they have at it, over an' over, all night long. Trouble is, next day, they cain't get all the worms out. Too many, y'know, an' most of 'em dead, an' so far up'n her works even a coker-coler douchin' won't do the trick. They's rottin' in there, buncha dead worms up her cooter."

"Yer pardon—" Abner hiccupped, spun away, and yarked into the bushes. "'Polgies, I ...'" He hurled a second time.

June couldn't help thinking if he spat like he puked, no wonder he'd won a Hock Party special judge's award. The boy-warlock may have had him on force, volume, and distance, but there really was a peculiar freestyle panache to the way Abner did it.

Maisy-Sue, meanwhile, kept going. "An' wouldn'cha know, she got a 'fection an' up an' bought the damn farm, all on 'count of him and them worms!" She finished with another *hmf*, hands on hips in a *so-there* pose.

"Thought you said you was gonna tell all of it," Spot said. "That ain't the all of it t'all!"

"Is so!"

"Is ain't not! 'Cause after'n she died, Wormy dug'd her up, took'd her back t' his place, an' turned her c'daver inta a worm-farm!"

"He's right," Abel said. "Fed 'em on her 'til she was bare bones. But that still ain't even the worst part—"

Wormy tried again to protest through his duct tape gag.

Abner made a time-out signal. "No more, c'mon now, gimme a break; gonna barf m'self into a rupture."

"We've gone this far," Xanne said. "Let's hear the worst part."

Spot rubbed his hands together, gearing up, but Maisy-Sue leaped in and beat him to the punch.

"I'se r'member now! Turns *out*," she said with fiendish enjoyment, "he'd gotten bits a' dead worms jammed deep up his dickhole durin' all the fuckin', an' when AllHell come along, they re-annermated! So's now he ain't got no proper peter t'all, but a zomberfied worm-dick!"

"We'll take your word for it!" The last thing June needed was visual confirmation, thank you very much. "I ... appreciate you bringing him in. And if you run across any others, let us know."

"Sure as we will!" Maisy-Sue said. "Be a real treat t' see that cunty highpockets Lorlinda get what she d'serves!"

Most of the Crawdy's crowd followed along as they left, turning the parade into an impromptu mass pilgrimage to the height of Bighead Rock.

Mere weeks ago, any vehicle larger than a dirt bike or ATV might've had trouble making the ascent, but construction on the senatorial rotunda had necessitated widening the trail into a road navigable, if with some difficulty, by trucks and heavy equipment.

The pace car with its mecha-organic treads, of course, made it easily. For the popemobile limo, the trip was more of a challenge; Juggernaut disembarked to reduce weight and provided the occasional push as needed.

June hadn't been up there since the battle. Nor had she wanted to. Nor did she want to be there now, but it had to be done.

Despite some salvage and cleanup efforts, reminders of the destruction were everywhere: burn scars and char marks, a cratered blast-zone ten yards in diameter, bullet-strafed swaths of terrain, blood stains indelibly soaked into the rugged earth, scatterings of scavenger-picked bones.

The rotunda, designed and intended to look like a classical Roman structure, had become more of a classical Roman ruin instead, a jumble of rubble and cracked columns and fractured stairs. And three Senators, crushed to paste when the whole thing came crashing down. Also mixed among the debris was the wreckage of an absurdly apocalyptic hodge-podge frankentruck. Presumably with the wreckage of its driver, one Heck Bodean, still pinned behind the wheel. Several witnesses had later seen a ghostly version of the truck, already firmly established in local folklore.

June barely cared about any of that. Drawn as if by magnetism, she went to the place where Favius had last set foot. She knelt there, weeping.

How magnificent he'd been, a warrior, a centurion, a Hell-lord, towering high above his enemies, muscular and huge, his armor gleaming, the faces stitched into his skin silently shrieking their eternal torment.

How magnificent, only to be struck down by that asshole warlock and his whore-slut angel! Not even struck down in fair combat but by eldritch sorcery combined with divine power! The spells binding the suffering faces to him snipped, the tormented souls cut loose, released to descend upon Favius in a swarm of vengeful wrath … annihilating him, obliterating him … so thoroughly *nothing* was left.

"You couldn't just discorporate him or send him back to Hell, could you?" she said bitterly. "Oh, no. That way, I might have been able to find him, join him, be with him again. So you had to fucking *eradicate* him, forever, leaving me here alone, when I'd finally found some goddamn happiness!"

They would pay. So help her, Lucifer, they would pay. Never mind she'd wounded the warlock, then stabbed the angel and sliced off her wings; that was a mere pittance! They would pay *in full*. They would endure agonies and miseries the likes of which the most fiendish Arch-Dukes might flinch to contemplate!

"June? Earth to June."

She caught her breath and looked around to see Xanne waiting a respectful distance away. "What?"

"We're ready whenever you are."

There they were, all of them. Silent, solemn, the marching band hushed, the soldiers at formal attention. The previous celebratory mood had changed, turning funereal and grave. Even the wildlife had gone quiet, and the churning Charybdian whirlpool at the base of the rocky promontory seemed to have subsided.

June arose, shaking out her cape, wiping tears from her eyes. Whispers of the dark muses flitted through her mind — oratory, rhetoric, poetry, notable speeches, paraphrasings of Shakespeare — but she pushed them all aside.

"There are no words," she said. "There simply are no words for what I'm feeling, here and now. No words big enough, powerful or strong enough, encompassing enough."

She raised her gaze to the pinnacle of the Dome, where Star Wormwood no longer blazed its baleful fire and the *Aurora Diabolicus* sheeted in ripples of bloodlight.

"No words … but actions," she went on. "Bring me the child."

They brought her the child.

The little girl, the boy-warlock's kid sister, daughter of the snake-lady Senator, both of whom had met their gruesome ends atop this same rearing headland overlooking the vast and vile expanse of the lake.

Whose father, once known as Brother William, had arrived here a passenger upon the same Holy Roller church bus that had brought June herself. They, and the unfortunate Shinns, were the only survivors of that foolish expedition. Crusader Markane and the others had all met fairly gruesome ends of their own. Being armed and armored with their faith, as well as Kevlar vests, riot helmets, guns, and grenades, didn't mean much in a place like this.

They brought her the child, and if anyone had qualms, they hid those qualms well. She really was a cheery, spritely thing, a charming ragamuffin, disheveled masses of curly hair held askew by colorful plastic barrettes. Snub-nosed, gap-toothed, bright-eyed, freckle-faced—adorably so, not a disaster like Spot.

And, by all accounts, a complete pint-sized psycho.

June had, thus far, been able to avoid actually meeting her. It'd suited her fine to foist babysitting duties off on others. She did not need some chatterbox brat underfoot, least of all one who expected to be adopted and named a royal princess.

"Do I get my pony now?" The girl—Sherri, her name was—wore a striped terrycloth romper and flip-flops. Her knees were scabby. Someone at the camp had given her a recent junior mani-pedi, her finger- and toenails done in hot pink.

Corporal Lewis, bearing her perched on his shoulders, chuckled and patted her leg. "Not yet. First, you need to say hi to the queen."

"Ooh goodie!" Then she spotted June and lit right up. "Wowie! Is that her?"

"That's her." He swung the child down. Something flickered in his expression, maybe remorse, but he masked it quickly. "Go on over and see her."

"Yeah," said Pork Chop, snout crinkling his lips back from his tusks. "Maybe give her a nice big hug."

June and Xanne both shot him narrow looks. He ducked his head, abashedly snorting, and scuffed a trotter in the dirt.

Sherri, oblivious, skipped right up to June. For a moment, she thought the kid truly *was* going to hug her, and her skin tried to crawl counterclockwise around her entire body. But Sherri stopped, beaming as she surveyed June head to toe.

"I like your cape! I want one; can I have one just like

that? Where's your crown? Your helmet-thing is cool, but you should have a crown. Are you going to live in a castle? Gollygosh, you're scary! Maybe not very pretty, but you sure are scary! Is that a real sword? Have you killed lots of people with it? I haven't killed anybody, but I helped Billy agonistitize Daddy, and I saw the snake-babies kill each other."

"Uh …" was the best June could do.

"Billy was my brother, but he's dead now, him and Mommy too; that's what the soldier-lady with the neato horns told me." She waved at Xanne. "Hi, soldier-lady!"

"Hi, kid," Xanne said.

"I found a dolly in the lake after you came to my house. A magic talking dolly. Mr. Goblin. He was my bestest, bestest friend." A scowl darkened her features. "But the *pig-man* shot him all to bits. Itty bitty shitty bits. I don't *like* the pig-man."

"Hear that, Porkie? She doesn't like you."

"Said I was sorry," he muttered.

Sherri, meanwhile, skipped closer to the edge and pointed. "That's our house, over there. I couldn't see the whole fight, but there were 'splosions and black birds and a flying truck." She giggled. "And the king-demon-guy yelled the f-word *suuuper*-duper loud!"

"Favius," June said, moving behind her. "His name was Favius."

"What happened to him? He got *zgorched*, right? By the other warlock and the angel? A for-reals angel? They *zgorched* him?"

"They did. But they're going to pay, and you're going to help."

"Me? I get to help? Yayyy! What do I—?"

The rest was lost in a pained yelp as June seized a fistful of Sherri's unkempt hair, barrettes and all, and lifted her until her flip-flopped feet tippytoed, then left the ground.

"*Ave Luciferos!*" June cried. "For the glory of Hell, for memory and vengeance, for Favius and the Morningstar, I offer this sacrifice!"

Whipping the gladius from its scabbard with her other hand, she held its razor-sharp edge to the girl's throat.

"Ow! Ow, hey! Ow! Lemme go! That *huuuurts*! You're pulling my *haaaair*!" Sherri struggled and kicked, flip-flops flipping off, hot pink fingernails scrabbling at June's wrist.

"Let it be known, wheresoever they are, be it in realms earthly, infernal, or divine, I do this in warning to, and in forever cursing the existence and very essence of, my sworn foes!"

"Lemme *go*, you meanie poopie-head bad queen!"

"Thus do I swear!" Her Voice doubled and redoubled, filling the Dome. Smoky redblack energy coiled in sinuous wisps around her, wreathing her limbs and torso, forming a storm cloud aura. *"Warlock **Gregory Nachtwald**! Angel **Ethriel**! This child's blood I hereby spill, her life I take, and her soul I commit to eternal damnation, because of **you**!"*

A single slice, almost effortless, and tender young flesh parted like soft bread before a knife. Sherri's yelps and complaints drowned in a sudden gushing gurgle as artery, airway, and vocal cords were severed by the deep, clean cut. June felt the blade scrape juvenile neckbone, felt the little body go rigid and then arch like a bow.

As with her brother, it was almost hard to believe someone so small could contain *that* much fluid. Should have been, what, two or three liters at most? Looked like fucking *gallons*, a leaping sanguinary fountain, a miniature firehose jetting out over the precipice to rain down from Bighead Rock.

She also felt, fleeting but intensely powerful, a *connection*. A connection with the Adversaries she'd Invoked by Name. Letting them *know*, making them bear *witness* as the last dregs of the child's vitality drained away. She sensed their horrified reactions, their desperate futility. Wanting to do something, *anything*, to intervene.

Too late. The deed was done. Sherri went limp, lifeless deadweight suspended in June's redblack-gloved grasp.

She turned to the crowd of onlookers and held the corpse out to them, still dangling by the fistful of hair.

None of them appeared to know how to respond. A few, like Corporal Lewis, bowed their heads or averted their eyes. Pork Chop looked torn between brutal satisfaction and "oh shit she really did it."

"She wanted to be a princess," June said. "Therefore, let her be entombed in glass, visible to all but untouchable. Such is my Will."

"So shall it be," Xanne and several others responded automatically.

No further speechmaking or ceremony seemed called for.

As conversation and activity resumed, June handed Sherri back over to Corporal Lewis again. He took her, so tiny and limp in his arms, bled pale, her feet bare, her head lolling. Such had been the force of the fatal gouting spray, hardly any had spattered her striped terrycloth romper.

With only the barest hint of reproach, he said, "She was just a kid."

"Yes," June agreed. "Which makes it that much the worse."

Which, of course, was kind of the point.

"Yeah." Lewis closed Sherri's wide, staring eyes. Unlike in the movies, it required more than a gentle pass of a hand; he had to apply some firm pressure. "Permission to stay with her until it's taken care of?"

"Granted."

He carried her off toward a patch of shade. June wiped clean the gladius—she thought about licking the blood from the blade but decided that might be overdoing it—and sheathed it, then joined Xanne, Iris, and the driver beside the limo.

"We'll continue on to Senator Carmichael's as planned," she told them. "Send someone ahead to let them know when to expect us."

An hour or so later, the main body of the processional was ready to move on.

A contingent had split off to return to the war camp, to put Wormy Bodean into custody to await full interrogation, as well as to arrange for the materials for and construction of the little girl's fairy-tale princess glass coffin.

No "love's first kiss" to waken her, though. No evil spell to be broken. No helpful forest animal companions, handsome prince, singing, or happily-ever-after. She was dead, full-stop d-e-a-d.

Just a kid.

Far from innocent; hardly anything here could honestly be called innocent. But, still and all, just a kid.

Whose throat June had slit. A cold, callous, deliberate, matter-of-fact, purposeful act. Not spurred by decades of bitter resentment, as the matricide had been. Not out of a twisted pity, like the *coup de grace* for Brother Ramon. It hadn't been self-defense, it hadn't been revenge, it hadn't been rage.

Sacrifice, plain and simple.

Nothing particularly personal against the kid—annoying brat though she'd been; someone would have needed to shut her up sooner or later, for the sake of sanity. And maybe June wasn't the biggest fan of children in general (understatement of the year), but as long as she didn't have to deal with them, overall she could live and let live.

Still, she supposed, under the circumstances, she should have felt at least a smidgen of guilt, a moral twinge. Some sort of remorse. The vestiges of a conscience, a shred of human decency.

Instead, she left Corporal Lewis to sit his solitary vigil beside the small tarp-covered corpse, and got back to business.

It wasn't as if the death of one child would undo what had been done. It wouldn't bring Favius back. The deaths of a thousand, a million, *ten* million wouldn't accomplish that—though, if she thought there was the proverbial snowball's chance in Hell it might, she would have lined them up and scythed them down without hesitation.

The best she could hope for was to see the warlock and angel share even a fraction of her loss. To *hurt* them, hurt them as *she* hurt, give them a sampling of *her* grief.

Still wouldn't be anywhere near enough.

Wherever they were now, she took some solace in knowing they *knew*. They knew, and there wasn't diddlyshit they could do about it.

And, if it made them want to try to do something? If it spurred them to seeking righteous justice? To take her to task and call her to account for her crime? Thereby bringing them back within her reach?

Well, that'd be perfect. Let them try.

A none-too-subtle throat clearing interrupted her pensive mullings.

"Miz Yer Highness?"

"What is it, Spot?"

"We'se 'bout set t' go, but, uhm, the Kellermans, they was wonderin' if'n they should mebbe oughta stick 'round. In case y' wanted t' see 'em or sumpin, since't as how they brung in Wormy an' all."

"Why? He's already been carted off to the camp, but any questioning will have to wait until this little excursion is over. If they'd like to be there for it, you can take care of the arrangements."

Be there to watch, of course. Watch a Bodean be interrogated, maybe by old-school techniques, maybe by adaptations of more modern methods—piss-boarding, she'd heard, was a favorite—or something altogether new and original. Clearly, these Kellermans shared Spot's grudge against the entire clan, heightened by Maisy-Sue's rivalry with Lorlinda over the status of Hock Party "cham-peen."

He bowed and scraped. "I'se'll do that for a certain, an' no doubt. Thankyas! Much 'ppreciated!"

"Make some popcorn, enjoy the show."

"Bet as I will!" Spot chortled, then paused, all 'xpectant-like, as he might have put it.

"Something else?" June asked when he showed no signs of shoving off.

"Uhm, well, jist, izzat all?"

"What do you mean, is that all?"

"Jist, onliest, y'know, they was wonderin' if'n there's t'be some kinda … well … comper'sayshern."

"Compensation," June repeated. "You mean a reward? A bounty? A token of gratitude? That kind of thing?"

"More'r'less, I guess? Not t' pr'sume, or—"

"I thought they'd … how did you put it? Come to pay their respects, show their loyalty."

His head bobbled like it was on a spring. "Oh, abs'lutely an' fer sher, no doubts 'bout that! All r'spects, loy'lty t' the moon an' back! Y' c'n count on th' Kellermans. Stake m' nuts on it!"

"Then why do they think they deserve a reward? Aren't they just being good citizens, doing their civic duty?"

Greasy sweat beaded on his acne-studded, pock-marked brow and trickled in oily rivulets through clusters of pustules at his temples. He scratched nervously at his jawline, popping a row of ripe zits like bubble wrap.

"Now hey there please Miz Yer Highness, hold th' phone a secon'; let's not git ahead of ourselfs," he stammered hastily. "I din't say they's thinkin' they *d'serves* no r'ward, an' *I* ain't sayin' they *d'serves* nothin' neither. Ain't how I meant it t'all, not hardly!"

"I'm glad we cleared that up." She let him dangle for a

while longer, then decided to let him off the hook. "However, it's a good point. They did go to all the trouble when they could have turned a blind eye. And we want to encourage people to do the right thing, don't we? In the best interests of the entire realm."

Gulping, Spot bobbled his head again. She briefly imagined dunking him in a barrel of peroxide; he'd probably fizz up like a giant Alka-Seltzer. Shit; he'd probably *dissolve* like a giant Alka-Seltzer.

"Showin' folks how gen'rous an' magnannermus y'are from time t' time ain't such a bad idear," he said. "Tol' Hiz Highness the very same more'n once, an' he reckernized some wisdom in it, all right."

"I'm sure he did," June said. "Of course, we both know he also recognized the wisdom in gratuitous displays of sadistic violence, torture, and abuse."

"At which he done a first-class job, an' so you'se been doin' too! First-class! Ain't no one c'n deny! Goes t'gether, though, don't they? Stick *an'* carrot?"

"True, very true." She glimpsed Xanne doing the two-fingers-tapping-the-wrist universal signal for "time to get this show on the road!" and bestowed a half-benevolent, half-merciless smile on Spot. "Tell you what," she said. "Invite the Kellermans to accompany us to the Senator's house, and I will see about coming up with something ... fitting ... in the way of royal largesse."

He bowed and scraped some more, so overwhelmed with relief she thought his wobbly knees might give out. "Def'nitely, you gots it, gonna go tells 'em right now!"

As he scurried off in the direction of Maisy-Sue and her husky brothers, June found Lyle for a quick touch-up, then boarded the limo. She was glad to see someone had squeegeed all the smear-marks and slobber from the transparent shielding. The AC was most welcome after being out in the balmy heat, and Iris had cool drinks waiting.

"What was Spot so in a dither 'bout?" Iris asked.

"My magnanimity and gratitude," June said. "Mustn't let the Kellermans feel unappreciated for bringing in such an obvious threat to national security."

"Pff, no secret, his and their grudges 'gainst the Bodeans. Never quite got to full-on feuding, with headers an' such, but they've all been sour lemons at each other for years."

"Headers?"

"Ultimate insult from way long ago. Didn't used to happen so much anymore, though after AllHell, the practice may've made a comeback." She considered. "If it ever was a real thing, I mean. Could be just backwoods legend. My father, he was of the 'pinion it was all talk; who would go t' so much trouble, drilling holes in peoples' heads t' fuck their brains?"

"Aaaand once again sorry I asked." June sipped her drink. "That's really how it was out here, even *before* the demons?"

"Maybe that's why Hell chose this place."

"Maybe."

Favius had been in the process of having plans drawn up for a palatial Roman villa worthy of the greatest emperors of old, lavish and decadent, a grand monument to power and excess. With many a Mephistopolian touch as well, of course; all the better to glorify Hell!

Late at night, between bouts of vigorous sex, he'd curl June in his arm and describe his vision to her in detail: marble, alabaster, mosaics made from precious stones and polished bone, statues, gilding, banquet hall, vomitorium, bathing complex with three different temperatures of swimming pool plus saunas, massage salons, grand gardens, olive groves, vineyards, an exotic menagerie, etc.

Trevor Carmichael, on the other hand, must've just let his imagination and horndog hormones run amok, and his parents' former lakehouse (which was no longer really a lakehouse, or even a house at all, strictly speaking) obliged, catering to his every hedonistic party-pad whim.

The results, June thought as she got her first good look at the place, were like an insane mash-up of Playboy Mansion, *MTV Cribs*, *Lifestyles of the Rich and Famous*, Caesar's Palace, the Marquis de Sade, and the 1979 "erotic historical drama" (aka "softcore porn") *Caligula* movie.

What Favius would've made of it, she couldn't begin to guess. Laugh? Approve? Take offense?

It was garish and gaudy, almost cartoonish in its obscene debauchery. The young Senator's amputation fetish featured prominently throughout, including a version of the Venus de Milo the Louvre wouldn't have touched with a fifty-foot pole, and a ceiling mural take on Goya's masterpiece of "Saturn Devouring His Son."

The shifting impermanence of everything only added to its surreality, as if the entire structure was CGI illusion, special effects, subject to change without notice. It made June uneasy in ways she couldn't define beyond the rock-solid certainty she was *not* spending the night. However luxurious a suite had been conjured for her, how hurt or insulted Carmichael might be by any perceived snub, no-way-no-how-no-thanks. She'd make the entire procession trek back to the camp, or sleep in the limo if she had to, before she'd stay there.

TBH, it took some mustering of nerve and girding of loins even to step inside. She couldn't shake the notion it might all disappear, warp out of existence in a split-second, taking everyone with it. Many in her entourage shared the sentiment, with no shortage of volunteers to remain outside standing guard.

Which, given the reputation Ol' Hornyshell had along this stretch of lakeshore, June was more than willing to grant. The Geiger-esque pace car probably could outrun or fight off a giant prong-dicked dino-turtle, but she wasn't eager to find out how well the popemobile's bulletproof shielding withstood *that* kind of assault. The other, more vulnerable vehicles wouldn't stand a chance, and vehicles of any kind were a rare, hard-to-get commodity these days.

In the end, she decided only a small contingent would accompany her inside for the evening's entertainments. No need to stress their host's hospitality, right? Xanne, Iris, Lyle, and Juggernaut … Spot … the Kellermans, since she'd extended the invitation … Meep, in case she needed to send any urgent messages … and a handful of others selected at random.

Trevor Carmichael had met them on the front steps. June hadn't seen him in person since shortly after the battle, when he'd approached her to plead on behalf of his sister, but even in that amount of time, he had undergone some minor changes of his own. Still a fit, handsome, well-bred college-aged pretty boy, his hair now flowed to his shoulders in a leonine mane, his lips had taken on a more plumply sensuous quality than before, and he had the hooded eyes of a dissolute libertine.

Instead of satin loungewear or velvet smoking jacket, as might be expected, he was dressed for a casual yet stylish afternoon on the French Riviera. He was flanked by rows of attractive, scantily-clad men and women … all notably missing at least one body part.

Introductions were made, refreshments offered, a brief tour given. It quickly became very apparent that the entire household, barring Trevor himself, had undergone some form of amputation, voluntarily or otherwise.

Many were fairly minor; an earlobe here, a pinkie-finger or baby toe there. Others were minus portions of, or entire, limbs ... or more. An armless beauty played piano with her feet. An athletic youth went about on all fours, the fours being the stumps where his elbows and knees used to be. A muscular man, truncated at the waist, propelled himself by means of swinging along on gorgeously toned arms. A slender woman, reduced to nothing but head and torso, moved in sinuous inchworm undulations.

Whether they were legitimately happy with their situation, masochistically kinky, insane, or doped out of their minds on the free-flowing substances available in every room, June wasn't sure and didn't want to ask. But none of them—with one exception—seemed to have any complaints.

That one exception, however? Oh, she would have complained plenty, were she capable.

"I thought you might like to see her again," Trevor said, ushering June into a round room where his sister Chelsea hung, suspended nude, in a kind of sex-swing/hammock.

Once again, if looks could kill ...

But, thankfully, in most cases (barring gorgons and such), they couldn't, so June was not stabbed to death by the daggers of sheer venomous hatred shooting from her former handmaiden's eyes.

And it seemed the vocal cord paralysis spell was still effectual, or else her delicate sensibilities might have been shocked; Chelsea's face went red, throat quivering with the effort as she mutely screamed and swore and no doubt spewed torrents of blistering profanity.

"I certainly don't think *she's* very glad to see *me*," June said, amused.

"She's never very glad to see me either," Trevor confessed.

June tutted. "Her own devoted brother? And after everything you've done for her."

"I know, right?"

The arrangement of netting and straps quivered as Chelsea

tried to leap at them, though what she would have done had she succeeded—bite their ankles?—was anyone's guess.

"Well, well," June said, circling her. "Look at you. Lost some weight, haven't you?"

Chelsea went from red to purple. If her head had exploded like in *Scanners*, June wouldn't have been too surprised.

She had indeed lost some weight, though. In addition to that of the arms Juggernaut had wrenched off at the shoulders, her legs now ended mid-thigh. With, June couldn't help but observe, several inches of the lower femur removed from each, creating puckered Fleshlight-ish orifices in the smooth stump-skin.

Orifices which, it was all too obvious, had been put to some use.

June extended a finger, then paused. "May I?" she asked Trevor.

"Please do," he said, breathing heavier. "You're the queen."

"Yes, I am." She touched Chelsea's right thigh-stump, running her fingertips over it, as Chelsea tossed and thrashed in the hammock. "Oh, are you ticklish?"

Chelsea's body bucked.

"Watch out," Trevor said. "She might try and pee on you."

"That wouldn't be very polite. Hardly befitting the sister of a Senator."

"I can have someone diaper her, if—"

"No, no." June smiled down at Chelsea. It was her special smile. "She'll behave. Isn't that so, Miss Carmichael?"

Shuddering, Chelsea turned her head away, squeezing her eyes tightly shut. Tears streamed from their corners as June probed curiously at the thigh-hole.

Trevor watched, licking his plumply sensuous lips.

"You've fucked these, of course?" she asked, slowly inserting her forefinger.

"Before they were even healed," he said huskily. "I couldn't wait."

June worked in a second finger. "Nice and tight, isn't she?"

"So tight."

"Show me?"

He wasted no time, undoing his pants and freeing a quite nice-looking cock. June had no way of knowing if it was the original model or had also undergone some enhancements, but regarded it with appreciation as he lubed it up and slid it into Chelsea's left thigh-hole, sighing in pleasure.

Never in her life would she have expected this either … to be finger-fucking one thigh-stump of the treacherous little bitch who'd backstabbed her while the treacherous little bitch's brother deeply dick-fucked the other.

Strangely hot, though. Quite a nasty turn-on. She suddenly understood Trevor Carmichael somewhat better. And the sight of his erection thrusting into that unnatural orifice, his lustful expression, the taut flex of his shapely ass as his hips moved in languid rhythm …

She altered the motion of her fingers to match while slipping her other hand under her battle-skirt to address the slick, needful warmth pulsating between her own thighs.

Chelsea, meanwhile, ungrateful creature that she was, didn't seem to appreciate the attention at all. She carried on thrashing, and did spray some pee, but it only rained harmlessly onto the tile.

Trevor's gaze flicked rapidly from the glistening shaft of his cock pushing in and out of Chelsea's stump, to June's fingers—she had three in there now—buried in the other, to the unabashed motions of June frigging herself. He came so hard his knees buckled, folding his upper body onto his sister, his head pillowed on her tits. Which, June did have to acknowledge, *were* exemplary. The hammock creaked but held. Chelsea bucked again, gnashing her jaws, snapping her teeth at him, but couldn't reach.

June's own climax followed moments later, waves of delicious thrilling heat rolling through her body. She rode them out, then stepped back, exhaling with a near-purr.

"My goodness, Senator; I was told you had some special entertainment in mind, but you do go above and beyond, don't you?"

"Majesty, I will entertain you in any way you desire." He withdrew, either still semi-hard or already gearing up for more—ah, the refractory period of the young and healthy!—and licked his lips again, sweeping her with a hungry look. "*Any* way you desire."

"I won't say I'm not tempted," she said, and it was true. "But I did make a promise, and it would be a shame to have to kill you."

"Kill me?"

"Mmm-hmm. After. My oath to Favius."

He wilted slightly. "Yeah, okay, fair enough."

As he adjusted his clothes, June turned to Chelsea again.

"And you," she chided, "you didn't seem to enjoy that very much. Hasn't your brother been treating you well?"

"I mean," Trevor said, zipping his fly, "no one's *fucked-her* fucked her. No oral, no anal either. She's had plenty of opportunities, but she always turns them down. Which is weird because—no offense, Chels—she used to be a total slut. The first night we got here, after a few drinks, she was all set to go down on *me*. Just to prove she was the better cocksucker and settle a bet, maybe, but still."

"Are you telling me, even *you* haven't—"

"Only the stumps. Since she *is* my sister, anything else seemed kind of … inappropriate."

Chelsea's eyes bugged at him with almost comical furious outrage. *Inappropriate?* she seemed to be silently shrieking. *You cut my legs off, fuck my stump-holes, let your sex-slaves jizz and piss all over me, and suddenly you're concerned about what's* **inappropriate?!**

"Well, no wonder she's in such a bad mood," June said.

"So, I was thinking," he went on, "for tonight's actual special entertainment, I'd like to ask *you* to call the shots."

"Me?" said June.

Her?! Chelsea's horrified, revolted gape said.

"Yeah. Whatever you want done, we'll have it done. Something cut off? Say the word. Nipples? Tits? Clit? You got it. Nose? Ears? Lips? Decapitation? Cut in half? Anything goes."

"That *is* very generous, Senator, but don't you think it might go too far? I wouldn't want to damage your property."

He shrugged. "You're the queen."

"Yes, I am." June regarded Chelsea, savoring her terror. "And, as it happens, I recently learned of a quaint local tradition I'd simply *love* to see demonstrated … particularly if your hired man is available."

Funny how quickly something could go from being an ultimate taboo to no big deal.

Cannibalism, for instance.

At first, when she'd begun to suspect what was really

going on in the war camp's mess tents, June had been aghast and appalled and sick to her stomach.

The very *idea*, etc. etc.

A line *never* to be crossed, from which there was *no* coming back, no hope of forgiveness or salvation.

All those stories about lifeboats of adrift shipwrecked sailors, the Donner party, people forced to do the unthinkable in order to survive, and how they could possibly live with themselves afterward. Isolated, primitive tribes. Serial killers both real and fictional. Dark web hookup sites catering to both predator and prey.

The most horrible, heinous, evil transgression. And so on.

She'd told herself, early on, she would *not* go there. Wouldn't fall that far, sink that low. Sex, murder, matricide, torture, okay. Cannibalism? Off the table. So to speak. Maybe she couldn't stop others from doing it, but she could keep *some* small corner of her soul untainted.

Noble. Lofty. Idealistic.

Yeah, right.

As if it'd make a difference on Judgment Day. As if she could stand there and say, "At least I didn't eat human flesh," after everything else she *had* done.

But, well, when in Rome … or in Hell …

And it really wasn't such a big deal, when you got right down to brass tacks. Meat was meat. Why should it go to waste? Why bury it or burn it or let it rot when it could feed the hungry? When resources were scarce and hard to come by, why squander any option?

Especially when it came to soldiers and supplying the troops; didn't Napoleon or some other historical general say how an army marched on its stomach? No one could be expected to fight and die for king, cause, or country while starving.

Besides, setting aside the various reasonings and rationales …

Well, it didn't taste half-bad.

In fact, properly prepared, it was fucking delicious.

It didn't even have to be done to Chef Emilio's elevated standards of high-end cuisine; down-home country cookin' could do the job just as well.

And, under the stern supervision of Mrs. Riggers, Senator Carmichael's culinary team had more than risen to the occasion.

Savory. Succulent. Fall-off-the-bone fork-tender. Melt in the mouth.

Slow-smoked, grilled, charbroiled, pan-seared. Juicy patties, marbled steaks. Thin-sliced cold cuts. Fried fat-cracklins. Platters of bone-in "wings" (with knuckles, the nails like chitinous shrimp-tails) ranging from honey-sweet to diablo-spicy. Steamed, stuffed dumplings.

It was quite a spread, accompanied by all manner of side dishes and salads and fresh-baked breads, served buffet style. The dessert selections were equally varied, be it fresh fruit dusted with coconut shavings, rich and creamy custard pie, or a blood-chocolate lava cake dark and decadent enough to need a new category of sin all on its own.

Upon a separate table, a nude man and woman lay side by side, their heads at opposite ends. Both were missing their right arms and legs, their bodies placed so close together that the hip-stump of each pressed against the shoulder-stump of the other, thus forming an artistic living platter upon which were a decorative array of hors d'oeuvres, sushi starters, and canapes.

The open bar did not disappoint either. Its centerpiece, an ice-sculpture in the form of an exquisite headless and limbless male torso, spouted chilled wine from all five stumps in a cascading magenta fountain.

Servants circulated, bearing trays of additional treats of a more recreational variety: joints, mushrooms, candy-dishes of pills. One carried a glass terrarium in which tiny, brightly-hued six-legged psychedelic frogs hopped about; another wore a scuba-sized tank of an opium pipe, from which snaked half a dozen inhaling-tubes.

There were also musicians, dancers, acrobats, contortionists, spontaneous sex-shows, and the occasional amputation as precursors to the evening's promised upcoming main entertainment.

"Okay, so he's a weirdo pervert," Xanne said, "but he *does* know how to put on one hell of a party!"

With Xanne's sentiment, no one could argue.

The Kellermans in particular; Maisy-Sue and her hunky brothers, having never experienced anything even *approximating* the likes of *this* before, were speechless. They gawked around as if they'd suddenly been dropped into an amazing alien world and the folks back home would never believe a word of it.

Spot was also speechless but because his mouth was full; he kept stuffing his face like there was no tomorrow. For someone as scrawny as him to have already consumed probably twice his own body weight was its own testimony to the powers of Gluttony. He was smeared with barbecue sauce from sternum to eyebrows, which couldn't be good for his complexion but at least masked the worst of it for the time being.

Iris wasn't so much speechless as quiet, possibly overwhelmed by the constant onslaught of stimuli or wracked by nerves. The plain, shy girl amid the popular, beautiful people. The awkward wallflower, the ugly duckling. Out of place and out of her depth. Or maybe, just maybe, it was something else; June had caught her sneaking glances at Abel Kellerman when she thought no one was looking.

Lyle, on the other hand, was not speechless. Oh, no; he was far, far from it. Lyle, devils-love-him, had gone into full Carson Kressley mode, gushing nonstop effusive and flamboyant commentary. He could have been covering a Hollywood premiere or New York society gala, switching from compliments to catty remarks quick enough to give a person whiplash. June might have been annoyed at him out-queening the queen, but he was just too funny to get mad at.

Rather, she only wished—as she always wished, every second of every day—that Favius could have been here with her to enjoy this outlandish spectacle. She thought even he, despite the cartoonish *Caligula* aspects to it all, would be favorably impressed.

Trevor's friend, the local horror writer / movie maker, had been on the guest list but unfortunately needed to beg off last minute due to deadlines and his nitpicky proofreader and pressure from his publisher. Apparently, however much of a toll the Painwave had taken on the rest of the world, it hadn't interfered much with the business of marketing sick, gory, blasphemous smut. The fact of there being a thriving audience for such fucked-up stuff continued to boggle her mind. What was *wrong* with those people?!

"He sends his apologies," Trevor said, "and an advance reading copy of his latest book to make up for it."

"That's … very kind of him," June said, diplomatically accepting the paperback without flinching or grimacing.

It had a black bar across the cover, printed with NOT FOR RESALE, but the bar did little to hide the graphic, grotesque nature of the cover art. When she made the mistake of turning it over to read the text on the back, the idea of an *en suite* vomitorium seemed perfectly logical.

"He's going to be sorry he missed the entertainment, though," Trevor went on. "Do you think it'd be okay if I had someone record it for him?"

"After what *I* got filmed doing?" She scoffed. "You can broadcast it, put it online, if you like. I'll have Meep ... where's Meep?"

"Right here, ma'am!" Returning from another foray through the buffet, balancing a plate piled perilously high and a brimming pint glass, he nonetheless managed a snappy salute.

"Before you dig in again, round up a camera crew." As the lad set down his load and dashed off, June turned to Trevor. "Might as well do this properly."

"Majesty." He bowed. Then, greatly daring, he caught up her hand and kissed it. "Such *fingers* you have ..."

"Don't you even think about cutting any of them off, Senator."

"I wouldn't dare."

"You're lying."

"Totally lying." He released her.

"Gawrsh-*sakes* but he c'n cut *mine* off *any* ol' time," Maisy-Sue blurted before clapping a hand over her mouth and blushing nine shades of *oh-shit-I-said-that-out-loud*.

Everyone looked at her, most with varying degrees of amusement, and Trevor with a speculative interest that diverted both Kellerman brothers' attention from Maisy-Sue to him.

"Now, beggin' yer pardon, Mr. Senator sir," said Abner. "She may be a grow'd woman who c'n make her own decisions an' all, but on our folks's behalf, we'd 'preciate you not—"

"Cross-an'-bless it, Abner!" Maisy-Sue swatted his arm. "How'm I ever gonna meet fellas if'n you big lugs keep buttin' in?"

"You meet enuff fellas already," Abel said. "Ain't you *met* half the fellas 'round the lake anyways?"

"Abel!"

"It's our *folks* I'se thinkin' of," Abner protested. "They's gettin' on in years, needin' help now more'n ever, an' how's you gonna take care of 'em an' keep up the house with any yer parts lopped off?"

"What, like it'd kill *you* stone dead t' warsh a dish or sweep a floor now'n'then?"

"That's wimmin's work—" Abel began.

"That's sexist diner-saur bullshit's what *that* is!" she retorted.

Xanne and Lyle overlapped each other: "Fuckin' A!" / "Preach it, girlfriend!" Spot didn't say anything, if only because of a mouth crammed overfull of sweet potato pie. Iris, seeming conflicted, also kept quiet, darting another surreptitious glance at Abel as if re-evaluating.

Trevor, who did possess some wisdom and discretion, or at least the good sense to not want his ass kicked, laughed it off. "Hey, family stuff; I know how it is. No worries. All friends here, right?"

"Right," June said in a tone to suggest the subject was closed. "We have plenty of enemies as it is without making new ones."

Spot forcefully swallowed his way-too-big bite, making his skinny neck bulge like a snake trying to get a gerbil down its gullet. He thudded a fist against his bony sternum, belched gustily, cleared his throat, and spoke up. "En'mies in common too … Bodeans 'specially. Sure, Heck an' Zeke an' Clarabeth's deader'n shit, but Lorlinda must still be out there somewheres, an' no tellin' what the rest of 'em might be up to."

"Tha'ss why we brung in Wormy," Abner said. "Reckon he oughta know somethin', or leastways know who *would* know."

"Jist *let* Lorlinda show her skanky-pants self 'round here!" snarled Maisy-Sue. "I'll twist her titties an' cunt-kick her *so* hard—!"

"When's you gonna r'sume the Hock Parties, anyway?" Abel asked Spot. "I mean, y'are, ain'tcha?"

"Been a li'l busy!" Spot said. "Tryin' t' help run a *kingdom* here, 'n case ya hadn't noticed!"

Abner leaned back, tucking a wad of chaw into his cheek. "Yeah, but been *weeks* now, an'—"

"An' you set'cher eyes on Maisy-Sue takin' the prize, what

with Lorlinda outta the picture," Spot retorted. "Ain't gotta be no rocket surgeon t' figgure that one."

"I don't *needs* her out the picture t' win!" objected Maisy-Sue. "I needs fair judges what ain't been swayed an' 'testants what don't *cheat*! A lev'l playin' field, like!"

"We done *had* this conv'sation before! Nobody been *cheatin'* —"

"I'm sure the Hock Parties will be back on schedule before too long," June said in an attempt to quell their bickering. "It'd be a real shame to let such a cherished custom fall by the wayside when it clearly means so much to so many."

How she got through this little speechlet without grimacing, she wasn't sure, but she did it. These hicks and their gross, nasty Hock Parties ...

"Hope so," Maisy-Sue said, giving June a grateful smile. "May seem silly, but it's 'portant t' us."

"Part'n our history an' culture," Abel agreed. "Our self-dennity, even."

"We gots *rights*," Abner added.

Rights, yes. Endowed by their Creator with certain inalienable *rights*, even the right of inbred yeehaws to spit on naked women. Maybe it fell under "pursuit of happiness?" Phlegmy, snotty, slimy happiness?

Across the room, she saw Meep signaling her, camera crew in tow, and realized how utterly ridiculous she was being.

Fretting about Hock Parties when something so, *so* much nastier was in store!

Young Senator Carmichael seemed a natural showman, who probably could've been a theater kid had such pursuits not been deemed "nerdy" and "uncool" by the popular, well-to-do circles in which he'd run.

"Thank you all for being here," he said, addressing the audience without a hint of stage fright. "I'd had some special entertainments planned for you tonight, but, by the generous grace of Her Majesty" —inclining his head toward June, seated in a place of honor, he paused to let them clap and cheer—"I'm delighted to be presenting something *extra* special instead."

The guests and select members of the household had been ushered into a windowless fan-shaped room June didn't think had been there before, or at least she hadn't seen it on her earlier tour. It may have manifested solely for the occasion, designed like a smallish concert hall, with tiered rows of seats and a central stage. The stage was obscured by a lush royal-blue curtain trimmed in gold, spotlights playing teasingly over it. Subtle background music issued from hidden speakers, a classical piece she couldn't immediately identify. Prokofiev, maybe?

The camera crew had set up in the orchestra pit, boom mics and zoom lenses and all. A couple of the cyclopean dragonfly-drone things hovered to catch the action from various angles and pan across the expectant sea of faces.

"Many of you know, or know *of*, my sister Chelsea," Trevor went on. He paused again for a rustle of reaction, not quite boos and hisses but close. "Many of you feel she should have been executed for her treacherous, treasonous attack upon the person of our queen."

"Backstabbin' *bitch*!" someone shouted.

Others chimed in.

"Death's too good for the likes of her!"

"Cru-ci-FY! Cru-ci-FY!"

"*Juno Regina*; long live the queen!"

"I must admit," Trevor said, dropping the formality. "It put me in a hell of a pinch. I mean, yes … betrayal, attempted assassination … but Chels still *is* my sister. Family is family, family ties are important; that's become a *lot* more clear to me, since being here, than it ever was before. You, my neighbors, have shown me that, by your example. Made me appreciate it in ways I never had."

A scattered ripple of "awww"s, sounding genuinely touched, arose. Trevor acknowledged them, nodding, displaying such heartfelt humility even June almost fell for it.

"So, what was I to do?" he asked them. "The rest of my family's far from here; they might as well be dead to me, and me to them. Chels is the only one I have left. But Chels, as pointed out, is a backstabbing bitch! How could I tolerate, let alone condone, her actions? A blight, a blot, on our family's reputation?"

The dark muses Favius had spoken of evidently must've favored Trevor Carmichael as well; he had the audience in the palm of his hand, rapt and sympathetic. Impressed as she was, June made a mental note to keep a close eye on him, because if he *did* turn against her, he could be a real problem.

"And I also admit," he went on, "my family's reputation, around here where it counted, was … pretty shitty. Our parents were elitist snobs who thought they were better than everyone else. Sure, they paid well; our dad's solution to anything was 'throw enough money at it.' Money and power were what they respected, no matter who they had to step on or walk all over to get it. That's how they raised us, and when Chelsea and I first came back to the lake, that's how we were. You, especially you locals and long-timers, had every reason to hate and resent us, and I wouldn't have blamed you. We showed no respect for what you'd built here, how you'd struggled, everything you'd been through."

He shook his head ruefully.

"We were wrong. So wrong. To us, this was just another vacation getaway. To *you*, with your roots and community and history, it's *home*."

From her place of honor, June had a good view of Ronny Riggers cradling the heads of his ma and pa grafted to his sides. Mr. and Mrs. Riggers were damn near moved to tears. So were several others. Maisy-Sue wasn't the only one who looked positively love-struck.

Only Spot, of the locals, didn't seem to have gone for it hook, line, and sinker; that, or he was wary of his own status being usurped, skeevy rat-weasel as he was.

"Home," Trevor repeated. "The idea didn't mean much to me until just recently. This … house, this strange and wonderful whatever-it-is, accepted me. *You*, my *neighbors*, welcomed me. I finally felt a sense of community, of belonging, of *home*, I'd been missing."

"And discovered stump-humping," Xanne muttered.

June shushed her.

"Then, my own *sister* …" He trailed off as if it were too terrible, too painful, to mention again. "When she survived her initial punishment, yes, I did appeal to the queen, but I did it for my own reasons, my own selfish reasons. Not for Chelsea. Chelsea, I told myself, hadn't suffered *enough*."

A fervent ripple of "damn-fuckin'-right" sentiment rolled through the room.

"For what *she'd* done?" he continued. "Yeah, no way

in Hell was it enough. She needed to pay. Pay with more than the loss of another couple of limbs. Pay in the coin of humiliation."

"Oh, that's a nice one," Lyle whispered. "Silver-tongued cutie's got some *skills*."

June shushed him as well, though she didn't disagree.

"There are people in this room," Trevor said, "who've witnessed and participated in that humiliation. Who've seen her degraded and defiled in a dozen disgusting ways. And who, I believe, would stand with me in saying it still wasn't enough."

An even more fervent ripple rolled through; they hung on his every word, on the edge of their seats.

"I tried to think of what might *be* enough, but I couldn't. The *magnitude* of her crimes, the shame she'd brought down upon me, upon our family … nothing seemed sufficiently … you know, ***pow!***" He extended an arm in June's direction, a spotlight following. "Our queen provided the perfect answer. An answer which speaks to the sense of roots, history, and legacy I mentioned. Which will strengthen the bonds of community, among long-time residents and newcomers alike, and bring us together."

The music had ceased. The audience seemed to hold its collective breath.

"And," Trevor said, "give my treacherous backstabbing bitch of a sister the punishment she deserves."

At that, all the lights went out, plunging the room into darkness amid a chorus of gasps. When the spotlights came up again, Trevor was gone. The royal-blue curtain rose in richly gathering folds to reveal the stage.

The set was minimalist, no painted backdrops or scenery. A simple wooden trough, familiar to anyone who had an agonicity generator or had seen the Shinns during their public utero-gourd gestation, occupied the center. It stood roughly waist-high, a tarp spread beneath.

Strapped into it lay Chelsea Carmichael, naked, arms gone at the shoulders, legs ending at the lower thigh. Her tits had never looked better. The jewel in her navel-piercing glinted, enticing. She was fully conscious, eyes open and flashing mixed messages of fear and fury. A person didn't need to be a lip-reader to discern the gist of what she was silently but strenuously mouthing.

At one end of the trough was a table, upon which rested a

bulky object draped in a towel. Next to the table stood Lester Riggers, all seven-foot-something of him, greasy-haired and grimy as ever, shirtless and shoeless, in his customary faded and patched denim biballs.

He blinked at the audience, a flicker of panic seizing his broad, lumpy face. Obviously not used to being in the literal spotlight, on stage, having everyone looking at him, cameras pointed at him … for a moment, it seemed he might chicken out, or pass out.

Then, he grinned, a cruel and nasty, leering, goatish grin.

"Hey, y'all!" Lester waved. "Ma, Pa, look! I'se gonna be on the tee-vee!"

"That's my *boy* up there!" Mr. Riggers crowed. "My *boy*!"

Mrs. Riggers beamed, eyes shining. "See you do us proud, Lester honey!"

The way they carried on, he might have been valedictorian at a college commencement ceremony or receiving the Congressional Medal of Honor. Ronny Riggers gazed at his brother with rapt hero-worship adoration.

"What's the deal?" Xanne asked.

"Wait for it," June said.

Iris drew a sharp intake of breath. "Oh, no, he ain't really …"

"Wait for it," June repeated.

Though no natural showman like Trevor, Lester—once past that initial moment of panic—embraced his role and fell to hamming it up bigtime.

"Hell-*lo*, Lake Misquamicus!" He flung out his arms like a goddamn rock star addressing a packed stadium. "How y' doin' out there? Havin' a good time?"

The audience cheered.

He cupped a hand by his ear. "I cain't *hears* ya!"

They whooped and hollered and did rebel yells.

"Fuck yeah, tha'ss what I'se talkin' 'bout! An' let's have some for Miz Chelsea, here! Ain't she a beaut?"

Volleys of wolf-whistles and cries of "hubba-hubba!" rocked the room.

"Tell ya," Lester said, "I usedta see her alla time, back in the day, struttin' 'round this here lakehouse in them teeny b'kinis … but daaaa-yum if'n she don't look even finer now!"

Chelsea, somehow, did not seem flattered by this praise

or pleased with the attention. Chelsea rather seemed as if she wanted to chew Lester's throat open and set the rest of them on fire.

June shifted into a comfortable position and took a nice, long, cool sip of black-grape wine. If there *was* a small, niggling qualm deep in the vestiges of her conscience—which there wasn't!—the potent alcohol should drown it nicely. Now was hardly the time to wonder if she'd taken this whole evil queen routine too far. Besides, "too far"? What a laugh! No such thing! Not after the Shinns and the little girl!

"Too far, my butt," she murmured, and drained the glass.

On the stage, Lester circled the trough, inspecting Chelsea from every angle, continuing to ham it up, reminiscing about his boyhood fantasies and what he'd wanted to do to her "since't we was kids."

"Only, as y'all local folks r'member, I was one tall, skinny geek then—Beanpole Lester, y' called me—an' fer shure no way a piece so fine's Miz Chelsea here'd give th' likes o' *me* th' time o' day!" He swelled his chest and flexed his muscles. "Done filled out some, though; Satan be praised!"

The audience responded with a hearty round of laughter punctuated by more wolf-whistles.

"Ev'n so," he went on, "you'd'a thunk I'se roadkill, way she turned her purty li'l nose! When's I was jist tryn' t' be sociable. So I gots t' say, it's a right dee-light t' be here with her now, an' I'se thankful as c'n be t' Mr. Trevor an' Her Majesty fer givin' me the opper-tun'ty."

A spotlight found June, and she lifted her refilled glass in a benevolent toast. Another picked out Trevor, who had taken a front row seat; he demurred in a manner almost humble.

"Go on, my friend," Trevor said. "You've more than earned it."

Exhortations and encouragements filled the air as Lester turned toward Chelsea again.

"Give it to her good, Lester!"

"Aw, yeah, git you some!"

"Make that cock-teasin' slutbag squeal!"

He leaned over her. "Sorry yet y' din't take me up on m'offer? I coulda been real nice t' ya, Miz Chelsea. Real nice. But you had'ta go an' be a highpockets bitch 'bout it, din'tcha?"

She spat in his face.

Lester recoiled, then guffawed, wiping off the spittle with

the back of his hand and licking it clean. "This ain't no Hock Party!"

Uncovering the towel-draped object on the table, he raised it overhead—a heavy drill, fitted with a three-inch circular hole-saw bit.

There he stood, like fucking He-Man invoking the goddamn powers of Grayskull. The classic movie-poster pose used by Luke Skywalker, Conan the Barbarian, Ash from *Evil Dead*, and many more.

Only, with a hick in grimy biballs, more suited to Leatherface in *Texas Chainsaw Massacre*.

The drill, not a new, sleek, modern model but an ugly, old, industrial hunk of metal, crude and primitive, dully caught the light. Lester held it high, letting them all have a good long look at it.

The majority of the audience—the military, former vacationers, newcomers, and outsiders—hesitated, as if not quite sure what they were seeing or how they were supposed to react.

With the long-time locals, it was a different story.

"Ho-lee shit!"

"That what I think it is?"

"Is he gonna—?"

"Hot damn, I dun' b'lieve it!"

"Fer serious?"

"No way!"

"Why, I never!"

"Fuck *me*, a real-live header?!"

"You best not be messin' with us, Lester!"

Xanne leaned close to June. "Uh, what's going on?"

"A header," Iris said. "He's gonna do a header on her."

"What's a ..." Lyle began, then comprehension dawned. "Oh myyyy."

"It's like Christmas come early," Spot said, awed. "Been wantin' t' see me a header so long, I cain't even."

Lester squeezed the trigger a few times, revving the drill in the air, making the circular bit whir into a blur—*vrrr! vrrr! vrrr!* His goatish grin was now that of a quarterback who'd just scored the winning touchdown in the Super Bowl. The lower portion of his biballs had tented prodigiously.

"Our granpappy told us stories," Abel said. "I thought he

was funnin'. Tall tales an' such."

Maisy-Sue huffed and blustered indignantly. "Why'd anyone wanna go an' fuck a gal's *head* when she gots a perf'cly good *pussy* y' don't hafta bore a hole through *skullbone* t' get at?"

"You wouldn' unnerstand," Abner told her. "'Nother man-thing."

"Stick it up yer condescendin' butt!"

"No, he's right," Abel said. "'Corrdin' t' Granpappy, a header's better'n *any* pussy. Or butt, fer that matter."

The rest of the audience had either caught on or had it explained and went silent as Lester prepared to get down to business, riveted with morbid anticipation. The air felt charged, electric. Nobody moved except for Lester—well, and Chelsea, trying like crazy to wrench out of the straps. She flinched as Lester stroked her hair, smoothing it over her scalp. He prodded at her skull, tapping it here and there like testing a melon for ripeness, trying to find the sweet spot.

Once satisfied with his decision, he lowered the drill, positioned it, pressed the circular bit firmly into place, and—

VVVVRRRRRRR!!!

A veritable pinwheel of shredded hair and blood flew in all directions, quickly joined by pale smoke and bone-dust as the teeth really dug in. The *vvrrr!* changed pitch to a shrill *vreee!* People flinched—worse than nails on a chalkboard—but it didn't last long before the *vreee!* became a *vrrunch!* and the bit was through.

Chelsea had gone stiff as a board, her expression a rictus more of shock and disbelief than pain, as if she just could *not* process or fathom what was happening.

Lester pulled the drill away. As it stopped spinning, he plucked a concave disk of hair, skin, and bone from its bit and showed it to the crowd the way a magician might "is *this* your card?" with the ace of spades.

The dragonfly camera-drones went in for close-ups, one focused on the plug of cranial matter in Lester's grasp, the other dipping down to get the round, bleeding gap in the top of Chelsea's skull; head wounds really *did* spill it.

A ceiling-mounted set of monitors, like at a hockey game, displayed the footage for the benefit of those in the tiered seats. It just needed a scoreboard, countdown timer, a scrolling statistics bar across the bottom, and maybe some Kiss-Kam interludes for the full effect.

Although she was no power tool or DIY expert, June could tell it was a very precise, professional cut.

Lester hadn't been a handyman all his life for nothing. He'd backed the bit off before its teeth could cut into the inner membrane surrounding the actual brain tissue, so despite the copious blood, the damage thus far was nowhere near fatal.

Must've hurt, though; Chelsea, still rigid, was trembling all over and, once again, appeared to be trying to scream.

He set the drill aside and picked up another tool from the table, not a surgical scalpel but an ordinary X-ACTO knife, none too new and certainly not sterilized. With this, he slit the membrane and peeled the edges apart, revealing the actual pinkish-grey crenellations of the cerebral cortex.

His next move was to carefully slice into the brain itself, bisecting the hemispheres.

And his next move after that? To unhook the straps of his biballs, letting the patched and faded denim drop in a heap at his feet. His cock sprang out, maybe not the most aesthetically pleasing pillar of man-meat anyone had ever seen, but impressive nonetheless. Long, thick, *very* veiny, somewhat crooked, with a knobby maroon tip protruding from a wrinkled turtleneck of foreskin, surrounded by a dense tangle of pubes, above a scrotum like two misshapen avocados in a crumpled brown paper bag.

Aesthetic or not, it got a wild round of applause. As Lester stepped out of the biballs and kicked them away, his parents tilted as far forward as they could, meeting each other's eyes around Ronny's paunch.

"That we'd live t' see the day!" Mrs. Riggers wept joyfully. "Our boy, havin' his first header!"

"Never been prouder t' be a pa," Mr. Riggers replied.

Ronny hugged them both to his sides. A real Hallmark moment, the absolute image of family togetherness, Norman Rockwell, eat your heart out.

Lyle, meanwhile, tipped toward June and remarked, "Lordy, last time I saw an ass *that* hairy was at the zoo."

Chelsea, from her vantage point, might not have been able to have a direct line of sight, but she could see the monitors displaying the hole in her head and what was aimed at it. The struggling fit she threw was a titanic, herculean effort compared to her previous attempts, but just as futile.

Lester primed the pump with a few loose-curled fist strokes, darting a quick glance in Trevor's direction as if to get the final okay.

"Do it," Trevor said.

After rubbing his knobby cockhead with her blood, he set it against the slice he'd made in her cerebellum and slowly pushed. Half an inch vanished as the audience unleashed another cacophony of hoots and hollers and yeehaws, then an inch. There, Lester paused, expression suffused with such eye-crossing ecstasy it almost made him a caricature of himself.

"Yyyyyyeaahh!" someone whooped.

"Git you some!"

"Hump that head!"

"Fuck 'er brains a good 'un!"

"How's it feel, Lester?"

"Mah ... sainted ... *Satan*," Lester rasped, easing another inch deeper, then another. "Best cunt I *ever* had m'dick in ain't got *nothin'* on this!"

"Don'tchoo nut too fast, now, son," his father instructed. "Wouldn't do t' have you go off hair-trigger!"

"Aw, but, Pa!" He gritted his teeth. "Damn if'n I ain't ready t' blow m'load already!"

"Shit, y'ain't even done a full fuckin'," someone else scolded. "Git it *alls* in there, boy! Balls deep!"

"He do, his dick gon' bust clean through her forrid!"

"Betcha *that'd* make her eyes pop!"

Chelsea stiffened, shivering, as yet more of his cock worked its way in, its crooked girth splitting and spreading and forcing the compact folds of tissues wider. Her eyes hadn't popped yet, but they bugged, giving her a distorted Marty Feldman aspect. A mix of blood and cerebrospinal fluid trickled from her ears.

Buried to the root, Lester paused again, his muscular frame taut with tension. He withdrew halfway, shaft glistening wetly. Then, buttocks flexing, he drove all the way back in.

His dick didn't "bust clean through her forrid," but June was pretty sure Chelsea was dead by then anyway.

Not that it stopped Lester.

He quickened his pace, and the sound—caught loud and clear by the boom mic and transmitted through the surrounding speakers—was a ghastly, gristly, mulchy squelching.

Nor did it stop the jubilant exhortations from the audience.

"Hooo-yeah!"

"Go, Lester, go!"

"Churn it like *buttah!*"

"Fill 'er up!"

Lester kept at it so hard and fast the trough shook, Chelsea's inert body jiggling with each thrust. He grabbed her tits to help hold her in place, mauling them with dirty fingers, thumbing her nipples as if trying to rub them right off.

"Attaboy!"

"Give them milkers a squeeze for me!"

His grip tightened on Chelsea's tits until they ruptured in his hands, blood and globs of fatty breast tissue oozing through splits in the skin. His hirsute ass-cheeks pumped in an even more frantic, erratic rhythm.

"Oooh, he's gettin' there!"

"Cream-pie that noggin!"

His urgent grunting gave way to a long, blissful groan, head flung back, jaw clenched, cords standing out in his thick neck. He held the tense pose for a timeless moment, a tableau of the most vile violation.

Then, with a colossal shuddering exhale, Lester relaxed. Almost collapsed, really; he had to brace himself against the trough to keep from falling over. His chest heaved for each raggedy breath. His muscles quivered and trembled.

"Ain't … *nevah* …" he wheezed, "had me … a nut … so … gawdamn good."

The room exploded in thunderous applause and tumultuous cheers. Standing-fucking-*ovation*, every member of the audience on their feet. If it'd been a bullfight or an opera, they would have thrown flowers; as it was, several articles of intimate apparel, wadded into damp projectiles, pelted the stage.

Lester extracted himself from the remains of Chelsea's brains. His semi-flaccid shaft was coated in gore; his dense pubes matted with it. Once again, the sound—thanks to the boom mic—was captured perfectly, a sucking clogged sort of *schlorppp*. A mixture of fluids similar to that trickling from her ears drizzled from the orifice, this biological syrup also now cloudy with semen.

Though, really, for all June could tell, that was in the mess leaking from Chelsea's ears now too. And her nostrils. And the corners of her bulging eyes and slack mouth. She thought of Chef Emilio using a piping bag to inject custard into puffs of *pâte à choux* until the pastry overflowed at the seams, then wished she hadn't thought of it because it rather spoiled her appetite for dessert.

Cream-pie indeed.

The curtain fell. The spotlights went out, plunging the room into darkness, before the dimmer house lights came up. Trevor was back onstage, in front of the curtain.

He waited for the applause to taper off, everyone settling into their seats again.

"Wow," he said simply. "I mean, I've seen some bonkers shit, but … *wow*."

It drew an appreciative laugh.

"I hope you've enjoyed this evening's special entertainment as much as I did," he went on. "By no means an end to the evening's *fun*, of course; the bar is still open, the night is still young. But first … let's hear it for our own Lester Riggers!"

The cheers and applause resumed as an abashed-looking Lester emerged from behind the curtain. He'd re-donned his biballs and didn't seem to know how to react.

Trevor clapped him on the shoulder. "Go on, my man, take a bow! You gave us a show to remember!"

His grin more sheepish than goatish, Lester did so, basking awkwardly in the praise.

"Show t' rememba!"

"*I'll* say!"

"Hell of a header!"

"Speech! Speeeeeech!"

Lester glanced uncertainly at Trevor, who gave him an encouraging nod.

"Uhm … well," he said, "ain't much a one fer speech-makin', so's … thanks t' Senator Carmichael an' Her Majesty … thanks all y'all fer bein' here … best day'a my *life*!"

The party went on, an orgiastic extravaganza of drinking, dancing, feasting, and fucking. The action spilled out onto the wraparound deck and backyard patio. So many bodies occupied the hot tubs there was barely room for the water.

Once upon a time, the noise might've led to annoyed

neighbors calling the police, but those times were long past, and none of the current neighbors would have dared. And most of them were there anyway.

June observed the goings-on with wry amusement but refrained from partaking of wilder activities. She felt oddly detached, not in the out-of-place and unwelcome way she had previously felt detached in many social occasions but in a way more … jaded, almost aloof. It wasn't a bad feeling. She could just sit and look on as if at a performance arranged for her benefit. One she had the power to change the course of at any second. A single word from her would turn fucking to fighting. At her idlest command, they'd do murder. They'd mutilate themselves and each other. She could bid any of them to go jump in the lake—the otherwise innocuous "buzz off" phrase tantamount to a death sentence here—and they'd do it.

Thy Will Be Done? she thought with a cold curve of a smile. *My Will Be Done!*

Too evil?

Maybe, but who gave a fuck?

Juggernaut stayed with her, a silent and imposing bodyguard, but she'd released the rest of her inner entourage to make the most of the festivities.

She saw Spot foraging along the buffet tables, Lyle flirting outrageously with a handsome bartender, Meep ogling a pair of girls entwined on a sofa, and … why, could that be Iris Tate out by the deck railing, engaged in serious private conversation with Abel Kellerman? Had she mustered the nerve to approach him, or had he noticed the way she kept shyly checking him out? Either way, good for her!

Xanne, meanwhile, was on the dance floor, lost in her own frenetic solo frenzy. She'd stripped off her uniform shirt, revealing a basic but decently filled-out military-issue tactical bra. Her skin shone with sweat, highlighting toned abs and arms. It looked more strenuous than recreational, an insane combat workout, that chick from *Flashdance* busting her ass. Any would-be partner who got too close received a boot to the nuts or an elbow to the face for his troubles without Xanne missing a beat.

Trevor Carmichael meandered over, none-too-steadily, beaming from ear to ear. He had a goblet in his hand and a dusting of crystalline powder under his nose. As he went to sit down beside her, he almost ended up in her lap.

"Whoops!"

"Whoops to you too," she said.

"Well?"

"Well what?"

"Well?" He waved his arm in a vague semicircle, sloshing wine. "What do you think?"

"I think you're a shamelessly indulgent pervert with no sense of decency or decorum; that's what I think."

"You say the sweetest things. A guy could fall in love."

"Save it, Romeo. I'm old enough to be your … aunt. Besides, we discussed that earlier, didn't we?"

"Okay, okay." Mock-pouting, he gave her a companionable bump to the upper arm.

Juggernaut stirred, and she signaled the Golem to take it easy; twisting the host's head 180 degrees might put a damper on the party.

Trevor, oblivious, pulled a small white box from his pocket, the kind often used for gift-giving pendants, earrings, or other items of jewelry. "Made a nice score tonight already, anyway. Look what I got."

He lifted the lid. Inside, resting on a layer of cottony batting, was *not* a pendant, pair of earrings, or other item of jewelry.

It was, on the contrary, a toe. A pinkie toe, feminine, cutely chubby. And, judging by the color and the still-seeping stump, quite fresh.

"Maisy-Sue Kellerman?" June asked.

"With Dad's old cigar cutter. She was into it too."

"Those brothers of hers won't be very happy."

"Pff. They're just lack-toes intolerant."

June sat very still for a long moment, then said, "I *can* have you executed, you know."

"You won't." He shifted so he sprawled halfway across her lap, gazing up at her with a dopey smile. "You like me."

"*Lack-toes intolerant*? Seriously?"

He laughed, hiccupped, laughed some more, and lolled his head. "So bad, it was, it really was, but I couldn't resist."

"Did you *try* to resist?"

"Not even."

"Senator, I do believe you're drunk."

"I sure am. Wanna make out?"

"We *had* that talk—"

"Right, but, see, we don't have to *fuck*-fuck; we can just fool around. Then you won't have to kill me after."

"I should kill you anyway."

"I promise I won't cut any parts off unless you say so."

June swatted him. "You're incorrigible."

"You keep incorriging me."

She shoved him, rolling him off her lap to thunk to the floor. He lay there, still laughing. "And that's enough of that," she said.

"Aww, come on. I'm in mourning. I lost my sister tonight."

"Yes, very tragic, very sad."

"Did you *see* how much dick he got into her head? And the way he gooshed her tits? Holy moly. Chels was a grade-A bitch, all right, but she had some *primo* tits."

"You're the one who offered her up for 'whatever.' And 'anything goes,' if I recall correctly. Weren't those your exact words?"

"Oh, they were, and I meant it. No regerts."

"No what?"

"Regerts ... never mind." He toyed with her ankle. "Delicate bone structure. Your foot would—"

June rose. "My foot will go somewhere you don't want it if you keep that up."

Trevor sighed, doing another pout. "As Your Majesty commands." He gave her a big, pleading puppy-dog-eyes look. "But, since you like me and I'm drunk and I just lost my sister, can I ask a teensy little favor?"

"You may ask, but no guarantees."

Suddenly not so drunk or in mourning after all, he sat up clear and alert. "A friend of mine, Jason Prentiss, is stationed at Checkpoint Jericho. I was hoping he could maybe be transferred, or appointed to me as commander of my household guard, or something. I've tried going through the proper channels, but the proper channels are still kinda wonky. The closest I got was finding out he was in some disciplinary trouble and being held on 'pending charges,' whatever that means. So, I hoped, you being queen, commander in chief, you might maybe pull a few strings, cut some red tape." He tilted his head and did the puppy-dog-eyes again. "Please?"

"Have you always been this charming and manipulative?"

"It's a gift."

"I'll look into it," she said.

Which wouldn't take much effort. Jericho was one of the Checkpoints she was scheduled to visit, along with Nazareth and Bethlehem. The three biggies, the ones best known to the outside world, which had previously had the most contact and seen the most traffic.

Jericho, as she recalled, was near the former Area 666 tourist trap. Her mother and the other church folk used to rant like crazy about that, as if a bunch of hicks selling tacky Hell-themed souvenirs was any worse than the perennial reappearance of Spirit Halloween stores.

Bethlehem had been the primary public face of the defensive perimeter, used as backdrop for stirring speeches on the anniversary of AllHell. After Favius took over, it had become home to the Blackwings, their elite airborne troops … led by the late Captain Adler, that two-headed eagle/Nazi harpy, whom June was personally just as glad to be rid of.

Nazareth, the largest and most well-staffed of the six, was the gate through which Favius had made his triumphant return, in a military convoy including government officials and the media. She'd been told its soldiers were gargoyles now. Not the regular cathedral downspout kind or the kind from a cartoon her mother had forbidden her to watch.

Nazareth was in fact to be the next stop on her royal tour.

Send Me An Angel

"There may be a way?" Ethriel echoed. "You mean, a way to …"

"To fix this," Greg said, his forehead still pressed to hers, her hand slim and cool in his grasp. "Heal you. Restore your wings. So they won't have to … erase you."

Her other hand rose from the spun-crystal cocoon serving as a hospital bed and curled around the nape of his neck. "Oh, Greg …"

He squeezed his eyes shut. "Unless that is what you want—"

"It isn't." Her voice quavered. "I never feared renewal before, but I never had so much to lose before."

Relief flooded him. "Me either. If they did it to you, they'd have to do the same to me, because—"

"No, no, don't say that. You're mortal; you have a life, and a *soul*—"

"I don't care."

"But, Greg—"

"I love you! How could I just … go on …?"

She drew his head down and kissed him. A soft, sweet, gentle kiss to which he surrendered himself utterly. In that moment, nothing else in the world—or any world—mattered. Earth, Heaven, Hell, the universe, the cosmos, as many other dimensions and alternate realities as you could shake a stick at … his all, his everything, was compressed into a timeless instant of here and now.

"Better?" she asked when she released him.

"Yeah." He sat up, smiling weakly, and wiped away a tear. "Sorry."

"Don't ever be. I love you too."

They kissed again, tenderly, then Ethriel settled deeper

into silken cloud-stuff bedding, sighing.

"Pain?" he asked.

"Mostly just so … tired," she said. "Funny, isn't it? Sleep's another of those things I never really needed, or thought about, until I went corporeal."

"If you want to rest, I can—"

"You can stay right there, mister."

"As long as they'll let me. And even then, they might have to drag me out."

"Don't think they wouldn't."

"I know, I know. A few of them would probably enjoy it."

"Making friends, are you?"

"Heh. One way to put it." He told her about Icaiah, about the white-flame seraph and the four-faced sumo, and related his surprise encounter with the raphim med students and their professor.

"You *have* been busy," Ethriel said, amused. "And here I thought you were just hanging out in a bar."

"That too." He clasped both her hands in his again. "In fact, it was him, Azrael, who told me how we could try and restore your wings. He said it wouldn't be easy, and it would be dangerous, but it wasn't impossible."

"Dangerous for whom?"

"Well, you, me, everyone." He shrugged. "Defying Heaven, pissing off Hell, crossing the boundaries, risking the divine karmic balance. You know, the usual."

"Greg, you shouldn't joke about—" Ethriel's words cut off in a gasp, her celestial eyes widening but her gaze going very far away.

"Ethriel? Oh shit, Ethriel, I'm sorry, I won't do it again. Tell them it's my fault, don't let them take it out on—"

She blinked and returned to him. "Cool it, tiger; it's something else. It's … it's Lorlinda."

"Lorlinda? Is she okay?"

"She's woven some of my hair and hers into a protective charm. The hoodoo woman, Delilah, taught her an incantation. To … to help shield her, keep her safe, when … when she leaves the tunnel. When she goes back in! Greg, she's going back in! Into the HellZone!"

"What? She can't! That's crazy!"

"She wants to find her family. Tell them what happened. Tell them about Heck."

"If anyone catches her, they'll kill her! *Worse* than kill her!"

Ethriel's gaze went hazy again. "She's got a … 'mota-scoota' … Brad and Dan are …"

"Stopping her? Please say stopping her."

"… helping her kit it up …"

"No, no, come on, guys, you can't let her do this!"

"They've tried to talk her out of it, but she won't listen. She's going … and she's going alone."

"Alone? No, that really *is* crazy. She'll never make it!" Greg raked his fingers through his hair. "God*damn* it—"

"Language."

"Gosh *darn* it, I promised Heck … it was his last request … how am I supposed to …?"

"Greg. It's her decision."

He exhaled heavily, shoulders sagging, and let his hands fall to his lap. "Her decision."

"And the charm *will* help. I can't be her guardian angel the way I was yours, but it'll still have some power."

"Okay," he said. "You're right, you're right, it's her decision. Just … aww, man. We left her in the lurch, there in the tunnel, after everything she'd been through, after she just lost Heck. I didn't even *think* about her, or Blaze, or anyone else."

"You were thinking about me." Ethriel touched his arm. "You saved me, brought me home. And for what it's worth, I'm sure they understand."

"Okay," he said again.

"Though my reach will be limited, I'll do what I can to keep tabs on her and nudge her away from trouble."

"As long as you don't push yourself too hard. She wouldn't want that either."

Ethriel drew him down to her, and they held each other as comfortably as position and situation would allow.

"I feel better when you're here," she murmured. "Stronger."

"Same."

"So, this insanely dangerous, boundary-crossing scheme you and Azrael cooked up …?"

"Hey now, I didn't cook anything up; it was all him."

"Well, what is it?"

"He said, and it fits with some of what Raphael told me, it has to do with the weapon that struck the wound. Favius's gladius. Which, according to them, isn't just Hell-forged but was imbued with additional demonic power. Some Arch-Duke, another Az-something name—"

"Azbunael," Ethriel whispered. "His skull, a Greater Relic, had been cast into the Sea of Cagliostro as an insult. It was drawn into the Reservoir and carried over in the Spatial Merge."

"Where it washed ashore, became the focal point for a cult of lake-folk, and … I'm not at all clear on the specifics of how … its essence got transferred to the woman we fought. The queen. She channeled a portion of it into the gladius, and—"

A convulsive shiver of memory coursed through her. "And used it to stab me, then cleave the wings from my back, hurting me far worse than otherwise would have been possible."

He nuzzled her, kissed her cheek, stroked her hair. "Pretty much. Whether she was even aware of what she was doing or not, who knows? I don't think she had any more idea how to control it than I did with the warlock stuff at first."

"While the weapon, the gladius, retains part of Azbunael's essence," Ethriel said pensively. "Mine as well, since it pierced my flesh, spilled my blood."

"Which adds up to a lot of divine and diabolical energies all wrapped up in one big messy tangled knot," Greg said. "If we can get ahold of it, we could—in theory—use those energies to mend your wings."

"Get ahold of it? The gladius? From *her*? Greg, she's not going to simply hand it over if we ask nice."

"I'm through asking nice. She may hate us—she's got her reasons; I can understand and respect that—but this is too important."

They held the embrace, heads tilted together, breathing synchronized, taking quiet solace in the nearness for an immeasurable length of time. Greg kept expecting Blianthis, one of the other raphim, or Raphael himself, to come in and tell them visiting hours were over.

Then Ethriel stirred. "I don't suppose Azrael had any helpful hints on *how* to get the gladius?"

"Well, given he *is* the Angel of *Death*—"

"Yeah, *that* much, I could have guessed."

"Otherwise …" Greg shook his head. "Stealing it, maybe, but I kind of doubt she leaves it sitting around."

"So, either way, sounds like we are in for another fight."

"We?" he repeated, trying to make light of it. "Whaddaya mean, *we*? We, nothing. This one's all on me."

"Greg, don't you even dare suggest—"

"Not suggesting. Being real."

"You said, and I quote, 'if *we* get ahold of it.' You said that first."

"Rhetorically."

"Oh, save your loopholes and pedantry for—"

"Ethriel." He clasped her hands again. "You're hurt. You can't right now. I have to do this. I *have* to."

She looked away.

"I hate it as much as you do," he went on, "but we need to face the facts."

A mask of misery drew her features into a tight grimace, eyes closed, chin quivering. A single tear, shimmering like a dewdrop, rolled down her cheek.

"Ethriel, please."

"You're right," she said. "I know you're right, I know it's true, but I *do* hate it, Greg, I do. And … I'm scared."

"So am I." He kissed the shimmering dewdrop tear away. Sweeter and more pure than Eden Springs. His throat clenched with a stifled sob.

Another long moment, less quiet solace and more fraught despair, passed between them, neither speaking. What needed to be said was too big to *be* said. Or maybe it didn't *need* to be said at all.

"Was that … an argument?" she asked.

"Sort of, I guess?"

"A lover's spat?"

"If that's what you want to call it."

"Shouldn't there be more yelling and throwing things?"

"Would it make you feel better?"

"Probably not. You?"

"No."

"Okay," she said. "We'll skip the yelling and throwing things part."

"Good."

"But I am still upset."

"I know."

"And scared."

"Me too."

They held each other, the quiet solace returning. Greg basked in her love and nearness, inwardly making steely vows to do whatever he could to fix this. Whatever it took. Whatever the cost.

Blianthis and Raphael appeared, manifesting through the cloudy wall, the latter once more in his white-coat-and-clipboard doctor guise, the former still matronly in her powder-blue scrubs. Greg put a protective arm around Ethriel as she clung to him. They huddled together, apprehensive, braced for the worst.

"Settle down," said Raphael. "Routine rounds, though there's very little routine about any of this."

Not without some reluctance, Greg disengaged and stepped back. Blianthis set about checking Ethriel's vitals, and though the process was nothing like the usual medical dramas—no blood pressure cuff, pulse oximeter, EKG machine—her manner was reassuring in its ordinary professionalism. He didn't know what any of the readings she cited meant, but the lack of alarm or urgency in her tone helped further calm his agitated nerves.

When Blianthis had finished, Raphael stepped up. Consulting his golden clipboard, making notes with his crystalline pen, he examined and questioned Ethriel. He hooked the buds of his stethoscope into his ears and pressed the bell to various parts of her body just like any regular doctor.

Then, unlike any regular doctor, he put aside clipboard and pen, rested the pads of his thumbs lightly against Ethriel's temples, and fanned his elegant fingers to either side of her head. Skeins of clear light coruscated between them. His divine Presence flared—great swanlike wings, an aura almost unbearable in its beauty, a halo woven of a billion golden stars.

"What's—?" Greg blurted.

Blianthis shushed him. "All is well, mortal."

All was *not* well; all was *miles* from well. It reminded him *way* too much of Donna's memory-wipe scene, that ultimate rape and betrayal even if with the best of intentions, saving a *life* at the expense of destroying a *person*. But he made himself shut up, wait, and watch.

The light grew, brightening and clarifying beyond the limits of human sight. The air hummed with vibrating resonance, rang with cascades of celestial chimes and harp string threnodies. A simultaneous sense of pressure and upliftingness washed over Greg, stronger than anything even he had yet experienced. He felt minuscule against it, infinitesimal, meaningless. He felt exalted within it, immense and encompassing, awestruck.

Then it faded, and Greg was himself again, as grounded and stable as it was possible for anyone to be in this place, or a warlock to be anyplace.

More importantly, Ethriel was still there. Ethriel was still *Ethriel*, tears shining unshed in her eyes as Raphael released her.

"If such is your wish," the archangel intoned, "so shall it be."

Ethriel relaxed, sinking deeper into the cloudstuff. "Thank you."

"Thank Him."

"Yes."

Resuming his doctorly aspect, Raphael picked up his clipboard and pen. He inscribed something, read it over, and held out both to Ethriel. "Sign here."

"Sign—?" Greg began, and Blianthis shushed him yet again.

Ethriel took the pen, scanned the clipboard, and signed.

Raphael then extended the items toward Greg. "Will you bear witness?"

He regarded what he could only describe as a thin sheet of opalescent white glass, covered in some intricate script millennia older than Aramaic or Sumerian. Maybe his grandfather, given enough time, could have deciphered it; to Greg, only a character here and there was even close to recognizable. Ethriel's signature glowed at the bottom in fluid calligraphy above a second line marked with an X.

"Uh, what, exactly, am I witnessing?"

"Standard DNDAR," Blianthis explained. "The patient hereby declines the treatment option of discorporation and renewal."

"A form? After all this, a form? What next, seeing how much her insurance will cover and how much has to be paid out of pocket?"

All three angels looked at him.

"Oh," he said, feeling like a complete idiot. "Of course. I

bet *they're* responsible for tax laws and student loans too." He scrawled his name under hers, next to the X. A tingle raced up his arm as he did so, letting him know this was no mere formality; this was a Document, legally binding enough to hold up in the highest of courts. Or the Highest, as the case may be.

"Plus credit cards, time share properties, and homeowners associations," Ethriel said, smiling with something more like her usual vigor.

"Color me shocked." Which, not really; hadn't he been making his living circumventing the health "care" system by flying in prescription drugs for a fraction of what Big Pharma gouged the typical consumer?

He returned pen and clipboard to Raphael, who looked the form over again and nodded, seeming satisfied.

"This should do," he said. "Barring dispute, although dispute under the circumstances is quite unlikely."

"Dispute?" Greg asked. Ethriel bit her lip.

"Quite unlikely," Raphael repeated. "Under the circumstances."

"Well, I—"

A furious redblack thunderclap out of nowhere interrupted whatever he'd been about to say. At first, he thought it was inside his head, until he saw the others reacting as well. Reacting in shock, in horror, in pain.

"*Warlock **Gregory Nachtwald!**"* roared a Voice, a rage-filled and wrathful terrible Voice. "*Angel **Ethriel!**"*

Her Voice, it was *her* Voice, the woman, Favius's queen, ripping through the cloudstuff, disrupting the very substance of Heaven. Ethriel cried out, Blianthis flung her arms over her head, Raphael dropped the clipboard.

A terrible window tore open, a window seething with baleful radiance, showing a view of the rearing battle-scarred promontory of Bighead Rock, the lake below and the *Aurora Diabolicus* above. Showing the ruins of a rotunda and a crowd of gathered onlookers in rapt attention.

Showing a little girl. A freckle-faced little girl, squirming, held aloft by the hair. In jumper and flip-flops, with the edge of a blade pressed to her young, tender throat.

"This child's blood I hereby spill, her life I take—"

"No!" Greg shouted, clenching his fists, silver fire exploding from his brow.

He saw Ethriel trying to leap up, unable to do so, falling

back with a distraught wail. He saw Raphael and Blianthis, stunned.

"—and her soul I commit to eternal damnation, because of *you!*"

He saw the blade—the Hell-forged bronze blade, the blade of a gladius—slice deep. Effortlessly deep, parting flesh and loosing a crimson torrent.

They couldn't stop her, couldn't save the little girl, couldn't do anything.

Not a goddamn thing.

The queen *knew*. And they knew that she knew. And she knew that *they* knew that she knew.

It was how she wanted it, her precise intention. To let them *know*, make them bear *witness*, in no way so simple as signing some *form*.

Witness **this**! the queen seemed to howl in their minds. *How do you like* **that***, you assholes? You murdering, cock-sucking, cunt-licking* **assholes***! The girl* **dies***, she dies in* **your** *Names, by* **my** *Hand and* **my** *Will!*

Savage with vengeance and hatred and purpose and bloodlust. Wreathed in dark power, in redblack storm cloud demonic energy. Strong. So strong, infernally strong.

Die, the girl did. Gurgling and gasping. Her last breath spluttering, blowing bubbles in the flood of hot blood. More blood than it seemed possible such a small body could hold. Gallons of blood.

With another thunderclap—but a thunderclap somehow reversed, a sonic boom turned inside-out—the terrible window slammed shut. The terrible scene vanished from sight, if not from memory.

As if it could or would *ever* vanish from memory ... as if it wasn't going to haunt and torment them for the rest of their days, mortal or otherwise.

Just a kid.

Like her brother had been, and it didn't save **him** *either. Did it, Mr. Hot Shit Big Shot Warlock?*

How the certainty came to him, Greg couldn't say. Nonetheless, there it was, undeniable. Further linking him to the evil, chaining him to the crime. A condemnation writ in violence, sealed in death.

Maybe there was a difference between involuntary

manslaughter via reflexive self-defense and calculated deliberate sacrificial murder ... maybe, but in the end, the results were the same.

Kids, just kids. *Dead* kids.

Because of him.

He found himself in Ethriel's arms again. Or she was in his. Or they were in each other's. It didn't matter. What mattered was holding her and her holding him, although both of them were too shaken to speak.

How much time had passed, he also couldn't say. The room was the same, but the cocoon of spun-crystal had enlarged from a twin to a double, its silky wisps wafting around them. Warm. Cool. Comfortable. Soothing.

For all the good it did. As soon as his awareness fully returned, so too did the guilt.

Burying his face in the crook of Ethriel's shoulder, he tried—and failed—not to weep. She hugged him and stroked his hair. Her breath hitched in shallow, watery sobs.

"It's not our fault," she told him. "It's *her*. That horrid, wicked bitch."

"The boy was my—"

"Greg, stop."

"They were just kids. Just *kids*!"

"I know. I know."

"Did you ... feel it? The connection? How fucking *spiteful* she was? I hate her. I hate her so damn much. I've never actually all-out hated somebody before."

"I felt it. She's evil, Greg. Whatever or whoever she used to be, she's evil now. She's *theirs*. As bad as any demon if not worse. Demons generally don't have a choice."

"I've got to stop her. Not only for the gladius. She has to be stopped."

She hugged him closer. "I can't stand the idea of you going up against her alone. And it's more than her; it's an entire army, *plus* the essence of an Arch-Duke ..."

"Yeah."

"As much as I love you, and it hurts to admit ... Greg, you're not strong enough. Not on your own. Not yet, maybe not ever. The greatest warlocks in history, with centuries of training—"

He forced a chuckle. "Okay, jeez, you don't have to rub it in."

It was the truth, though. Thanks to his crash course from

his deceased grandfather and his innate bloodline talent, he was far from a slouch in the warlockery department, capable of taking on some pretty impressive adversaries.

But *Juno Regina*, backed by Azbunael's power?

Yeah, dream on; fat fucking chance.

"Which is why," cut in a dry and dusty Clint Eastwood drawl, "you need an ace in the hole."

Greg sat up fast. "You?!"

"Me."

The best a startled Ethriel could do was prop herself onto an elbow, her eyes wider than ever. She stammered a few incoherent syllables.

Azrael waved a casual hand. "Take it easy. Thought I'd drop by is all. See how you two were doing."

Ethriel stammered some more, clearly at a total loss. First, the personal healing attention of the Archangel Raphael himself, and then to have the very Angel of Death walk in unannounced?

While there she was, an injured low-tier minor leaguer of lesser seraphim rank at best?

With her mortal lover, no less. And naked to boot.

Not that nudity was such an issue here; making it a shameful sin and taboo was more the province of post-Garden humanity.

Still, a sudden modest impulse had her groping at the silken wisps in a feeble effort to conceal the naughty bits.

For which, Greg could hardly blame her. He'd been relieved, upon waking in the lecture hall surrounded by raphim med students, to find his magically created clothes had not forsaken him.

"Take it easy," Azrael reiterated. "You need your rest. I told the Doc I wouldn't agitate anyone unduly, and I'd appreciate it if you helped me keep my word."

She sank down, having gone from stammering to speechless. The disbelieving *am-I-dreaming* wonder in her expression could not be conveyed.

Understandable; Greg felt it too. It'd been one thing to run into the guy by accident at a bar; him taking enough of an interest to seek them out and pay a hospital visit went way past unexpected.

"You, uh, heard what happened?" he asked, clambering

from the bed and smoothing his disheveled coat.

"Little cherub told me. News travels fast. This Juno, she called you out."

"She killed a child to do it. A child!"

"Yep. Cold. Lady's got a grudge." Azrael leaned against the cloudy wall, arms crossed, fixing Greg with his gunslinger's gaze. "She'll mop the floor with you, kid, if you let your conscience interfere. You have to be cold too. Cold, hard, and sharp."

"If I can."

"You better. Not to wax melodramatic, but, there's nobody else."

"There must be something," Ethriel said plaintively. "Someone who can help."

"Policy, sweetheart. You know the rules as well as I do."

"So we're going to sit safe up here and watch, not lift a finger, while Greg's life and soul—a *lot* of lives and souls!—hang in the balance?"

"You did a great job down there," Azrael told her. "Given what you were thrown into the middle of and what you had to work with? Above and beyond. Admirable. Brave. Quick-thinking. Michael couldn't have done better."

She blushed. "Me? Oh, I … you shouldn't …"

"Say it? I said it, and I'll say it again. To the Warrior's own face, if need be."

Greg held his breath for a second, bracing for another Archangel to burst in, with eagle's wings and sword of fire. Ethriel tensed, doubtless in anticipation of the same.

Azrael, unbothered, continued. "You've stirred the pot, and in a good way. With everything going on Earthside, the whole Host's talking. Questioning our noninvolvement. Speculating maybe we've—or He's—been turning a blind eye too long."

"I didn't mean to cause so much trouble—"

"Pots need stirring. And this lake situation is a pot that needs to be taken off the stove before it boils over."

"How, though?" Greg asked. "You're right; if I go down there by myself, I'm toast."

"Like I said when I came in, kid … you need an ace in the hole."

"Such as what? Ethriel's injured, our allies inside are gone or scattered, the world outside's a giant mess since that Painwave—"

"Such *as* ..." The Angel of Death trailed off meaningfully, sliding them a slanted Clint Eastwood half-grin.

"*You?!*"

"Me."

"But ... but isn't that ... wouldn't that be ...?" Ethriel fumbled.

"Against the rules?" Azrael finished for her. "Contrary to policy? Not allowed? Absolutely. I operate on an assignment-only basis. Without direct orders from Himself, my actions are limited."

"Then, what are you saying?" Greg asked, having the glimmer of an inkling but hardly daring to hope.

"Loopholes, kid. One of your specialties. I may not be able to intervene directly, but there's no reason I can't lend a hand here and there."

"Wouldn't that be ... risky? For you? I mean, I've already gotten Ethriel in enough trouble—"

"I had as much to do with that as you did," she said tartly. "Who seduced whom in the motel room?"

Azrael cleared his throat. "Staying on topic ..."

"Sorry." She blushed again.

"Anyway, risky? Maybe so, maybe no. I've got a certain amount of leverage. After all, what's He going to do, fire me? Nobody else would take the job. It'd be a reprimand at most, and some causes are worth a reprimand."

The clicking tap of a crystalline pen on a golden clipboard caught their attention, and they all turned to see Raphael, in his white coat, with a disapproving frown.

"I thought we agreed you wouldn't agitate my patient," he said to Azrael.

"Unduly," Azrael said. "Agitate *unduly*. And no one's agitated. Are they?" He glanced at Greg, then Ethriel. "Are you?"

"No," Greg replied.

"Not agitated at all," Ethriel chimed in.

"They look agitated, Doc?"

"This is a place of healing, peace, and serenity," Raphael said. "A balm to both body and spirit. A haven of rest. A sanctuary—"

"For His sake, Doc, spare me the sales brochure."

"For His sake, spare *me* the sardonicism, Azrael. You

know I can't have sedition brewing on my watch."

"That's an unfair exaggeration."

"Is it? Would Gabriel think so?"

"Gabriel's a—"

The pen flared with divine light as it rapped the clipboard again, striking a high and clear musical note. "I'll thank you not to complete that sentence."

"Fine, fine. Have it your way. Sentence uncompleted."

"Thank you."

"He is, though."

"Perhaps we could continue this discussion elsewhere." Raphael did not make it sound like a request. "Privately."

"Sure thing." Azrael inclined his head to Ethriel in a manner which suggested touching a dusty hat brim, though he wore no hat. "Sweetheart, been a pleasure, feel better soon."

"And an honor, sir."

"Nah, save it." He held out a hand to Greg. "And you, kid, see you around."

Never in his life either would he have expected to find himself shaking hands with the Angel of Death, but it happened. Azrael's grip was firm, neither warm nor cold.

You know where to find me. In his head, nothing like his own inner commentary or the occasional message-remarks from his dead grandparents. Neither read nor heard but plain as anything.

Unbidden, his mind flashed an image in response—a round design of three chalices pouring into each other. *I do.*

"See you," he said aloud.

Raphael gestured. "Allow me to show you out."

"Lead the way, Doc."

They vanished through the wall, the cloudstuff rippling as it closed in their wake, leaving Greg and Ethriel alone again.

"Did that all really just happen?" he asked.

"Pretty sure it did," she said. "Wow."

"For a minute there, I was afraid they were going to get into it."

"Right? This is *way* above my pay grade."

"I don't know about that," Greg said. "You may be seriously underestimating your promotion."

"Even if I am, it's still nowhere near." She exhaled wearily. "And I'm just so *tired.* How can I be so tired when I've barely moved?"

He stroked her hair and kissed her forehead. "Recovery's its own full-time job. You need to rest."

"Promise me you won't go off and do anything stupid while I do."

"What? Lie to you? Here? In Heaven?"

"Humor me."

"I promise I won't do anything *too* stupid."

"Close enough."

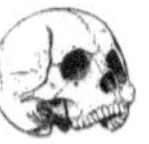

Once more unto the breach.
Here I go again on my own.
Out of the frying pan, into the fire.
Express elevator to Hell, going down!

None of them seemed exactly right, so, with a sigh and a shrug, Greg just muttered, "Fuck it, let's do this," under his breath as he summoned up his magic.

The Pearly Gates—again, not *the* Pearly Gates, but the side entrance through which he'd initially barged his way into Heaven—had swung shut behind him. He stood alone amid an otherwise featureless cloudscape, shadowless, bereft of even the slightest breeze, the temperature as neutral as the fluid filling a sensory deprivation chamber.

The sigil seared into his brow came alive in lines of silver fire, radiating outward in a laser-show cone to etch the seven-sided pattern into the air. It wavered, steadied, resolved, and formed a portal large enough to step through.

So, fortified with defensive wards, attack spells close at mind, he stepped on through.

Way to make an entrance.

Only, there were no Stargate-esque special effects, no whooshing wormhole space/time dilation, no universes or dimensions unspooling before his very eyes.

He just … stepped through.

Vwomp, and there he was.

The humid Florida heat, amplified like a greenhouse by the Dome, washed over him in a sweltering wave. So did the lake stench, part shithouse and part slaughterhouse, with an underlying sulfuric miasma. He'd gotten acclimated to it before and would again, but damn, that first whiff made his eyes water.

It did not, however, make his eyes water so much he couldn't discern his surroundings. Forget safe, sheltered, liminal spaces; dicking around with tunnels wasn't a luxury he could afford on this foray. Every sense on high alert, ready to come out swinging, he found himself facing …

Absolutely nobody.

The rubble-strewn, battle-scarred, char-blackened promontory of Bighead Rock was deserted.

Fetid updrafts from the lake belled his coat. The *Aurora Diabolicus* bathed him in its awful bloodlight. Gritty skirls of dust and ash swept across the rocky ground. The only living movement he saw was that of a six-legged lizard basking on a boulder and a few scrawny bird-things pecking at crawling bugs.

Way to make an entrance? Waste of a good entrance, more like.

She *had* been here, **Juno Regina**, in this very spot. He'd seen it in the monstrous vision. He felt the redblack storm cloud residue of her Presence. She'd been *here*, holding the child aloft by the hair, gladius in hand. Here with her followers. Putting on a show for them. Reveling in it. Soaking up her power, steeping in her vengeful hate.

But she wasn't here now. Had moved on.

Greg lowered his guard, but only a little. Moved on or not, this was *her* realm. Although he detected no active arcane energies, there might still be alarm charms. Unseen magical traps and tripwires. Oracles monitoring him on crystal ball security cameras. For all he knew, the pecking bird-things could be her spies, the basking lizard a disguised demon.

Seeing the place, with its remnants of destruction, brought the memories back, more pointed and painful than ever. While some clean-up work appeared to have been done— corpses disposed of, weapons salvaged—plenty of debris had been left behind.

Most notable was the ruined rotunda, a heap of broken columns and cracked marble atop the crumpled junkyard scrap metal that had been Heck Bodean's souped-up, apocalyptically "modderfied" frankentruck. Heck had brought the house down, all right, turning what started as a crazy-ass crash into a demolition wrecking ball … plus several crates of extremely flammable high-test hellshine.

The resulting explosion hadn't been *as* spectacular as the one Blaze managed when he—again, fueled by high-test hellshine—accidentally set off the entire arsenal of fireworks he wore strapped to his lanky body. Peterson Pyrotechnics;

their boy did the family business proud. Left a crater like a bomb blast.

Blaze, though, survived.

As for Heck ... well, that was another matter.

They'd all seen it, the ghost-truck, barreling out of the rotunda wreckage with revving engine, grinding gears, and screeching burn-rubber tires. Hazy, translucent, eerily glowing, clearly an insubstantial phantom.

Insubstantial yet solid enough to slam ramming-speed into the two Golems bearing down on the desperate but defiant foursome—Greg, Ethriel, Blaze, and Lorlinda— preparing to make their last stand. One of the Golems, its clay already kiln-fired near solid by Blaze, shattered into chunks at the impact. The second, despite its massive bulk, was bowled over.

Of the four of them, only Greg had perceived what happened next. The sudden jumper-cables inrush as Heck's newly-nascent power leapt to him, infusing him with energy, replenishing his direly depleted stores. And with it, Heck's parting message: '*Member your promise, magic-man.*

His promise, yes. To, if anything happened to Heck, do his best to get the others out of there. Lorlinda, Blaze, and the doll with some guy named Andy's spirit trapped inside it. Except, during the chaos, they'd lost track of the doll. Whether Andy had still been in the truck when it crashed and burned or been thrown clear somehow, no one knew.

"If you're there, Heck," he said, "if you can hear me, thank you. You saved our butts, man. I did get Lorlinda and Blaze back to the tunnel, anyway; two out of three. No idea where Andy ended up, sorry. Lorlinda figured he was as good as gone. She ..."

It felt inadequate, but he couldn't bring himself to go on. Too much, too big, too complicated, long story. Ethriel injured, needing urgent help, translocating with her ... what she'd told him about Lorlinda's decision to return to the HellZone, to try and make it home on, not a wing and a prayer but a "mota-scoota" and an angel-hair friendship bracelet ...

"Maybe you're aware of all that already," he went on. "Maybe you *are* still hanging around, one way or another, and keeping an eye on her too. If I find her, I'll help out however I can. Assuming I live through this myself."

An optimistic assumption, ace in the hole or not.

Heck, if he *was* there, didn't answer. There wasn't so much as a spectral whisper or wisp of ectoplasm.

Greg surveyed the rubble, noting again the crushed scraps of metal, grimly aware that Heck's corporeal remains must still be among them, entombed behind the wheel.

"You really did save us," he said. "I wish there was more I could do for you. But, for what it's worth, again, thank you."

Turning from the collapsed-and-exploded rotunda, his gaze involuntarily sought a patch of rusty-looking earth. His throat tightened. A sick pang jabbed at his insides. The blood had soaked into the dirt and dried, and the … pieces … had been removed, but it might as well have been marked with a neon sign.

A big, blaring neon sign reading MURDER.

With smaller silver-fire fine print spelling out the details of how Mr. Hot Shit Big Shot Warlock Gregory Nachtwald had turned his power against some eight-year-old boy and reduced him—before the very eyes of the boy's own mother—to a 3-D jigsaw puzzle of dripping red chunks.

Approaching the spot, he knelt.

Billy, Azrael had told him. *His name was Billy.*

"Billy," Greg said. "I'm sorry. I could make excuses, offer explanations, rationalize, but … what would it even mean? In the end, you're still just as dead and gone, and I did it. I'm responsible. I own that responsibility. I'm sorry. Azrael's right; I'll carry it with me to the end of my days. I know it's not enough. I just hope it's … something."

As before, addressing Heck, he received no answer, or any inkling his words had been heard. Still, it seemed to somehow lighten at least a portion of the dark burdens weighing heavy on his soul.

"And, if it helps," he added, "I'm sorry about your mom and your sister too."

As he got to his feet again, a glint caught his eye, a shine reminiscent of light reflecting off a windowpane. It was over toward the inland side of the promontory, where the open rocky expanse gave way to scrubby brush thickening into more verdant foliage near a sparse tree line.

He caught the glint again as branches swayed, and

ventured closer for a better look. Something was definitely there, something large and glassy. But not a windowpane … more of a glass-sided structure … a … rectangular box, about four feet long …

The bottom dropped out of his guts.

A casket. A glass casket, elevated on a platform. A sprig of wildflowers, still fresh and unwilted, had been placed atop it.

Hadn't he, back among the raphim, thought how the cocoon in which Ethriel lay was like the resting place of some enchanted princess in a fairy tale?

Wrong on that one … here was the real deal.

Maybe not as fancy as the one from Snow White, maybe cobbled together from old windowpanes, but the intention was the same.

"Oh, come on, no," he groaned.

The body within—the *small* body within, the small *child-sized* body within—lay in the classic serene posture, arms folded over chest. It had been draped from collarbones to toes by a lightweight throw-blanket, lavender, patterned with outline designs of castles, crowns, and carriages.

Forget enchantments, though. Forget poisoned apples or sleep-cursed spinning wheels. Forget Prince Charming and all that shit. No kiss was going to magically revive her. She was *dead*.

Dead, the gruesome, fatal throat slash considerately concealed by a cloth wrapped around her neck but the bloodless pallor of her face leaving no doubt. Against that pallor, a cute smattering of freckles stood out in stark contrast. Her lips and eyelids were tinged blue-grey, her eyelashes almost startlingly dark upon her pale cheeks. Her hair, a wild mop of curly clumps and barrettes in the vision, had been brushed, now held in place by a plastic-and-tinsel tiara.

Wasn't it enough to have killed her? Sacrificed her in such a ruthless, violent way? Did they have to put her on *display* like this? A morbid spectacle for all the world to see?

What next? Why not a *plaque* proclaiming precisely whose fault it was this little girl had died? Name and shame! Immortalize the deed!

Hell, going by what he knew of the queen, such a plaque was probably on order. It would be just her style.

His brow and fists crackled silver, yearning to lash out.

At a stealthy sound from behind him, he whirled and almost did, but held off, not wanting to let another hasty action give him yet more to regret.

Seeing the barrel of a military assault rifle leveled at his chest, he realized maybe he should have gone with that first lashing-out hasty action instinct after all.

The soldier holding the rifle, getting a good look at him, may have been thinking along similar lines—shoot first, ask questions later. He was fit but on the thin side, a day or two unshaven, not showing any outward signs of demonic influence. His uniform was rumpled but fairly clean, sporting a two-bar chevron insignia. Corporal stripes? A broad black band was secured around his upper arm.

They stared at each other in a tense standoff.

"You're him," the soldier said. "Nachtwald. The warlock."

"Yeah," Greg said. "I am. And you are …?"

"None of your goddamn business."

"Okay."

The standoff/stare down stretched out, neither of them blinking. Greg had reined in his power but not entirely; the sigil glowed on his brow, and sporadic silvery tendrils sparked around his fists.

"I ought to blow your fucking head off."

"Are you going to try?"

"Are you bulletproof?"

"I'd really rather not find out."

Another few intense, unblinking beats passed. The rifle's barrel did not waver. The soldier's stance didn't either. "Give me one good reason not to put it to the test."

He spoke evenly, but the fact he hadn't already done so made Greg suspect his heart wasn't in it.

"Well, your queen might want me alive so she can torture me in ways that make the Spanish Inquisition look like a fraternity hazing."

"Think you're funny?"

"Sure doesn't feel that way right now."

"So what you're saying is, I'd be doing you a favor if I shot you."

"Maybe."

"And maybe I should. You know what happened here. You know about the girl."

Greg broke the standoff, glancing over his shoulder. "I do. I wish like hell I didn't, but I do. She was—"

"—just a *kid*," the soldier finished with him.

This time, rather than staring, they simply looked at each other. Not soldier and warlock at spellpoint and gunpoint, but two regular guys swept up in a shitshow beyond all sane comprehension.

Then the soldier slung his rifle. "SNAFU is as SNAFU does," he said. "Zap me if you're going to. At this point, I'm half past give a damn."

Instead of zapping him, Greg glanced again at the casket. "You put the flowers."

"Yeah. Been … staying with her … should have reported back by now … suppose that makes me AWOL, but at this point, I don't give half a damn about that either." Fishing a crumpled pack of cigarettes from a pocket, he lit one and inhaled.

"Did you know her?" Greg asked, shaking his head when the cig pack was tipped in his direction.

"Hardly. A few days. Was sent to pick her up and bring her to HQ, then took babysitting detail. I didn't mind. We got along okay. So she was a little nutso. Who around here isn't?"

"Amen to that. I'm Greg, by the way."

"Tony. Uh, Corporal Anthony Lewis, yada-yada, if it still matters. And hey, listen, Her Royal Bitchness isn't *my* queen. Not anymore. Which I suppose also makes me guilty of treason as well as being AWOL; big fucking whoop. I'm done."

"If I could have stopped her from—"

"Yeah, I figured. I saw you during the fight, how it went down with the boy, how hard it hit you."

"And if I could take anything back—"

"Figured that too."

"She was the boy's sister?"

"Sherri. Their mom was a Senator, had some reptilian thing going on. The General—"

"Decapitated her. A whole family, gone."

"There was a dad at the house, but he was pretty badly fucked up too. They had him hooked to one of those agony generators or something. I can't explain it. Bad scene. It was all such a bad scene. Soon as we got there, the girl opens the door and this talking *doll* comes running at us, if you can believe it."

"Talking doll?" Greg very much could believe it, a jolt of excitement zinging his nerves. "What kind of a doll?"

"Star Wars, I think."

Andy! he thought. *Lorlinda's going to be—*

"Pork Chop, the guy with me, opened up on it so fast I barely got a look," Tony went on. "Wasted the fucking thing."

—devastated; fuck. Lorlinda's going to be devastated.

After a final drag, he dropped the butt and crushed the smolder from it under the toe of his boot. "Upset the kid something fierce. She called it Mr. Goblin. Said she found it in the lake and it was her best friend, could walk and talk just like a real person. Who knows?"

"Hey, like you said, around here ..." Greg trailed off.

"No shit. So we brought the kid to HQ. She had it in her head the queen would adopt her, make her a princess. Porkie thought different. I did too, but I let it go, told myself it was none of my concern. Not my kid, right?"

"Sure. Wouldn't want to go against the queen."

"Should have." Moving past Greg, he set his hand on the casket. "I goddamn fucking well *should* have."

"It's not too late," Greg said. "You still could."

Corporal Lewis stood silent and motionless as a statue for so long Greg was sure he'd pushed his luck too far.

Nice try, dumbass. Now, he's going to shoot you, and you'll have to find out the hard way if you're bulletproof or not.

"If you're saying," Lewis finally said in a quiet, calm, and measured tone, "what I think you're saying ..."

"Hey, just throwing it out there. No harm, no foul." But he gathered his arcane strength all the same.

"Go against her. You mean be a turncoat. You mean join your team."

"Admittedly, my team isn't such of a much at the moment, but, basically, yeah."

Very, very slowly, Lewis turned. His gun remained lowered, his gaze piercing and intense. "What about your angel?"

"She's benched for this one. I'm sort of solo."

"Your other friends? The guy with the fireworks? The crazy tailgunner chick?"

Greg uplifted open palms. "Not currently available."

"So, it's just you and me?"

"Unless you have other suggestions."

"Shit." Lewis glanced pensively skyward. The bloodlight of the *Aurora* played across his face. "I must be nuts even to consider it."

"Who isn't, around here?"

"To paraphrase what the Caterpillar said to Alice."

"I think that was the Cheshire Cat."

"Either way. You realize what you're asking."

"I know. It's a big ask. But I get the feeling we're on the same side. You don't support what they're doing. What *she's* doing."

"I didn't care at first," Lewis said. "I went along, sure; plenty of us did, no matter what we really thought. Sure, we're sworn to serve our country, not some fucked-up maniac bent on world domination ... but we saw what happened to those who resisted or fought back when Favius took power. Toe the line, or else."

"Under the circumstances, hardly unreasonable," Greg said.

"Plenty more, though, totally bought into it. All that evil, demonic influence flying around too ... people started changing right on the spot. *Physically* changing, transforming, sprouting horns and stuff. Had to make a snap decision before they decided you were fresh meat."

"No one could blame you for that."

"Maybe. Then, there you are, stuck with it, while things get worse and worse. People—your *own* people, fellow-fucking-*Americans*—being tortured, raped, butchered, *eaten*! *Also* by your own fellow-fucking-Americans! Some of whom have gone actual-goddamn-NAZI. Your former commander's had his *face* peeled off and his faceless *head* jammed onto a spike when his head's not even *dead* yet, trying to yell orders!"

He paced fitfully, angrily, voice rising, so worked up he was damn near frothing. Greg stood back and kept his mouth shut and let him get it out of his system.

"And then, oh and *then*, your own *government*, the US of-fucking-*A*, launches a nuke at you! On American soil! Which you probably deserve, because you're all a bunch of traitors or spineless chickenshits, but that goes FUBAR too; everything goes FUBAR. Somehow, suddenly, who's in charge? This whacked-out, mother-killing, vindictive psycho-cunt whose first official act is to *sacrifice* a little *kid*!"

Lewis stopped, winded, red-faced, gasping for great gulps of air. The scant local wildlife had rapidly dispersed, the bird-things scattering, the six-legged lizard abandoning its boulder.

Greg gave him time to pull himself together, scanning their vicinity with all the magical and nonmagical senses at his disposal to make sure the disturbance hadn't drawn the wrong kind of attention.

Dropping into a crouch beside the glass casket, Lewis braced his elbows on his knees and let his head hang. "Son of a bitch," he said hoarsely. "Sorry. Guess that'd been building up a while."

"No worries."

"At least it was to you. Be my ass if I'd blown my top in front of anybody else."

"As far as I can tell," Greg said, "your secret's safe with me."

"For now. She's got spies all over the place. Whatever you're wanting to do, we gotta do it *fast*."

His every instinct, arcane and otherwise, assured him Corporal Lewis—Tony—was on the level. If his instincts were wrong and it came back to bite him … well, he'd cross that bridge if and when he came to it.

"I've got a jeep parked down the trail," Tony said. "Be less conspicuous than the flashy way you get around."

"Good call."

After lingering another minute at the casket, paying their solemn respect and regrets to Sherri, they set off.

"Might also want to lose the coat," Tony added. "It's pretty conspicuous, too. So's the mark on your forehead but not from as much of a distance."

"Another good call." Greg concentrated, willing the alterations to his wardrobe.

"What the *fuck*? Okay, that's a nice trick."

He'd replaced the Constantine / Castiel look with a mix of military casual: camo cargo pants, boots, t-shirt, khaki fatigue jacket, cap with bill tugged down to help conceal the sigil. Slightly dirtied and rumpled to match the level of Tony's attire. In lieu of dog tags, his silver medallion hung on its customary strand of beads around his neck.

"You mentioned earlier," Greg said as they descended the

sloping trail past wiry tufts of pube-like grass and bramble-bushes, "there were others who went along with it, no matter what they thought. Snap decision to save their skins. How many others?"

"No idea. Hard to tell. All it takes is a whisper of suspicion to get some poor fucker interrogated or outright executed."

"Damn. I wouldn't mind a few more allies."

"I'd like to say they'd step up if they had the option, but it'd be a risky gamble. Once it's on, if they saw a chance to turn the tide … may be another story. As it stands right now, I wouldn't even know who to approach."

"What about prisoners?"

"Less than a dozen in the stockade, last I checked. Most of them in rough shape. Though, you remember the chariot-pullers? That Ben-Hur naked galley slave bullshit? Your angel broke their chains—"

"Yeah, and they didn't waste any time charging into battle," Greg said, recalling how they'd cast off heavy yokes and manacles, seized whatever weapons they could, or just went at it with fists and feet and teeth, attacking their erstwhile captors with a battle-rage to rival Viking berserkers of old.

"The survivors escaped. There've been patrols searching ever since, with no luck. If we could find them …"

"Big if, but worth a try."

They reached the jeep, which was parked off to the side of the trail—a trail which had recently been widened, brush cleared to allow for the hauling of construction materials to build the now-ruined rotunda—behind a thin screen of sickly-looking yellow vines. It was road-worn, dented, and bedraggled, caked with lake-muck to the fenders, its windshield splatted with demonic bug guts. A metal pipe framework hung with barbed wire netting offered passengers token protection from the usual Lake Misquamicus infernal flora and fauna but wouldn't be much use against anything large or determined, and provided zero shelter from the weather.

Tony cleared the vines. Greg settled into the passenger seat, thinking this was the first time—not counting the night spent in the inoperable El Camino, and their insane assault by flying frankentruck—that he'd been in a car since parking at the rinky-dinky airport to board his Cessna and take off to pick up his shipment.

A goddamn lifetime ago. Someone else's lifetime. Someone *normal's* lifetime. Someone with no clue about warlocks, demons, and angels.

Someone who, simply as a matter of habit, had automatically transferred the lucky medallion his grandmother had given him from one vehicle to the other, the way he always did.

Had he neglected to do that one little, minor, routine thing … well, he'd be dead. Full stop, end of story.

It also occurred to him, as Tony started the engine, he'd only paid for a two-day parking pass at the airport.

"Would also help," said Tony as they reached the intersection where the trail up to Bighead Rock met what passed for a more main road along the shoreline, "to know where we're going."

Not that "main road" was giving it much credit, unpaved stretch of dirt and gravel that it was.

"Well, where are we?"

"I don't have a map. The war camp and Crawdy's are off that way. Senator Stump-Humper's place is the other."

"Uh, Senator *what*?"

"Carmichael or something. It's what they call him behind his back. Rich college boy whose parents owned a lakehouse. Got a kinky amputation fetish. His sister was Her Royal Bitchness's handmaid, the one who backstabbed her after she did a number on your angel."

His attention having been rather diverted—Ethriel hurt, the Golems, the desperate huddle, Heck's ghost-truck, the spectral infusion of energy, the translocation spell—Greg had only been peripherally aware of anything else taking place just then. He had a vague mental image of a young woman, drenched head-to-toe in blood (*Billy's blood, you* **murderer!**) and greenish-white ichor (*Billy's* **mother's** *ichor, which was* **also** *your fault!*), scantily clad and sexily curvy. Initially paralyzed, she'd recovered and gotten up, holding the item that had appeared to be a bronzed and bejeweled long-handled marshmallow toasting fork.

For real, the amount of absurdities and incredulities going on around here … how could anyone *not* be crazy???

"It was the next stop for the procession, or parade, or whatever the hell you want to call such a flagrant pile of ego-stroking bullshit. Can you imagine if the *president* ever tried to pull a stunt like that?"

Greg, for all he'd just been thinking about absurdities and incredulities, couldn't. Some scenarios were just *too* stupid to be real. "So they went there, to this guy Carmichael's house?"

"Yeah, for a 'royal visit' and a night of 'special entertainment.'" He made sarcastic air-quotes with his fingers.

"All right, wait. His sister, the queen's handmaid, backstabbed her? Literally, I presume?"

"Literal as it gets."

"His *sister* does this, and she's still going to his *house*?"

"Oh, well, you missed the part where, after she did the backstabbing, one of those clay Golems yanked her arms off, and rather than finish her off, the queen let her live but gave her to her brother as a sex-toy after he kissed sufficient ass."

"… *what*?"

"Or something like that. I don't know; I don't want to know. I was just as glad to have the excuse of staying behind with the kid while they got the casket built. Why I've been in no hurry to catch up."

"Where else was this royal tour thing headed?"

"The bigger Checkpoints. Nazareth, Bethlehem, Jericho, I think, maybe a couple others. I heard some talk about Bible Creek, but nothing confirmed."

Rubbing his brow, the lines of the sigil weirdly comforting beneath his fingertips, Greg pondered. "So, we could either follow, try to get ahead, or stake out this war camp and wait."

"You still haven't told me what the mission objective is. Besides 'go up against her,' that is. Which, in this instance, means what, exactly?"

"She's got something I need, and I doubt she conveniently leaves it sitting around where anyone could—"

"Not the fucking marshmallow fork?"

"No! God. No."

"Well, whatever it is, you'll probably have to …" Tony dragged a thumb across his throat. "Or is that already part of the plan?"

"What do you think?"

"I think if it's *not* part of the plan, it damn fucking well *should* be, because she's only going to get worse, and you and your angel are tippy-top of the Shit List."

"Of that, I am *very* much aware."

"If we do go to the camp, I might be able to sound out some people as possibles, or see if there's any intel on those chariot-pullers. And there are the prisoners in the stockade. Oh, and that Bodean guy, if he's still alive."

"Bodean guy? What Bodean guy?!"

They drove, uncontested, right into the war camp. Tony flicked a salute to the sentries, they flicked bored salutes back, and on they went.

Nobody even looked twice at Greg.

"Some security you got here," he said.

"With so many off escorting Her Royal Bitchness, camp's operating on a skeleton crew. And things tend to get lax with no officers around."

"Just as well for us, then."

"I was counting on it."

Taking it all in as they drove along, Greg remarked, "Gotta say, this isn't quite what I was expecting. What with the way the Wall turned out and everything."

"You mean you've seen Boy Scout Jamborees better organized, disciplined, and defended?"

"Well ..."

"No need to be polite on my account."

"Okay, then; I've seen *tailgate parties* better organized, disciplined, and defended."

"There you go."

"Not that I'm complaining."

Some effort at orderliness clearly *had* been made, but the result was still a mixed sprawl of tents, sheds, troop trucks, RVs, port-a-potties, open-sided pavilions, and structures thrown together out of whatever materials were available. The overall effect was less "rigid military discipline" and more of a cross between "shantytown" and "music festival." Prominent displays of what could loosely be called "artwork" added bizarre touches—murals, mosaics, sculptures. There was a lakeside monument, marking, as Tony explained, where Favius had first arrived from Hell. And a grisly shrine commemorating the queen's matricidal act—

"Hold the phone!" Greg said. "For real?"

"For real. You don't even want to know what happened next."

"I probably don't, but tell me anyway."

Pointing out a raised dais, Tony began telling him anyway.

"On second thought," Greg cut in hastily, "you're right; I *don't* want to know."

"Let's see, what else? Over there's where she had these two holier-than-thou anti-abortion types force-fed fertilized utero-gourd seeds to show them what it was like being pregnant against their will. That was some sick shit for sure. Especially with the man."

Greg listened, thunderstruck, to the whole story, thinking he really had to stop telling himself how nothing could surprise him anymore.

"This couple," he said, when Tony finished. "The Shinns. Would they be possible allies?"

"Fuck, no," Tony said. "They were old, out-of-shape, and useless to start with. Now, they're also post-partum, post-op, practically catatonic, and on suicide watch. Even if we could get to them, the only ones they'd be any danger to would be themselves and their ... gourd-babies."

They circled, at a respectful distance, the mammoth luxury RV designated as the royal residence. To Greg, to his magesight or warlock-vision or whatever, it was lit up brighter than an entrant to a holiday decorating contest. Charms, wards, and hexes covered every inch, layered extra thick at every door, window, air vent. Any hopes of infiltrating it were dashed, as were most hopes of attacking it. He was good, but without a boost from Ethriel, his full power would be like waves crashing on a cliff face. Sure, over time, the waves took their eroding toll and wore down the stone, but such was the work of centuries or millennia, and centuries or millennia, he did not have.

"If you're contemplating blowing it sky-high," Tony said, "don't bother. The heaviest artillery we've got would bounce right off. Bombs, grenades, landmines, same deal. And by your expression, I'm guessing it's a no-go on the magic too."

"Pretty much."

"This item you need, would it be in there? Because, if so, you may be S-O-L. That's—"

"Shit Outta Luck, yeah, no kidding."

He tried extending his astral awareness into the RV, with the idea of getting a quick scan of its interior, but backed off before reaching the wards. Not only did he stand about as much chance of getting through as Chris Hemsworth's motorcycle jump in *Cabin in the Woods*, but it was sure to trigger all sorts of alarms.

What was the saying? In for a penny, in for a pound? He'd trusted Tony this far already …

"The sword," he said, deciding to go ahead and go out on the limb. "The gladius Favius had, the one she picked up and …"

He couldn't bring himself to put it in words, the memory too vivid and painful. Hearing Ethriel's shriek of pain. Seeing her fall, bereft of her celestial armor, naked and frail and vulnerable. Seeing Juno's hateful, savage satisfaction as she swung the blade, shearing off Ethriel's wings of golden light at the shoulder blades, leaving ragged, ichor-oozing stumps.

"*That's* the item you need to get?" Tony asked. "Can't pick anything easy, can you?"

"And take all the fun out of it?"

"Bet you play video games on max diff ultra challenge mode."

"As if. Believe me, I *wish* this was easy. But, as someone told me recently, 'suck it up, kid; free will or not, life is no cakewalk.'"

"Who told you that?"

"Either Clint Eastwood or the Angel of Death."

"Huh?"

"Never mind. I don't suppose you know where they do keep it, the gladius. *Is* it in there?"

"She took it with her. They've got her done up in armor—*his* armor, refitted for her. Helmet, cape, the works. Including a war belt. Gladius hanging on one side, that damn marshmallow fork on the other."

If nothing else, at least now, after getting the full story, Greg finally understood what the marshmallow fork business was about. Though, given what it had initially been used for, he would have been just as happy to remain ignorant of the details.

"So, back to square one," he said. "No entire separate quest into some heavily-guarded booby-trapped inner sanctum."

"No, just a major boss-battle."

"It was going to be a boss-battle either way. I've still got to deal with her, and she's not just going to hand the gladius over without a fight."

"No, she'll use it," Tony said. "She'll use it on you. Do her level best to give you a sharp Hell-bronze enema."

"Thanks for the image."

"*After* she cuts off your—"

"I get it, okay? I get it."

Leaving the RV undisturbed in its layers of spellwork, Tony continued their tour of the camp. Few soldiers, and fewer civilians, were about, and they went right on not noticing the stranger in their midst.

True, he was with one of their own. True, they probably assumed he was from another unit; the company was already a mingled melting pot, and nobody knew everybody. True, as Tony had said, they'd gotten lax in the absence of officers. True, they were primarily concerned with outside threats, but that's what the Wall, Dome, and Checkpoints were for.

His mind kept flashing to movies, where a quick costume change—usually after a tackle-and-scuffle with a guard—was all it took to get into an enemy stronghold. It worked for Indiana Jones more than once, even if Indy had to do a bad German accent. It worked for Luke Skywalker, short for a stormtrooper though he may have been. It even worked for the Scarecrow, the Tin Man, and the Cowardly Lion, putting on fuzzy hats and bulky stiff-flared overtunics, joining the line marching into the witch's castle.

As a kid, he'd been convinced they were chanting "O-REO" and it always made him crave cookies. Even now, corrected after looking it up online, a tenacious vestige of the belief persisted.

So did the craving, reminding him he hadn't actually eaten anything substantial since being in the hidden tunnel, noshing from Brad's stockpile of canned goods and snacks. Where there had in fact been a decent stash of Oreos. He grinned at the recollection of Lorlinda teaching Ethriel how to gently twist apart the embossed wafers to get at the creme filling.

"Now, some folks," Lorlinda had said, "claims they's *Satanic*, Oreos. 'Cuz of simbalizm or sommat. Ain't that a hoot-an'a-half?"

"That's the Cross of Lorraine!" an indignant Ethriel replied upon close inspection. "The Knights Templar used it. And the *Jesuits*! What *next*, banning devil's food cake?"

The majority of the soldiers may have gotten lax with their

officers away, but those on duty at the stockade were still on the ball. Furthermore, even had the incarcerated been of an inclination to rebel, not to mention in any capable physical or mental state to do so, it'd take a full-scale prison break, which would not have gone unnoticed.

As much as it dismayed Greg to leave them there, under inhumane conditions, he had to concede to practicality. Tipping his hand too soon was bound to put the entire mission in jeopardy.

Plus, he knew once he got started, there'd be no turning back. The more he saw of the war camp, the more he yearned to wipe it off the fucking map. It and damn near everything else inside the Dome.

He'd thought the demon-satyr Zilch, with his mutilated slave-thralls, was an outlier example on the extreme end of the horrific continuum. What a naive idiot he'd been!

Look, just *look*, what passed for commonplace! And not only among the long-term residents who'd had years to adapt to their infernal environment, succumbing gradually to corruption and damnation because they had no other choice. Even new arrivals, regular people, who hadn't been here a full fortnight, wholeheartedly embraced the most atrocious, abominable evils!

Agonicity generators. Rampant cannibalism. Amputation orgies.

Celebrating matricide. Sacrificing children.

Emasculation and unnatural impregnation.

And they just … took it in stride. Went with it. Gleefully threw aside any concept of taboos, morality, or decency, and fucking *reveled* in it!

"If I asked you how much you've participated in and partaken of," he said to Tony, striving to keep his tone neutral, "would I regret it?"

"Only if I answered honestly."

"Goddamn it."

"For what it's worth, compared to …"

"You think that makes a difference?"

"Shouldn't it? If someone, say, ate at the mess tents without knowing what was in the stew, does it make them Jeffrey Dahmer?"

"I see your point there, but what about after they *do* know what's in the stew and keep going back to the mess tent just the same?"

"Well, they could not get the stew, but then risk being singled out and hassled by their buddies. Was at boot camp with a vegan, and the shit he got? He didn't last three weeks. Went Section 8."

"So, what, he should have shut up and eaten whatever they served him?"

"You've never been in the military, have you?"

"Well, no."

"Bet your mom didn't have a cutesy sign posted in the kitchen saying, 'House Menu: Take it, or Leave it,' either."

"Not my mom. My aunt, but she never cooked. Still, okay, okay, forget I brought it up. Nobody's perfect."

"Hey, judge me if you're gonna, just keep in mind I did what I had to do in order to survive and not make a big-ass target of myself." Tony paused wryly. "Until I signed on with *you*, that is, which'll get me a lot worse than a court martial if it all goes south."

"Then let's make sure it doesn't." Greg forbade himself from any further questioning along those lines. *Let whoso is without sin cast the first stone* and all that. He might not have personally eaten human flesh, but his own slate was far from clean.

Thunderbolt. Pillar of salt. Tribunal of archangels. Any or all of which could still be in store for him.

"Where did they stash the Bodean guy?" he asked instead. "You said they wouldn't have put him in the stockade yet."

"Holding cell for questioning, the poor son of a bitch. I doubt he knows a damn thing, but why should these torture-happy assholes let it spoil their fun?"

"So even if he can't give them any info about Heck and Lorlinda, they'll torture him anyway." Greg glowered.

"Make an example of him, to encourage anybody who *does* have info to come forward before it's their turn."

"Then reward them for it. Carrot and stick."

"You're catching on."

The "holding cell" turned out to be a sturdy metal Home Depot prefab, windowless, the sort of outdoor storage shed you might keep your riding mower in. Its double doors were secured with a heavy padlock, and a solitary soldier was stationed out front.

Well, "stationed" with a folding lawn chair, a patio

umbrella, a portable radio tuned to a staticky station broadcasting doomsday fire-and-brimstone ravings, a bondage magazine, and one of those little plastic spray-bottle / fan gadgets to spritz a cooling mist whenever he pulled the trigger. His attire made Tony's "military casual" look seem formal: boardshorts, a U.S. Army star-logo tee shirt, Crocs, and oversized sunglasses.

"Yo," he said as the jeep parked and Greg and Tony clambered out. "S'up?"

"If I said, 'surprise inspection,'" said Tony, "would that get you off your butt?"

"Come *on*, dude. Too hot for that BS." He tugged the sunglasses partway down his nose to peer over the rims, revealing multifaceted bug's eyes. "Corporal," he added, with the barest minimum of respect for rank.

"Private."

"Who's this guy?" His insectile gaze flicked over Greg, taking in the lack of insignia. "Some spook?"

"You tell me," Greg said.

"We're here to do some preliminary questioning of a person of interest, preparatory to more thorough interrogation." Tony held up a small, battered, spiral-bound notebook.

The soldier hooked a thumb over his shoulder at the shed. "*That* fuckwit? Good luck. Might as well question an egg-salad sammich."

Greg, leaning into the spook angle, smiled thinly. "Leave that to us."

"In fact," Tony added, "How about you take fifteen, soldier? Have a smoke, get some shade, save yourself overhearing anything above your clearance."

"Twist *my* arm." He got up, dropping the magazine and the spray-fan into the seat of the lawn chair. "Keys're on the peg."

And off he went, at a lazy amble in the direction of a large, low tent serving as a commissary.

"Bozo just bought himself a world of hurt," Tony said, not without some satisfaction, as he retrieved the keys and opened the padlock.

"This seems too—"

"Don't you fucking jinx it."

"Sorry."

If it was "too hot for that BS" outside, where there was at least the occasional passing shadow or desultory breeze, the interior of the metal "holding cell" was a rice cooker. A rice cooker containing not rice but a mélange of rotting vegetation, foot fungus, and BO. Dank and rank, dark, fetid, steamy-humid, with slick moisture condensing on the inner walls and streaking the floor ...

The red-tinged daylight permeating through the open doors didn't do much to improve the ambiance, only spilling a thinly baleful glow across the most minimal of furnishings: a cot, a chemical commode, and a folding aluminum tray table holding a plastic pitcher.

Upon the cot, squinting and shielding his face as he tried to peer at the shadows looming in the doorway, was a miserable-looking sweat-soaked wretch. Naked but for underpants that had been neither tighty nor whitey in a long time, he had thinning hair, jug ears, and more bruises than an apple bounced down five flights of stairs.

"Waylon 'Wormy' Bodean," Tony consulted his notebook.

"I din't do nuthin'!" he whined, cringing. "I din't hurt no one. All's I done was *look*; ain't no law 'gainst lookin'! C'n I helps it if'n them young hussies go an' leave their winders wide open? S'like a invertashun! They'se practercully beggin' fellers t' have a peek! An' Maisy-Sue, she *allus* flauntin' her goodies; jist ask ennerbuddy!"

"Apparently apprehended in the act of voyeurism," Tony continued.

"So I gather," Greg said.

"I swears, I swears t' Lucifer an' Satan, I'se innercent! Them Kellerman boys had no cause t' rough me over s'bad! Even if'n they did, done be done! They got their justice! Why they'se gotta brung the royal *law* in on it ..."

"We aren't here to talk about the Kellermans," Tony told him.

Wormy went suddenly wary. "... then what's it you *do* want?"

The bug-eyed soldier came ambling back from the commissary with an energy drink and a bag of chips just as Tony was replacing the keys on the peg. "Yo, any luck?"

Tony scoffed. "Like you said, we'd've been better off questioning an egg-salad sandwich. Fucking waste of time. Why we're even bothering to keep his useless ass alive is beyond me."

"Copy that. But, hey, beats being on clean-up detail, amirite?" He settled into his lawn chair again, gave himself a refreshing spritz-mist, and opened his magazine.

"Clean-up detail will be the *least* of his worries," Tony muttered as they returned to the jeep.

"How long do you think it'll take anyone to notice?" Greg asked.

"Dinner bell or shift change, probably. Either way, gives us a few hours."

Exiting the camp proved as easy as getting into it had been; a quick exchange of perfunctory salutes, and off they drove. Although it was in their best interest, and to their advantage, Tony was disgusted.

"Some tight goddamn ship we're running. Top brass would shit a ton of bricks."

"Gift horses. Don't knock it." Greg summoned the magical map he'd crafted with Wormy's help. It was a crude thing, a rough sketch of squiggled roadways and waterways and approximate landmarks, floating like a silvery hologram in the air before him.

"Okay, lemme see." Pulling over and idling, Tony took a look, comparing it to a more tangible paper map. "Some of these, I know. The camp, Crawdy's, Bighead Rock of course … Senator Stump-Humper's lakehouse … the one where we found the girl would be over here …"

"Not far from where my plane went down," Greg said, "which must mean Zilch's vineyard is out that way, toward the Wall."

"This must be Checkpoint Uriel, making this Keene's ranch, where they raise the damn emusaurs. Then we've got Dumbfuck Gully and Shit-Yer-Pants Road—"

"Gotta love those quaint, charming, rustic place-names."

"This, the Yard, is some huge combo auto salvage, junkyard, and town dump. It's also Bodean Central. Supposedly, most of the extended family lives in the general vicinity, or within a couple-mile radius. With moonshine operations scattered throughout the further-ranging wooded hilly sections."

Greg tapped an X beside a squiggle. "Now, Wormy said his cabin was here, along … what did he call it?"

"Another of your charming rustic place-names: Crotchrot Crick."

"Ah yes, how could I forget?"

Wormy had also said, since his particular branch of the

family tree—which sounded less like a tree and more like a Gordian knot of tenacious brambles—had had a falling-out with the branch from which Heck and Lorlinda descended, they weren't on the best terms or in close communication.

"Sommat t' do with a prize-winnin' cornbread recerpie," he'd explained, shrugging. "My great-nana on my da's side, she 'herited it from *her* nana an' was s'posed t' share it with her cousins, only, she kep' it t' herself an' her own daughter. My da's ma, *my* nana, that was. Who wouln't share it neither. Oh, the others pulled all manner o' sneaky shit an' threats an' blackmail, tryin' t' get their hands on it. More'n twenny *years*, this went on, an' did it get ugly? Did it ever! Ain't *nobody* c'n hold a grudge like wimmin; take that t' the bank. Then, my aunt Vern up'n died 'thout passin' it on, so now th' gawrshdamn recerpie's lost f'rever! Best cornbread I ever et too. Fuckin' shame."

The main takeaway from the tragic tale being, as far as Greg was concerned, that Wormy only had the vaguest idea where what he referred to as "them lot" lived, let alone ever visited.

"Onliest one worth a dog's fart was ol' Jeb anyways. A body jist couln't *not* like Jeb, feud'r no feud. We'se all called him 'Uncle Jeb,' no matter what kin we was; kep' it simpler, I reckon. Now, Jeb, he owned most ever'thing prop'rty-wise 'tween th' Yard an' Grady's Crossin,' from here t' 'bouts here."

The area Wormy had indicated as being "from here t' 'bouts here" showed on Greg's map as an oblong encased in a silvery dotted line. On Tony's map, it was a basically featureless expanse of dull greens and dun browns, split by the occasional meandering thread of blue.

"County surveyors might as well just stamp DO YOU HEAR BANJOS in big red letters," Tony said. "You want to try driving it, or do you want to do your thing?"

"Translocating blind is tricky, but if it works, it'll save a lot of time."

"And attract a lot less attention."

"Also a plus."

"Though, I don't mind telling you, the prospect of being poofed from one place to another gives me the heebies."

"It's not so bad, once you get used to it."

"Yeah? Are you used to it?"

"Not really, no."

"Great. Makes me feel lots better."

"You don't have to go along," Greg said. "This isn't exactly part of the main objective. I owe it to Lorlinda and Heck."

"And I owe it to that little girl. We're both *in*, okay? Let's do this already."

They found a place to park and conceal the jeep, then picked their way on foot through the malformed and diabolically mutated Florida undergrowth until they reached a modest clearing with a ring of grotesquely fleshy and pulsating mushrooms poking up from the spongy mulch.

"They look like dicks," Tony said.

"Wait until you see one of those actual utero-gourd trees."

"Thanks but no thanks."

"Anyway, this is good, this is a bonus. All that fairy-tale stuff about magic portals has some basis in reality."

"Reality? In case you missed it, reality's out to lunch."

"Fact, then. Whatever. Something like this, it's a thinning, where the barriers are more permeable, making it easier to travel."

"I'll take your word for it."

Greg stepped into the ring, immediately feeling its fungal power burgeon around him. Tony watched a moment, as if waiting to see whether or not anything nasty happened—obscene violation by demonic mushroom-dicked monsters, for instance. When nothing did, he steeled himself and joined him.

"Take my hand," Greg said.

"Sure, why not? Holding hands with another guy in a circle of dicks. Totally normal."

"I told you you didn't have to go along."

"I'm going, I'm going." He grabbed Greg's left hand. "This isn't going to send us someplace weird, is it?"

"Weirder than where we already are?"

"When you put it that way ..."

Closing his eyes, Greg mustered his energies and felt the sigil on his brow tingle. He concentrated on the silvery contours of the map, aiming for the approximate center of the dotted-line oblong. The translocation spell came with certain built-in fail-safes, so it wasn't likely to materialize them inside a solid object or high in the air, but some factors couldn't be accounted for. Like whether or not anyone else would be around; when he and Ethriel had jaunted into the liminal space of the tunnel, they'd appeared right in front of Heck, Blaze, Lorlinda, Andy, Brad, and Dan.

Way to make an entrance, Blaze had said, his remark defusing what very quickly could have become a volatile situation.

"Ready?" he asked.

"Fuck no," Tony said, "but don't let that stop you."

Even through his closed eyelids, the brilliant silver-white flare burst left a smeary negative-colored blotch on his retinas. The air pressure and temperature underwent brief but drastic drops, a nanosecond's ear-popping chill, accompanied by the spinny-fally sensation of weightless vertigo more commonly experienced when on the edge of sleep.

Tony didn't make a sound, but the sudden crushing clamp of his grip spoke volumes. Greg felt something crack and hoped it was only a knuckle.

Then, with a faint elevator-coming-to-a-stop wobble, it was over. Instead of spongy mulch, their feet stood upon loose, gritty earth. The lake-stench had lessened, the mushroom-clearing hush replaced by a cards-shuffling riffle of wind-stirred leaves.

"The *hail*'re you?! An' the *hail* you doin' in th' beanfield?!"

The voice was a woman's, with a rusty twang. Greg opened his eyes to a weathered but not un-pretty face framed by brownish curls straggling from under a floppy gardening hat. Stoutly built, broad through shoulder and hip, she wore baggy denim mid-thigh-length cutoffs, a man's plaid shirt with shirttails tied at the waist and sleeves rolled to the elbows, and battered lace-up boots.

Her hard-worked hands held a hoe at the ready, poised to let them have it with the edge of the metal end. She looked like she could do it too. Had done it before, maybe. Hacked up previous trespassers with farm implements, buried them in the field, and gone about her day with no one the wiser.

"Ms. Bodean?" Greg figured it was worth a shot.

Beside him, having let up the clamp-grip a little, Tony hadn't yet reoriented himself from the translocation. "Whu-thuh?" he mumbled.

"I'se Sadie Bodean, right 'nuff, but that ain't what I asked."

He was *sure* he'd heard Heck or Lorlinda mention the name before, so he took another shot. "My name's Greg. I'm a friend of—"

Her jaw dropped. "You'se that warlock fella! Saint's taints, you cain't be out here! Gots t' get you inside 'fore somebody sees."

"Wait a minute," Tony said. "What's going on?"

"No waittaminutes; put a move on, soldier-boy!" She gave them a nudge from behind with the hoe's wooden shaft as if goading a pair of recalcitrant goats. "You too, warlock, if'n you half a brain in your head."

She hustled them from the beanfield, past a vegetable garden and a fenced chicken coop, around a ramshackle farmhouse where an elderly man and a—skeleton?—yes, a skeleton in a faded paisley dress sat side by side in creaky old rockers on a crooked plank porch, and bustled them into a barn. Dust motes and hay chaff danced in bloodlight beams slanting through the gaps of missing boards. A cow with extra horns poked her head from a stall and lowed conversationally.

Sadie rounded on Greg. "What in th' blue fuck tarnation was you thinkin'? Droppin' in un'nounced like that? Might've earned y'self a split skull."

"I, uh … sorry." Once again, way to make an entrance …

Tony shook himself all over and took a deep breath. "Anytime someone wants to explain, feel free."

"Lorlinda told us 'bout you," Sadie said to Greg. "But who's *he*? Sure ain't no angel."

"Lorlinda's here? She made it?"

"*Was* here. Turned up t'other day on a mota-scoota. After we'd heard what happened over t' the Rock, we thought sure she must'a been dead too … with Heck, an' Zeke, an' Maybelle; it 'bout broke our hearts. Shee-it, we'se even been mournin' *Clarabeth*; she may'a been a kin-killer, but she still was kin. Then, s'prise, there's Lorlinda, an' what a tale she had t' tell!"

"Where is she now? Where did she go?" Greg asked.

"Begged her an' Heck's mommas t' go inta hidin', said that crazy queen gonna be huntin' Bodeans, puttin' bounties on us, wantin' t' punish us for what her an' Heck—*an'* you an' your angel—done. She tried t' c'nvince more of us t' go with, but weren't nuthin' doin'. Pap-Pap, he an' Gammy ain't ever gonna leave the homeplace, so me an' Jammer sent the li'l'uns t' my sister's, then came here t' look after 'em."

"I can't say for bounties," Greg said, "but some of that's already started. They had a Bodean in the holding cell at the war camp—"

"Judas fuck! Who?"

"Uh, Waylon—"

"Wormy? He ain't gon' be no use t' nobody far as revengin' on Heck an' Lorlinda. Him an' his, us an' ours, barely be famb'ly but fer the tecknerkal sense."

"He told us about the cornbread recipe," Tony put in.

"He also told us where we might find Lorlinda's people, which is how we landed in your beans," Greg said. "You may not be safe here."

"May not be *safe*?" Sadie echoed. "Safe, like it's been since't AllHell? Like it's been since't Pro'bishon an' the revenuers? Like it's been since't fer-fuckin'-*always*? Don'tchoo tell *me* where th' boars shit in th' buckwheat. Ain't our first rodeo, Mr. Warlock, not by a *loooong* chalk."

"Sorry if I spoke out of turn," Greg said. "I didn't mean any insult."

"Naw, no, sorry too. I'se gets a li'l hot unner th' collar sometimes; Jammer sure as could tell y' that. But y' hasn't answered me: who's this here soldier fella? He from the camp?"

"I was," Tony said. "Came in with the convoy. I know 'just following orders' is a weasel-ass cop-out, but most of us had no damn idea what we were walking into. Played along as far as I could until … until I couldn't."

"He's an ally," Greg said. "A friend. I trust him."

Tony shot him a skeptical glance. "Not sure how much *I* trust me, but, okay."

"Oh, don't worry; I'll still zap you if I have to."

"Glad we cleared that up."

"Awright, then," said Sadie, "now's we'se all on th' same page, what'cha want? Takin' a big risk poppin' in here, bringin' a bigger risk 'long fer the ride."

"Partly to warn you, if you needed warning," Greg said, "though it turns out you don't. Mostly, looking for Lorlinda. I'd promised Heck I'd try to keep her safe. Which I thought she was, until I found out she'd left the … hideout."

However much he provisionally trusted Tony, and

however much Sadie might have already known, he didn't think it'd be smart to go around talking about the tunnel. Secrets were secret for a reason, especially one so secret Heck had kept it even from Lorlinda until it was the only option.

"Her an' Heck's mommas gave her an earful fer *that*," Sadie said. "Read her the riot act, how she shoulda stayed her butt there rather than go mota-scootin' off through the backroads an' willywags on her own. 'Specially fer their sake; they'd'a rather took th' heat on theirselfs than lose her too. Do the same if'n it was any of my li'l'uns." She chuckled wryly. "A'ccourse, there's times aplenty I'se'd been 'bout ready t' choke th' life outta the boogersnots m'self, but I never ackshully *would*. Weird that way, motherly d'votion; go figger."

Neither Greg nor Tony had any comeback for that.

Sadie, not waiting for one, carried on. "When Lorlinda gits a notion in her noggin, though, ain't no talkin' sense t' her. Stubborn as the day is long, that gal. 'Sides, she had some hoodoo help an' her angel-charm."

"Her what?" asked Tony.

"Later," Greg told him. To Sadie, he said, "It worked, then? It helped? She made it all right?"

"Well, she had her some 'ventures an' close-fuckin'-calls, an' if'n y' ask me, it's a pope-kissin' miracle she made it at all. I gets th' feelin' she downplayed it some so's not to upset their mommas. Seen a diff'rnt truth in her eyes, I did."

"So, she convinced her and Heck's mothers to go into hiding, and she went with them?" Greg asked. "Do you know where?"

"Th' fuck good would that do if'n it'd jist be tortured outta us?"

"They'll torture you anyway," Tony said.

"But they won't get nothin' from it when there's nothin' t' be got."

"That won't stop them."

"Nor'd I 'xpect it to. They'd do it 'cause that's how they are, 'cause they'se sadistic fucksticks an' they likes it, an' 'cause they reckon it'll 'timmerdate ever'body else inta knucklin' under. If'n we don't, or cain't, give 'em what they want, we c'n go out satersfied on one score, at least. May not be a great win, may not be much win 'tall, but makes it not a full win fer them neither. We won't be abserlutely skunked, will've held t' our loy'lty an' princerples. An' *they'se'll* have t' swaller one bitter-fuckin'-pill, bein' outsmarted, outdone, an' denied, by backwood trash *Bodeans*."

"I'd *say* I feel sorry for anyone who gives *her* any shit," Tony remarked after they bade their farewells to Sadie, "but I'd be lying. They damn well deserve whatever the hell they get."

"Agreed," Greg said. "I was tempted to ask her to join us. She seems like she could really kick some ass."

"Why didn't you?"

"One: their family's been through enough already. Two: if and when the queen's people *do* show up and try throwing their weight around ..."

"I'd pay good money to see that ... from a distance."

So as not to take the chance of being seen by any nosy neighbors as they were leaving, Greg had translocated them from the barn to a disused moonshine distillery about a mile away.

On closer inspection, "disused" was euphemistic; large twisted shards of verdigris-greened metal, strewn in an impressive radius and half-buried in tangled foliage—one wedge was embedded in a tree trunk which had since grown over and enfolded it like those pics of old bicycles left decades in the woods—spoke of something more drastic and sudden. Cataclysmic blowout seemed more accurate. What remained of some lean-to structures and a derelict wagon were similarly nearly reclaimed by nature.

Greg didn't want to take his "closer inspection" any closer than that, lest he uncover the corroded bones of whichever ancestral Bodeans may have been working here when the tank went kablooey. He doubted it; he suspected others, in the process of salvaging what could be salvaged from the wreckage, would have taken care of any remains. Nonetheless, he preferred not to go on such a morbid treasure hunt.

"Now what?" asked Tony.

"Now I give you one last chance to bail," Greg said. "I could translocate you out of here, out of the Dome. You can leave this entire clusterfuck behind you and—"

"And what? News flash, pal, it's gone clusterfuck out there too. Didn't you hear about that Painwave thing? By what reports we've gotten, it's wall-to-wall riots and anarchy."

"In here's not going to be much better."

"I appreciate the offer, even if you are just trying to ditch me—"

"If I was trying to ditch you ..." Greg bipped across to the other side of the exploded tank. "I just would," he finished as he reappeared.

"You showing off now, or what?"

"Just making a point."

"Point made." Tony crossed his arms. "Now my turn to make my point. I'm not bailing. Her Royal Bitchness needs to be brought down. If I walk away and don't do everything I can to help, that kid is gonna haunt me the rest of my damn life. She probably will anyway, but it'll be worse if I don't at least try."

"Your point made as well."

"Then I repeat: now what?"

"Now I try to home in on Lorlinda, wherever she is, and see if I can get us there."

"You don't sound reassuringly confident."

"Yeah, well, there's a reason for that." Going to a set destination, even an unfamiliar one, was more reliable than finding a potentially moving target. "Anyway, keep watch; I've got to concentrate."

If he *was* in the wrong to trust Tony, this was another time as good as any to find out. Not that he was putting him to the test; more a basic matter of fact. Would he feel like the world's biggest idiot? Oh, no doubt, but it'd be nothing new.

He curled a fist around his medallion, the septagonal sigil pressing into his palm. His other hand, he held in front of him with fingers fanned. He shut his eyes and did his best to clear his mind of extraneous clutter.

Ethriel and Lorlinda. Their strange friendship, bonding over girltalk and giggling in the subterranean bunker. Weirdly wrong, weirdly right.

Strands of their hair, woven together into a bracelet.

Seek it, find it.

There.

He fixed it in his mind, less waypoint than tracking beacon.

"Got it. Here we go."

Earth, Wings, and Fire

Two Checkpoints down, one to go, and June was more than ready to be done with the whole "royal visit" thing. A fucking tour of the realm ... whose bright idea had that been in the first place? Some political campaign manager or publicist left over from the original convoy?

Note to self: find out, then have their bones dissolved from within, leaving a floppy flesh ragdoll, a skin-sack of meat and blood and organs, still sentient and alive.

The mental image pleased her, and wondering how long a person might last or how well they might function in such a state kept her mind occupied most of the way to Jericho.

The last stop. The last stop, and then back to the camp. Back to the lavish comforts of the palatial RV, where Chef Emilio had a full kitchen at his disposal. Where she had her bed, her big and proper—if far too empty—bed. Her private bathroom with jetted tub.

It had turned out more feasible for the procession to make just a single long round-trip of it rather than several separate smaller jaunts. Quicker, easier, less hassle. But it did mean a bit of roughing it. She didn't actually end up sleeping in the limo; a fairly nice travel trailer, hitched to a troop truck, did the trick. It provided her tolerably comfortable and secure accommodations, and even had room for Iris, Xanne, and Lyle to bed down. The rest of the company bivouacked as best they could in or around the other vehicles. They may not have had the most restful nights, but nobody complained.

Nobody dared. No matter how swelteringly hot or stickily humid. No matter how teeming the nocturnal insects—and if Florida mosquitoes had been bad enough *before* AllHell, well ...

At any rate, the ordeal was almost over. Jericho, and done.

After that, if her adoring loyal subjects wanted to see their beloved ruler, they could hie their asses to court. Let them come to her instead of expecting *her* to slog through the rustic boonies.

Because fuck that. Fuck that right in the ear. She *was* the goddamn *queen*, after all.

The suggestion *had* been put forth that, since they were making the round-trip anyway, they might expand the tour to drop in on the other three Checkpoints while they were at it. So the soldiers there wouldn't feel snubbed, overlooked, or left out.

To which June had also been of the opinion, fuck that, fuck that right in the ear.

By all accounts, Checkpoint Moses was some waterlogged swampy crumbled Lovecraftian temple, presided over by a monstrous mega-gator who may have once been human and presumably chowed down on everyone else who'd been stationed there.

And Checkpoint Uriel? A high, daunting, desert mountain laden with stupid gamer-type quests and challenges and booby traps? With a hermit madman prophet waiting at the top, an insane zealous masochistic flagellant?

Not to mention Checkpoint Gabriel, which June was in no great hurry to ever see again. It might not bear much resemblance now to what she'd seen when the Holy Roller passed that way, having become a bad acid-trip version of the jungles of Vietnam; still, she had zero interest in going there.

With *less*-than-zero interest in being anywhere *near* Bible Creek. Whatever the inbred cult of creeker-freaks was up to, worshiping *her* through the cobbled-together remnants of an Arch-Duke's grenade-blasted skull, she wanted no part of it. The memories, and humiliation, of being on that altar continued to sting.

So, no.

No expanding the tour. No Moses, no Uriel, no Gabriel. Let them go ahead and feel snubbed, overlooked, or left out … tough titty. She'd send Blackwing couriers with politely-worded messages, but that was it.

She was tired of the popemobile and the wristy-wavey-wave. Tired of the salutes and speeches. Tired of the petty bullshit.

And she also just could *not* shake the feeling that,

somewhere in her dominion, something was very wrong.

True to her earlier resolution, she hadn't stayed the night in what passed for the Carmichael lakehouse after the banquet with its "special entertainment." Much to the young Senator's disappointment; he'd kept on with the flirting and heavy innuendos until June had finally instructed Xanne, with Juggernaut as backup, to tell him to knock it off.

He'd done so, and if his disappointment was somewhat mitigated by Maisy-Sue Kellerman practically throwing herself at him, he'd have to settle for that consolation prize.

Naturally, the brothers were none too thrilled, and when Maisy-Sue announced she might "be stayin' on a day 'r three, so's we'se c'n git better 'quainted," Abner had decided he would stay on as well. This led to another bickering row among the Kellerman siblings, Maisy-Sue insisting she didn't "need no busybody shapper-own!" and Abner swearing it was "jist so's y' ain't go lettin' him cut off nothin' 'portant!"

Abel, perhaps wisely, mostly kept out of it, aside from a couple well-meaning forays to try and play mediator. Or he may have had other motives. June, at breakfast the next morning, walked in on him and Iris looking quite companionable, swapping shy glances over by the waffle bar.

So it was that, when the procession was ready to roll, Maisy-Sue and Abner stood on the deck with Trevor and key members of his household, waving goodbye, while Abel swung astride an emusaur whose previous rider had wildly overindulged to the point of needing to be unceremoniously slung into the luggage compartment underneath the band bus. Abel, in his jeans, his plaid shirt hanging fully open, and his longish blondish hair catching the breeze, could have modeled for the cover of a western-themed romance novel … except for, of course, the emusaur. Nonetheless, June could hardly blame Iris for leaning against the popemobile's bulletproof shielding, chin cupped in her hand, gazing dreamy-eyed.

As Lyle put it, "My-oh-my, but he *is* one hunk of backwoods beefcake to be sure."

Note to self: if he's interested, find Abel some sort of job around the camp, something of decent status, no low-level grub or grunt work.

*Note to self, additional: and do **not** fuck him, no matter how* *hunky he is; you cannot afford another jealous murdery backstabby handmaid.*

Of course, she doubted Iris would go *that* far, but, better to avoid the complication altogether.

The journey to Nazareth had gone smoothly enough, and up close, its demonic renovation was extremely impressive. It was rock and metal, stone and iron, a mashup of the medieval and the modern, with a hefty helping of Hell thrown in.

The Wall reared high and formidable, bristling with spiky parapets and ramparts. Upon broad weapons platforms, enormous ballistae and catapults waited at the ready, capable of hurling deadly payloads at ranges upward of a mile. There were gunslits, arrowslits, portcullises, ironclad drawbridges, cannons, and huge cauldrons. The main fortress itself was an impenetrable bulwark; what it lacked in luxury, it more than made up for in offense, defense, armories, and sheer menace.

As for the Gargoyles ... having not yet seen them in person, June found herself inadequately prepared. She was used to Juggernaut, had been used to the other Golems, great near-indestructible clay behemoths that they were. She'd been more than used to Favius, his majestic muscular glory, a powerful dominant presence in his war gear (or *out* of it, wink-wink-nudge-nudge; *damn*, but she missed him!).

After everything she'd thus far experienced, therefore, being met by a solid shield-wall of Gargoyles left her surprised at her own surprise.

They were as much rock and metal as their fortress, stone-skinned, jasper-eyed, iron-clawed, gravel-voiced. Armed and armored to the nines and beyond with everything from full plate to high-tech visors, from rocket launchers to battle axes.

"Now, *this*," said Xanne, "is some military *hardware*. No fuckin' wonder those chickenshit dicks in DC had to resort to trying the nuke. Any frontal assaults here must've been like toothpicks and spitballs going up against a herd of pissed-off rhinos."

Indeed, the view from the outwardmost parapet confirmed it: a desolate and ravaged no-man's-land stretching across miles of what had until recently been a more-or-less ordinary expanse of undeveloped, only vaguely tainted northwestern Florida real estate. The torn-up terrain smoldered here and there, pocked with impact craters and bomb-blasts, strewn with wrecked tanks and artillery.

By the looks of it, none of the attacking forces had gotten within a quarter-mile of the actual Wall, let alone done any appreciable damage. Or if any damage *had* been done—insignificant at best—it had already been repaired.

How many lives, how many good and decent mortal American lives, had been lost in those futile attacks? No way of knowing; any dead remaining unclaimed would have provided a juicy smorgasbord for local scavengers. Or already rotted, providing an even juicier smorgasbord for maggots, worms, and flies. Broiling, boiling, seething, and teeming in the sun.

The sun.

It was also pretty weird to see the sun again. The sun and sky, unobscured by the *Aurora Diabolicus*, the parapet from which they made their observation being one of the few sections protruding past the Dome.

Being out there made June uneasy. Made her feel vulnerable and exposed. Not weakened but ... precarious. And disoriented.

The sky wasn't supposed to be blue. The sun wasn't supposed to be a bright ball but a smeary blur. The air wasn't supposed to be fresh—

Well, okay, with the scent of death wafting up from the battlefield, it was far from fresh, not *fresh*-fresh by any means, but it was a minorly unpleasant whiff compared to the thick-enough-to-taste miasma of Lake Misquamicus.

"Yes, thank you, well done, exemplary," June had told the Nazareth commander. "If it's all the same to you, though, I'd like to go back inside now."

She had no idea what his name was because he spoke with the dulcet tones of a rock crusher arguing with a cement mixer. When he'd introduced himself, bowing as deeply as his stony body and bulky armor would allow, the closest she could guess was "RRKHAK." But he understood normal speech well enough and readily complied.

Making it a short stopover, claiming they had to hustle if they hoped to be at Bethlehem on schedule, went off without a hitch. If anything, June got the strong impression that the Gargoyles were just as glad to have them gone as she was glad to be going. They had a kind of rumbly superiority about them, as if, as far as they were concerned, any non-Gargoyle was a soft and squishy liability, too weak and fragile to be of any use.

Not that she'd been in any huge hurry to get to Bethlehem either … the Blackwings had always annoyed her. How much of her annoyance was due to her instant hate-at-first-sight reaction to Captain Adler projected unfairly onto the rest of the unit, she wasn't sure, but also didn't really care. Bunch of lockstep jackboot Nazis, in their own way every bit as smugly superior as the Gargoyles. *They* could fly, which automatically put them above the pathetically ground-bound in every sense of the word. *And* they had *far* sharper, snazzier uniforms than anybody else.

Okay, maybe her opinion *was* colored by her dislike of Adler, but it wasn't *only* that. Arrogant flying fucksticks, all glossy black leather, shiny boots, and epaulets.

But they *were* diligent, vigilant, and single-mindedly loyal. They *had* sustained terrible losses during the battle at Bighead Rock, dozens of them shot down or incinerated in a colossal fireball. They *did* provide valuable surveillance, air support, and quick courier service.

So, off to Bethlehem the procession had gone. Not slouching toward it like some rough beast waiting to be born, or whatever the fuck that poem was, but neither were they going to any great lengths for neatness and precision, because everyone knew those arrogant flying fucksticks would outshine and show them up in every possible way.

Which, yea verily, they did.

Full-scale pageantry, the jerks. Making the formation flyover a small group of them had done at the beginning of the procession paltry by comparison.

Stunts, loops, dives … intricate flag and banner routines … skywriting in plumes of colored smoke … perfectly synchronized, not a pinion out of place.

It really was spectacular, sensational, breathtaking.

Goddamn showoffs.

And, after, they strutted. They preened. They fucking *preened*.

Captain Adler's replacement didn't have two bird-heads, just one. But that one was proud and sleek and streamlined, with a backswept feathered crest and a beak polished to a high sheen. He called himself The Nightfalcon, eschewing any military rank or title. The snugness of his uniform showcased a gorgeously gym-sculpted bod, with a butt so fine as to render even Lyle momentarily speechless.

Oh, and he knew it too, The Nightfalcon did. More vainglorious and narcissistic than that guy in *American Psycho*, he needed not a partner but a mirror with a hole in it.

Under his leadership, the tone and tenor at Bethlehem had already somewhat shifted. Gone were Adler's driving obsessions for annihilating anything threatening their airspace, or doing deadly strafing runs and raid-strikes to targets outside the Dome. Now, it was all about the flash and flair.

Given this *was* a royal visit from the queen, The Nightfalcon and his troops made an effort not to be *too* condescending … to her, anyway. In public, to her face. She had the distinct feeling, honed by a lifetime of experience, that they unleashed the snide comments and sneery remarks as soon as she was out of earshot.

They also made clear their opinions of Blackwings serving as couriers. It wasn't the task itself, but the sense of treating them as mere messengers. Errand boys. Package deliverers. With a "what next?" implication of their possible subjugation to further indignities, like carrying passengers.

"Too bad 'Lyft' is already taken," Xanne had said, earning herself a few piercing glares.

Even June's assurances that the couriers were most highly valued and respected wasn't sufficient for The Nightfalcon's ego; he wanted more tangible recognition. Actual badges of honor. Titles. Perhaps an exclusive knightly order.

"Be calling himself The Knightfalcon in no time, if you do," Lyle told June later, in private. "Might want to nip this one in the butt."

"Bud. Nip in the *bud*."

"Guuuuurl, we'd both like to nip him in the butt, and you know it."

"Lyle's right," Iris said. "Not 'bout the butt thing, I mean—"

"It *is* a damn nice one, though," Xanne cut in.

Iris shot her a crinkle-nosed look; her former meek reticence had diminished significantly over the course of their journey. "I *mean*, 'bout him putting on airs, making much of himself. He's apt t' be a problem, and someday right soon, if you don't remind him who's queen."

"I suppose." June sighed, tilting her head per Lyle's direction so he could apply eyeliner on the left. Funny how what had once seemed to foreign, alien, and uncomfortable to her—having someone else fuss over her hair and makeup—had become natural as breathing. "As if I don't have enough aggravation to deal with. Speaking of which, any news from the camp? I can't shake the feeling something's gone wrong over there."

"Nothing since Nazareth," Xanne said. "Want me to dispatch a Blackwing? Or send Meep? He's getting faster all the time. He'll be running *across* the lake like the kid from *The Incredibles* before you know it."

"No matter how fast he runs," June replied, "that still sounds like a bad idea. Send a Blackwing. As for Nightfalcon—"

"*The* Nightfalcon," corrected Iris. "With a capital The."

"Yes, him. I'll tell him I'm considering the order of knighthood idea, ask him to start working on ideas for emblems ... coats of arms ... you know, that heraldry shit. Should keep him busy and buy me some time to make up my mind. Dissension's the last thing we need right now."

Her meeting with Nightfalcon—with *The* Nightfalcon, pardon me!—went fairly well, since June made it a priority to pander to his vanity, laying on the compliments with a fucking trowel. She kept the rest of it vague, avoiding making any promises. No royal decrees, nothing to be put in writing or set in stone, nothing that would hold up in a court of law.

Not that they *had* courts of law; in *this* realm, it was all *her*, babycakes. ***Juno Regina,*** law and order and life and death as she pleased.

The Nightfalcon, meanwhile, ate up the pandering and compliments, preening so hard it was a wonder he didn't pull a muscle. The prospect of designing a heraldic blazon had his backswept feather-crest just about quivering.

"Special uniforms for the Knights Courier as well, I think," he said. "Something more elaborate, to let them really stand out. Elaborate yet dignified."

At the first sign of plumed Musketeer hats, starched Elizabethan collars, or powdered wigs, she was going to pull the plug on the whole charade, but she didn't let it show in her expression. Instead, she manufactured a gracious smile.

"I shall entrust the matter to your impeccable taste."

"Very form-fitting, of course," he went on. "Aerodynamic."

"Of course."

He clacked his beak thoughtfully—he'd had an underling literally buffing it when she came in, using a device like a handheld shoe polisher—and brushed at an invisible speck on his sleeve. "The knighthood ceremony will need its own stirring musical theme too."

"Oh, obviously," June said, wondering what he'd look like plucked bald as a stewing chicken, and whether his feathers would make for an even comfier mattress than emusaur down.

Allowing herself a further flight of fancy, she envisioned him kneeling before her as she tapped his shoulders one after the other with the flat of the gladius, then used it to lop off his arrogant, preeny head. *I dub thee Sir Shut-The-Fuck-Up-You-Vain-Egomaniac.*

Somehow, they got through the entire visit without any serious altercations between members of the "airborne elite" and the "ground-bound dirty-feet." Verbal jabs and petty passive-aggressive crap was another matter, but it never got physical ... aside from one close-call, when a Blackwing lieutenant, who'd known Xanne before, let drop (with blatantly faux innocence) a reference to a certain nickname. June had interposed Juggernaut to deter any further escalation, and Xanne held herself in check with only minimal grumbling, but Satan help them both the next time their paths crossed.

Then, on the procession went, wending around the lake toward the roaring inferno that was Checkpoint Jericho. Its fire—its **FIRE**—could be seen from quite a distance, and its heat felt from almost as far.

"A cold day in Hell is sounding pretty good right about now," June said, fanning herself despite the agonicity-powered AC being cranked to its highest setting.

"Hmm?" Iris hadn't been paying attention. Abel, his emusaur pacing the popemobile, now wore his shirt tied by its sleeves around his waist, his rugged torso gleaming, beadlets of sweat caught like tiny diamonds in his lusty crop of gingerish chest hair.

"Nothing."

Note to self, additional additional: Lucifer have mercy, if Iris doesn't nail him soon ...

The swoop-flutter arrival of a Blackwing courier saved her from finishing the rest of that thought. It was the one Xanne had dispatched to go check on the camp, a woman with golden bird's eyes and a pert beak set in an otherwise normal human face, and a fluffy featherlike texture to her hair.

A signal from Xanne brought the line of vehicles and riders to a halt. The Blackwing landed smartly beside the xenomorphic pace car. Something in her posture, the restless flick of her wings, and the quick, darting motions of her head, indicated agitation.

As if there was indeed news to report. And not the kind of news that might go over well, but the kind to elicit considerable queenly ire.

"… squirmy, slimy, scum-suckin', low-belly, treach'rous worm-dick! We ought shoulda wrung ever'thing he knowed outta him then an' there an' kilt his ass. I'se *told* y'all them Bodeans was nothin' but trouble, an' now, look! Jist *look*! Din't I *say*—?"

Xanne seized Spot by the grubby shirt-front, yanked him to his tippy-toes with his nose mere inches from hers—which couldn't have been pleasant for either of them—and snarled, "Shut your fuckin' noise-hole." Her eyes flared red as brake lights. With a bony crackle, her devil-horns grew another inch.

Spot, sensibly, shut his fuckin' noise-hole. He may have also wet his pants a little. When Xanne released him, roughly pushing him away from her, he stumbled over his own feet and seat-planted hard enough to make his jaw clack.

"Are you quite finished?" June asked them both, striving to keep her tone level.

Xanne huffed gustily, rubbing at the bases of her horns. "Okay, *that* hurt. Ma'am, sorry, ma'am. Momentary lapse."

Needless to say, the report the Blackwing—Private Kestrel—had brought from the war camp had not, in fact, gone over well.

It wasn't so much the loss of Wormy Bodean; June had figured he wouldn't have any useful information anyway. As far as making an example of him went … what would be the point? By the sounds of it, not even his close kin gave two shits about him. Hell, they'd probably send a thank you card.

To be sure, the lazy incompetent sentry who'd let it happen, and hadn't even noticed for several hours, needed to be punished. Harshly. Extremely harshly. He was currently in the stockade, under reliable guard, awaiting his fate. There'd be no court-martial, no defense attorney, no appeals. He had fucked up; ergo, he would pay.

Though not as much as the actual traitor in their ranks would when he was caught and brought to justice. Disloyal, turncoat bastard! How *dare* he? Yes, all right, maybe the stuff with the little girl had been a *tad* on the excessive, but was it reason enough to betray his oath, his unit, his uniform, his fellow soldiers, and his by-Satan *queen*? Corporal Anthony Lewis would rue the day he'd let sentiment stand in the way of duty!

Rue the day … seriously?

Fuck it. He'd rue the day *plenty* by the time she was done with him.

Most infuriatingly irksome of all, however …

"No one else got a good look at him, this so-called 'spook'?" she asked. "No one else thought twice about it, let alone thought to get his name or check his credentials?"

"As he was appropriately attired and in the jeep with Corporal Lewis," Kestrel said, "they presumed it was a matter of some legitimate business." While she was not *as* smugly arrogant as many Blackwings, more than a trace of it came through now; the unspoken *what would you* **expect** *from ground-bound dirty-feet?* loud and clear.

"So they gave this … person … the run of the camp. Unquestioned. He and Lewis entered, did as they pleased, and left again. Without raising a single ripple of suspicion."

Kestrel's beak prevented her from visibly smirking, but June was sure she was on the inside. "So it would seem, Your Highness."

"None of our mages noticed a single-goddamn-thing either?"

"The wards and spellwork around the royal residence were not triggered or tampered with in any way. As those were their priority, it had not occurred to them to be on the alert for other magics."

June fumed in silence for several seconds, tendrils of smoky redblack seething around her fists and coiling through her hair. The others kept quiet, watching her, apprehensive. Leaving it for her to say what all of them were thinking.

When she did say it, she said it through gritted teeth, her nails digging crescents into her palms, tense with rage. "It was him. It must have been; who else could it be? That asshole warlock. Nachtwald. It was *him.*"

Xanne argued in favor of calling off the rest of the tour and heading back straightaway. Whereupon, her attitude suggested, she was ready to start busting heads from one end of camp to the other.

But, since they were already so close to Jericho and the quickest homeward route meant continuing along their plotted course rather than making the longer reverse trip, June decided they would keep on going. Including the scheduled stop at the Checkpoint, which had been planned to be a brief one anyway. Jericho had a smaller contingent—four soldiers—than Nazareth and Bethlehem.

It was also, as had been noted, on *FIRE*. While her advisors felt fairly confident most of the procession wouldn't broil alive, they couldn't be a hundred percent certain. Less so when it came to the vehicles and mounts. Nobody was eager to see the damage an angry, flaming emusaur might do. And even if nobody actually burned, the roaring incinerator heat on top of the day's already-climbing temperatures made the prospect of lingering longer than they had to about as appealing as swimming in an active volcano.

Thus, at Jericho, there would be no ceremony or speechmaking. A quick how-do-you-do, thanks for your service, blah-de-blah, seeya, bye.

Oh, and putting in the transfer request—not that it was a "request," coming from her—to have that Jason Prentiss guy assigned to Senator Carmichael's security detail. At least, that was how it would look on paper, to keep the red-tape bureaucrats happy. If dear Trevor really wanted his friend around for more salacious reasons, fine; she wasn't about to file official documents with phrases like "amputation fuck-buddy" in writing.

On they went, with June just as glad to not have excited crowds lining the road. She was in no mood for the smiling and the wavey-wave. Her thoughts were dark, storm clouds jagged with forks of crimson lightning.

Gregory Nachtwald. The asshole warlock himself. He'd returned, but without his angel—the densest mental doorstop in the war camp couldn't have missed a for-fuck's-sake *divine being*; no matter how well disguised, there would be impossible-to-hide traces.

Was it possible she'd hurt the holy whore-slut even worse than she'd thought? Or, dare to dream, killed her? It'd been bad, no doubt about it … the way the gladius had pierced the angel's side, drawing amber-honey ichor, might not have been immediately fatal, but a slower death from lingering unhealable internal injuries would be just as satisfying. Likewise, shearing off those radiant, dazzling wings … a debilitating, crippling blow at the very least … the ultimate insult and injury combined. What use was a wingless angel? Perhaps she'd been put down, put out of her misery, like a horse with a broken leg.

Could that be it? Could Nachtwald have come back on a crusade of maddened, grief-stricken vengeance? As if *his* loss might somehow possibly match *hers*! Preposterous. His could barely approximate!

He must have been snooping around the camp with more than rescuing some worm-dicked hillbilly on his mind, whether or not said worm-dicked hillbilly was related to his erstwhile allies.

Despite what the mages had told Private Kestrel about the RV's spellwork not being tampered with, June wasn't about to trust any hastily drafted third-raters when a warlock of Nachtwald's abilities was involved.

The bitch of it was she'd been looking forward to relaxing in the welcome comfort of the RV, and her own bath and bed. Couldn't very well do that now, could she? After all the times Favius had warned against hubris, it'd be such a basic blunder she'd never forgive herself.

Jericho's edifice of **FIRE**, a towering inferno as it were, now dominated the landscape. The popemobile's AC, chugging at full power, was on the verge of blowing the agonicity generator's synapses, yet only mustering a lukewarm, tepid wheeze.

The procession stopped. The limo driver opened the door. June stepped out into a fucking crematorium that made a lukewarm, tepid wheeze seem like an arctic chill.

"Whew lordy!" Lyle declared, mopping his brow. "When they said Hell on Earth, they weren't goosing the gander.

257

Spontaneous combustion while you wait!"

"Let's make this quick as goddamn possible," June said to Xanne. "Get it over with."

Xanne shouted for parade assembly, but the heat was clearly hitting them all hard. The troops formed up, drenched in sweat, some already blistering. The band launched into a rather ragged rendition of Johnny Cash's "Ring of Fire"—when all was said and done, June *would* need to have a word with the band director—as best they could before their brass instruments began to melt.

Iris also appeared about to melt. The sight of Abel Kellerman shucking his jeans, leaving him only in boots and boxer briefs, probably didn't help. It certainly didn't lower June's own thermostat, and she forced herself to avert her gaze.

Unfortunately, her gaze first averted to Spot, panting like a dog locked in a hot car on a summer day. His pimples may have actually been boiling over with oily pus. She averted her gaze again.

Her limo driver, with his leathery skin and polarized sunglasses, looked least affected. Well, him and the skeletal horse among the riders; the other horses showed varying degrees of discontent.

No emusaurs had yet ignited, but their quilly feathers had taken on a dry, tindery, about-to-curl texture, and they shifted from foot to foot as if trying to minimize direct contact with the smoking earth. Which June could feel baking through the soles of her own sandals.

Whose brilliant idea had this tour been, again?

A set of large fiery double-doors swung outward, and an envoy of lumpy pyroclastic pumice-people emerged. If searing charcoal briquettes covered with a flaky coating of whitish-grey ash took humanoid shape, every movement further cracking that ashy coating to reveal the furnace-hot orange glow beneath, the results might've approximated the figures now approaching.

"Hail, Queen Juno!" the one in the lead proclaimed in a gruff, crackling incinerator's voice. "Captain Nora Schultzmann, OIC of Checkpoint Jericho." Schultzmann saluted, emitting a shower of embers.

Although quite stocky, the overall bodily contours did suggest the feminine. The rank had to be taken on faith, as none of them wore uniforms or insignia.

"Captain," June said, giving a brief nod.

*Do **not** thank them for the "warm" welcome, do not, just fucking **don't**!*

To the captain's right was what could best be described as an obese lava-man, his rolls flowing over each other and being reabsorbed in an almost hypnotic manner. To her left was a more slender, androgynous form, resembling a mobile, lit-from-within version of the bodies found at Pompeii. These were introduced as Privates Russ Ingersoll and Shae Saunders, respectively.

"We were under the impression," said Xanne, after a hasty, perfunctory round of pleasantries, "your duty roster numbered four. Is the other holding down the fort?"

An irritated ten-inch gas-flame jet shot straight up from a fumarole in the fissured top of Captain Shultzmann's head. "Private Prentiss is in custody, pending trial on counts of desertion, defiance, and disobeying direct orders."

"And theft," the refugee from Pompeii added. "Stole my bike."

"But, mmm-*mmm*," chortled the lava-man, "does he smell like barbecue! Makes me hungry every time I go down to the dungeon."

"Is he alive?" June asked.

Schultzmann shrugged indifferently, which caused a great shedding of ashy flakes from her upper body. "He heals almost as fast as he burns."

"Lost his looks, though!" The lava-man chortled again.

June pursed her lips, nonplussed. If Senator Carmichael was expecting a sexy, studly soldier-boy and got Freddy Krueger's younger brother instead, he would not be very happy. How to handle this curveball? She was at a loss.

Luckily, Xanne stepped up to the plate. "Well then, excellent; you've dealt with an awkward situation admirably, under trying circumstances. I see commendations in your future. Have him brought out. We'll transport him to Camp Favius and hold him there until a proper trial can be arranged."

They brought him out in a cage of fire, and damned if he *didn't* smell like barbecue, as the lava-man had said. Or one of those Hawaiian luaus where they roasted a whole pig in a sand pit and pulled it up, sizzling with juices.

But, as Schultzmann had also said, he healed fast, almost as fast as he burned. His skin char-blackened before their very eyes, then peeled off in long crispy curls, revealing newer but already blistering skin beneath. Which charred again, repeating the cycle.

And, as June herself had thought, he *did* look like Freddy Krueger's younger brother. Scorched bald all over, a naked man-shaped mass of sears and scars, the overcooked meat of his feet nearly falling from the bones, and his groin …

No, the state of his groin wasn't anything she wanted to look at, thanks. She got as far as thinking about a hot dog dropped into a campfire and shoved it from her mind.

The fiery cage sat atop a wheeled cinderblock platform, pushed along by a bevy of flame-gremlins and pumice-imps. They rolled it to a stop, glanced to Captain Schultzmann for permission, got it, and capered around June in an excited, chittering gaggle. Some salaamed, wafting yet more waves of heat her way.

"Yes, all right, that'll do, thank you," she said. In her armor, she had a pretty good idea what a foil-wrapped baked potato felt like in the oven, and she was worried her cape would go up in a blazing whoosh.

The imps and gremlins retreated. As they did so, the cage's bars extinguished into puffs of smoke. The prisoner collapsed to his hands and knees, though the cinderblocks could have easily been used to fry eggs.

"Jason Prentiss?" June asked.

He raised his head, trying to look at her, but his eyes were occluded bubbles swelled near to the bursting point. His lips were fused most of the way together. The cartilage of his ears and nose had gone malformed and uneven and about to slough off. A rough, hoarse, affirmative-sounding croak was the best he could do.

Two soldiers marched him—well, guided his blind and clumsy steps—to one of the vans, secured him inside, and clambered in with him. Two other heavily armed soldiers joined them. Excessive precautions, no doubt, but word of what had happened at the camp had gotten around, and nobody wanted to be next on the disciplinary shit-list.

Private Saunders, the Pompeii-looking one, passed Xanne a bundle of paperwork—asbestos sheets, unless June missed her guess—and a thin charcoal rod to use as a pen. In a matter of minutes that seemed much longer, half the procession on the verge of heatstroke or seeing delirious mirages in shimmering pockets of superheated air, the necessary documents were signed, countersigned, and approved.

The formalities thus concluded, they made their goodbyes and got the fuck out of there. None too soon, in June's opinion. As Jericho shrank behind them, she stripped down and splayed herself in front of the AC unit. If its tepid, lukewarm wheeze *wasn't* actually an arctic chill by comparison, it was at least a semi-cooling balm.

She would have preferred being neck-deep in a tub of ice water, guzzling a frozen margarita from a glass the size of a punchbowl, but this and a "glacier blue" store-brand electrolyte drink were the best she was going to get for now.

Iris Tate slumped in her seat, wilted as steamed lettuce, damp cloths draped around her neck and over her forehead. "Anybody'd cracked smart 'bout how 'least it was a dry heat, I swear I might've slapped their face."

June squinted sideways at her. "That's not *you* cracking smart about it being a dry heat, is it?"

"… aw dammit …" She lifted a hand, palm open.

"No, no. Royal pardon. Just don't say it again."

"Yes'm. I mean, no'm. I won't."

"Good. I think we've suffered enough for one day, don't you?"

Cheating Death

Adding to the ever-growing list of things Gregory Nachtwald never in his life would have expected …

How about translocating smack into the middle of a deep-bayou zydeco party?

Bombarded from all sides by energetic Cajun and Creole rhythms, the thickly spicy scents of gumbo and jambalaya, surrounded by writhing half-naked dancers streaked in body paint, he reeled back in surprise and sensory overload. If Tony hadn't grabbed him by the arm, he would have ended up falling flat on his ass yet again.

Way to make an entrance.

The silvery flash of their abrupt arrival brought the festivities to a sudden discordant halt. People spun to face them. Many large, muscular people, poised to attack.

Though the spell had taken a fair bit of his energy, Greg whipped up a protective ward, lines of eldritch light forming the familiar septagonal sigil around himself and Tony.

Tony swung up his assault rifle, but Greg swatted it down.

"Hold your fire."

"But—"

As it happened, more than a few similar assault rifles were leveled at them. Along with assorted other weaponry. Some rustic, some top-notch military hardware, and a few decidedly arcane. A curvaceous Black woman with dreadlocks and stark-white deathmask makeup held a staff topped with a trio of skulls, their hollow eye sockets glowing marshfire-green; Greg knew right away her power was formidable. So was that of a Black man dual-wielding yard-long whiplike coral snakes, while several more of the deadly reptiles twined about his torso.

"It's the warlock," said a burly guy in a Utilikilt, his

tanned skin covered with blue Celtic-looking warpaint.

"… Corporal *Lewis*?" asked another, who wore jockeys and a tank top and tiger stripes.

"Davidson?" Tony peered dubiously at him. "You're out of uniform, soldier."

"Isn't he on *their* side?" snarled another, sporting a crude prosthetic where one arm ended at the elbow. It appeared to have been made from alligator jawbone, held on by strips and straps of gator-hide.

Greg realized these were the former military POWs, the surviving chariot slaves whose bonds Ethriel had broken, who'd joined the battle against Favius's troops and then escaped in the ensuing chaos.

"We're not here to cause trouble," he said, stepping forward, palms turned out. It may have presented as a peaceful gesture, but if it also just so happened to be good for blasting a wide-range conical magic shockwave, well, bonus. "We just—"

"Eeeeeeeee!" a shrill cry interrupted. Someone barreled through the crowd, elbowing bystanders willy-nilly. "Holy fuckaroni! Greg! It's you, it's rilly *you*, saints-an'-sinners, I'se c'n hardly *b'leeve* it!"

Lorlinda Bodean leaped at him in a flying tackle, the protective ward not hindering her in the slightest. She slammed into him full-tilt, damn near sending him flat on his ass *again*, but he kept his footing and caught her in his arms.

"Lorlinda!" He swung her in a wild circle as she squealed with delight. "*So* goddamn glad to see you!"

Everyone else, if not exactly fully standing down, eased off their hair-trigger high alert on a provisional basis.

"Whatchoo *doin'* here?" she asked as he released her. "How'd'ya find us?"

Gently grasping her wrist, he ran the pad of his thumb over the intricately woven friendship bracelet. "This. Ethriel told me—"

"She awright?" Lorlinda cut in anxiously. "*Please* tells me she's awright; I couln't hardly *bear* it if'n—"

"She is. For now. Uh, long story, can get into that later. You, though? You're all right?"

A slightly crazed giggle issued from her, with a slightly crazed look to match. "'Nuther long story, too long t' get inta … but I'se fine, best as c'n be, anyways. Made it, din't I? Tha'ss what matters."

"And found some friends, I see."

"Oh, yeah." She turned, raising her arms and her voice. "Ever'buddy, s'okay, this here's Greg. I done tol' you 'bout him. He's a good 'un."

"Then what's he doing with one of *them*?" demanded the man with the alligator jawbone prosthetic, glowering suspiciously at Tony.

Another long story, but Greg summarized as succinctly as he could, his case augmented by character references from Davidson and a couple of the other ex-soldiers, and a bone-casting by the dreadlocked deathmask woman. She tossed a strew of vertebrae in an arc in front of Tony, studied the pattern, and gave a nod.

In the end, everyone was satisfied—except maybe the prosthetic guy, who remained skeptical—and the various weaponry went on standby. Tensions lessened, people dispersed, the zydeco band struck up more music, and a few dancers renewed their writhing gyrations. Others gathered by the food, where jambalaya was being dished up from a large pot, a table was heaped with the steaming bounty of a crawfish boil, and older ladies in colorful head-kerchiefs handed out bowls of gumbo served with potato salad and 'slaw.

"Reckon we all's cain't help but be some parer-noid," Lorlinda said, leading Greg and Tony away from the lively heart of the party. "No 'ffense or nuthin'?"

"None taken," Tony said. "If I was in their shoes, I would've reacted the same way."

Now that he had the opportunity, Greg got a better look around. It was a bayou village of sorts, stilt-shacks and rope bridges suspended over sluggish waterways, treehouse huts reachable by ladder, pole-punts moored along docks of warped and weathered boards. He saw nets and fish traps, drying racks, baskets. As dusk came on, jars of hellfire-flies served as lanterns. The elderly enjoyed their porch rockers and pipes; kids ran and chased and threw things.

"Where are we?" he asked.

"Near t' Shallowstown," Lorlinda said. "Deeper inna swamplands, though. Checkpoint Moses be off thataway a couple miles, I think. They say it's gone all creepy, with ruins an' vines an' such, an' a giant gator-god."

"How did you end up here?"

She did the crazy giggle again. "Bishop's balls, I'se wond'rd that myself. See, I found this mota-scoota, musta been stashed there fifty years. A Vespers or sommat, like when bells ring at a monner-stary? I dunno. Brad and Dan, they fixed it up fer me so's I could git where I'se goin' faster. Scairt half t' death, I was, bein' on m'own, but I couln't jist set an' do nuthin'."

"Ethriel said you were trying to get home."

"S'right. Done did it too! On th' way, runned inter this buncha fellas, an' they'se 'membered me from Bighead Rock. All chained up t' th' Gen'rul's chariot, they were, 'ntil Ethriel set 'em loose. They was hidin' out in th' wilderness with no idear where t' go or what t' do, so they vol'nteered t' sign on with me." She laughed and shook her head, pigtails bouncing. "Like I'se any kinda leader-type? Shee-it. Still, figgured, why not? Worst's I c'd do was git us all kilt, an' that'd likely happen with 'r without."

"We were at the farm," Greg said. "We met your … cousin? Sadie."

"Yeah, her an' Jammer come t' look after th' homeplace once't I told'em I'se takin' our mommas away. Pap-Pap, he weren't goin' nowheres, an' Gammy neither. Tried, I did, but … we'se c'n be stubborn as a mule-pack, us Bodeans."

She brought them to a rope bridge spanning a wide stretch of murky water broken by the occasional stubby tree, slime-slicked rock, mossy log, and telltale wakes marking the surfacing of alligator snouts. On the other side was one of the stilt-shacks, fairly large, with a rickety branch-railed deck encircling the exterior. Smoke curled from a bent tin chimney, and dim light shone through sheets tacked up like curtains.

"Then, well, I din't dare risk goin' anywheres folks's might rat us out, an' I r'membered Miz Delilah sayin' how she had kin 'round here—y' seen that gal with them skulls?"

Greg nodded. "A powerful mage. Glad I didn't have to tangle with her."

"Too right." Lorlinda shivered a little. "Tha'ss Mortisse. She c'n raise th' dead. Zombies, like. Real nice gal, though, when's y' get t' know her."

After dropping this casual necromancy bombshell,

Lorlinda stepped onto the bridge, motioning for Greg and Tony to follow.

"They took'd us in, been shelterin' us these past days," she continued. "Had plenny room; lost half their number t' the gator-god. Buncha houses left empty. Also, they ain't had no dealin's with th' Gen'rul an' his queen an' all neither. Not that they's rebels, 'xactly. Or weren't 'til we shown up an' spoke our'n piece."

This was Lorlinda? She hardly seemed the same person, a striking change from the sweet but ditzy girl Greg had last seen only a few days ago. More mature, more serious, stronger.

But then, this place had a way of doing that. Was certainly the effect it'd had on him. He wondered, though it gave him a pang to do so, what Heck would have made of this new Lorlinda. She even looked the part; yes, she still had the messy-cute Harley Quinn pigtails, but she dressed more like Furiosa. Well, Furiosa with a tacky sunset-hues misspelled FLORDA fanny pack belted around her waist. Gone were the bottom-hugging daisy dukes and the skimpy-thin top with ample braless jiggle.

They crossed the bridge, which dipped and creaked and swayed, and the telltale wakes of reptilian nostrils converged below, ready to carpe diem the shit out of anyone who fell in.

Not this time, not today. Carpe somewhere else.

Lorlinda opened the door. "It's me!" she called. "We gots comp'ny!"

She ushered them in, where they were met by two women, not identical twins but very clearly closely related. Very clearly closely related to Lorlinda as well; they had the same backwoods beauty and must have had, in their not-so-distant youth, the same fantastic figures. Even now, they were well worth a look, doing amazing things for simple Walmart smocks.

"These here are Jos'phine an' Av'line Bodean, me an' Heck's mommas," she said, then introduced Greg and Tony in turn.

However, unlike Lorlinda, the sisters were reticent and somber, heavily burdened by their cares. They murmured polite words of welcome, gazes shadowed and far away. As if merely going through the motions, their hearts not in it, their thoughts wrapped up in grief. Aveline, the older by a year or so, bore an almost palpable weight, mourning the loss of both her sons. Josephine's relief at her daughter's return had been tempered by the distress of leaving the only home she'd ever known to seek refuge among strangers.

It made for a stilted, awkward visit, which even Lorlinda was just as glad to conclude sooner rather than later. Promising to be back after the party, she led Greg and Tony out again, then scrubbed the heels of her hands up the sides of her face.

"They'se been like that," she said, keeping her voice low. "Ain't easy fer none of us, but hit them extra hard." Brushing at a tear, she tried for a brave smile. "Me too, accourse … after Heck … an' I couln't even bring m'self t' tell 'em 'bout Andy, since't it'd be too much t' xplain."

"Lorlinda, about Andy—" Greg began.

"He's gone, I knows it. Miz D said th' spellwork come undone."

"Tony was there when it happened."

"He was?"

"I was?"

"The doll," he said. "The one the little girl called Mr. Goblin. It, well, it had this guy Andy's spirit in it. He was with us at Bighead Rock but got separated somehow, and must've ended up in the lake where the girl found him. He and Lorlinda were … close."

"Ohhh fuck." Tony grimaced, turning to Lorlinda. "Sorry, I didn't … I … there was no way to … it was just so fast …"

"S'awright." She sniffled. "How'd you've had any idear? Jist … were it you what done it?"

"No. Porkie did. Pork Chop. The guy I was partnered with. He saw this weird talking doll running at us, and …"

"S'awright," she repeated. "Allus better t' hear the truth, howev'much it hurts."

Always better to hear the truth or not, Lorlinda still needed to excuse herself for a while: "I'se gots t' have me a li'l uglycry, and ain't nobody needs t' see that."

She suggested in the meantime, they head back on over to the party, which they did, loading up on food and finding seats to watch the dancing. A few former soldiers came over to chat, asking after Ethriel, expressing their gratitude for her freeing them, questioning Tony as to what had been going on at the war camp, etc.

They also spoke glowingly of Lorlinda, damn near making her sound like a hillbilly Joan of Arc who'd been sent by God to lead them to victory.

"We heard the engine, you know, that waspy whine," Davidson said, "so we laid wait to take a look. Then this peach-and-cream vintage Vespa comes putt-putting along. I swear it must've been from 1973. Tricked out with defenses, panniers slung on the sides. And there she was. We'd seen her during the firefight, operating that railgun-rig, though at the time, none of us knew her name."

"We were in a real nut-pinch too," added Braveheart— which was how the others addressed the guy with the blue Celtic body paint. "All we had was whatever we'd been able to grab on the run, hostile territory, no plan. She knew the land, pointed us toward shelter and supplies. We talked it over and decided to accompany her to her family's place. They said we could stay if we liked, but when Lorlinda decided to escort the ladies somewhere else, of course we stuck with her."

Davidson took over again. "Which is how we ended up here. Had some trouble on the way—"

"Putting it lightly," grumbled the man with the alligator jawbone prosthetic, rubbing the join where it merged with his flesh.

"—with Vore-Voles, giant snakes, swamp-monsters, and the freakiest creepiest fucking *tree* out of your worst nightmares," Davidson went on. "Hairy shit. Still, we made it without losing a single man, parlayed with the bayou people, and here we are."

"Not so bad, if you don't mind the zombs," Braveheart said. "And the chow's Grade-A." He cracked the shell of some sort of steamed lake-mollusk, slurping out the gooey bits. "Though we're ready, standing by. Give us five minutes' notice, we're on the march."

"On the march where?" Greg asked.

"Wherever she—and you—are headed."

"Whoa, okay, hang on ... I was just looking for Lorlinda to make sure she was all right. I wasn't planning on dragging her back into the shit."

"Dude, she's got an army," Tony said.

Greg gestured around. "Of a dozen?"

"A squad, then, if you want to be picky."

"And us, *n'oublie pas*," a woman's voice chimed in. Mortisse stood by their table, grinning at Braveheart. Beneath her painted deathmask, her features were strong and striking. "If, that is, you don't mind the zombs."

"Did I *say* I minded the zombs?" Braveheart replied, grinning back. "I never *said* I minded the zombs. Well, maybe the one with the big gnarly *hole* in his middle, so you can see through him. Aside from that ..."

"Everyone, listen, while I appreciate your ... uh ... enthusiasm, let's not get ahead of ourselves," Greg said.

Mortisse turned to him. "What is there to get ahead of, *sorcier*? You resist *le règne de l'enfer*, which will otherwise ultimately destroy us all. We are against it, which makes us with you. *N'est-ce pas?*"

It may have seemed a strange sentiment coming from a necromancer, but his own recent experiences and education had given Greg perspective. He'd seen for himself how readily "warlock" could get automatically lumped in with "evil" magics, when every branch of the arcane arts and eldritch sciences had multiple facets and could be used in multiple ways. Intention, purpose, and effect were what mattered.

By such reasoning, even the practice of raising the dead deserved the benefit of the doubt.

The party was going strong, plentiful hellshine and rum contributing to the increased disinhibition of the dancers. A raucous, cheering ring surrounded Mortisse and Braveheart, whose moves together would've earned a rating just shy of NC-17. Tony had gone off with Davidson to hobnob with other soldiers and looked to be having a fine time.

Greg sat on a bench at the edge of the festivities, watching, wishing Ethriel could be here to enjoy them as well. He steered clear of the potent alcohol, sticking with a homebrew sassafras cola that blew A&W root beer off the map.

Lorlinda, returning from her "li'l uglycry" with a freshly washed face and a stiff upper lip, slid onto the bench beside him.

"Sorry 'bout that; needed t' have it out," she said.

"No worries. Sorry to be the bringer of bad news."

"Y'wasn't. Miz D already tol' me, r'member?"

"Well, then, sorry to be the confirmer of bad news."

"Wh'ever he's at now, I jist hopes he's happy."

"Amen to that."

"An' Heck; y' hear 'bout Heck? 'Bout folks been paranormal encounterin' his ghost-truck? All pale glowy greenish-white an' see-through, they sez. Jammer swears he saw it hisself, out on th' road t' Grady's Crossin'. Went right by him, din't slow or stop, but it was Heck sure 'nuff. Gived Jammer a big ol' shit-eatin' grin, flipt him the bird, an' drove on."

"You know, I can totally believe that."

"He allus said, Heck I mean, how's he wanted t' go out no way but b'hind the wheel."

"He also went out a hero," Greg said.

"Like a boss, how Blaze put it." Lorlinda smiled with a touch of sadness. "Missin' 'em terrible. Blaze too. Don't git me wrong, I'se glad he went home t' his folks an' is safe outsida here, but lordy-Lucifer, weren't he the goofiest hotshot firecracker y'ever met?"

"Definitely."

She watched the dancing for a moment, then asked quietly, "An' Ethriel? She for-reals gonna be awright, or was y' sugar-coatin' it t' spare my feelin's? Long story later, y'said … well, don't git much later'n this, so late it's gonna be early soon."

He went into as much detail as he could, sometimes hampered by his inability to put Heaven into mere words. At other times hampered for more strategic reasons; aces in the hole were more effective when kept secret. If he glossed over certain aspects, such as conversations in the dive bar and matters resulting therefrom, he tried to make up for it with impressions of Icaiah's snarky fussiness, anecdotes about the raphim med students and other angels, and so on.

"Sounds like they's as nutty p'culiar up there as we-all are down here," she said.

"Yeah, and I also get the idea it's just as peculiar downstairs, if not more. So much for faith in an orderly, organized system, huh?"

They watched the dancers a while longer, then Lorlinda spoke again. "Why'm I gettin' the feelin' there's a bunch more y' leavin' out?"

"Because there's a bunch more I'm leaving out," Greg admitted. "For now, anyway."

"An' you din't come back jist t' look fer me."

"There's something here I need to retrieve. To help Ethriel recover. There's also … some unfinished business."

As much as it wrenched his guts to do so, he told her

about the little girl, Sherri. What the queen had done, how she'd called him and Ethriel out. How that had introduced him to Tony, how they'd formed their alliance. Going to the war camp. The business with Wormy, which led to visiting the homeplace, meeting Sadie, and eventually translocating into the bayou.

"Peepin' at Maisy-Sue?" Lorlinda scoffed and shook her head. "He never did have no sense. No taste neither. Fuck-a-duck, though, he's lucky her brothers din't stomp him inta worm-jelly 'stead of handin' him over. Even luckier *you* fellas escaped his dumb butt. His an' mine, we ain't close d'spite bein' kin—ol' cornbread feud—but that don't mean I'se'd wanna see him exercuted."

The party finally began winding down, the zydeco band packing up their instruments, the kerchief-wearing ladies doing the same with the leftovers. People drifted away in groups or pairs or singles. In the comparative quiet, night-critter noises tentatively resumed.

Above, the *Aurora Diabolicus*, like the Red Death, held sway over all. But its eastern edge showed the advancing hint of dawn, and the slightly cooler temperatures would soon turn warm and muggy again.

"So y' needs t' retrieve sumthin,' sumthin' t' help Ethriel," Lorlinda said. "An' that y' had unfinished bizniss with th' queen. Like, fightin' bizniss? Killin' bizniss?"

"Yeah, pretty much." Greg exhaled heavily.

"Gots a plan?"

"Working on it."

"Onliest road from Jericho t' the camp what could handle bigger vee-hicles runs 'tween here an' Shallowstown. Th' way I drove Heck's truck t' th' tunnel when's he was hurt. If'n we moves fast, we c'n innercept 'em. Couple-three places 'long the way as oughta be eye-deel fer ambushes—"

"Lorlinda, wait, what's this 'we' stuff? I can't ask you to—"

"Din't ask, din't hafta. Accourse I'se with ya. Reckon the army fellers'll be too. Prolly Mortisse an' her dead'uns, mebbe Reuben an' some vol'nteers from th' bayou-folk. They'se been champin' at the bit fer a chance t' throw some monkey-wrenchin' inta the works."

"Lorlinda—"

"Greg. I'se serious This is 'portant. Most 'portant thing since't takin' on Gen'rul Favius. Like I'mma sit on my bee-hind an' do nuthin? Nuh-*unh!*"

"It's too dangerous—"

"So was las' time."

"I promised Heck—"

"Heck'd be sayin' the same fuck-an'-damn thing, an' you knows it."

"Please. What about your mothers?"

"They'se'll unnerstan too."

"But, Lorlinda—"

"Fer Satan's sake!" She flung her hands in the air, huffing. "Lissen up an' lissen good. I'se *in*, an' you ain't stoppin' me. 'Sides, turns out I gots a knack fer it. Fer this ... leadery an' stratergizin' stuff, I means. Sure as never woulda thought, same's Heck never woulda thought he'd got any warlockin' mojo, but cross-an'-bless me if'n it ain't true!"

He opened his mouth. Nothing sensible came out. In his peripheral vision, he saw Tony and Davidson a few yards away, watching intently. So was Reuben, the coral-snake man, his sinuous charges coiling around his arms.

Lorlinda seized the lapels of his rumpled coat and gave him a shake. "An' you think *Ethriel'd* want me lettin' you go off an' do this by y'self? Popeshit t' *that!* So don'tcha *dare* even *try* translocatin' outta here on y'own, or anythin' sneaky-like! Y' hear me?"

"I hear you," he said.

"Y' better." She gave him another shake, then hugged him so tight he could barely breathe, and burst into tears.

Greg held her, patting her back. "Hey, no, it's okay. You're right. I was being an idiot. My grandfather would rip me up one side and down the other. *Stubborn half-assed martyrdom, Gregory?* he'd say. *Haven't you learned anything? That I'd waste part of **my** eternity training you, only to have you undertake some suicidal fool's crusade ...*"

It wasn't just his grandfather's *words* but his grandfather's *voice*, and no mere imitation either. As if the deceased old man really *was* speaking through him from Beyond. From that quaint, occulty, book-lined black-and-white study in Purgatory, smoky-velvet torch songs on the radio.

"Yeesh." He shuddered. "Point made, I get it, thanks. Let's not do that again, huh?"

Lorlinda was looking up at him, confused.

"Another long story," he said. "Now, my grandmother, she'd be telling me …" He hesitated, waiting to see if it would happen again, if she would ring in from her own cozy corner of the afterlife; caller 2, you're on the air.

A warm fresh-baked cookies sensation suffused him, and a sense of kindly amusement, but nothing more.

"She'd be telling me," he went on, "to graciously and gratefully accept whatever help was offered. So, I will."

She stepped back, wiped her eyes, and smiled tremulously. "Bet'cher butt y' will. Now, let's git us a fuckin' *plan!*"

"This is nuts," Tony said. "You do realize, this is nuts."

"Yep." Greg finished etching another septagonal sigil, using a metallic silver Sharpie.

"Just figured I'd say it up front and get it out of the way."

"As long as you don't say you have a bad feeling about this."

"What if I do?"

"Say it or have one?"

"Either?"

"If you have one, keep it to yourself. If you say it, I'll put you in a Han Solo costume."

Tony glanced down at his current outfit, the casual military look now mixed with other random pieces of gear gleaned from the bayou folk and Lorlinda's squad. "Classic Solo, original trilogy? I could make that work."

"Next you'd want a blaster."

"Hell yes, I'd want a blaster."

"Maybe later." Greg moved on to the next in line.

The man was built like a football player gone somewhat to seed, solid but softened. His complexion was a dark bluish-brown, his gaze cloudy and vacant. With the way his head canted to the left and the rope mark encircling his neck, it didn't take a rocket scientist to determine cause of death. A latticework of scars covered his body, some dating back to childhood.

"'Merica," Tony said sourly. "Makes me sick this kind of shit's still going on in this day and age."

"Humanity, bad enough even without demonic influence." Greg Sharpied a sigil onto the dead man's broad brow. "Yay, us. I'd like to think maybe some positive changes will follow that Painwave thing, but I'm not banking on it."

With the party having gone on until late became early, they'd all slept from dawn until midafternoon. Tony bunked down with Davidson and the guys, while Greg couched it in the front room of the stilt-house where Lorlinda and the mommas were staying. Then came a few hours of prep, and their makeshift rebel alliance set out just before dusk. Traveling by day was riskier, as well as harder on the troops. Mortisse's Zombrigade most of all, though the Dome-filtered daylight didn't make them as torporific as direct sunlight would have done.

Lorlinda's and Heck's mommas, along with the bayou women, children, elders, and other noncombatants, stayed put, with a modest guard just in case worse came to worst. A few scouts had been dispatched in pole-punts along the sluggish waterways, while the rest of them went on foot. Lorlinda's "mota-scoota" was trundled along on silent running by a teenaged girl with medusoid cornrows, who was under instructions to "scootie-patootie" back to the village and warn them if things went badly.

Greg's previous Lake Misquamicus nature walks, disconcerting enough during the day, hadn't left him fully prepared for how much spookier and weirder it got by night. No moon, no stars, but the rippling deep-garnet glow casting everything as if seen through a filter, outlining the strange shapes of trees, making the inky pools of shadow appear all the blacker. Void-black, nothingness-black, like you could step into one and just be … *gone*, instant oblivion.

Not to mention the fucking *eyeglow*. The fucking *eyeglow* was fucking *everywhere*, from tiny pinpricks to saucer-sized luminous disks to a pair of poison-yellow orbs bigger than hubcaps and brighter than headlamps.

Those last belonged to a behemoth of a sabertoothed beaver, which fortunately showed no signs of aggression. It merely lolled in its pool, watching them pick their careful way across the causeway formed by its ten-foot-wide dam of logs and mud.

Miraculously, no one made any beaver jokes. Not then and there, out loud, at least.

They'd kept moving. Meals were eaten on the go, rest breaks brief and perfunctory, and by around three in the morning, they'd reached Lorlinda's chosen destination—a hill thick with cypress and Spanish moss. It provided cover, vantage points of long stretches of the lake road, the high ground, and promising opportunities for sabotage and/or ambush.

There, they'd settled in to make their final preparations. After that, it was only a matter of wait-and-see.

So, they waited. Septagonal sigils etched in silver Sharpie upon their brows, armed and alert. A sabotage crew headed by Braveheart had rigged some surprises, including a special surprise involving an old bridge over a boggy delta where several sluggish waterways met the lake. The River Kwai, it was not, but they did the best they could.

Thanks to a debriefing from Tony, they had a rough estimate of what to expect, give or take any changes made since the royal procession had left Bighead Rock. Reports from the pole-punt scouts supported his tally with some additional information.

"They've got a Blackwing with them," a sniper named Hendrix said. "Just the one, probably as a messenger. I'll bring her down first so they can't send for reinforcements."

"And there's a speedster?" Greg glanced at Tony for confirmation.

"Meep, yeah. A runner, who's really been able to pour it on since coming here. Young guy, barely old enough to shave. I'd like to think he's a decent person caught up in the mob fervor and would come to his senses, but we can't risk it."

"Oh, shit, Meep?" Hendrix looked glum. "Roger, I'll make him my second target. You want him dead, or should I just go for a leg?"

"Leg," Lorlinda said. "If'n we c'n spare some, or get 'em t' switch sides, let's try. They ain't all bad. Them as fights fer th' queen, them's as loyal, gotta go. But if'n they wanna s'rrender or's jist reg'lar folks, they d'serves the chance." She swept the troops with a cautionary gaze. "But only, an' that's *only*, if'n doin' so ain't endangerin' y'self, us, an' ours."

Greg nodded. "Our primary objective is the queen. The less backup she has, the better. Don't attack her directly, though. Leave her to me."

"Unless'n y' gits an opper-tunerty," Lorlinda added, scowling at Greg. "Y'see a clear shot? Fuckin' go fer it. We don' need no one-on-one boss battle bullshit. This ain't 'bout bein' hon'rable, an' you damn well knows it. Think *she's* gonna fight fair?"

"Absolutely not. If anything, I'm counting on it."

"Y' still hidin' somethin', some sneaky trick up yer sleeve, ain't'cha?"

"Of course I am." He winked.

She stuck out her tongue. "Chaps my bee-hind t' be kep' inna dark; still, I'se guessin' it's how it's gotta be."

Soon, the royal vanguard rode into view, the rest of the company straggling along behind. It was far from the parade-neat arrangement Tony had described, all orderly units and marching in step. The long, tedious journey had worn on them. They were road-weary, tired, overheated, sticky, bedraggled, and only wanted to get home. The horses—and horse-type creatures—plodded one hoof after another. The emusaurs ambled. The banner-carriers and flag-bearers had stowed their banners and flags, and either trudged beside or hitched rides on the various vehicles. The band members had done the same with their instruments. All in all, they more resembled a caravan of refugees on the final stretch, motivated to keep moving by the prospect of finally being able to sit the hell down and not go anywhere for a while.

Could almost feel sorry for them, Greg thought. *If not, that is, for the whole demonic evil regime thing.*

Following the riders was a low-slung, nasty-sleek biomechorganic convertible nightmare that could have come right out of a bizarre *Cars / Aliens* crossover. A woman with jutting no-nonsense devil horns rode in the back seat—Major Duval, according to Tony, recently promoted to chief military advisor—while a mostly-human female Blackwing perched on the trunk, wings folded.

The rest of the procession consisted of a few jeeps and vans, some trailers, a couple troop-trucks, and an armored limo-turned-popemobile hung with what had started out as patriotic bunting and garlands. Needless to say, the decorations, by now, were rather tattered and droopy.

And there, protected by transparent bulletproof shielding, *she* sat upon a stately chair.

The queen herself, in all her glory.

Juno Regina.

Greg zoomed in with a pair of binocs Davidson had loaned him, to get a good look at his opponent.

She, like the rest of the procession, was clearly feeling it. Not at her camera-ready best, by any means. Tony had described how they'd done her up in Favius's refitted armor, with wild hairstyle and savage eyeliner. Though sweaty and lank-haired and smeared, she presented a far fiercer picture than the woman Greg had faced on Bighead Rock.

And her power …

Even at this distance, he could sense it, stronger than ever. More refined than ever. More dangerous than ever. Before, she hadn't understood what she was capable of, had tapped into those energies by raw emotion-fueled instinct, and still done terrible damage. This time, she would have a better handle on it, more control.

"Tha'ss Abel Kellerman," Lorlinda said when it was her turn with the binocs. "Ridin' an emusaurus. Don't sees Abner nor Maisy-Sue. Oh, an' there's Spot, th' pimple-dick fuckwit; anybody kills *his* grease-stain ass, I'se'll kiss 'em full onna mouth, I'se will."

This remark elicited considerable interest among the troops, but Lorlinda was oblivious, her attention fixed on the enemy.

"Her new han'maid, y' said's Iris Tate?" she asked Tony. "Neva met her m'self, but her pa used t' do tax stuff fer Uncle Jeb an' Buster an' the boys."

"The way I heard it," Tony replied, "she's got a serious case of hero-worship on for the queen. Don't expect any backstabbing from her. If anything, she'd be the type to leap into the line of fire." He glanced at Greg. "Be ready for that."

"Noted, thanks."

Her tone darkened. "Him with th' piggy-head mus' be yer pal Pork Chop, who blowed up my poor los' li'l sugar-pie."

"Remember, we agreed, no one-on-one boss battle bullshit," Greg told her.

She stuck her tongue out at him again and gave the binoculars back to Davidson.

"Limo driver's another to keep an eye on," Tony said. "Ex Secret Service, plus whatever the lake did to him."

The vanguard reached the bridge and started across it without so much as a pause to investigate. Either they were too confident, too tired, or both; it didn't matter. Those riders who were being vigilant directed most of their vigilance at the broad, boggy delta itself; if there was a place for quicksand and inexorable sucking black-hole mud morasses (that fucking traumatic Swamp of Sadness scene in *Neverending Story*; "Artax! Noooo!"), this would be the place.

The xenomorph-esque car crossed next, not exactly rolling and not exactly crawling. Hendrix drew a bead on the Blackwing, tracking her, patient as a … well, as a sniper, which he was.

"We go soon's the bridge does," Lorlinda ordered. "Hold 'til then. Reuben, snakes on standby?"

"*Oui, cherie*. Rain of snakes, standing by."

"Zombs in position," Mortisse reported.

"Is now a good time to say I've got a bad feeling about this?" Tony muttered to Greg.

"Are you saying it because you *do* have a bad feeling, or because you really want that Han Solo outfit?"

"Outfit. And blaster. Don't forget the blaster."

Greg traced an arcane pattern of silvery light in midair, which spun around Tony in a blur, then left him standing in trousers, white shirt, vest, and techy low-slung gun belt.

"Son of a bitch, you actually did it!" Tony drew his weapon, familiarizing himself with it. "This thing work?"

"Wouldn't be much use if it didn't." He triple-checked to be sure all his wards were charged and activated. Each sigil should provide its bearer heightened defense; not full invulnerability but a definite edge.

Under ordinary circumstances, maintaining so many would've been a serious drain, not leaving him much in the tank for anything else. These, however, were not ordinary circumstances. It felt as if he had a generator tucked away inside him, thrumming with eldritch energy.

None of the others noticed him discreetly slipping an onyx-banded titanium ring from his pocket onto his left forefinger.

About two-thirds of the procession had crossed the bridge by the time the royal limo reached it, with the rest providing a rear guard. They displayed sensible caution in terms of weight limits, the larger vehicles crossing one by one, because the bridge was far from new and much of the infrastructure around Lake Misquamicus had suffered considerable neglect in the years since AllHell. The sheer mass of the Golem, planted solid and stoic on a trailer-hitch arrangement at the rear, had to be of additional concern.

The bridge may have groaned a little, but it showed no sign of collapse …

… until the limo was at the halfway-point, and Lorlinda said, "Now!"

Braveheart slammed the plunger.

It wasn't one big **KA-BOOM!**; it was a series of smaller, simultaneous *ka-blams* and *ka-bangs* as the improvised explosive devices detonated. And if it wasn't as pyro-technically spectacular as Blaze's fireworks extravaganza on Bighead Rock had been, it made up for the lack in the absolutely gorgeous way the supports just disintegrated into splintery shrapnel.

In slo-mo, it would have looked goddamn amazing. In real time, it still looked goddamn amazing, just, over quicker. Smoke billowed. Concussive shockwaves hammered the air. The span bucked and buckled and fell, dropping straight down into the muck, taking the limo, the Golem, two emusaurs, and a dozen soldiers with it. A jeep behind the limo, which had ventured partway onto the bridge, now tilted precariously with nose pointed at the drop and rear wheels uselessly spinning several inches above the road.

In the same moment, the Blackwing pitched sideways from her perch, a gout of blood where her temple used to be. A horse-thing plunged into a concealed pit-trap. Gunfire rattled. Spears flew. Masses of coral snakes plummeted from the cloudless sky, a red-yellow-black torrent like streamers of old-fashioned ticker tape, only alive and deadly. They fell upon and among the members of the disorganized procession, turning confusion into chaos. Then zombs and men, sigils blazing on their brows, burst from hiding.

Once again, it was on. It was fucking *on*!

Greg focused his will, translocating a short hop to hover where the bridge used to be. Much of the wreckage was already going under, being slurped inexorably into the quicksand and black mud. He saw soldiers thrashing in it, saw an emusaur viciously turn on its rider in a frenzy of beak-jabs and claw-slashes. He saw the limo, canted sideways and half-submerged, muck sluicing in through the open passenger door, the driver clambering out a window. He saw no sign of the Golem; whatever else, they were not built for buoyancy.

As for the queen …

The bulletproof shielding had held, hadn't so much as

cracked. Most of it protruded from the morass in a weird bubble, splattered and splashed with more muck. Within it, dazed from being flung about in the impact, Juno struggled upright. It took barely a moment for her to assess her situation—not good; the entire limo would go under in less than thirty seconds—and barely another moment for her furious gaze to find Greg.

Find, lock on, and silently promise him a thousand hideous deaths, each more painful than the last.

He drove the heels of his hands downward. A surge of energy shot from them. Rather than shatter the bubble, as he'd hoped, the force drove the stricken limo deeper. Which wouldn't do; while he wouldn't have minded entombing her alive, buried in fifty feet of wet silt, it'd make getting his hands on the gladius that much more difficult.

Nearly all of it was immersed. He could no longer see Juno, partly through the swampy sludge and partly because the interior had gone murky ... no, had gone a smoky, crimsonish hue he knew all too well ...

It still wasn't a **KA-BOOM**, but the massive mushroom-cloud eruption of roiling, seething, horrible *redblack* made the demolition of the bridge seem as trivial as the clattering end of a game of Jenga.

Dark Phoenix rising.

The original run of comics had been well before his time, but there were *Essential X-Men* omnibuses and reprints and memes, so he was familiar enough with the iconic imagery.

Dark Phoenix rising. Not in a blazing birdlike corona of flames, not in a skintight superhero costume, but the effect was much the same.

Wreathed in *redblack*, forming the suggestion of a demonic skull with huge down-curving ram's horns. Wearing a Hell-forged bronze corselet, battle skirt, greaves, and bracers. Hair streaming wild from beneath a headpiece part helm and part tiara. High-collared cape billowing. War belt with gladius at one hip, marshmallow fork at the other (at least now he finally had the whole story as to what *that* was about, batshit insane as it was).

In his peripheral awareness, everything else came to a sudden standstill. Combatants paused mid-conflict to gape at the sight. Soldiers sinking in mud and quicksand briefly ceased their struggles, too thunderstruck to move. Zombs, emusaurs, horse-things, and coral snakes as well ... no one was immune.

Including Greg himself. Warlock or not, talk about an "oh shit" moment. Had he sincerely believed he could handle this? She was *Juno Regina,* infernal queen, imbued with the powers of an Arch-Duke of Hell, driven by vengeful hate, rage, and fury the likes of which no mere mortal could *begin* to comprehend—

He shook it off. A calm, clear, controlled sense of purpose settled over him.

"*Nachtwald,*" Juno said, sneering, turning his name into a curse. "Where's your little whore-slut angel?"

"Couldn't make it. Scheduling conflict. She sends her regrets."

"Oh, does she, now? How kind. I'll have to send something in return. Your head, maybe. Your heart. Or do you think she'd prefer your dick?"

"Well, she does prefer my dick." *Keep it cool, don't be baited.*

"You mock me? *Me?*" Juno shrieked, her Voice reverberating so the very Dome above them quivered.

"Hey, *you* called *me* out," he said. "You sacrificed a *child* to do it. Just a kid, a helpless kid. So, now, here I am. What do you want?"

"To see you suffer an eternity of agonies such as no soul in history has ever known!"

"Yeah, yeah. Besides that."

With an inarticulate howl, she attacked, launching a fusillade of smoky redblack cannonballs from her fists. His sigil flared, deflecting them, and he retaliated with a barrage of silvery energy-darts. Which her own aura also deflected, leaving them both untouched, but had sure looked cinematic as fuck. Big budget special effects time, the two of them hovering above the ruined bridge, flinging arcane energies back and forth as the fighting resumed below. Concerned though he was for Lorlinda and Tony and the rest, Greg couldn't be distracted. They had their parts to play; he had his.

"It's still not too late, you know!" he yelled, dodging a colossal redblack Balrog-whip.

"Yes it fucking is!"

"It doesn't have to be!"

"You destroyed Favius! Took him away from me! Think

I'm going to forgive and forget? *No* redemption arcs! Shove it up your ass!"

"Rather not, thanks." He willed two shining disks into being, each the size of a bank vault door, and crashed them together like a pair of cymbals with her in the middle.

The shining cymbals fractured to fragments, but the blow staggered her, sending her reeling back while her energies coalesced again.

"How she *screamed* when I cleaved those wings off!" she taunted. "*Such* a scream! She's useless now, isn't she? Maimed and crippled! No good to Heaven, to you, to anyone!"

Don't take the bait ... don't take the bait ...

"Or have they already put her down?"

Don't ...

"Like the weak, feeble, pathetic creature she is?"

"Shut *up*!!!" Silver energy scythes flew from his fingertips, whirling at her in a slicing tornado.

A concave curving redblack wall formed, catching the tornado and veering it off course. Her Balrog-whip lashed again. Its barbed tip pierced his wards, tore his coat, and dug into his thigh.

It hurt worse than anything he'd experienced or imagined in his entire life. Hurt so much he barely heard himself scream. Hurt so much he barely felt himself fall, only to be jerked to a halt in midair.

Suspended, swinging, a fish on a hook, the barb an excruciating torment embedded in his flesh. Embedded deep as the bone, scraping his femur. He clawed at the whip's vile redblack substance, clutching it in his fists, trying to lift some of his weight with his arms.

In a detached, rational corner of his mind, he noted the barb hadn't pierced his artery, and supposed he should be glad of that at least, but was finding it challenging to be glad of anything just then.

Juno crowed a cruel laugh and flicked the whip. Greg hung on desperately. Even with the artery unpierced, profuse blood sprayed in pinwheels as his body was flung this way and that. More of the merciless redblack length looped around him, binding his legs, cinching his arms to his sides.

She reeled him in, retracting the whip slowly, enjoying his

pain. When she held him suspended before her at a crooked angle, she tilted her head to meet his eyes.

"Did you honestly expect to beat *me*?" she asked.

Gritting his teeth, he said, "In a fair fight? No."

"A fair fight! Ha! As if *I'd* fight *fair* after what you've done?"

"Figured you wouldn't."

"So you're throwing your life away for nothing."

"Am I?"

"Aren't you? In case you haven't realized, *warrrrrlock*, I have you now. You are mine, my prisoner. You will pay. The most fiendish princes of Hell will wince to witness your torments."

The whip constricted, squeezing his ribcage, making it difficult to breathe.

"Monologuing," he gasped. "Villainy 101. Weren't you listening when I told Favius—?"

Another rude yank, a short hard snap, made his cervical vertebrae understand the term "whiplash" on the most fundamental level.

"Do *not* speak his name!"

"Okay, but you're making the same cliched mistake he did."

"Oh, and I suppose this is when you take advantage of my distraction?" She drew him close again, smirking. "Nice try, asshole. I'm going to unravel your guts from both ends."

"I could still have a trick or two up my sleeve," he said. His bones ached, and his muscles were going numb from the crushing pressure. "An ace in the hole, as it were."

"A trick up your sleeve, an ace in the hole," she mimicked. "You're so full of shit."

"Am I? Did you really think I'd make it this easy?" He threw her words back at her. "Did *you*, honestly, expect to beat *me*?"

But two could play at that game, and she snidely did. "In a fair fight?"

"As if *I'd* fight *fair*?" Return volley. "After what you've done?"

Juno hesitated, a hint of nascent doubt forming in her eyes. "Are you trying to be funny?"

"No. I was trying to warn you." He twisted his left wrist, working it free of the agonizing coil. "Give you one last chance to change your mind. Too many people have died already. I don't *want* to kill you, but I will if I have to."

"Kill me? Kill *me*???" The storm cloud of deadly *redblack* burgeoned again, ram's horns and jagged scarlet lightning.

The whip tightened further. Joints creaked and cartilage crackled. Something popped wetly inside him, something rupturing. He groaned.

"And just how," Juno asked, sweetly as a spider to a webbed fly, "do you propose to do that?"

Almost all the air had been forced from his lungs. His limbs tingled. His head swam. He was millimeters from passing out, but she pulled him closer still.

Closer. So close. The closer, the better.

"With …" he wheezed hoarsely, "with some help from a friend."

Bending his wrist, extending his left forefinger … the one encircled by a band of titanium and onyx … he pulled the metaphorical trigger on his ace in the hole.

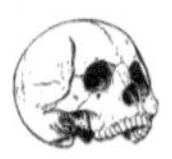

She died.

Just like that.

It wasn't cinematic. It wasn't dramatic. There were no last words uttered with a dying breath. No final moment of comprehension, awareness, resignation, fear, or despair.

She simply fucking *died*.

There and then gone. Snuffed out with the totality of a candle. Snap, poof, dead.

The redblack vanished. Juno, limp and lifeless, began to fall.

Freed from the whip-coils, Greg darted to catch her.

He almost missed. Almost flubbed it. Almost fell himself.

Which would have been even less cinematic, both of them plummeting into the quicksand muck below with ignominious splats.

But he pushed through the lingering pain and wobbly disorientation, mustered his magic, caught her, steadied himself, and regained some altitude. Her inert body hung slack in his arms. Head lolling, limbs dangling. Seeming so much smaller somehow, so … diminished. Normal. Ordinary. No longer a fierce, fearsome, vengeful, demonic warrior-queen. Only a woman, a sad and lonely middle-aged woman, in garish makeup and absurd armor. A woman poisoned by bitterness. A woman who'd merely wanted to be loved.

He was in tears by the time he touched down on a grassy hummock near the edge of the delta. Hectic activity continued all around him—skirmishes, shouts, arcane upheavals, a great trembling rumble—but it felt far away.

Settling the body onto the ground, he closed her blank, empty eyes. "It had to be this way," he said. "I'm sorry."

Quick, though. Painless. That was something, at least. A kinder fate than she deserved, as some might have said.

He drew the gladius from its sheath on her belt. *It* was *not* dead; a terrible vitality still pulsed within it, locked and blocked yet potent. Holding it in his hand both nauseated and tempted him.

So much *power* had been channeled into the weapon. Power there for the claiming. There for the owning. Power that could easily become his—

"Fuck off," he told it. Shrugging out of his torn coat, he wrapped the gladius into a bundle and encased the bundle in a cage of silvery fire. "Other plans for you. *Better* plans for you."

The trembling rumble intensified. The quality of the ambient light changed, thinning and brightening. He looked up. At the apex of the Dome, a wavery hole had appeared in the rippling *Aurora Diabolicus*. Then widened and spread. Beyond it was sky, the slightly hazy blue of a typical muggy Florida spring day. The opening continued to grow, the *Aurora* melting in flowy sheets, receding toward the Wall. The sun became fully visible, no longer a smeary blob filtered through bloodlight. Fresher air rushed in, mingling with stagnant lake-funk, forming localized weather systems of foggy clouds.

And the Wall? What was happening to the actual Wall?

Greg remembered his frantic full-tilt sprint when the *Aurora* had initially descended to form the Dome, the drastically altering Wall rearing up to meet it. Rearing up in immense slabs and spires, towers and fortifications to rival Mordor.

He remembered his certainty he wasn't going to make it. He wouldn't have either, except for Ethriel's miraculous reappearance, golden and glorious, grasping his hands and lifting him, bearing him through the narrowing gap at the last possible second.

Was the Wall also receding? Shrinking to its former

configurations? Chain link fences, barbed wire, panels of corrugated tin? What about the Checkpoints? The corrupted soldiers stationed there? Would they revert to their previous human forms?

No way to tell from here.

What he could tell from here, as the seismic rumbling subsided, was that the corrupted soldiers who'd been with the royal procession remained that way, unchanged.

What he could also tell was that the seismic rumbling had affected the lake the way an offshore quake could affect the sea. Where the boggy delta's sluggish watercourses had mingled with six billion gallons of liquid infernal filth, a broadening expanse of sickeningly moist silty lakebed now lay exposed.

Exactly how the tide went *waaaaay* out right before a tsunami.

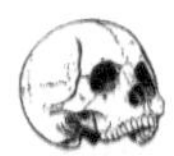

"Oh, shit," he said.

The fighting had stopped. Everyone still able to do so was gazing up in bafflement at the blue sky or assessing the scene. Or, for those who'd been keeping tabs on the airborne conflict between Greg and Juno, hustling toward the hummock.

There were, of course, plenty unable to do anything. Anything but sprawl where they had fallen. Dead, dying, gutted, bleeding out, badly injured, unconscious; the casualty list would be substantial for both sides.

Most of the actual battles had been concentrated at either end of where the demolished bridge used to be, two-thirds of the procession having made it across before the limo, while the rest brought up the rear; Lorlinda had divided their troops accordingly.

Overall result? Decisive win for the rebel alliance. Not a complete shutout; the enemy made them earn it and scored their share of points.

Still, a win was a win.

If they could survive to claim it.

His mind's eye showed him an aerial view of Lake Misquamicus, the center of which had swelled into a mountainous bulge, leaving a similarly exposed and sickeningly moist band of silty lakebed all along the entire encircling shoreline. Stranded fishlike things and other semiaquatic denizens flopped and flapped in the gore-streaked mud.

"Tidal wave!" he yelled, projecting his Voice to the limit and then some. *"The **lake**, get **away** from the **lake**, get **uphill**, **high ground**, move it, move it, flash **flood**, fucking **tidal wave** incoming!"*

As he yelled, he grabbed the silver-caged bundle of his coat and launched himself skyward again, his mind's eye continuing its grim clairvoyance.

Surface tension or seismic harmony held the lake-bulge in place for a few seconds … then released. Gushing outward in an expanding ring, billions of gallons of it, blood and rot and bile and sewage, flotsam and jetsam and other detritus. The initial wave crest towered to a height of more than fifty feet (sixty-six feet to be precise, because, c'mon, what else?), moving at ungodly speed.

His hidden inner generator of stored energy was nearly depleted, but he tapped into it hard, mining it to the very dregs. Electric tendrils arced from his fingertips, branching and splitting, reaching for the empowered sigils he'd sketched on the brows of his allies.

The drain was too much, the strain unbearable.

Lift … lift …

Wringing his power like a damp washcloth for every last minuscule drop.

"Yyyyeaaaargh!" he cried.

Ripping him asunder, pulling him to pieces, losing cohesion.

LIFT!

They lifted. Well, *he* lifted *them*, levitating them as high as he could, shaking with the effort. Their reactions to this abrupt, involuntary taking-to-the-air didn't help. Most of them understandably freaked out, kicking and screaming, swearing, rattling off random gunshots in a blind panic. Lorlinda and a few others were shouting orders and reassurance—*cease fire, hold still, it's okay, it'll be okay, it's warlock-magic*, etc.

With the lake's basin being an irregular oblong, not perfectly round, the leading edge began overlapping and crashing in on itself and breaking up as it encountered obstacles and variations in elevation. It roared toward shore, slowing in speed but gathering momentum, washing inland for more than a mile in some places, surging with immeasurable force.

Those he held aloft saw it coming, the huge wave of bloody filth, the frothing curls at its top less like watery whitecaps and more like reddish-greenish-brownish-yellowish foamy barf. No surfer would want to hang loose or hang ten on that; there was gnarly and then there was *gnarly*!

It passed beneath them, swallowing the wreckage of the bridge, the vehicles, the road, and everything else. The grassy hummock was swamped in the blink of an eye. Uprooted trees, debris, and bodies both living and dead were swept along in a bilious torrent.

The hill of cypress and Spanish moss, from where they had launched their attack, was above the flood's danger zone. Greg brought his levitate-ees in for safe landings, ended the spell, and keeled over.

He revived to the scent of cookies baking, the buzzy hum of a sewing machine, and the feel of a narrow couch that had never been much good for napping on. Opening his eyes to the sight of floral upholstery draped with delicate lace doilies confirmed it.

"Grandma?"

The buzzy hum cut off. He heard the rustle of movement, and she appeared in the doorway between parlor and the sewing room, in her usual soft cardigan, little-old-lady glasses perched on her nose instead of resting on a pearl chain around her neck.

"Feeling better, dear?"

"I guess so," he said, sitting up and taking inventory. All original body parts present and accounted for, systems operating more or less normally. Running a tad low, could use a tune-up. "Jet-lagged and hungover, maybe, but not too bad. How long was I out?"

"Oh, you know how tricky time can be around here." She smiled at him, tousled his hair, kissed his cheek, and bustled into the kitchen. "Your friends will be worried, but they won't think you're dead."

"I'm not?"

"No, dear, though if you'd pushed it much closer ..." Tutting, she returned with a tray bearing a cup of tea and plate of cookies. "The company you keep, my word."

"What, my friends?"

"A certain Angel of Death, in particular. How you got

tangled up with *him* ..."

"Hey, he's a decent guy. If not for him, I probably *would* be dead now. Lorlinda and the others too."

"Don't get defensive. You did what needed to be done. I'm very proud of you, Gregory, but as a grandmother, I am allowed, if not contractually obligated, to fret."

"Fair enough." He rubbed his temples and shook his head. "Where's my coat?"

"I'm just stitching it up for you. It was looking quite tattered and raggedy."

Alarm jolted him so he nearly slid off the couch. "The gladius—"

"Yes, that horrid thing. I put it in one of your uncle's pool cue cases. It's waiting for you by the back door."

He sagged with relief. "So I got it? We won?"

His grandmother nodded. "Drink your tea, dear."

After cradling the warm cup in his palms, he inhaled the fragrant steam, then took a welcome sip. "And ... and *her*? Juno, the queen?"

"Let's just say it went as planned. I'm sure your grandfather will have some criticisms, of course, but then, he always does."

Which he was *not* looking forward to, and would be just as glad to save for much, much later. "The Dome ... when she died, it ... melted away, vanished."

"You broke the hold of dominion Favius had established. It could no longer be sustained. Other changes he invoked, such as the Wall, reverted to their former state."

"What about the soldiers?"

"Dear, my information is limited. I've told you as much as I can. The rest, you'll need to see for yourself. Here." She handed him a remote control. "You drink your tea and eat your cookies, watch some television while I finish mending your coat, and then we'll take it from there, hmm?"

Off she went, back to the sewing room, where the buzzy hum started up again. He could have fixed the coat himself easily enough, since he'd conjured it in the first place ... or conjured a new one ... but it made her happy, and it did give him some time to reassemble his thoughts.

He clicked on the television—no slim flat screen HD here—and flipped through the channels. His options were limited to Turner Classic Movies, A&E, PBS, a channel rerunning vintage game shows, another re-running vintage sitcoms …

"Try channel six, dear," his grandmother called.

And there, with the herky-jerky quality of a cell phone video or amateur livestream, was Lorlinda Bodean, brandishing a big-ass gun.

"C'mon, fellers! Time t' show these cocksucker fuckernutters some southern hospertality!"

"Goodness me; such *language*."

"I'll turn it down."

"Thank you, dear. Young people these days …."

Rather than just turning it down, he muted the volume and put the closed-captioning on instead. Best choice, really, since the audio was a total combat cacophony. Gunshots, grenades, screams, swearing, the grisly squelch of disembowelment, splattering blood.

The visual aspect pulled no punches either. As graphic as could be, all the more so for it being real. No special effects. No squibs or fake severed limbs. No actors delivering convincing death scene performances.

It would have failed as a movie. Poorly filmed, poorly choreographed, unedited, jumping around with little regard for continuity or plot. Utterly lacking in terms of musical score. Production value leaving a lot to be desired. A crazy-quilt of thrown-together segments, piecemeal found footage from different sources. Anyone who didn't already know the characters would've had a bitch of a time trying to make sense of it.

But Greg did know the characters. He slid from the couch on purpose to sit on the carpet with his nose nearly to the screen—the way his grandmother had often chided him *not* to sit as a child—taking it in.

The *how* of it didn't matter. What mattered was filling in the blanks, what else had been going on during his confrontation with Juno.

Lorlinda, leading the charge, blowing the shit out of anyone who tried to get in her way. Half her squad at her back, overwhelming the disorganized soldiers who'd crossed the bridge before its destruction, mowing them down from a distance and then closing to lay into them melee-style.

She personally singled out the boar-headed dude, Pork Chop, who gawped at her, perplexed, until she said, "This's fer Andy, y' doll-shootin' sunuvabishop!" Where she'd gotten ahold of a goddamn *rocket launcher*, Greg had no idea. When she was done, nothing remained of Pork Chop but a heap of smoking meat, two trotters, and his tusks.

The devil-horned Major Duval rallied her troops as well as could be done under the circumstances. Dealing with former fellow soldiers was one thing. Once they overcame the initial surprise, numbers and weaponry were on their side, with the added high-octane emotional impetus of punishing bastard-ass traitors.

Dealing with the zombs was another matter. These weren't the Romero kind, attacking in a mindless ravening horde; Mortisse directed them strategically. They also weren't the kind that could pass on their undead infection, but no one had informed the enemy of such. As a result, many who were bitten opted to fast-track it and shoot themselves in the head, which helped even the odds.

His sigils, Greg was grateful to see, also helped quite a bit. Even with his attention diverted waging his own battle, the protective wards deflected bullets which might have otherwise proved fatal.

As for dealing with a sudden bombardment of coral snakes dropping onto them by the dozens? Instant wholesale pande-fucking-monium. Grown men, hardened military men, shrieking and leaping about, flailing wildly. Some ran right off the edge of the broken bridge, plunging into the mire, covered in snakes, fangs battened into necks and faces.

Tony Lewis brought his own brand of pandemonium to the party. The gunfire and grenades, okay. Gung-ho warpainted half-dressed ex-POW rebels? Fine. Zombs, and Mortisse's dark spectral-skull fear hexes? Weird, but not totally unexpected in a place like this. Rain of snakes? Bigtime freakout eek factor, but again, reasonable enough given the swampy surroundings. A guy in a Han Solo outfit, zinging off laser blasts left-right-and-center while whooping like a maniac? Much more into WTF territory.

Somehow, in the ever-shifting course of the battle, Tony and Major Duval ended up squaring off. Her horns extruded another two inches from her scalp, her eyes blazing scarlet orbs. She'd also sprouted reddish bat-wings and a spade-tipped tail.

"Xanne, looking good," Tony said. "Did I ever congratulate you on your promotion?"

Her lips curled, revealing sharp teeth. "I'd rather talk about your impending *de*motion. From corporal to *corpse*."

In the spirit of Han-shot-first, Tony fired a split-second before she sprang.

She twisted mid-leap, the laser searing a sizzling welt across her shoulder instead of burning a hole through her throat. It didn't slow her, barely fazed her.

He fired again, center mass, but by then, she was on him, swatting the blaster from his hand, her claws shredding him wrist-to-palm in the process. They crashed to the ground in a tangle, throwing punches. Duval drove a knee into Tony's crotch; Tony dislocated her jaw with an elbow. He followed up jabbing a thumb at one of her scarlet eyes, while she punched her clawed fingers through his skin to seize his left collarbone.

"Tony, no!" Greg raised a hand as if he could reach into the screen, but met only the smooth, cool, solid barrier, faintly fuzzy with old-school TV static. He watched, horrified and helpless.

Duval yanked. Tony's collarbone snapped with a loud, thick *kkrakk*! Part of it pulled free in her grasp, sheathed in a fistful of torn flesh, jagged end protruding. This jagged end, she stabbed at his chest, as if trying to stake a vampire. It skidded to the side, gouging a bloody trench. Tony punctured her eyeball with his thumb, and she screeched.

As he got a throttling grip on her neck, she headbutted him. The space directly between the bases of her horns struck him in the forehead, bullseye on the glowing eldritch silver sigil.

It might as well have been a bomb going off. Greg pushed himself backward from the television, expecting a faceful of glass at the minimum, but the screen held. The picture went all zigzag bands of color, flickered briefly to a shot of Paul Lynde saying something naughty on *Hollywood Squares*, zigzagged again, then cleared.

There lay two very obviously, very dead people. The reaction, like a magical version of matter/antimatter colliding, had been violent enough to throw them a yard apart. From mid-sternum on up, little was left of either.

"Aw, fuck, no," Greg groaned. Quietly, mindful of his grandmother in the next room, humming along with her sewing machine. "Tony ... damn it ..."

The next scene showed Davidson escorting some bayou men with a wounded young soldier slung between them. He really did look barely old enough to shave, and had been shot in both knees. Nice and precise. Hendrix knew his stuff. The runner called Meep wouldn't be speedstering anywhere anytime soon.

The video then took on a different perspective, zooming in on the boggy delta, the sinking bridge wreckage and mostly submerged limo. Greg had previously caught a glimpse of a lizardy-looking guy in a muddy black suit and sunglasses hauling himself out through the driver's side window, but lost track of him.

This time, the focus was on some blondish, shirtless hillbilly Hemsworth deliberately diving into the morass, headfirst and trailing a rope, *a la* Westley going after Buttercup in the Fire Swamp. And, again, *a la* Westley, resurfacing   way-too-long-for-anyone-to-hold-their-breath later with a bedraggled, semiconscious woman clinging to him. Accurately assessing which way the wind was blowing, he hefted her over his shoulder and slogged off in the direction of Shallowstown.

The view lingered once they were gone, making Greg wonder if the "movie" had come to an end. Before he could pick up the remote, though, it dipped *into* the delta. Seeing anything other than reddish-brown water and silt should have been impossible. Still, down it went, cruising monster-cam style, deeper and deeper, through thicker and thicker muck, all the way to the bottom.

Where, mired to the neck and unable to move, was a blocky clay head with crudely-formed features and dull reddish slits for eyes. The Golem, the third Golem, stranded in the depths.

At that point, the screen went briefly black, followed by an "Off The Air" test pattern. As if on cue, his grandmother came in with his coat—laundered as well as mended—on a hanger.

"Here you go, dear. Always nice to visit, but you should probably be on your way."

"There, sees? I'se *toldya* he'd be back!"
Greg opened his eyes to the dissipating silvery afterflash

of his arrival, cypress trees and Spanish moss stirring in a strengthening wind, clouds scudding across blue sky, and another circle of faces peering inquisitively down at him.

Not angels this time. Far from. But still the good guys. Lorlinda. Davidson. Mortisse. Braveheart. Somewhat the worse for wear, to be sure. Sweaty, grimy, blood-spattered. Lorlinda had one arm in a sling. A stained bandage was tied around Braveheart's head. Mortisse's painted deathmask had smudged into more of a sad mime. Davidson displayed the onset of an epic set of bruises.

Beyond them were a loose ring of soldiers, bayou folk, zombs, and a few apparent prisoners.

And beyond them, below the higher-ground refuge where he'd deposited them ... a sodden flood zone aftermath of displaced debris. Overturned and crumpled vehicles, uprooted trees, chunks of broken asphalt roadway, bridge wreckage, bodies.

The main surge had receded, though the lake's surface was choppy and unsettled, sloshing frothy surf along the shoreline. Its stench was viler than ever, everything previously sunken to lower levels having been upchurned anew.

"What happened?" he asked Lorlinda.

"After y' brung us here—saved our bacon fer sure, thanks; an' some kick it was, flyin' like that!—y' keeled over an' got kinda blurry semi-see-through. Came an' went a while, fadin' in an' out, y'know, how radia stations do? I figgured it mean y' wasn't dead, only somewheres else. Somewheres lim'nal, an' we jist needed t' wait. Then, well, here y'are."

"You weren't wearing your coat at first," Davidson said. "Had it rolled up in this net of electric wire. Then suddenly, you were wearing it, and holding onto that briefcase-thing."

"Pool cue case. And my coat needed mending. My grandma ... never mind. Long story. How ... how did we do?"

Lorlinda's expression sobered. "Lost quite a few of our'n. Not as many as we might've—'gain, thanks t' yer mojo. But, yer friend Tony—"

"I know. I ... I saw some of it while I was ... away. Him and Duval. You and Pork Chop. Other stuff. What about the enemy?"

"We had 'em on the ropes even b'fore y' took'd out the queen, an' soon's she fell, they could tell they was done fer.

Sent their m'rale right down the shitter. Them as din't die in the fightin', a few surrendered, a few got captured, an' the rest either 'scaped or got caught by the flood. I'se reckon they's scattered hell t' breakfast, whoever done survived."

"The flood, *mais oui*," Mortisse said. "The dominion *maléfique*, it was broken, *non? Défaite*. Undone. Le *Dôme* and Wall, they are no more. Many died with them as well. Many soldiers at the *points d'entrée*, who had been changed but could not withstand *le traumatisme du renversement*."

"Now, that tidal wave," said Davidson, "that was some serious shit. Came most of the way up this hill. For a minute there, I thought we were gonna get our feet wet after all. Was it just here, or was the whole lake affected?"

Braveheart's grin was hard-edged. "If it was the whole lake, those fuckers at the war camp better have been wearing their water wings. It's right on the damn shore."

"Crawdy's too," said Lorlinda. "Prolly got wiped clean off the map, an' good ridd'nce. Speakin'a which, though, dunno if'n Spot made it or not; seened him makin' tracks soon's the fight started, the yeller-belly."

"And the queen?" Greg asked, glancing toward the grassy hummock, which was now a soggy mess. "Her body, I mean?"

"Warshed clean away, 'thout a trace. She *was* dead, though, weren't she? She ain't gonna be one of them horror movie slashers, like, what cain't be kilt fer keeps?"

"No," he said. "She's dead. As dead as dead can be. I have that on absolute authority." The pad of his thumb rubbed the onyx and titanium ring. *Thanks to someone else's mojo, far stronger than mine.*

Even without trying to be stealthy, getting back to the bayou village was no picnic. They had to pick their way through a lot of storm-mess, as well as being slowed by having wounded and captives among their numbers.

The queen's former royal cosmetician had been the first to surrender. He swore he'd been drafted, coerced into service, doing what he had to in order to survive. A couple of the marching band members and standard-bearers said the same. They were guarded but well treated.

Reuben, whose talents weren't limited to coral snakes, had managed to catch and calm two horses and an emusaur;

these were put to use as beasts of burden, pulling makeshift litters carrying those unable to walk. Hendrix, having apologized for the necessity of the double knee-shots, stuck close to Meep; the young runner didn't seem inclined to hold a grudge.

Of the queen's handmaid, there was no sign. Greg related what he'd seen, the hillbilly Hemsworth rescuing someone from the sunken limo, and Lorlinda said it must've been her and Abel Kellerman.

"I ain't wishin' no ill-will 'pon 'em, if'n they got out. Long's Iris don't take it inta her noggin t' avenge the queen, what with her hero-worship an' all. Y' said they was headed fer Shallowstown?"

"That's how it looked."

Ceelie, the teenager with the medusoid cornrows, did frequent scouting runs on Lorlinda's Vespa. She reported that Shallowstown had gotten a real wallop from the flood surge, but the people who lived there had heard Greg's warning—he hadn't realized his Voice would carry so far—in time to mostly make it onto their rooftops. Lots of property damage, comparatively little other harm done.

The bayou village, it turned out, had fared better, being further inland and upstream, as well as having most of the structures built on stilts. The water (or, "water") level had risen several feet, enough to reach the undersides of some houses and swamp a few bridges. Three pole-punts and a bunch of fish traps had been swept away, but no lives were lost.

Then there was Jason, who'd been found handcuffed and naked in the back of a van. All-over balder than an egg, with bright pink healing skin, he looked like an alopecia patient recently released from a burn ward. He'd explained the events leading up to his situation, including deserting his post and getting thrown in the fiery dungeon, but hadn't been given much info after that.

"I got the idea I was some sort of hostage or bartering chip," he said, slathered head-to-toe in gooey alchemical aloe ointment. "That Trevor had done a favor for the queen, maybe had something she wanted. I don't know, man. I was *so* fucked-up from being barbecued for days on end, I could hardly think."

The cosmetician, Lyle, confirmed Jason's theory. "That pretty-boy Senator sweet-talked her into having his friend here transferred, reassigned to his household security. When we got to Jericho and found they were holding him on charges instead, Xanne—Major Duval—did some fancy red-tape footwork to take him into custody. I expect, once he'd healed, he would've been pardoned so the Senator got his wish."

"So what're *we* s'posed t' do with him?" Lorlinda asked. She turned to Jason. "Lissen, I don't means t' trash on yer friend an' all, but ..."

"They don't call him Senator Stump-Humper for no reason," Lyle added. "What we saw at his house? His idea of entertainment? Oh, honey, lawd no."

"If'n his house even survived, what with the tidal wave," Lorlinda went on. "Might as be smarter t' stick with us 'til y'se healed up an' had some time t' sort y'self out."

A sentiment everyone could embrace, now that the current crisis had passed. New crises might be on the horizon, depending on how the outside world reacted to the Dome and Wall reverting to pre-Favius status, but the outside world still reeling from the Painwave gave them some breathing room.

Two rosy-cheeked, bare-bottomed, chubby baby cherubs were playing planetary pool when he walked in, a substantial amount of celestial currency on the line. They regarded Greg, and the pool cue case at his side, with glowers more suited to mob bosses.

"Closed game," one said. "Peddle your papers elsewhere, mortal."

"Yeah," said the other, fluffing dove-white wings belligerently. "Who invited *you*?"

"I'm here to see him." He nodded toward the bar, where a figure remarkably resembling Clint Eastwood sat with a shot glass and bottle of liquid galaxy.

"That so?" challenged the first cherub. "Hey, Az, you know dis guy?"

"Don't get your halos in a twist," replied the figure in a dry and dusty drawl also remarkably resembling Clint Eastwood. "The kid's all right. How about you mooks flap off for a while?"

"I got seven grand riding on—" protested the second.

"Flap off," the Angel of Death repeated, not turning but

his narrow gaze pinning them via the mirror behind the bar. "You can pick it up later."

Disgruntled, but not about to push their luck, they flapped off. By the time Greg crossed the room and settled onto the next stool over, Haphthiah had a sphere of Eden Springs waiting. The nephilim bartender winked at him before resuming his duties. As before, classic rock played softly from hidden speakers.

"So, you made it."

"Yeah. Thanks to you." Greg removed the titanium and onyx ring from his forefinger and slid it over.

"I just lent a hand, kid. You're the one who faced the music. Took some nerve."

"How close was I? To, you know ..."

"Kicking the bucket? Buying the farm? Like I told you, in order for it to work, you had to take it to the limit. Maybe not at Death's door—yea verily I stand at the door and knock—but on Death's front porch, let's say."

"And she's really gone? As in, *gone*-gone?"

"Not here, not *there*, not anywhere. One way ticket to oblivion, no backsies. You don't have to worry about her subcarnating for an encore." He put the ring back onto his own finger. "When I do the job, the job stays done."

"Good. Glad to hear it. She was scary. Scarier than Favius."

"Hell, fury, woman, etc." Azrael knocked back another shot. "Pray you never run into Lilith, kid."

"Uh, okay, noted." As before, the Eden Springs was cool, clear, pure, and heady, making him feel renewed. His soul, as well as his body, rinsed of the residue of the past few days.

"Seen your girl yet?"

"First thing." Where he'd also encountered Raphael again, which had taken care of his lingering physical wounds. Mostly. The place where the barb of Juno's *redblack* whip had dug into his thigh was, like the scar on his chin from the gladius, going to leave a mark.

Once certain things were under control at the bayou village, he'd said his goodbyes—receiving another brains-out-his-ears hug from Lorlinda—and hied himself Heavenward. This time, he'd been met at the Gates by none other than Icaiah, who of course had been all huffy and prissy and indignant about it.

"As if I haven't anything better to do than play mother hen."

"Nice to see you too."

He'd found Ethriel even more wan and dispirited than when he'd left, which Blianthis told him was only to be expected given the severity of her injuries. Even with the best care the raphim could offer, her divine essence continued seeping away.

"If you're going to try what I think you're going to try," she'd said, matronly as ever in her powder-blue nurse's scrubs, "it should be soon. Maybe not STAT; she's not critical yet. But, soon."

Greg thumped the pool cue case onto the bar. "And I got the gladius. Now what?"

"Now," Azrael said, decisively screwing the cap back onto the bottle and standing, "we see if Haph's brother is in the mood to work us up a little miracle."

They left the Three Chalices, Greg very aware of how other Heavenly denizens cleared a deferential path for Azrael. He was also aware of the way they glanced at *him*, a living warlock in the company of the Angel of Death.

"Out of curiosity," he said, "what's all that about?"

"They're scared."

"Of me?"

"Well, mostly of me, but of you too. Get used to it, kid."

His previous explorations had taken him through several areas where the backstage, behind-the-scenes, administrative work of operating an afterlife went on. He had not, however, ventured into the more industrial sections, and wasn't quite sure to make of what he saw. Cloud machines, like giant cotton-candy makers, spinning puff after puff of purest white ... a factory-type chamber mass-producing harps and halos ... a golden machine topped with a giant prism ...

"What's that?" he asked.

"Rainbow generator."

"But I thought ..."

Azrael shrugged. "Sometimes, He still uses them to send a message or make a statement. Promising not to drown the world, and so on. There's another down the hall for comets. And you should see the setup for the End Times." He paused. "Actually, nah, you shouldn't. It's a bit much even for us old-schoolers."

"I'll take your word for it."

"Smart kid. Here we are, the Crucible."

As he swung the door open, a wave of heat basked out, but it was nothing like any heat Greg had previously experienced. Certainly unlike earthly heat, let alone infernal. It was the heat of Creation.

"Whoa," he said as it blew back his hair and coat.

The entire space shone with light, emanating from a cylindrical shaft plunging into what could have been the heart of a supernova. Stationed all around it were tools of metallurgy on a cosmic scale. Cauldrons capable of rendering and refining rare elements from entire asteroids ... anvils large enough to hammer out Saturn's rings ... forges in which new stars could be formed ...

"You okay, kid?"

Greg gulped. When he'd first beheld the halls of the raphim, it'd been too much to take in, and this was ... this was more, this was bigger, this was ...

"Kid?"

"I'm here," he said faintly, clinging to coherence by the thinnest of threads.

"Should have warned you. Sorry. Over here. It'll be less a brain-buster."

Azrael led him to another door, much smaller, that opened onto a room, also much smaller. And less brain-busting, but only just. If parts of the Wall around Lake Misquamicus were Mordor, this was a combination of the dwarven smithies under the Lonely Mountain and depictions of Vulcan's volcanic workshop.

Presiding over it was one of the nephilim, similar in appearance to Haphthiah but three times as tall and proportionally built. A true giant, hugely muscular, with an awful lot of platinum-gold fur for someone spending this much time around the furnace of Creation.

"Haph's brother," Azrael said, by way of introduction. "Hephaestel. Heph, Gregory Nachtwald, the warlock I told you about."

"Hephaes ..." Greg began. "Wait, as in ...?"

"Not exactly. Close enough. Forget trying to figure the mythology, kid; you'll give yourself a headache."

When there he'd been, just thinking about Vulcan, who, to the Greeks, had been known as ... no, best to take Azrael's advice. He was in for a doozy of a headache already.

Heph, like Haph, didn't speak, but smiled amiably. He

listened, head cocked in an oddly golden retriever way, as Azrael told him they needed something reforged. A demonic something, imbued and infused with the darkest of dark powers, bound to an Arch-Duke of Hell and a Greater Relic, but also with a measure of divine angelic essence mixed in.

Greg unlatched the pool cue case and opened it, revealing the gladius. It seemed to throb with evil all the more, a blasphemy, an abomination, an affront against the very fabric of Heaven. Even Azrael drew back, disinclined to get too close.

And him, like a dope, just toting it around …

Hephaestel, though cautious, seemed more intrigued than perturbed. Waving them aside, he pulled on a heavy glove and lifted the gladius from its resting place, rumbling thoughtfully deep in his broad chest.

Saying nothing, Greg and Azrael stayed out of the way, watching as Heph examined the weapon.

He hefted it, experimentally swung it, turned it this way and that. He tinked the blade with a hard, blunt, hornlike fingernail, holding it to his ear to listen to its tone. He affixed a gadget like a jeweler's loupe over his eye and scrutinized every inch. He ran a thick, callused thumb along its edge. He sniffed it. He tasted it—Greg and Azrael both winced—touching the metal to his tongue. He sprinkled it with various gritty powders, drizzled it with oils and acids, and passed it through gas-jet fumaroles, noting the chemical and alchemical reactions.

Finally, with a satisfied chuff, he nodded, thumped himself on the sternum, pointed to the gladius, pointed at the equipment, grinned widely, and nodded again.

"There you go, kid," said Azrael, clapping Greg on the back. "Let's make this happen."

They watched from the sidelines as Heph went to work, disassembling the gladius and placing its components into a vessel of some otherworldly alloy.

"So, how was it?" asked Azrael. "Pulling the trigger?"

"Didn't feel great. Sucked, actually. Not something I'd want to do again."

"Yeah, makes two of us."

As the gladius rendered down, gooey globs of redblack burbled to the surface, like the stuff inside a lava lamp. Heph skimmed it off with a long-handled ladle, funneling the viscous substance into a block of opalescent alabaster.

"What's that?" Greg asked Azrael.

"Containment unit."

Next, Heph ran the remaining molten metal through a series of siphons and filters, further refining it. Originally Hell-forged, the bronze was tainted with brimstone, charnel soot, and other contaminants. It also carried minuscule traces of every life the weapon had taken and every injury inflicted, these rising like vapor to collect and condense and drip, distilled, into a vial.

"Once it's sufficiently purified," Azrael said, "he'll cast the mold. It'll cool and solidify, he'll crack it out, heat it again to do some touch-ups, temper it in holy water and anointing oils, go over any rough spots, give it a final polish, and we'll be in business."

"How long will that take?"

"Can't rush perfection, kid. If you want to go be with your girl, I can bring it over as soon as it's done."

He hesitated, torn. Wanting to be with his girl, definitely; he'd only had time to do a quick summary of events Earthside, and it had wrenched at him to leave her side while she was so frail. But also wanting—even somehow *needing*—to see this strange process through to the end. It felt like a sacred obligation, an important part of the quest.

"I'll stay."

And stay, he did. He and Azrael mostly stood in silence, not having to say much. Heph, of course, said nothing at all, aside from the occasional chuff or rumble.

At last, it was finished, the shining masterpiece presented for their inspection. It was beautiful. It was exquisite.

It was …

"Are you shi—uh, messing with me?" Greg asked.

"What'd you expect?"

It was a bell.

A beautiful, exquisite, divine *bell*.

"All that, all this, for a … a movie reference?"

Azrael slanted him a wry Clint Eastwood half-grin. "How else do you think an angel gets their wings?"

They returned to the halls of the raphim, to Ethriel so wan and fading. She stirred as they came in, trying to sit up, but lacked the strength. Blianthis helped her. Raphael observed, pen poised over clipboard.

Azrael unveiled the bell, which had been draped in finest samite, and handed it to Greg. "Go for it, kid."

It rang clear and true.

Ethriel gasped.

The room filled with the radiant, glorious light of her restored wings.

Bloodbath Aftermath

*"Tidal wave! The **lake**, get **away** from the **lake**, get **uphill**, high ground, move it, move it, flash **flood**, fucking **tidal wave** incoming!"*

Everyone in the vicinity heard the warning.

Not everyone in the vicinity heeded it.

Some were simply unable to. Like the leprous, gangrenous, rotting, maggot-infested husk of a man affixed upside-down to a large wooden X. Insane but still conscious, gagged, no longer bearing the slightest resemblance to a careworn George Clooney. Dozens of fishhooks pierced his flesh—lips, ears, nose, fingertips, nipples, but most of all genitals, particularly the suppurating tip of his penis. Wires led from the fishhooks to a television, VCR, and vintage Atari.

He heard the warning, and he may have even understood it, there in the lakehouse where he'd at long last been reunited with his estranged wife and their children.

It hadn't been exactly the happiest and most heart-warming of reunions. Yes, he'd gotten it on with his wife out on the dock, even if she'd become a finely scaled *creme-de-menthe* snake-lady with paralyzing venom for bodily fluids. Yes, he'd reconnected with his kids, as they'd connected *him* to the agonicity converters so they could watch cartoons. But the wife and kids were gone now.

If anything, when the tsunami of infernal filth crashed into the house, knocking it off its foundations and battering it to pieces, eradicating generations of scandalous family secrets, he was glad.

Now, at another lakehouse, a larger and fancier one (which, strictly speaking, wasn't really a house anymore, though what it *was* could be the subject of much debate), the warning went not just unheard nor unheeded but mostly just lost as background noise. With a party going on—a party was almost always going on—the music, chatter, laughter, sex-sounds, and screams of the newly mutilated tended to overpower anything else.

Furthermore, the partygoers, thanks to copious amounts of alcohol and assorted mind-altering substances, absorbed in their perverse pursuits, wouldn't have noticed a bomb going off. Downstairs was wall-to-wall gorging, orgies, and dancing. The majority of the participants were missing at least a finger or toe, if not entire limbs.

Club-footed Ronny Riggers clomped around cradling the severed heads of his parents grafted into his stout sides. Mrs. Riggers rode herd on the kitchen staff, critical and domineering. Mr. Riggers kept a sharp eye out for any property damage; fun was fun, but no one would go breaking furniture on his watch!

The fourth member of the Riggers family, Lester, was hidden away in the utility room, floggin' the hog for all he was worth as he rewatched for the umpteenth time the video of himself doin' a header on Chelsea Carmichael. Damn, but what a fine-ass piece she'd been! Never mind her arms and legs'd all been cut off; she'd still had them *fiiiiine* titties, and busting his nut inside her brain-pan was the highlight of his life.

Upstairs, in the master bedroom, Trevor Carmichael was engaging in some romantic amputational foreplay with Maisy-Sue Kellerman, who moaned like crazy as he worked the hacksaw in slow, teasing strokes. Its serrated teeth grated sexily against elbow bone, her semidetached forearm wallowing in a puddle of blood.

Out back on the patio, Maisy-Sue's brother Abner, who'd given up trying to deter her, leaned on the rail, chugging beers and chain-smoking. He liked all the booze and wild fornicatin' well enough, but the rest of it just wasn't for him. *Gimme a reg'lar ol' Hock Party any day,* he was thinking, when he heard someone hollering about tidal waves. *Must be stoned outta their gourd.*

The hot tubs on the upper and lower decks offered a picturesque view of the lake. Some of the naked people packed into those hot tubs noticed the not-so-picturesque view of a monstrous churning mass barreling toward them, but their reactions at best amounted to: *whoa, this is some gooood shit.*

Turned out, not even a house that wasn't, strictly speaking, a real house could hold up to a full-on supernatural disaster.

Neither could the war camp, Camp Favius, there on the lakeshore near the monument marking the place where the Hell-Centurion had first set foot upon God's green earth.

Where the military convoy had arrived in triumph, ready to activate the Ameri-Golem and take back the realm in the name of the USA, cementing their status as the uncontested #1 badass muthafuckas on the entire planet.

If it hadn't gone quite as planned, resulting instead in Favius seizing power, slaughtering the politicians and top brass who'd hoped to look all patriotic and victorious on the news, that had worked out okay too. Wasn't this also where they had returned Favius, where he'd claimed his dominion and queen?

Make no mistake, the warning came in loud and clear.

And it did not go ignored, oh no. Far from.

It was heard.

Fake news.

Some sort of trick. A trap. A distraction or misdirection.

That asshole warlock, who'd obliterated Favius with angelic aid, who'd infiltrated their camp and freed a prisoner with help from a turncoat traitor of their own, had to be trying to get at them another way.

Tsunami alert? Flash flood? Tidal wave?

Yeah, right.

He *wanted* them to flee, abandon their posts and scatter for higher ground. Betray their queen. Run like sheep, like chickenshit chickens, like rats. To be picked off and leave the camp undefended.

As if they would fall for such a transparent ruse!

At once, officers barked orders. Buglers bugled. Soldiers scrambled. Formations formed.

A private, who'd been a California surfer-dude before enlisting, noticed the exposed lakebed and distant rising swell. His attempts at pointing it out only earned him a spittle-flying cuss-laden rebuke from a sergeant, followed by a lieutenant threatening him with latrine detail.

As a result, the soldiers were on full alert, armed and ready, prepared to stand their ground. Let the warlock give it his best shot; they were itching to shoot back!

They changed their tune real quick when the wave hove into view, tall as a six-story building and moving fast, sludgy maroon cresting with yellowish-brown froth.

For all the good that did.

Some belatedly decided maybe running was the better option. Some opened fire. Some ducked and covered. Some, ironically, prayed.

None of it made one whit of difference. They were eradicated. Bowled over, dragged under, tossed like corks, crushed, and drowned. Tents might as well have been houses of cards. Buildings fared little better, collapsing and being torn apart in violent eddies. Prefabs were just as often swept up and carried away. The stockade held, but the prisoners within died gurgling in their cells. Tanks, troop trucks, vans, and other vehicles tumbled and rolled, awash at the mercy of the relentless tide. The surfer-dude, though, managed to snag a chunk of plywood and rode it to safety.

Mr. and Mrs. Shinn, who'd been moved into a spartan little cabin after birthing their utero-gourd babies, probably weren't even aware of what was happening as the flood poured in, swiftly engulfing them where they lay strapped to their beds. Out of their minds as they were anyway, they might not have cared if they *had* been aware.

The on-duty nurse, however, had lately begun experiencing minor premonitions. She'd been ill at ease all day, troubled by a growing urge to get herself the holy hell *gone*. By the time the warlock's warning reached her, she'd already grabbed little Manny and Melony from their cribs, buckled them into the panniers of an ATV, and was on her way.

As for the RV, the huge ultra-luxury RV serving as combination throne room and royal residence? With the king-sized bed June and Favius had put to such vigorous and frequent use, the jetted bathtub, and the full kitchen where Chef Emilio (who, btw, was with the procession, but didn't make it; coral snakes got him) had crafted works of culinary art? The RV warded and hexed to the nines with everything every spellcaster left in camp could muster?

Fucking *annihilated*.

It still being fairly early afternoon, hardly anyone was at Crawdy's. The gravel-and-dirt parking lot was all but empty. Two old farts with nowhere else to go sat on the ramshackle porch, shootin' the shit, while a dumpy gal mopped the previous evening's mess from the floor, and a buck-toothed adolescent climbed a ladder to replace some busted lightbulbs.

Something something *tidal wave* something *lake, high ground* something something *flash flood* something …

"Y'hear that?" the kid on the ladder asked the dumpy gal.

"Mus' be th' radio."

"Since't when we get the weather channel?"

"Jist you git them bulbs done an' quitcher jabberin'."

On the porch, the two old farts gazed at the lake, one repacking his pipe while the other whittled at a chunk of driftwood.

"Hunh," said the one.

"Don' see that ever'day," said the other.

The first leisurely lit his pipe, puffed, then said, "Strange."

"Mite strange," the whittler agreed.

Half a minute later, the whole dang place was washed off its foundation in a jumble of splintered planks and busted windows. A live wire struck a spark near some cracked 'shine jugs, causing a minor explosion, but the turbulent torrent swallowed the flames.

Further along the shoreline, toward what locals had taken to calling Turtle Beach, several females had waddled their way to the dunes to lay this season's clutches of eggs, buried in sandy nests.

It'd been a bad year for Ol' Hornyshell, whose era as undisputed alpha-male had come to a shameful end when the young dino-turtle bucks teamed up and harassed him from his rightful territory.

He didn't so much mind loss of access to the females, as he really had grown to prefer humping vehicles—maybe it was the way their metal shells crunched and crumpled beneath his weight, the way their tires squealed as they sought vainly to escape, and the way their rougher edges scraped at his scaly double-pronged dick—but there was the principle of the thing. Upstarts thinking they could **SKREE-ONK** louder than him? He'd show them.

Such were what passed for thoughts in his small dino-turtle mind, thoughts abruptly disrupted when a sudden powerful current caught him. Buffeted on all sides, swirled dizzily around, the familiar lake a heaving maelstrom, he struggled to plant his feet or swim to the shallows.

Another rolling upheaval flipped him ignominiously onto his back, armor-plated tree trunk legs waving ridiculously in the air. He spun, dipped, bobbed, spun some more, unable to right himself. Then the surge plowed him up the beach, bulldozing his spiked shell through nests, squashing eggs into greenish goo.

He fetched up against a boulder, pinned there until the tide receded. But even then, he was upside down, with his legs pedaling at nothing, unable to right himself, as helpless as the hatchlings who'd now never hatch.

Not too far from Turtle Beach, near the rearing promontory of Bighead Rock, was a cozy little cottage with a few outbuildings and a yard decorated with rustic art, including a wooden whirligig sculpture depicting a male figure pumping his wooden dick in and out of a hole in the top of a female figure's wooden head.

At an umbrella-shaded patio table on the deck, a certain horror writer / movie maker of considerable repute in genres often described as "sicko shit," glanced up from his laptop.

Lake Misquamicus hadn't been anywhere close to normal for years, but he'd never seen it like this before. Or gotten a flood warning. Or had massive roiling swells converging from different angles.

Converging and then, in that fluke of nature waves sometimes displayed, colliding and canceling each other out, leaving him and his property entirely untouched.

His "bosom companion," Jubblies, an ambulatory humanoid composed entirely of breasts, jiggled over to him with an icy-cold bottle of Collier's lager. He popped the cap, gave her a friendly boob-honk, and returned his attention to the laptop.

Time to see what stickerly nit-pickery his proofreader was going on about now …

AFTERWORD

Did we make it? Are you still with me, here on the flip side? Are you okay? I realize things in this one got kinda more intense than I'd initially anticipated. Can thank or blame June/Juno for a lot of that; turns out she still had plenty of grievances to air.

Plus, there was the header. I mean, of course I had to do a header sooner or later. How could I not? It's one of Lee's signature things, and I wanted to try it out in my own ludicrous fashion by playing it up as much as I could.

Funny thing, though ... I still cannot bring myself to do a Hock Party. As I've mentioned elsewhere, reading those scenes by Lee and Ryan Harding have brought me closer to legit outright puking than anything else I've read (excepting perhaps Lee's "The Dritiphilist"). So, I wussed out there and could only tease about it. I'm sorry. Maybe, one day, I'll muster the nerve.

What most surprised me, though, was how much I enjoyed tinkering with the notion of Heaven, with its hierarchy and biblically-accurate angels, and its theme-park nature where the real work goes on behind the scenes, out of the view of the paying guests. I may also now have a crush on the Angel of Death, who insisted on playing a bigger role than expected.

All that said, the logical question is: what next? Since Lee followed up his trilogy with *Lucifer's Lottery* (which is what got me here in the first place), do I do likewise? I don't know yet, and it's partly up to him anyway.

What I do know is how much this entire experience has meant to me. My life has undergone some drastic upheavals over the past several years, but at the same time, I was able to do all this. Real "best of times / worst of times" situation. These crazy books have seen me through the most difficult experiences I've ever endured.

Sinus cancer, for instance, with its assorted surgeries, procedures, disfigurements, complications, and miseries. For a while there, I honestly thought I wouldn't be able to write anymore. I thought I was done, time to give up. But I couldn't let myself. I started *Lakehouse,* and it gave me something to hold onto, something to strive for. Like the saying goes, "when you're going through Hell, keep going."

Then came an ordeal I found much worse (even with the clownshoes shitshow of current events going on since 2020). I was my mother's full-time live-in caregiver for the final two years of her life, and it made everything else seem paltry. I'd rather have cancer in my face all over again than deal with another situation like that. I was, quite probably, clinically insane from sleep deprivation and stress for several months there. What helped me survive, along with my internet community, was writing *Warlock* and having that world to escape into.

Even after Mom passed, the struggle was far from over, dealing with the estate and probate and assorted legal stuff that'd gone unaddressed for decades. But I finally landed in the safe haven of my dad's high-desert homestead. I daresay I've done some of my best writing since then, this book included. So, if I have to take the bad to get the good, well, okay; it's worth it.

The ongoing love and support I've received from so many of you has been invaluable. I cannot thank you enough, and I will never be able to find sufficient words to express my gratitude to Edward Lee. Whatever does come next, I wouldn't trade this for anything.

Before I go, one last note to those who may be wondering: that whole "writing in 666-word segments" shtick? Yes, I did that in this one too. Contents may have settled or shifted during edits, but in their first drafts, each bit came to a tidy 666. Because, hey, why the Hell not?

SEMPER GAUDIUM ET IOCUM SEQUERE!!!

WHO IS CHRISTINE MORGAN?

Christine Morgan, author of the Splatter-punk Award winning LAKEHOUSE IN-FERNAL and co-author of the Wonder-land Award winning NYMPHO SHARK FUCK FRENZY, as well as many other works, currently lives as a high-desert hermit bossed around by cats. A two-time cancer survivor, dubbed "the Martha Stewart of horror" for her baking and weird crafts, she has way more sharks and dinosaurs than someone of her age probably should. She can be found online at https://christinemariemorgan.wordpress.com/

MORE BY CHRISTINE MORGAN

- Spermjackers from Hell
- Lakehouse Infernal
- Warlock Infernal
- Nympho Shark Fuck Frenzy
- Trench Mouth
- Almost Normal Horror
- The Night Silver River Ran Red

MORE FROM MADNESS HEART PRESS

- Squirming All the Way Up
- Ten Words for a Wicked Woman
- PINS
- Bound with Briars
- Blade Job
- Curse of the Ratman
- Lights Out
- Pure Hate
- The Bighead
- The Television
- Trip Chainsaw
- Whispers of the Dead Saint
- Kennel
- Thrust Into Battle
- Czech Extreme
- The Reattachment
- ALL MEN ARE TRASH